I0732907

REVENGE

2

GODS & MONSTERS

LAUREN DAWES

Revenge
(Gods & Monsters #2)

First Edition, 2014 by Momentum (Pan Macmillan Australia Pty Ltd)
Second Edition, 2017 by Lauren Dawes
Third Edition, 2021 by Lauren Dawes
Copyright © 2014 by Lauren Dawes

www.authorlaurendawes.com

The right of Lauren Dawes to be identified as the
author of this work has been asserted by her under the
Copyright Amendment (Moral Rights) Act 2000

E-book: 978-0-9876409-6-3
Print: 978-1-922353-69-6

Cover by Deranged Doctor Designs

For Phil and Evie

GLOSSARY

Aesir (n) – The sky gods. It is their belief they are superior to all other races in the Nine Worlds.

affinity (n) – the weapon that a Shadow Walker uses as their preferred weapon. It is said that the weapon will choose the Mare while they are training for the Final Test

agarwaen (adj) – after a Shadow Walker has completed their training and survived the Final Test, this is the title they are awarded; literally translated as blood-stained.

Asgard (n) – The former home of the Aesir.

fade (v) – to dematerialize to another location with a thought.

Fall, the (n) – The time when the Norse gods were no longer worshiped and therefore lost their power. The Fall was the tipping point that destroyed the Nine Worlds, breaking down the highly organized and coveted hierarchy built by the Aesir. Factions split and different species within those Nine Worlds were strewn across the human world. Some prospered while some merely survived. The gods favored the cities created by humans while others, like the dwarves, preferred the furthest outposts of human civilization.

Final Test, the (n) – At the end of a Mare's training to become a Walker, a gladiator-style battle takes place where the last man (or woman) standing is awarded the title agarwaen.

Frigg – Odin's wife; the goddess of fertility, love and marriage.

Hel – The goddess of the underworld

Jotunn (n) – a giant.

Mare (n) – a dark elf. Pure-blooded Mares are believed to be extinct after a campaign by Odin over a thousand years ago to eradicate their species. To escape persecution, dark elves bred with light elves creating half-breed children whose features helped them to pass as light elves.

Morier(ea) (n) – a derogatory term for a Shadow Walker; literally translated as dark one.

Odin – The father of all gods and men. Sometimes referred to as the *All-Father.*

Quinary (n) – a group of five Mares training to become blooded Shadow Walkers. At the conclusion of the Final Test, one of the five will become agarwaen. They will be the victor of their quinary for that year.

Shadow Walker (n) – Shadow Walker is the ancient name for any Mare trained to be an assassin because of their ability to 'wrap' shadows around them to conceal themselves. However, due to the extensive interbreeding with the light elves, the ability to shadow walk was lost but the name remains the same. Shadow Walkers were feared for their ability to enter a person's dreams and manipulate them.

Sleipnir – an eight-legged horse owned by Odin.

Svartalfheim (n) – the original world of the dark elves, located between the land of the light elves and the dwarves. The majority of the dark elves who lived in Svartalfheim before the Fall were slaughtered there by Odin and his Valkyries.

Valhalla (n) – An enormous hall within Asgard that housed fallen battle heroes.

Valkyrie (n) – A beautiful female warrior created by Odin to take the bodies of men slain in battle to Valhalla. Their immortality is only possible while their swan feather cloak is in their possession. If this cloak is stolen, the thief is entitled to seven years of service from the Valkyrie. However, if the feathers are plucked from the cloak, the Valkyrie's immortality leaves them and they can be killed by a mortal wound.

Vanir (n) – The Vanir are the old gods who ruled before the Aesir. Sworn enemies of the sky gods, they are the masters of sorcery and elemental magic.

Vanaheim (n) – the land of the Vanir, which was situated below Asgard, constantly reminding the elemental gods of their place below the Aesir.

Vanir (n) – the Vanir are the old gods who ruled before the Aesir. Sworn enemies of the sky gods, they are the masters of sorcery and elemental magic. They live on Vanaheim.

"Tay? Adrian's de—"

"Yeah," she interrupted. "I heard you the first time."

Adrian's dead. Adrian's dead. Adrian's dead.

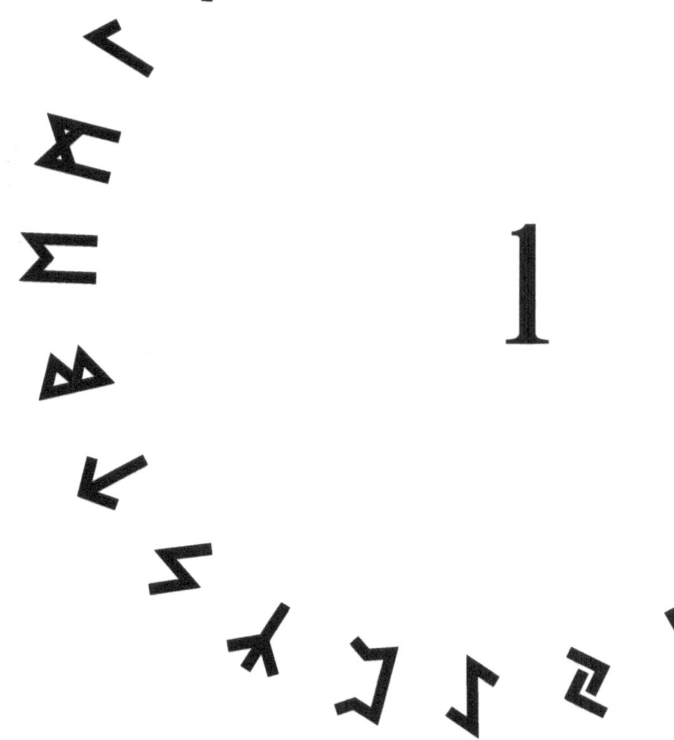

1

Taer didn't want to open her eyes.

She knew what she would find if she did, and she wasn't ready to experience it again. A deep, disembodied gasp finally forced open her eyes. All she could see was red. It was everywhere, pooling on the floor beside her head, splattered on the walls. Tacky, warm blood covered her face and neck.

The desperate sound of gasping made bile—hot and vitriolic—creep up the back of her throat, burning the delicate skin. Swallowing it back, Taer rolled her eyes around, trying to make sense of the scene she once again found herself in.

The gasping became louder then, and she recognized it for what it was …

Hopelessness.

Suffering.

Death.

Focusing all her energy on her heavy limbs, Taer willed her fingers to move. She could feel a fine sheen of sweat on her forehead, but her hands remained motionless, and the gurgling breaths grew louder—sharper. Taer let her eyes roll in their sockets, hoping to catch a glimpse of whoever was responsible for the desperate noise.

The sound ripped through her once more, tearing her heart to shreds with every beat that it took because she now knew who was making those fraught sounds.

Adrian.

Taer wanted to scream out to her brother, but her body betrayed her and her tongue lay useless in her mouth.

Adrian.

He was in agony.

He was dying.

"Adrian." His name was barely a whispered croak from deep down in Taer's throat, but she cringed away from the sound.

She was to blame for his death. The crushing despair she felt overwhelmed her, threatening to suffocate her. How could she have let it happen? Tears leaked from the corners of her eyes and the back of her throat burned.

How could she have killed her brother?

"Taer, wake up."

Taer woke with a loud gasp. Blinking rapidly, she looked around the darkened room.

"Are you okay?" a woman asked. Still struggling to breathe, Taer managed to focus on the blonde-haired, blue-eyed Valkyrie sitting beside her on the bed. She knew this room—she had woken up in it for the first time more than a month ago, on the day her life had changed forever. She knew the Valkyrie, too—it was Eir, the healer.

Eir brought her hands to Taer's chest, her palms beginning to glow slightly. With a relieved groan, Taer slumped back into the pillows, feeling the tightness in her chest loosen.

After what felt like forever, Taer's breathing eased.

"You were having another nightmare," Eir said, repositioning her hands over Taer's throat. The near constant pain that lingered there eased just as the pain in Taer's chest had. Despite Eir doing her best to heal the muscular and arterial damage to her throat, Taer still suffered from pain. She didn't know how much longer her body would need to heal the slash to her throat that she'd received from her brother's former guild master, and in a way she never wanted it to go away.

"Do you want to talk about it?" the Valkyrie asked, flexing her hands into small fists a few times before placing them primly in her lap.

"No," Taer replied sharply. As she tried to sit up the sheet fell from her body, and looking down she noticed her tank top was soaked with sweat. Her nightmares were getting worse.

She knew what the Valkyrie was trying to get her to do, but she wasn't ready for that yet. If she spoke about Adrian, she would break down and there was no way in hell she was going to cry over the death of her brother.

"I'll be fine," she said defensively when Eir looked at her with concern.

Eir nodded and returned to the bed on the other side of the room. She was one of Bryn's Valkyries, and also the goddess of healing. Taer had been sharing her room since Korvain had brought her to the Valkyries to be healed. And with her house now nothing but a charred ruin thanks to the same guild master who had murdered her brother in cold blood, there was nowhere else she could go. She had no home. No brother. Nothing …

Taer had her tank top over her head when Eir spoke again. "I understand, you know." Her words were barely audible, and in the cocoon of cotton surrounding Taer's head, she couldn't be absolutely sure that she'd heard her right.

Taer bit her tongue. She had to remember that Eir had lost someone too. Her twin, Kristy, had been killed in front of her by the god Loki. Although she must have been suffering just as much as Taer was, Taer couldn't find it in herself to give a fuck right now.

Pulling another tee over her head, Taer's eyes flickered over to the Valkyrie as she sat with her knees pulled up to her chest. Her loose blonde hair curtained the side of her face, making it difficult for Taer to see her expression and gauge her emotions.

Taer knew she should have said something comforting, but she had nothing but rage and sadness in her. She didn't even think it was possible to comfort someone else when she was still so messed up inside. Turning her back on the Valkyrie, Taer stripped the sweat-soaked bottom sheet from the bed and went to get another.

After making up her bed, Taer settled back on the mattress, letting the pillow cushion her head. She was afraid to close her eyes, afraid to dream of her brother again. Although she hadn't actually seen his death, Korvain had told her that he had died lying sprawled across her chest. Sometimes, she thought she could feel his blood soaking into her skin—and not always when she was dreaming.

"Taer!" Korvain barked. "Are you even listening to me?" Taer withdrew from her dark thoughts and tried to focus on her brother's best friend. The glowing ember of her anger flared at his provocative tone.

"Yeah, I'm listening," she replied defensively, keeping her eyes on his face. The Mare folded his arms over his muscular chest, stretching his shirt across his wide shoulders and firm pecs. She had no fucking idea what he'd been saying. Her thoughts had been consumed with finding ways to get to Darrion. It had been a month since Adrian's death, and she still hadn't been able to find out where the bastard was holed up.

"All right, what did I just say?" Korvain asked. When all Taer did was stare impassively, his lips turned up into a smug smile, the tips of his enormous fangs peeking out. He moved towards her without warning, sweeping her legs out from beneath her.

She landed heavily on her tailbone, the thin blue mats covering the bare polished concrete floor of the Eye doing nothing to cushion the impact. Taer pressed her lips together to muffle the small grunt from escaping her throat. "Sonofa—," she started to growl under her breath as she moved to get up, but when the air shifted around her, she looked up and the words turned to ash on her tongue.

A shiver ran down her spine like a knife being wielded by an expert hunter skinning his latest kill. Korvain towered over her, and his violent eyes were all she could see. A vicious, raw sound came from his throat, setting the hairs at the back of her neck on end. Her instinct to get away from him was warring with her angry desire to stand and face him.

"Pay attention, Taer! I was teaching you how to avoid getting caught with a leg sweep. And if you'd been listening," he hissed, "you would have known how to evade that last attack."

She stood back up, maintaining eye contact with the male. She had to crane her head back a little for that, but she wasn't going to give him the satisfaction of winning this argument.

There was a time—not too long ago—when she would have

been embarrassed to look at him, especially after she'd practically thrown herself at him and told him that she loved him … but things were different now. Adrian was dead, and she was going to kill the bastard that had put her brother in the ground.

Korvain must have seen the renewed determination in her eyes, because his thickly muscled arms wrapped around her back, dragging her against his hard chest. Taer could feel her eyes beginning to burn, could feel those traitorous tears threatening to spill over. Biting the inside of her cheek, she held them back. She would *not* cry. She would not cry in front of Korvain.

"We'll get him." He pulled away, forcing her to meet his eyes. "I swear on your brother's life that we will, Little—" Korvain shook his head. "*Taer*," he corrected. His eyes churned with pity. "You've been forced to grow up, Tay."

Taer felt his words hit her, rippling through her blood as their meaning struck home. She would never be his "Little Fox" again.

She had lost her innocence. She'd had her baptism in blood. She had crossed over to the other side and returned—bloodied and bruised—looking at the world in a whole new way.

He let her go and turned around. When he spoke again, his voice was painfully soft. "I lost my best friend when your brother died. He made me promise I'd look after you if anything happened to him, and dammit, Tay, I won't lose you to your anger and grief."

He turned towards her again, clutching her tightly by the upper arms, forcing her to look into his bottomless black eyes. "Your training is my top priority right now."

She wanted to scream that her top priority was killing Darrion, but she didn't need to say a word. Korvain could read the determination flowing off her body.

"The reason we're training is so that when the time comes, you'll be able to finish that motherfucker off by yourself."

Korvain released her arms, running both of his hands through his short hair. "We should stop for today," he muttered. "You're upset, and I've probably pushed you too far."

"No!" she replied, her voice hoarse. "I need to keep going," she explained when Korvain raised a dark eyebrow at her.

"We've been training for hours, Tay. You need to get some fuel into your body and you need to rest."

"I don't need food. Or sleep. What I *need* is to learn how to kill Darrion."

He turned his stormy eyes to her. "I know you've been having nightmares, Taer, and believe me I see the fucking irony in that." Taer started at his words, but she chose not to acknowledge his assumption. The last thing she needed was to have him worrying about her even more than he already was. "If your body isn't working at one hundred percent, then neither is your brain. I need you sharp, so when I say we're done, guess what? We're fucking done."

"Fine," Taer conceded. "Give me an hour to get my head on straight. I'll eat. I'll rest, too, if that's what you want, but after that, we train until the club opens. Deal?"

Korvain's shadowed eyes narrowed on her face. "If I see you eat and rest in that hour, I'll continue to train you," he bargained.

Taer swallowed her irritation, but from between her clenched teeth, she said, "Deal." Like hell she was going to close her eyes, though. She followed him up into the lift and into the apartment they now shared.

"Sit. I'll make you something to eat," Korvain commanded, pulling things from the fridge and setting them out on the bench. Taer bit her tongue and did as she was told. A minute later, a haphazardly slapped together turkey on rye was placed in front of her. Taer forced herself to eat it while Korvain watched on.

Seemingly satisfied, Korvain walked away, stripping the shirt over his head as he did. Taer caught the flash of black ink running the width of his shoulders. It was his contract with Darrion, inked with blood, and she wondered whether it was still active considering Darrion was currently off the grid.

"I'm going to take a shower," he called over his shoulder. "And Tay?" he added. She turned to look at him. "Get some sleep. You look like shit."

———————

Eir's eyes opened, her body waking slowly from the small nap she'd taken before having to go work her shift at the hospital. Although she didn't feel like it, she knew she had to go. She had to maintain some sort of semblance of her life before her twin sister had been ripped from her by a deranged god.

The door to her room was slightly ajar, allowing Bryn and Korvain's faint whispers to filter through.

"How's Taer doing?" Bryn asked, her voice gentle. The leader of their dwindling little group had taken the young Mare into her care almost immediately when Korvain had brought her to be healed after Darrion's attack.

"She's doing all right," the Korvain replied, sighing. "I just wish she'd talk to me about it."

There was a long pause.

"Do you want me to talk to her? Or maybe Eir could? She lost her sister, so maybe they could help each other."

Eir squeezed her eyes shut, but a solitary tear slid free. Kristy. Gods, she felt so hollow inside with her twin gone. Watching the light fade from her sister's eyes had killed something inside of her.

They'd given Kristy and the other Valkyries the funerals they'd deserved the day after Korvain had rescued her and Bryn from Loki, but it would take a long time before Eir could forget. Grief didn't abide by time. She could only imagine the pain Taer must have been going through, too.

Korvain's coarse, rumbling voice drifted back into her bedroom. "I'll ask her."

She pushed the light blanket from her body and sat up. Picking up the small, silver fob watch from her bedside table, she noted the time. She had about an hour and a half before her shift at the hospital started.

Kicking her legs off the side of the bed, Eir sat on the edge of the mattress and finger-combed her blonde hair. Braiding it with practiced fingers, she secured the end and got up, stretching out her back until her muscles felt loose.

She crept to the door, listening carefully to hear where Korvain and Bryn were. Eir liked Korvain—now she'd got over the initial shock that he was actually a Shadow Walker. And Bryn seemed happy for the first time since she'd left Odin's service.

When the apartment door opened then closed, Eir padded out into the hallway. A touch to her shoulder from behind stopped her, spinning her around.

"Eir," Korvain said, taking back his hand and folding his arms across his chest. She took a small step back, that old fear rearing its ugly head. He noticed the subtle shift in her behavior and loosened his arms, letting them drop to his side. He made a show of displaying empty hands.

"Sorry," she replied, taking a deep breath and shrugging. "Old habits."

His dark eyes were watchful. "You don't have to apologize. I get it."

She wondered whether he did get it. Eir guessed Bryn hadn't told him that Odin had personally ordered them to kill all Mares on sight while they were still in his service. The Valkyries had even gone on killing missions to known dark elf settlements to slaughter them all.

Bryn had been the most voracious in her drive to kill every single Mare in the Nine Worlds, all in her desire to please the All-Father.

How things had changed.

She lifted her eyes to his face once more. "Did you need me for something?"

Korvain reached up to scrub the back of his skull, and his bicep flexed and relaxed, reminding her that he was still dangerous. He was a tamed tiger right now, but he could unsheathe his claws at any time to protect what was his.

"Yeah. I was kind of hoping you'd speak to Taer about … about how she's feeling. She won't speak to me, and I know she's bottling things up." Eir nodded sympathetically. "She hasn't even cried about Adrian's death yet. Has she said anything to you about losing her brother?"

"No." She paused, wondering whether she should tell him what had happened that morning, and every morning since the death of Taer's brother.

"Do you know something?" he pressed, reclaiming the small steps he'd taken away from her.

She blew out a breath, meeting his dark, intense gaze. "I had to wake her up this morning. She's been having nightmares, but today's one was unusually violent. She was in a cold sweat. Her vitals were all over the place, and I had to slow her heart rate down."

"Gods," he muttered, his hand raking through his hair again. "I had a hunch about the dreams, and she didn't correct me earlier."

"After I stabilized her, I asked whether she wanted to talk about what she'd dreamed of. Her response was emphatic, and I didn't want to push her."

Korvain's concern for the young Mare radiated from his body, his harsh face etched with lines from the corners of his eyes and mouth. "Fuck, what am I supposed to do?"

She placed a tentative hand on his forearm, letting her natural healing ability take over, taking away some of his pain. "If you want my opinion, I'd leave her be for a little longer. Adrian's death is still a bleeding wound for her … she didn't have the opportunity to see his body and say goodbye." Eir paused to swallow past the sudden lump in her throat. "Give her a while longer to grieve."

Her voice cracked over the last word. Korvain moved towards her, wrapping his arms around her and pulling her against his chest. She stiffened in his embrace for just a moment—both terrified and unwilling to fall apart in front of him—but as soon as he uttered, "I'm so sorry, Eir. I didn't think," the tears began to roll unashamedly down her cheeks.

She wasn't sure how long he held her like that, but eventually he gently pushed her from his body, thumbing away a stray tear from her cheek. Eir took a moment to realize what a contradiction Korvain truly was. He was a Shadow Walker—one of the most feared assassins in all the Nine Worlds. He was death, yet, here he was, holding her, cradling her and supporting her while she fell apart. Bryn was incredibly lucky to have him in her life.

The apartment door opened and closed at that moment, making Eir take another step back and hastily swipe at the tears still clinging to her cheeks. She looked at Bryn as she stepped into the kitchen. "I should get ready," she said. "I have to go to work soon."

2

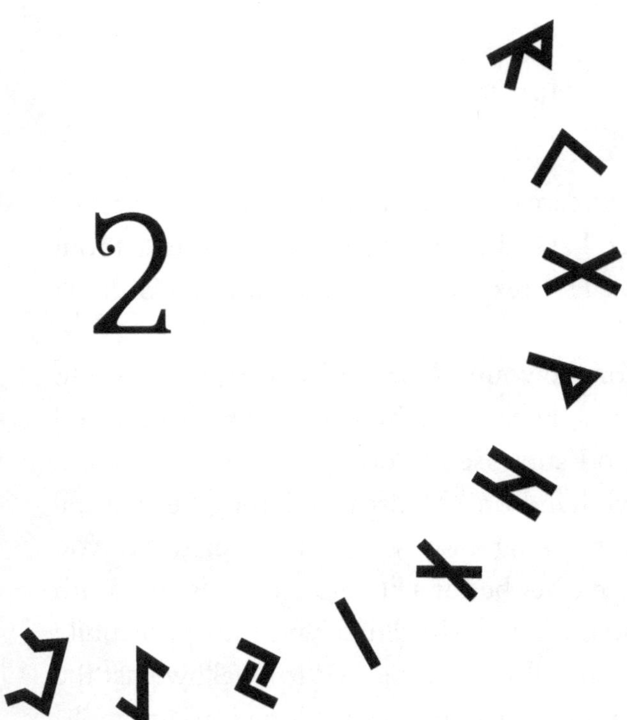

Taer had made sure to keep the smile plastered on her face as Korvain told her to get some sleep. He had to start work downstairs and expected her capitulation on this one thing after he'd held up his end of the bargain of a few hours more training.

But restful sleep just wasn't on the cards for her. Not anymore. She'd come to that realization and accepted it. Besides, she had work of her own to do, and all this waiting around was making her skin itch.

She watched Korvain disappear into the master bedroom he shared with Bryn, waiting until she heard the door click closed before she slipped inside the room she shared with Eir. Moving quietly, Taer retrieved the Beretta 92 Steel she'd 'acquired' to replace the one she'd lost in the fire, checking it over. Pulling on the leather holster, she slid the weapon into place and threw a jacket over her sweats and tee, making sure the collar would cover up her scar.

The quiet determination she had been sitting on for the past few weeks was finally paying off. Her injuries had prevented her from going out and tracking down the Mare who had murdered her brother, but now she was healed. Now she would be able to follow the leads she'd come up with while she rebuilt her strength.

Taer stuck her head out of the room. She could hear the shower running from behind the door to the master bedroom. Soundlessly, she slipped from the apartment and made her way down to the lower levels of the club, stepping out of the rear door and walking into a wall of icy air and the bitter perfume of car fumes and rotting garbage.

She walked towards the end of the alleyway that ran along the side of the club, emerging on the sidewalk. It had rained recently and the cement was slick from the recent downpour; puddles of water stood in the depressions of the bowed sideway, their surfaces shivering with the wind that seemed to blow straight through Taer.

Wrapping the jacket more tightly around her body, she walked away from the club, making sure she was a few blocks away before fading to one of the last known addresses of a Mare who was one of Darrion's longest serving Walkers.

She figured if anyone knew where the former guild master was, it would be him. Stepping from the shadows of a dilapidated house, Taer looked up at the apartment building Nieven was rumored to live in. It looked as depressing as every other building on the street and seemed a fitting home for that piece of shit.

She watched the place for a few minutes, her eyes darting over to the surrounding buildings every time there was the slightest hint of movement. The minutes seemed to drip by and yet nothing happened. It was quiet … perhaps too quiet.

Just as she was about to pull away, about to give up on Nieven as a possible lead and return to the club, a man walked up to the property—his walk a little too casual to be really casual.

"Nieven," Taer spat under her breath, his name a curse on her lips. She took a step closer to her target, her gaze predatory as he walked up the stairs of the apartment building and disappeared inside. She let out a breath and faded to the top of the stairs, watching the front door close. Waiting a few more minutes, she ghosted inside the building, remembering some of the skills Korvain had taught her while she was recovering from her wounds.

She kept her footsteps light, following the Mare undetected. She sneered to herself. How in the hell had this fucker become a Mare when he couldn't even tell when someone was following him? The cocksucker deserved to die for his ignorance, but not until Taer had pumped him for the information she needed.

Down the hallway and around a corner, Taer continued to follow him, her fingers touching the grip of her Beretta as she moved along the wall. Nieven took one last corner before his footsteps stopped.

Taer stayed hidden, listening carefully as his key slid into the lock, the teeth chattering along the tumbler like gunshots in the silence of the building. Keeping herself flat to the wall, she peered around the corner in time to see the Mare enter his apartment, the door slamming behind him. Taer walked towards the door, looking the doorway over. There were no runes to protect against fading. There was nothing extraordinary about the security measures either—just a deadbolt.

Nieven had become complacent—after only a few weeks. With Darrion gone, it appeared as if every member of his guild had lost their fear. Fading directly into the room would be too dangerous, but she didn't have to wait too long to figure out what she was going to do.

The dull rush of a shower running vibrated through the thin wooden door, telling her that Nieven was no longer in the room. Giving it a few more minutes, Taer faded directly into the apartment, just beyond the front door. Palming her weapon, she looked around the apartment, taking note of everything she could see.

The white walls were grubby with marks and nicotine stains. Not one stick of furniture was new, nor was it complete. Taer had to wonder why the Mare lived like he did. From what she understood, many Walkers made good money, and when they didn't, they would work in the human world like … *he* had.

Shaking off her unwanted thoughts, Taer followed the sound of the water, navigating through the one and only bedroom to the bathroom door. It had been left slightly ajar, a sliver of dirty yellow light cutting across the dingy, olive green carpet. Taer's feet straddled this light as she waited for the Golden Second.

She remembered Korvain's lesson on that. She had been laid up in bed for about a week, alternating between healing sessions with Eir and long periods of rest, so her body would heal naturally. She'd gone stir-crazy just lying there.

"How much longer am I going to be here?" she asked Korvain as he sat on the chair he'd dragged into Eir's room from the kitchen.

He indulged her with a rare smile. "As long as it takes. You need to heal."

They were not the words she had wanted to hear. "We're wasting time," she said, shooting him a fierce look. To her dismay, he only laughed.

"You need to get strong enough to start weapons training with me, and I won't start until you're ready. And right now, you aren't ready."

"I'm ready," she replied hotly. She was ready to get her revenge, and the

more time they wasted, the more time Darrion had to get away. She couldn't let him. She just couldn't.

Korvain's weary sigh cut through the room. "Tay, have you ever heard of something called the Golden Second?"

"What's that?"

Leaning back in his chair, Korvain studied her face. "It's that perfect second when you've come face to face with your enemy, and they've realized that they didn't even know you were there. It's that split second where you have the upper hand, and that advantage is hard for them to take back."

Taer hadn't really understood what Korvain had meant when he'd spoken about the Golden Second, but she understood it now—standing there, waiting for Nieven to appear. He had no idea she was inside his inner sanctum. He had no idea that he would more than likely be dead by the end of the hour.

The shower cut off with a sharp squeal from the taps.

The drip of water.

The snap of a towel.

Taer raised her arms carefully, the Beretta trained on the spot where Nieven's head would appear. The door opened, more light spilling into the room and onto Taer. He had a towel wrapped around his hips and was running another one roughly through his hair.

Her lips twitched up into a sardonic grin when he finally noticed her and stopped abruptly. His eyes darted around the room—no doubt looking for a weapon—but Taer had already anticipated he would do this.

"Don't," she said quietly and stepped toward him. She pressed the cold steel of the muzzle against his temple to drive her point home.

"Who are you?" he breathed, dropping the towel he had been

using to scrub at his scalp.

"I want information," she replied.

His pulse fluttered against his skin. "I don't know where Darrion is," he replied.

"Who said anything about Darrion?" Her voice was cold and even.

"You're not the first to come looking for him. I'll tell you what I told the last guy: I don't know where Darrion is. He hasn't contacted me."

Against her better judgment, she pushed on. "*Who* asked you where Darrion was?"

The Walker shrugged, and Taer pressed the muzzle in tighter. Nieven winced and his breath caught in his throat. "I didn't get his name."

Had Korvain already pressed this guy? When? And why hadn't he told her?

The muscle in Taer's jaw flexed.

"Where's Darrion?" she asked, moving her finger from the guard and onto the trigger. She had no problems with blowing this guy's head wide open. Hell, it would probably improve the decor.

"I told you, I don't know." He tried to step away, but Taer moved with him. She would find the bastard one way or another. Nieven had the balls to stay tight-lipped for a few moments longer until Taer removed the gun from his head and pressed it against his crotch. The Mare yelped and attempted to step away, slamming against a wall.

His fear would prevent him from fading, and he damn well knew it. She repositioned her weapon, aiming right between his eyes, and canted her head to the side. "His location. Now."

"I already told you. I don't know."

Was he stalling, or would she be able to get more information from him? Or had his usefulness worn out? She met his defiant gaze, her lips flexing into the barest smile.

"Wrong answer."

The sharp tang of gunpowder filled the room, the sound of the explosion ricocheting in her eardrums. Warm blood splattered her face and neck, her eyes closing against the spray. Nieven's lifeless body sagged to the ground, the back of his head a mess leaking out all over the filthy carpets. She bent down, staring at the look of surprise on his face. Had he really thought she wouldn't kill him?

It didn't matter. Nieven had been disposable. There were plenty of other people out there who would have the information she sought. Taer stood up from her crouch, put the safety back on the Beretta and faded from the apartment.

3

Darrion had been playing outside with his sister when he first heard the screams coming from down the road. Standing up from their game of runes, he shielded the sun from his eyes and squinted down into the valley that spread out beyond their house.

Dotted along the road were small houses made of stone and thatch, much like the house Darrion had been born into and grew up in. Suddenly, a flash of color caught his eye. He looked a little harder, squinting against the sun.

"What is it, Dar?" his little sister, Ara, asked. "Why are people screaming?"

Darrion looked down, taking in the smudge of dirt on her cheek. Ara had taken after their mother with her dark hair and eyes. She looked more like a Mare than he ever would. "I don't know," he replied, casting his eyes back out toward the road. A few houses were burning, their roofs having been set alight.

Further down the valley, more Mares were fleeing their houses now, looking hastily over their shoulders. Small children were being carried in the arms of their frightened parents, their screams of fear echoing between the vast mountains that hemmed in their village, traveling to Darrion's ears and sending chills through his blood.

"Dar?" Ara asked again, pulling at the bottom of his tunic for him to pick her up. Scooping her into his arms, he held her close and watched as more slashes of color flashed around the settlement. Whoever they were, they were coming closer.

Ara began crying when she saw a rider on a horse cutting down one of the female dark elves running with her young child clutched tightly to her chest. There was that flash of color again … except it was more than one color.

Gold.

Scarlet.

Blue.

Black.

More colors than Darrion could count, but he knew in that moment who they were.

Valkyries.

The loud whinnying of a horse drew his attention. The eight legs of Sleipnir were clear to see, and astride that horse was Odin—the All-Father.

"No," Darrion cried out softly. "No." He had thought they'd be safe here. Clutching his sobbing sister closer to his chest, Darrion turned and ran towards home. Those horrible screams followed him until he drowned them out by slamming the wooden door behind him.

His mother looked up, startled, from her sewing. "Darrion, what is it?" The yarn in her lap fell to the floor as she stood up, the spool unraveling along the wooden floor. The fear in his eyes must have told her everything she needed to know, and she began wringing her hands together until her knuckles turned white. Darrion's sister was wailing now, and his mother moved to take her.

"Hush, Ara." She turned her dark eyes to Darrion. "What has happened?"

"They're coming … *he's* coming."

A strangled cry broke from his mother's lips, but she said nothing more, just held Ara closer.

"Where is Father?" he asked, moving toward the small window and looking out past the rough fabric covering the crude opening. He could see the first few dark elves who had fled the village making their way past their house now.

And still his mother said nothing. Darrion swung around, seeing that her wide eyes were fixed on the door. "Mother! Where is Father?" He'd raised his voice, shocking her out of her fear.

"He's … he's out tilling the fields."

Cursing under his breath, Darrion knew he had no choice. He turned towards the door.

"What are you doing?" she asked frantically.

He met his mother's eyes first, then his sister's. "I'm going to fetch him home."

Tears dripped down his mother's face. "You can't. They'll kill you."

"We'll be sitting ducks here without him." He could see that she knew he was right, but her natural instinct to protect her children was warring with her common sense.

"I'll go instead," she said. "I can fade to him and be back instantly."

"No, Mamma!" Ara wailed, tightening her grip around their mother's neck. Darrion knew this was the only way they could survive. He wouldn't be old enough to fade for another fifty years … if he survived today's attack, that was.

"Ara, come and stay with me. We'll hide and wait for Mamma to come back … come on," he coaxed, pulling her from their mother's arms and into his. He raised his eyes to his mother. "Go. We'll be fine."

Darrion watched his mother fade from the room and then turned toward the hidey-hole that had been built into the wall when their house had been constructed. He pulled open the door and eased Ara inside.

A bloodcurdling scream just outside the door spun his head around. Ara began crying harder, and that was the last thing they needed—to draw attention to themselves.

"Hush, Ara. It's all right. It was only the scream of a horse." His words did nothing to ease the little girl and she cried even harder.

"What if it's Ascal?" she heaved through her wracking sobs.

"Your horse is in the back field with mine. It was not Ascal." That seemed to work. She stopped sobbing, looking up at him with tears tracking slowly down her face, streaking the mud in fine dark lines down her cheeks. "Now stay here. I'm going to keep an eye out for the Valkyries."

Standing up, Darrion pushed the door to, but didn't close it properly in case he needed to dive in. Walking quietly towards the window, he tried to block out the sounds of violence vibrating through the wood. Looking out, he saw his neighbors lying in pools of their own blood, their bodies left where they'd fallen on the road outside their fence.

"Darrion!" his father whispered in a harsh voice. The boy spun around, relief flooding him to see that both his father and mother were back. "Come away from there. Now."

He did as he was told, creeping back towards his parents. Ara sprang from the hidden cavity, throwing herself at their father's legs.

"Darrion, get inside the hidden room."

Wasting no time, he did just that, sliding inside and moving over to make room for Ara, but before she could squeeze in beside him, there was the sound of splitting wood, and his father hissed at him to close the door and hide. Darrion didn't want to hide away like a coward while his mother, father and sister faced the goddesses who had been hunting them down for hundreds of years.

The front door exploded in a rain of sharp wood, and the anguished tone of his father's voice forced Darrion to close the door to his hiding place. With his heart pounding in his ears, he peered through the tiny space between the wooden slats and watched on in horror.

A Valkyrie stepped through what was left of the door. Her golden blade dripped with the blood of the dark elves she had slaughtered, and her hard, beautiful face was expressionless as she looked over his parents and sister as if they were nothing more than vermin.

"Please," his mother begged. "Spare us."

A sneer lifted the Valkyrie's full lips and she stepped to the side as Odin walked in through the broken doorway, his one green eye surveying the room and all the people within it.

Ara screamed when she saw him, burrowing her face under their mother's hair. Odin was the god their parents had told them about, the god who haunted their nightmares. His mother had said that if they were ever naughty, the All-Father would swoop down on his eight-legged horse and carry them away forever.

His father stepped in front of his mother and Ara, shielding them from the All-Father's view.

The god laughed, the sound booming around the small room. "You think you can protect your women from me?" he taunted, still laughing.

"We only want a peaceful life. We only want to raise our child and teach her our ways."

Odin's expression darkened, the room darkening in turn. Darrion felt his scalp prickle with fear, and he recoiled from the small hidden door.

"Do you think we'd let you raise your spawn so she can hunt down and kill *my* people? Your entire species must be wiped from the face of the Nine Worlds."

Darrion's mother whimpered, shuffling away from the Valkyrie, who had just taken a step closer to them all.

"Please," his father begged. "We won't—" but his words died as the Valkyrie thrust her golden sword into his chest. His mother screamed uncontrollably. She dropped to her knees beside his father's body, Ara falling from her arms and onto the floor next to her, sobbing.

Darrion's fingers dug into the rough wood beneath his fingers; the splinters burrowed into his skin, but he hardly felt the sharp stab. The sound of sobbing was suddenly cut off as the same golden blade pierced the hearts of both his mother and sister.

Darrion clamped both hands over his mouth to stop the scream burning the back of his throat from breaking free. The blood of his family leaked out onto the floor, mingling to create one huge puddle—a deep, rich crimson, the same color as Darrion's burgeoning rage.

As he watched on, he could feel the hatred writhing beneath his skin, an almost living thing in his blood that demanded he avenge the death of his parents and his sister.

Odin and his Valkyrie turned their backs and left the house as if what they had just done required not a single lingering glance.

Once their shadows were gone and the sound of their retreating footsteps was nothing more than a distant memory, Darrion removed his hands from his mouth and the harsh, rough sounds of his breathing filled his ears. He stayed hidden until night fell—until he could be sure that Odin and his Valkyries were really gone.

Eventually Darrion fell asleep, awaking only when hushed footsteps echoed on the cold, wooden floor. Blinking the sleep from his eyes, he looked through the small crack in the hidden door and saw a man standing there, looking at the bodies of his family.

"Such a waste," he said in a low voice and turned to leave. Darrion could sense he wasn't one of the Aesir. Taking a risk, he pushed open the door, revealing his hiding place.

The man stopped abruptly, his shoulders tensing, but he didn't turn around. Darrion scrambled to get to his feet, his muscles sore from being cramped up for so long. The man turned and Darrion got his first look at him.

With his long gray hair and a flowing gray beard, the almost luminescent green of his eyes looked out of place on his otherwise wizened old face. He was tall and lanky, barely a shred of muscle on him, but Darrion wasn't about to underestimate the man.

The man knelt, bringing himself down to Darrion's eye level. "What's your name, son?"

Darrion remained quiet.

"I'm not going to hurt you. I'm here to help you. What's your name?"

"Darrion," he replied. What else did he have to lose? His parents and sister were dead. He was only a boy. What hope did he have of survival other than becoming a beggar?

The man smiled. "Darrion, my name is Njord. I am—"

"A Vanir," Darrion gasped, taking a step back, eyes searching for something he could use as a weapon.

"Yes," Njord replied softly—almost angrily. "But I've grown tired of Odin's ridiculous war against the dark elves. He is killing them for no other reason than for fear that they will bring down his coveted world."

The words were spoken with such venom that Darrion had no doubt that they were true.

"The Vanir are rising against Odin and the Aesir for their unfounded and prejudiced persecution of your people," Njord said.

"What does that have to do with me?" Darrion asked, his voice a bare squeak. Fear was running through his body, turning his blood to ice. The Vanir were the gods who were in power before the Aesir. The two groups had always been civil, but it sounded as if things were about to change.

"You are valuable," Njord said. "You just don't know it yet."

"What would you know? You are a god of old—a magician. What would you know about our struggle? About revenge?"

"I know a lot more than you think," Njord said vehmently, causing Darrion to shrink away. Taking a few steps towards the boy, the hard thump of his boots punctuated the seriousness of the words that followed. "I can teach you how to handle a knife, how to be at one with the weapon. I can teach you how to rule others, to be respected and feared at the same time. I can give you your revenge on Odin. Don't you want that chance?"

Darrion was hardly listening to a word he'd been saying until the phrase "your revenge on Odin" caught his attention. Yes. That was what Darrion wanted—revenge. And the only way he would get it was if he was trained to kill.

And this man—this god—was willing to train him. Darrion stood a little straighter and looked Njord square in the eye.

"When do we start?"

4

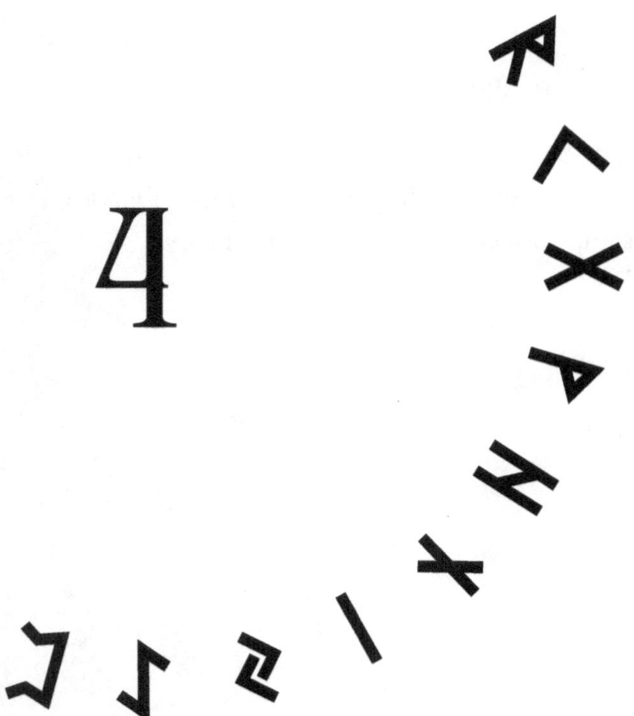

The club was absolutely heaving with people; gods and humans were rubbing shoulders, drinks were being spilled, women were being hit on, and Mason had to keep his eyes moving and his instincts sharp. Being able to hear people's thoughts had always seemed to be some kind of burden, but right now, he saw the fucking silver lining. With the recent events involving Bryn and the other Valkyries still hanging over his head—weighing on his conscience—Mason listened out for any information that might fill in the blanks Bryn had refused to.

When he started to hear the thoughts of—what he'd later found out had been—gods, he knew he was in for a whole world of pain. The only way to get away from the cacophony of sound was to concentrate on not hearing anything, like hitting the mute button on a remote control.

Slowly, the buzzing began to die down until all he was left with was the sound of the gods' actual voices, mingled with the human voices, chattering in his ears. Letting out a relieved breath, he focused on Bryn sitting at the bar. Her eyes were on the glass in her hand, her mind obviously far away from what was happening around her in The Eye.

Mason refrained from listening in to see what was bothering her, finding the violation distasteful. Instead, he busied himself by scanning the crowd again. A brunette sidled into his line of sight, the whisper of a smile on her lips.

"Hi, handsome," she said, her voice rolling out in a guttural purr that only a three-pack-a-day smoker could pull off. Mason's eyes flicked down to her cleavage, which was proudly on display in a low-cut dress. After getting a good long look at the goods, his eyes returned to her heavily made-up face.

"Can I help you with something, ma'am?"

"Ma'am?" she said, laughing. "Who would have thought I'd find a gentleman here."

Mason ground his molars together. The politeness was a side effect from his time in the Marines, and one of the habits he just couldn't shake.

She ran her finger down her neck and over the swell of one of her breasts. "Could you tell me where the bathroom is?"

Jerking his chin in the direction of the back corner of the building, he said, "Over there, past the black curtain."

Looking pleased with herself, she touched his forearm lightly. "Thanks." Turning, she swaggered away, her hips swaying and holding Mason's attention for a little longer than normal.

"I thought you preferred blondes," Bryn said behind him. Mason turned around to see his boss standing there, her arms folded loosely across her chest. The golden sword tattooed on the side of her neck reflected back glimpses of their surroundings.

Mason laughed. "I don't discriminate when it comes to women."

The Valkyrie snorted and shook her head, a small grin on her face. "You always know what to say to make me feel slightly better."

Of course, Bryn hadn't had a lot to smile about recently. The light that had been in her eyes a few moments ago was now gone.

"Hey, are you all right?" he asked, touching her shoulder.

Her blue-ringed eyes rose to his face. "I'll be fine."

"You still haven't told me what happened to you."

She took a step away, looking down at the ground, her hands curled into tight fists. She refused to meet his eyes. "Some other time, Mason."

He wasn't going to push her if she wasn't ready to talk, but that didn't mean he wouldn't be there when she was ready. "I'll hold you to that," he replied, letting her hear his conviction.

She got busy surveying the customers in the bar to avoid his concerned stare. "We're busy tonight. Better keep your eyes and ears open."

"They always are."

A month had gone by already. Mason hadn't heard any more about what had happened, other than Bryn had been taken by a god who was convinced she was the key to killing Odin. He didn't know how much longer he could wait to hear the whole story. Whatever it was, it had broken something inside her.

And that broke something in him. Mason would have killed for Bryn. He should have been looking out for her, but it had always been the other way around. She'd given him a job when he'd really needed one. Mason had known she was different right from the start. Apart from her stunning looks, and the golden tattoo on her neck, she gave off an almost palpable vibe of "otherness".

Mason returned to watching men come in, carefully looking them over before allowing them access to the higher levels of the club. If they weren't wearing the right thing, or hadn't made a prior booking to be there, he refused them entry.

The Eye could afford to be that exclusive.

He was just letting the last group past him when he felt a deep thrum in his blood; the deep thrum that was Korvain, calling him, searching him out. Mason couldn't feel it all the time—only when Korvain was actively looking for him. He turned his head just as the Mare pushed into the club from behind the "Staff Only" door. Even though Mason was technically Korvain's boss, he knew who was top dog and when to follow orders. Mason hadn't survived the marines without learning that important lesson.

Fear gripped Mason by the balls, a shiver traveling down his spine, setting his fight-or-flight instincts on high alert. As the guy prowled into the room, humans and gods scattered, trying to get as far away from him as possible. Mason knew what he was—a Shadow Walker, and also the last full-blooded Mare in existence. The bastard was powerful. Mason had tasted it when he'd taken a blood oath and bound himself to the male. Hell, he could taste it even now as if it hung in the air.

"Mason," Korvain said, his dark brows drawing down over shadow-filled eyes as he glowered at those who stared. Mason looked up and noticed the three-foot exclusion zone Korvain had inadvertently created.

"What's up?" Mason asked, meeting the guy's eyes. Mason liked the Mare, mainly because he had Bryn's back. They were definitely on the same team when it came to protecting that Valkyrie.

The guy moved his body closer to Mason, herding him toward the wall, blocking him from view and shielding their conversation. "I just need to reiterate the fact that you need to keep what you know locked down. Nobody can find out what you know."

Mason swallowed. Korvain would kill him if he ever breathed

a word about the other world of gods and goddesses. "I told you before I wouldn't. Besides, I thought our blood oath took care of that?"

Korvain smiled unpleasantly, baring his fangs. Up close, they looked at least two inches long, gleaming despite the low light. "That blood oath isn't a gag order."

"I wouldn't talk about Bryn and the others. They're too important to me."

Korvain kept up the threatening smile, but the hardness drained from his eyes. "That's exactly what I wanted to hear." He looked at his watch and moved his big body away. "I have to go, but keep your ears open tonight. If you hear the name Darrion, I want a report as soon as I get back."

Mason let out the breath he didn't know he'd been holding. "You got it, but where are you going?"

"I have to go get one of the other Valkyries from work. Bryn doesn't want any of her girls traveling without an escort."

"Until Darrion is caught?" Mason asked, piecing the puzzle together all on his own. He had no fucking idea who Darrion was, but he was on Korvain's shit list, which couldn't have been a good place to be.

"Yeah," Korvain said. "Keep your ears and eyes sharp."

Mason looked out over the crowd. Every single set of eyes was on them. As Korvain strode from the room, those eyes followed him. When the door slammed shut behind him, the whole room seemed to breathe a sigh of relief.

Yeah, Mason knew exactly how they felt.

5

Galen watched his partner finishing off their current hit in the reflection of the floor-to-ceiling windows of the high-rise apartment block nestled in the Chicago skyline.

The male cowering at the end of Rhys's knife was making soft mewling sounds in the back of his throat. With a wicked grin, and his blue eyes flashing brilliant gold for a split second, Rhys plunged his knife into the human's throat, the pitiful bleatings turning into his final gurgling breaths.

Galen refocused his eyes onto the dark waters of Lake Michigan beyond the glass. Lights from the surrounding buildings bounced off the nearly flat surface, creating a kaleidoscope of blues, yellows and reds. It was almost serene, until he caught glimpses of the fresh blood splashed on the front of his shirt in his reflection.

He shrugged.

Occupational hazard.

Galen turned back around to face Rhys, who was just getting to his feet, his hands and forearms slick with blood. Galen's eyes drifted down to the corpse, a sadistic smile tugging up the corners of his mouth.

Craine was going to be happy with them.

"We're done here," he said. Rhys nodded once and faded from the room. Galen wandered over to the front door, stepping over the body casually, and unlocked it. He didn't have to worry about the human authorities tracking them, recognizing them, although their crimes were already notorious.

As Walkers, they would never be discovered and never be caught.

As Craine's wet men, they were untouchable.

When Galen faded back to the apartment, he found Rhys at the kitchen sink, washing away the blood caking his skin. Galen didn't know why their boss had wanted their latest target liquidated, but what Craine wanted, Craine got.

And in all honesty, he didn't give a fuck.

He'd been born and bred for this shit.

Killing. Blood. Torture.

He thrived on the hunt, on the kill. Pulling his T-shirt over his head, he dumped it on the ground as he entered his bedroom.

With blood still sticky on his stomach, he had a shower and wandered back into his room. Slipping his arms into a fresh shirt, he looked at his reflection in the mirror as he buttoned up the black silk. He double-checked he didn't have any other blood left on him; nothing said serial murderer like blood spots on your neck, after all.

Flashing himself a confident smile in the mirror, Galen returned to the kitchen, where he found Rhys in a fresh set of clothes.

"You ready?" he asked. Rhys's pale blue eyes glittered with excitement. Nothing got him harder than killing. Galen almost felt sorry for the female that Rhys would decide he wanted that night. "Ice?"

Without a word, Rhys faded from the kitchen. Galen took a moment to take stock of the apartment they shared. They were currently unaffiliated with the Chicago guild master, and that was the way they wanted it to stay. Of course, being owned by another Mare did have its advantages—safety, mostly—but that reason didn't really seem to have much credence anymore.

Before the Fall, if any Mare wasn't connected to a guild, whether as a Walker or in any other position, they had more chance of being killed by Odin; the old adage of strength in numbers was definitely true. But *since* the Fall, since Odin had lost his power and his Valkyries, Shadow Walkers had been on their own, unless their term with their master happened to be a damn long one.

Closing his eyes, Galen faded from the apartment in Chicago, rematerializing in the alleyway beside the bar, Ice. Running a hand through his hair, he stepped from the shadows and joined Rhys, who was waiting patiently—as always—against the brick wall. Indicating the way with his head, Galen led them inside the bar, stepping through the door and into the near-arctic environment the owner, Skadi, liked to maintain.

Towering over the high bar, the female Jotunn was serving mead made from the traditional recipes from the old country. Her ice-blonde hair was hanging in her silver-frosted eyes, her well-proportioned body moving with lithe grace. As the muscles in her upper arms and forearms moved, the ripple of the albino snake-skin tattoos that ran all over her body moved with them. She looked up when the door slammed behind Galen and Rhys, her bored expression unchanging.

Galen's eyes shifted around the bar, taking note of who was in the room. Rhys did the same, but when his body language changed—became tenser—Galen followed his gaze. It was stuck on Tyr sitting at the back of the room. The god's whole body was slumped forward over the table, the stump where his right hand used to be resting beside his drink.

This could be problematic. Rhys was generally all right—he still looked like a light elf—but Galen's black hair gave away his dark elf heritage. The standing order to kill all dark elves hung perpetually over his head, and there were still some among the Aesir who had become bounty hunters just for the fun of it.

But the more he studied the god, the more he realized that Tyr—the former god of war—would not give them any trouble. Rumor had it that after the Fall, Tyr got lost in human vices like alcohol and drugs. Although they didn't really have the same negative effect on gods as they did humans, Galen could see how worn Tyr had become.

Rhys grabbed them a table while Galen moved towards Skadi at the bar, acutely aware of how her eyes followed him.

"Two tankards of ale," Galen told the ice giant, leaning his forearms on the bar. He was only there for a second before cursing and stepping back as a thirty-foot albino serpent slithered around his legs. If there was one thing he couldn't stand, it was large snakes, and when it came to Skadi, everything she owned was big.

It took a few minutes for the snake to inch past his feet, and by the time he stepped back up to the bar, two overflowing mugs had been set in front of him. Placing a couple of bills on the rough bar top, Galen took the drinks and made his way over to Rhys.

He shivered when he sat down, catching the last two feet of the snake's pale, thin tail slithering around the other end of the bar.

"That fucking snake defies logic," he muttered under his breath.

"What?" Rhys asked, tipping back his tankard and draining half his beer.

"Skadi keeps the temperature hovering near freezing in this damn place, yet that *thing* crawls around here like it's got a goddamn rocket up its ass."

Rhys's lips twitched—just about as close to a smile as the guy got—but he didn't say anything more. Galen kept an eye on where the snake had disappeared around the bar while he took the first long drink from his ale. Rhys stood up a minute later, wandering over towards the bar.

His mug was empty already.

Fuck, the guy either needed to get flat-on-his-ass drunk or laid … and soon. Galen relaxed back into the booth and took another sip from his glass, his eyes moving around the outer perimeter. There were probably twenty or so gods and goddesses, giants and elves in the bar tonight.

But he didn't care about ninety-nine percent of them—all he was looking for was a female he and Rhys could use for a couple of hours—and then his eyes latched on to a goddess he hadn't ever seen around before.

She was standing by the jukebox, carefully selecting some music to play. Her corn-silk hair was curled, inching down to the small of her back, highlighting her small waist and large bust. From his current angle, Galen couldn't see what color her eyes were, but if she were Aesirean like he thought she was, they were probably going to be blue.

Rhys returned to the table, another drink in his hand. Galen pointed out the goddess to Rhys with a covert nod of his head in the direction of the jukebox. His best friend's eyes zeroed in on the female, dragging down her body and lingering on her ass. His tongue swiped along his bottom lip.

Ding, ding, ding.

We have a winner.

Galen stood up and wandered over to her, leaving the near-mute Rhys to sit back and watch the magic happen. As he got to within a few feet of her, his nostrils flared, taking in the delicate scent of rosewater. She looked up, startled, as he sidled up beside her.

"Hi," he said, holding her pale blue gaze.

She smiled demurely and looked away for a moment, a blush sending a flush of color across her cheeks. "Hello," she replied, keeping her eyes on the jukebox.

"What's your name?" Taking her free hand, he brought it to his mouth, brushing his lips over her delicate knuckles. She wasn't the usual type he'd go for. He preferred a woman who looked like she could take what he and Rhys dished out.

She didn't look like she could, but she was the only acceptable choice, the only unattached female in the place other than Skadi.

"Amanea," she replied, brushing some of her long hair back and sweeping it behind her ear … her slightly elongated ear. She was a light elf—not one of the Aesir as he'd thought.

"Amanea," he repeated thoughtfully. "Beautiful whisper."

Amanea's eyes widened before she dropped her gaze again, blushing.

"Come and have a drink with me and my friend," Galen coaxed, pulling at her hand. The light elf looked over in Rhys's direction and froze—a mouse ensnared in the hypnotic stare of a stalking cat.

Leaning in, Galen whispered into her ear. "He's harmless, I

promise … besides, I can protect you." Pulling back, he watched Amanea's body relax slightly. With one more gentle tug, he had her following him back to the table. "What are you drinking?" he asked, still grasping her hand as she lowered herself down into one of the chairs.

"Red wine?" she replied, her inflection making it more question than answer.

"You got it. Be right back."

Flashing Rhys a *behave, asshole* look, he headed toward the bar, ordering a red wine for Amanea and another ale each for him and Rhys. He watched anxiously over his shoulder, checking to see whether Rhys had scared her off yet. He tended to do that.

After what felt like a millennium, Galen returned to the table, only to find Rhys sitting there … alone.

"What the fuck?" he growled, setting their drinks down too roughly, sending amber liquid sloshing over the lip.

"Some fucking light elf came over and collected her."

Galen inspected the bar, spotting her talking to another man. "Fuck," he cursed sharply, sitting down and downing the wine before starting in on his drink.

"There'll be others," Rhys drawled dryly in reply. Galen tried to ignore how his friend's eyes morphed color as he said the words, but he knew better. Rhys couldn't last much longer.

Galen he kept his mouth shut, though, biting back the words. She was the *only* eligible female in the bar, and it was probably Rhys that had scared her away, or made her look like she needed rescuing. But Rhys scared a lot of people away. It was probably the way he stared at them like he wanted to slit their throats for no other reason than that they were breathing the same air as him, but it could also have been the fact that there was something hidden behind his eyes—something dangerous that made the hairs at the back of their necks prickle and their hearts race.

If only they knew …

Years ago—before the Fall—Galen had rescued Rhys from a near fatal beating by some Aesirean fuckers who had decided that his mixed blood was a good enough reason to attack and nearly kill him through some cruel and unusual torture. Rhys had sworn his life to Galen that day, but Galen wasn't into the whole servitude bullshit. Still, they had been inseparable since then.

Downing the rest of his drink, Galen let out a heavy sigh. It looked like neither of them was going to get their cock sucked unless they picked up a pro. Galen looked at his watch. There was still time to find a woman, but by the flashes of gold in Rhys's eyes, they had to go find one fucking fast.

Indicating it was time to leave, they both stood up and moved towards the door. When a low snarl vibrated from Rhys's throat, Galen's eyes cut to his face, noting the way his best friend's eyes were staying solid yellow for longer now.

They had to find a way for him to expend his volatile energy and soon.

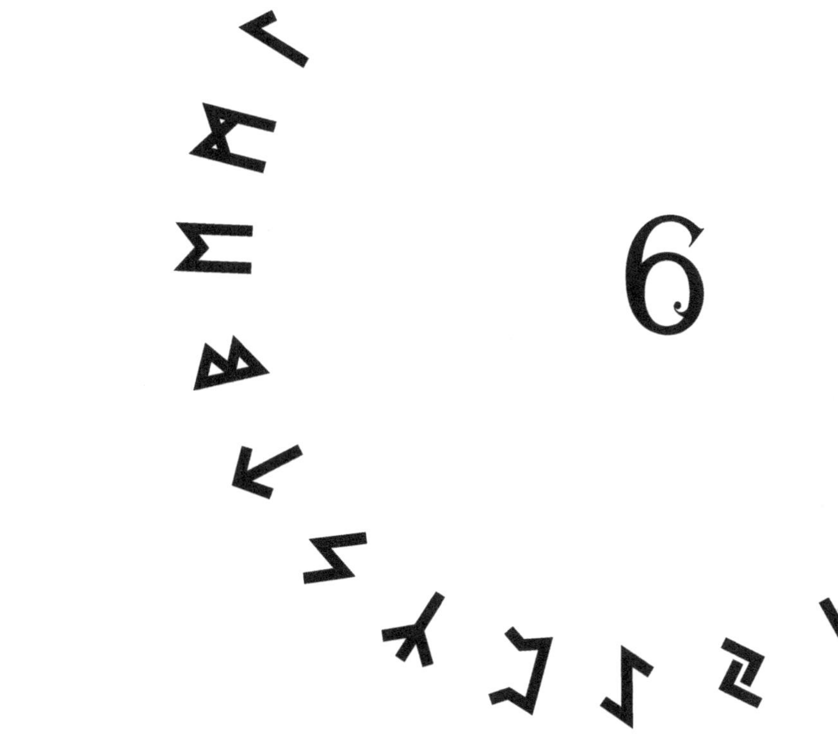

6

As Loki listened to the Aesirean prattle on about the All-Father, he was smugly pleased that at least some things hadn't changed. The gods still liked to gossip, and Odin was still their favorite topic of conversation.

Leaning casually against the hot dog cart the guy was working from, Loki asked, "So you heard he's in Chicago?" He had changed his appearance slightly just in case anyone recognized him.

The god loaded a dog with relish and handed it to the human waiting in line. "Yeah. That's what I heard."

"Why would he go there?" Loki took his first bite of the hot dog in his hand, finding the flavors and sensations unexpectedly pleasant. He chewed thoughtfully, waiting for the Aesir to answer.

Running the sleeve of his shirt under his nose, the god shrugged and looked out at the unseasonably sunny Boston day. "He was only staying here because Frigg was here. But now that she's dead, why would he hang around?"

"His Valkyries?" Loki quizzed.

The god barked out a laugh. "Odin hasn't been in Bryn's good graces for a very long time. I doubt he'd hang around for them."

Loki thought about that for a moment, but dismissed the idea. Odin would never leave Bryn unprotected—not when she was the key to his very survival. But that little titbit wasn't public knowledge. If the All-Father were in Chicago, it wouldn't be for an extended stay. He would come back to Boston … unless he had a *very* good reason not to.

"So what's in Chicago?" Loki asked casually, wiping his fingers with a paper napkin and dumping his trash into the small bin attached to the cart.

"His son is," the god replied, taking out a warmed bun for his next customer. Turning to Loki he added, "Thor is there."

Loki let the words sink in. He couldn't believe how single-minded he'd been. He'd been going after Odin by taking away all those he loved. His wife was gone. Half of his Valkyries were dead. But Thor was still alive. How could he have overlooked the god of thunder? Thor had been present at Loki's imprisonment, had taken pleasure in his pain, had laughed along with his father as Loki writhed in agony.

Contemplating the information carefully, Loki walked away from the Aesir, already planning how he could possibly use Thor against the All-Father. Loki still wanted Bryn first, especially after she had escaped him last time. But if he should fail in a second attempt, the All-Father's most favored son would be the perfect substitute.

Knowing that preparedness was the key to a well-executed plan, Loki faded away from Boston Common. The vibration ran through his whole body for mere seconds, and then he was standing in the vast, modern, steel-and-glass city of Chicago. Not knowing where to begin, Loki started walking, keeping his eyes and senses open for anything that might lead him to Thor or Odin.

It wasn't until nightfall that he stumbled across a building that had been shielded from human sight with very old Vanir magic. Standing across the road, hidden in shadows, Loki watched light elves and giants, Aesirean gods and dwarves enter the establishment, all without drawing any attention from the humans sharing the sidewalk with them.

Changing his features subtly, Loki ensured he looked like a demigod of some description by changing his green eyes to brown, and lengthening and darkening his blond hair until it brushed against his shoulders.

Satisfied with his ubiquitous appearance, Loki crossed the road and pushed open the door. Stepping into Ice was like stepping back into the past. The bar was run by the very ice giant who had helped Odin imprison Loki all those years ago. It was her snake that had been used to torture and torment him while his mind had rotted away in that cave. It had been her who walked away, mourning the loss of her serpent rather than the eternity of pain and agony she had condemned him to.

For an ice giant, she was beautiful, but the last time Loki had seen her, she had not had the albino serpent tattoos covering both her arms and disappearing into the short sleeves of her shirt.

It appeared that time had changed her, too.

Loki walked further inside, taking a seat near the back of the bar, making sure he could see the entire floor and all its occupants. All the races of the Nine Worlds were there, talking and drinking together. On occasion, he saw one of the Aesir he had known before his imprisonment, but it was one of the gods that caught and held his attention longer than any other.

Tyr was drowning himself in a tankard of ale. Seeing his stump lying motionless on the table beside his cup made Loki smile. He remembered the day Tyr had lost his hand very well indeed.

After observing everything, and taking note of everyone's location in the building, Loki made his way over to a group of gods who were playing pool on the opposite side of the bar. There were four of them altogether, and from what he could tell, they were all Aesireans. Loki stopped a dozen feet from the table, his shoulder resting against the wall casually.

"We're almost done with our game, buddy," one of them said, the echo of his shot still resonating around the room.

Loki pushed off the wall and approached the men. "I don't want to play. I need to ask you all a few questions."

Another man in the group chalked the end of his cue before lining up his shot. The white ball cracked into the solid green, sending it rolling into a corner pocket. "What kind of questions?" he asked, looking up from his shot.

"About … Odin," Loki replied, gently testing the waters. All four men stopped what they were doing and stared at him. Then they began laughing at him. Confused, Loki asked, "What's so funny?"

One of them stopped laughing long enough to say, "The All-Father is nothing but a joke now. I'm not even sure he's still alive anymore."

Loki's rage kindled within him. Odin might not be as powerful as he had been, and he was Loki's mortal enemy, but he was a god who still demanded respect. And anyone who disrespected him would feel Loki's anger. His hands curled into fists, ready to lash out. His muscles were tensed, ready to strike, when he stopped himself. He had to control his temper. Killing four Aesireans now would not get him the information he needed.

Exhaling, he fixed them all with a hard stare. "Taking the All-Father for granted is not wise."

The group laughed out loud again. The first man stepped forward, leaning on his pool cue with two hands. "What could he possibly do to us now, huh? He's lost his Valkyries. He's lost his power. Nobody believes in him anymore." The god turned away, sliding his cue back into the rack hanging on the wall. The others did the same, all of them walking past Loki and back to the bar to order some more drinks.

Frustrated, he turned around and made his way to the door. He should not have brought it up so casually. He stepped out into the cool night air, resting his back against the wall beside the door. He knew Odin had to be in Chicago—especially now that he knew Thor was also there—but where was he? And who would know where to find him?

Loki was so lost in his thoughts that his head snapped up suddenly when the door opened beside him, the noise of the bar trailing out after a couple of men as they left. One was blond, the other dark-haired. Loki's nostrils flared when the faint odor of blood carried on the breeze hit his nose, and he immediately knew what the pair were. Apart from the altercation with Bryn's Walker while Loki was trying to snatch one of the Valkyries from the street, it had been a very long time since he'd encountered any dark elves with such undiluted blood.

"You need a woman, Rhys. You're so close to the fucking edge right now," The dark-haired male said to his friend, leading them away from the club, away from Loki.

"I'm fine, Galen" the other man replied, his voice strained, his body tense. His hands were bunched into tight fists at his sides, his shoulders hunched up. The blond—Rhys—looked over his shoulder, pinning Loki to the spot with a piercing glare, and causing Loki to lower his eyes. Pretending to study the ground intently, Loki waited until he heard their footsteps retreating, and then waited a few beats before following them.

He stayed far enough away to avoid detection, but kept them within sight. If they were Walkers as he suspected they were, he could find a use for them. Perhaps he could send them to hunt down Odin, Bryn, or even Thor.

He tracked them to the edge of Humboldt Park, then looked around, trying to figure out what they were doing. It was deserted at this time, and the only humans around looked to be either whores or drug dealers. As they walked along North Avenue, a woman in a short dress stepped into their path.

Sidestepping behind a tree, Loki listened to the exchange between human and dark elf.

"How are you doing, sugar?" the woman asked, and the stench of stale cigarettes and alcohol drifted from her body. "You looking for a date?"

Loki waited for the Walkers' response.

"Not me," Galen said. Gesturing in his friend's direction, he added, "Him."

The whore's eyes wandered over to Rhys. She bit her lip nervously, and Loki could practically see the fear wafting from her body from where he was.

"Well?"

She searched for someone behind her for a moment, but then she seemed to shake herself, and the siren's mask was back on again. The smile she gave Rhys was full of promises. Slinking over to him, she draped herself over his shoulders, her mouth close to his ear. Loki could see her lips moving, but couldn't hear what she was saying.

"Do we have a deal?" the other Walker asked.

The woman looked over her shoulder at him before latching her lustful stare back on Rhys. "Oh, yes. We have a deal."

"Fine." The word seemed to be gritted out from between his teeth. "How much?"

"Five hundred, and believe me, I'm worth every penny."

The woman peeled herself off Rhys and reached out her hand, her fingers curling up a few times. Galen reached into his pocket and pulled out some money, holding it in front of the human's face. She snatched the bills out of his grasp and swiftly shoved them down the front of her dress.

Galen cocked a brow. "Aren't you going to count it?"

The whore gave him a small shrug. "I trust you." As she turned to lead them into the park, Loki heard Rhys utter, "You shouldn't," under his breath.

"We don't have another choice," Galen muttered in reply.

Frustrated, Rhys replied, "You don't have to stay around for this."

Galen rounded on him, getting up into his face. "I'm not leaving you. We're brothers. Where you go, I go. Besides," he paused, following the woman's movements with his eyes, "I kind of want to see what she can do now." He grinned at Rhys, who didn't return the gesture. Wrapping an arm around his friend's shoulders, Galen dragged him into the park.

Loki followed them, hearing Galen say, "It's either this or the alternative. At least you get to have your dick sucked this way."

Rhys grunted, but allowed Galen to lead him away.

As they moved deeper into the park, Loki could see the woman they'd paid up ahead, leaning against a chain link fence surrounding children's play equipment. There were a few streetlights dotted around the perimeter, but only one of them was still working, its gloomy yellow light barely illuminating a two-foot radius.

Loki found a place behind the trunk of a large oak, able to watch the exchange unseen.

"Where do you want to do this?" the woman asked, her hand reaching up to touch the bare flesh at the center of her chest.

Galen looked around, taking in the broken lights and the general emptiness of the immediate area, and replied, "Here will do."

The whore smacked her lips together, pushing herself off the chain link fence. It groaned and rattled, the small sound echoing around the vast park. Her hips undulated under the thin fabric of her dress, as she positioned herself in front of Rhys, running her hands all over his upper body. Loki noted that the Walker looked as if he would rather be skinned alive than have her touching him. A savage, animal sound vibrated through the night air, making the woman pause for a moment to look behind her.

"What was that?" she whispered to nobody in particular, still peering into the darkness engulfing the three of them.

"It was nothing," Galen said impatiently. "Look, you've been paid. Can you please get down to business?"

The woman smiled. "Of course, sugar." Popping the gum from her mouth, she unzipped Rhys's pants and snaked her hand inside. The Walker's head tilted back, his eyes closing to shallow slits.

"So ready for me," she purred throatily, staring up into Rhys's face as he succumbed to the sensation of her hand on him.

Loki's eyes gravitated to Galen. He had thought the Mare would be getting in on the action—after all, those who fight together tend to do everything else together—but he was hanging back, his attention not on what was happening in front of him, but rather on their surroundings.

He was detached … emotionless.

But he was expectant, too.

The woman's contrived moans soon turned into pained gasps, and eventually desperate screams. Loki noted how Rhys's grip tightened on her body, pinning her in place and stopping her escape. Loki wondered whether Galen would stop what was happening, what was clearly no longer a consensual act.

Instead, he waited, his head swinging to the side when a new voice warred with the high-pitched screams of the woman. Loki watched as a man dressed in baggy jeans, a sweatshirt and a baseball cap marched towards them, one hand reaching behind him. The sharp snick of metal on metal rang out into the night.

"Let her go!" he yelled, brandishing a weapon in front of him.

The woman stopped screaming long enough to yell out to him. "Glide! Get this guy off—" Her words were cut off by an even louder scream than before, ragged gasping hiding her new sobs.

Rhys barely gave the human any attention, but when the pimp brought up his weapon, aiming the barrel at Rhys's head, Galen spoke up.

"I wouldn't interrupt him right now." He delivered the words in a steady drawl, looking relaxed and at ease despite the fact that the pimp had a loaded gun aimed at his friend's head.

The pimp turned towards Galen. "Tell him to let her go, or he gets a bullet through the head," he warned, thumbing off the safety on the side of the gun.

Rhys finally looked up, and Loki saw his eyes glowing a soft yellow. When his top lip peeled off his teeth in a fierce scowl, Glide took an unsteady step back, his hand shaking slightly.

"Last warning, asshole," he said, his voice unsteady.

Rhys didn't stop, forcing Galen to step forward. His actions were a blur. Within seconds, he had broken the pimp's neck with a resounding crack. The woman, who had not taken her eyes off her supposed savior, began screaming when the human's body hit the ground.

Her hoarse howls rent the air, guaranteeing someone would surely come to investigate. Hauling the pimp's body over his shoulder, Galen barked, "Finish," to Rhys and slipped off into the darkness, the man's limp arms dangling near the small of his back.

The woman whimpered as she watched him leave, knowing she would not be released from Rhys's savagery. She looked as if all the fight had gone out of her, her slight body sagging in his arms.

By the time Galen had returned, Rhys was throwing his head back and roaring his release. His whole body shuddered, and he was completely unaware that the woman had lost consciousness.

Rhys blinked rapidly, clearly returning to his senses, and he blanched—his grip loosening. Before the woman's body could fall, Galen took up the slack. With gritted teeth, he told Rhys to go home.

Rhys looked at the female, something akin to regret in his eyes. "What about—"

"I'll take care of it."

Rhys's gaze hardened and, with a snarl, he faded away from the park, leaving Galen alone with the unconscious woman. Lowering her to the ground, Galen dug a hand into his pocket and withdrew a phone. After hitting a few numbers, he held the device to his ear.

"Yeah, there's an unconscious woman at the north-east corner of Humboldt Park, near the kids' play equipment."

Loki could hear the voice of the emergency dispatcher on the other end of the line trying to get more information from him, but Galen ended the call and shoved his phone back into his pocket. He pulled out a wad of cash from another pocket and shoved it inside the top of her dress.

Before turning to leave, Galen paused and knelt beside the woman. "You were right. You were worth *every* penny."

7

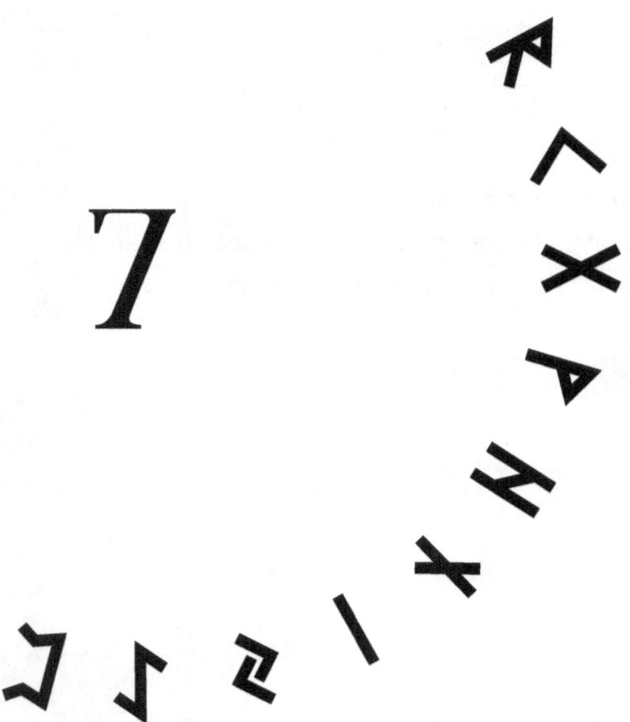

Taer found she was having the same dream she'd had so many times before. And it appeared to be the same as it always was, except as she listened to the final rasping breaths of her brother, a dark, maniacal laugh echoed through the room, congealing the blood in her veins.

She wasn't alone.

The air shifted around her suddenly, the sound of footsteps coming closer, punctuating the otherwise near silence. Squeezing her eyes shut, Taer waited for them to disappear; she willed them away. This was her dream, after all. The closer they got to her, the more her body was wracked by shivers.

"Open your eyes." The dark voice dripped with malice.

Taer woke with a gasp and sat up rigidly in the bed, unable to shake the echoes of that voice from her ears. Her heartbeat was so loud it was drowning out her harsh, labored breathing. Like before, her chest was tight—so damn tight that it felt as if something heavy was lying across it.

Like dead weight.

Like your brother's dead body.

She swallowed down on her dry throat, wincing at the way the scarred skin stretched with the movement. Her hand clutched at the base of her throat, her fingers rubbing against the raised tissue.

Her eyes slid to the other side of the room. Eir was still asleep, her back turned towards her. The blanket thrown over her body was rising and falling, and Taer let out a relieved breath. The last thing she wanted to do was wake the Valkyrie up. She'd practically worked a twenty-four-hour shift at the hospital the day before.

Throwing the blankets from her body, Taer swung her legs around and off the bed, letting her toes curl into the carpet. She sat there for a few moments, letting her racing heart slow down before getting up. She tugged at the bottom of her over-sized tee to straighten it and opened the door quietly.

She padded out into the living room and curled up on the couch with her legs drawn to her chest. Resting her chin on the top of her knees, Taer stared at nothing in particular on the floor.

She liked how quiet and dark this apartment was. At their house, before it had been burned down by Darrion, there was always some sort of noise or light. She'd always wake up in the middle of the night after a dog barked or a siren wailed up the street. She had felt safe there, but she supposed that was because her brother and Korvain were there. Now it was just her and Korvain, and her heart ached. She missed Adrian so much.

"Couldn't sleep?"

Taer was jolted from her thoughts by the whispered voice, her legs stretching out, her body prepared for a fight.

Eir was leaning against the wall, her pajamas rumpled and her hair disheveled.

Taer shook her head. "Sorry," she muttered, looking away. "I didn't mean to wake you."

"You didn't."

Taer looked back at the Valkyrie. Eir shrugged, looking down at her hands, flexing them into delicate fists before releasing them. "My palms are still bothering me a little."

Taer stared at the goddess. Everything about her was gentle—from the way she spoke to the way she acted so selflessly, but Taer had learned early on that weakness and compassion would get you killed.

"Do you mind?" Eir asked, indicating to the other side of the couch. Taer shrugged, self-consciously pulling at the top of her shirt as she watched Eir sit down. The Valkyrie let out a heavy sigh and rested her head back against the couch cushion. Taer watched her eyelids flutter shut and could sense the burden that weighed on her shoulders.

Eir had lost her twin sister at the same time that Taer had lost Adrian, yet Eir seemed so much more … put together than she did. Taer was running on the desire for revenge, whereas Eir was still willing to help people, to go to the hospital and share her gift of healing.

"I don't know how you do it," Taer murmured faintly, causing Eir's eyes to open suddenly. After seeing Eir's puzzled expression, Taer added, "How you can still want to give to people—to the humans—when your twin sister was taken from you?"

Eir blinked at her and shrugged. "Everyone deals with grief in a different way."

Taer brought one leg beneath her body and turned towards Eir.

"I'm not pretending she hasn't died," the Valkyrie said, studying Taer's face. "A part of me died with my sister, but I can't let that feeling swamp me, because if I do ..." Eir stopped, her words drifting off.

"If you do, you feel like you'll never find your way back to the light again?" Taer asked, staring down at her hands in her lap. She was there ... lost in the darkness.

"Yes," Eir replied almost inaudibly. "Just like that. I never want to forget Kristy, but sometimes when I think about her for too long, I feel as if I'm falling down into a black pit of despair, and no matter how hard I fight, I fear that I'll never really be able to pull myself free again."

Taer shuddered, knowing exactly how that felt. She'd found herself in a dark place after Korvain told her what had happened to her brother. When she was alone with her thoughts, she found herself dwelling on the actions that had led to Adrian's death. Maybe if she had faded straight away to remove herself from the situation when Adrian had told her to, none of this would have ever happened. But she'd taken a step towards Darrion to move around him, and he'd grabbed her arm, making her unable to fade.

Adrian had only been trying to protect her.

The rage she had seen in his green eyes had scared her, but not as much as being pinned to Darrion's chest had scared her. She'd felt sick, trapped there, knowing he could do whatever he wanted to her. Taer's hand wrapped around her throat again in an attempt to shield herself from the memories.

"I think I'll try and get some sleep," Taer lied, her words drawing Eir's eyes to her face. She began to get up, but Eir's warm fingers wrapped gently around her forearm, stopping her.

"You know you can talk to me about Adrian."

Taer shrugged. "There's nothing to say," she said, her voice hard and unyielding.

"Taer." Eir's tone was softly chiding.

"I'm fine." Taer turned away, her hands curling into tight fists.

"I'm just worried about you—Korvain is too. We just want you to be all right."

Without turning around, Taer uttered the most untruthful words she'd ever said in her life. "I am all right."

Before Eir could respond, Taer retreated back to the bedroom, put on some jeans, a high-collared jacket and her boots, then headed for the door of the apartment, sliding her Beretta into the waistband of her pants as she moved. Once she was outside, she leaned back against the door and squeezed the bridge of her nose, letting out a sigh. There was no way she was going to be getting any more sleep tonight, so she might as well do something useful.

Taer breathed in the chilly night air and began walking. Her thoughts immediately turned to Darrion. *Talking* to Nieven had been a dead end, just like she knew it would be, and although putting a bullet between his eyes had made her feel better—like she was twisting the knife into Darrion's carefully constructed guild—she was still without any solid leads.

Darrion was a narcissistic, tyrannical megalomaniac.

But he wouldn't have been able to walk away from his guild so easily, which meant that he had to be close to Boston, at least.

Taer wrapped her arms around herself but kept her senses open. She was heading towards a bar where a lot of beings from the Nine Worlds spent their time. She needed information, and after getting nothing of worth from that cocksucker Nieven, she couldn't think of any other place to go.

The War Hammer was run by a dwarf named Alistyre. From the outside, it appeared to be a disused industrial building like Odin's Eye, but unlike Odin's Eye, it wasn't frequented by humans. The dwarves had a kind of magic that hid it from them in plain sight.

After stepping through the haze of magic, Taer pushed through the door. Despite the early hour, the place was packed. Every single set of eyes turned to her, looking at her dubiously. Raising her chin and pulling her shoulders back, Taer walked confidently towards the bar.

A Mare she'd never seen before stepped in front of her, bringing her to an abrupt stop. "Hey, honey," he drawled, his accent giving him away. He wasn't from around here. Darrion had been gone a little over a month and already the vultures were swooping in.

"Get out of my way." Taer's lips curled away from her teeth as she spoke, baring her fangs to him.

The guy just grinned lazily at her, revealing his own—rather less than impressive—fangs.

"Oh, come on, baby. Don't be like that. I'll be real good to you." His hands got a little too familiar then, grabbing her ass and pulling her into the cradle of his hips. It took Taer a few beats to realize the bastard thought she was a whore.

Taer's mouth turned to a playful pout. "You caught me out," she purred, reaching behind her, her fingers grazing the butt of her Beretta. The familiar ripple of the black grip against her fingertips made her smile even more brightly. "But you haven't caught my friend out."

"Friend?" he asked, looking behind her expectantly for another woman. Taer pulled her weapon out and pressed the barrel to the center of his chest.

She shrugged innocently. "My friend."

All hell broke loose around her. There were yells and orders that she drop the gun, shouts that there was a strict policy in the War Hammer that no one carry a weapon. Ignoring them all, Taer pressed the muzzle in tighter, moving the asshole backwards as she moved towards the bar.

Only when she was standing in front of the dwarf bartender did Taer remove the gun from the man's chest and place it on the bar top. The bartender grabbed for the weapon immediately, staring at Taer like she had actually pulled the trigger. She could only assume he was Alistyre.

The elf slid out from between Taer and the bar, slinking away with a figurative tail between his legs. Taer watched him go in the mirrored wall behind the bar. Only once everyone had gone back to their drinks did she look back at Alistyre.

The dwarf was just as Taer expected him to be—short, slightly round and generally cantankerous from what she'd seen so far. He leveled a glare at her, his flint-colored eyes hard. His rusty beard hung shaggily from his face, tangled and dirty, and the faint odor of earth and stone clung to his clothes.

Ignoring his irate look, Taer got straight down to business. "I need information."

The dwarf laughed, the sound like two boulders rubbing together. "What makes you think I'd give you information now that you've come in and terrorized my customers?" He was trying to intimidate her, but he had nothing on Korvain when it came to intimidation.

"I'm looking for a Mare," she pressed on. "And I need to know whether you've seen him, or heard anything about him."

The dwarf laughed again—louder this time—the sound booming around the bar. Taer noticed a few eyes rise at the noise. She'd figured this would be the fastest way to get her information, but if Alistyre didn't start talking soon, she'd have to go to Plan B. Taer looked around, getting more and more agitated.

"Who are you looking for?"

Taer turned towards the voice, her eyes scanning the face of the light elf who had approached her. His eyes were a gray so pale they were almost white and his hair was much the same. Just with one look, she knew he was from very pure blood. But what would a light elf know about Darrion?

She ignored him, turning her attention back to Alistyre. "Who are you looking for?" the elf repeated.

Taer looked at him from the corner of her eye. What did she have to lose? She'd gotten nowhere so far. "The master of the Boston guild," she answered, lowering her voice.

His expression changed, his eyes darkening slightly. Abruptly, he took her by the elbow and dragged her towards the back of the dim bar. Taer fought the urge to break free of his grasp, letting him lead her to a booth surrounded on three sides by high partitions.

The light elf folded his tall, lithe frame down into the other side of the booth. "Sit," he said, his tone hard and unyielding. He had high cheekbones, a long straight nose and a jaw that seemed a stranger to a razorblade. He was the epitome of male beauty, but the air of danger about him told Taer he was more than just a pretty boy. "Who are you, Little Girl?" he demanded.

She stared defiantly and remained silent. She had no idea whether she could trust this guy. She wasn't about to spill all her secrets to him, even if he was one of the sexiest males she had ever laid eyes on.

His top lip twitched. "Little Girl it is then."

Dick.

Taer gritted her teeth, staring at him from under her dark lashes.

Sinking back in his chair, the elf rested his forearms on the table and let out a deep breath. Taer caught his scent, the aroma of spicy cinnamon getting tangled in her nostrils.

"Do you know who I am?" he asked.

Taer shook her head. "No idea."

"My name is Aubrey."

"Is that supposed to mean something to me?" Taer retorted bitingly.

He chuckled at her outburst. She glowered back at him, balling her hands into fists.

"Let's say, for argument's sake, that this Boston guild master is someone I'm familiar with. Why would I give you anything?"

"*Why?*" she replied sharply. Aubrey arched one pale brow at her. "He owes me money," she lied. Taer waited for him to call bullshit, but he said nothing. "I always collect on my debts."

His lips lifted in a pleasantly bland smile. "He must owe you a great deal."

You got that fucking right.

Taer looked at the scarred tabletop so he wouldn't see the rage and pain simmering within her. He wouldn't answer her question, so she wouldn't answer his. They were at an impasse. She met his eyes once more, hoping all he could see now was her determination.

His finger began tapping the table, rhythmically drumming out a steady pattern. "Where can I find you if I hear anything about this … Mare?" Although it didn't show on his face, there was definitely amusement in his voice.

Taer didn't know how to respond. She could lie, but what would be the point of that? She was well protected at the Eye. Nobody could fade in or out of the building. "Odin's Eye," she replied.

His eyebrow arched again. "With the Valkyries?" She nodded. "How interesting," he said, studying her carefully.

Not enjoying being scrutinized so closely, Taer glanced at the gold face of his expensive watch, seeing that it was close to dawn. She stood up, Aubrey's eyes following her movements. "Where are you going?" he asked congenially.

"I'm leaving."

She didn't wait to hear what else the light elf had to say. She wasn't even sure she should have told him as much as she had, but desperation can drive people to do rash and stupid things.

8

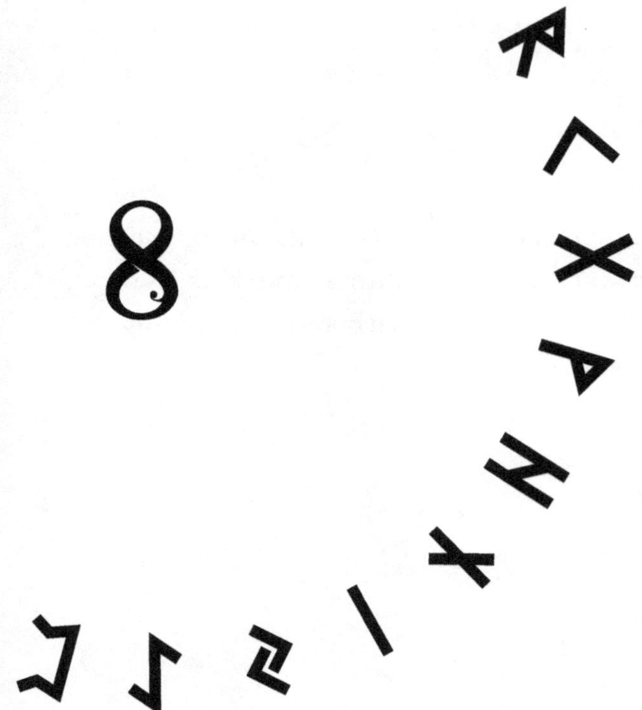

Mason had been lying in bed, staring at the brushstrokes on the ceiling for at least the last four hours. He'd woken from the same dream that always assaulted him, but Sophie had been there for him—just like she always was when he needed her—bringing him down, forcing his racing heart to settle.

The weight of his dog's head against his belly was welcome, the heat of her body beside his own grounding him, reminding him that he wasn't in that building anymore. Lifting his hand, Mason laid it on top of her large head, right between her ears, and stroked her soft fur.

She groaned lightly in her sleep, and Mason envied how quickly she could fall asleep. He would probably be lying there for another four hours, thinking about what had happened.

The screams reverberated through his skull each time he tried to close his eyes, reminding him that he had made it out, but others hadn't. With a sigh, Mason sat up, disturbing Sophie as he did. She blinked up at him with soulful, caramel-colored eyes and slid from the bed.

He'd been given Sophie after arriving back from Iraq. The marine shrink had said that his panic attacks wouldn't be so bad if he had someone there to talk to. Mason just had no fucking idea it would be a female German shepherd who would become his life-preserver in the sea of guilt he'd been treading in for just over ten years.

Mason had only been a kid when he'd signed up for the marines. Now, at the ripe old age of thirty-one, he felt—and looked— much older than he should have. The war had taken its toll on him—had taken more from him than it should have—and also left him with a fucked-up ability to read the minds of the gods— not that he'd known that at the time.

After two long years of suffering, he was ready to give it all up … that was until he just happened to be walking past the Eye one day eight years ago. Bryn and Mav had been watching him from the doorway. As he'd passed, Bryn had told him to get his ass inside and park it at the bar.

He'd known then that she was different. He could hear her thoughts—her thoughts about him. She could tell that he was close to eating a bullet; in fact, that was exactly what he'd been about to do. He'd had a Beretta M9 tucked into the waistband of his jeans.

Loaded.

Ready to turn the back of his skull into mush.

"What's your name?" she'd asked, sitting back and crossing her arms over her chest. Mav stood at her side, her model-perfect face wearing a stony expression. All Mason was picking up from her was hostility.

"Mason," he'd replied, looking around the interior of the bar. He remembered being impressed with the layout and set-up.

Bryn's eyes slid to the side, looking at Mav. An unspoken conversation passed between the Valkyries before Bryn turned back to him. "Planning on doing something fucking stupid in the next ten minutes, Mason?"

One of his brows rose, but he said nothing. He didn't owe them a damn thing. In fact, he remembered being pretty pissed that Bryn had interrupted his plans. He'd been staring hard at the bar, looking everywhere but at Bryn and Mav, when Bryn had cleared her throat.

"We need a head of security here at the Eye. I want that to be you."

"Me? Why? You don't even know me." Pity and fear had churned in Bryn's head as she stared at him, imploring him to just say "yes" to her offer.

"You need a job, right?"

Mason's spine had stiffened. How had she known? He'd been fired from his job the day before for turning up late. But he couldn't help it. His nightmares had kept him awake, and he could only really sleep when the sun was up. So that was what he did.

"Then you have one here. If you want it."

He'd looked between the two goddesses for a moment, finally saying, "I want it."

There'd been a smile in Bryn's voice when she'd said, "Good. You start in ten minutes."

Mason had worked that evening, and kept returning to work ever since. Bryn had saved him.

With a sigh, he got out of bed, Sophie padding silently beside him on the carpet. After washing his face, Mason changed into a pair of sweats, pulled his marines tee over his head and slid his arms into a jacket before tying up his shoes. A bit of fresh air was just what he needed.

"Come on, Soph," he called gently, grabbing her leash from the hook beside the door and clipping it to her collar. Stepping out of his apartment building, Mason turned towards Boston Common—a place he and Sophie usually went every morning to shake off the nightmares. Sophie was a lot more attentive than normal, sticking close to his side rather than pulling forward eagerly. He let his hand burrow deeply into the fur at the ruff of her neck, feeling the warmth of her body settle him.

The sun had barely begun to rise when he made it to the fifty-acre gardens, a slight fog hanging about a foot off the ground. There was hardly another soul in sight, and Mason didn't bother to check either. He liked the silence in his head.

Making his way towards the Frog Pond, he let the icy breeze blow away the terrors still clinging on stubbornly like leeches bleeding his mind. Stopping, he crouched down to tie up his shoelace when Sophie suddenly started pulling frantically at the lead. Mason tried to peer through the fog to see what had her so riled up, but could barely see more than twenty feet in front of him.

"Sophie. Sit," he commanded sternly, returning his attention to his laces. The next thing he knew, he was on his ass, holding onto a leash minus the dog. Jumping up, Mason tried to see where she'd run off to. It was so unlike her to disobey a command from him.

Panic lanced through him, but this time it had nothing to do with his nightmares. If Sophie ran onto the road, no car would be able to see her with the fog cover until it was too late.

With a curse, he started jogging, opening himself up to people's thoughts. Boston seemed to be a big fucking beacon for the creatures of the Nine Worlds, so he was always blocking out the white noise. Per capita, there were more gods and goddesses living there than any other major city in America.

He'd just come up to the Sailors and Soldiers Monument when he heard the thoughts.

I'm so sorry I couldn't save you, Kristy…Oh! What was that?

Spinning to his left, he started forward again, blindly following the words.

I wonder where you came from … your owner must be around here somewhere.

Damn, he wished this fog would lift.

And then, as if his wish had been granted, the sun burst out, burning the fog away faster than he'd ever seen before. It was so bright that Mason had to shield his eyes for a moment, and when he could see again, he found Sophie sitting at the feet of a gorgeous blonde woman.

Eir had had her face buried in her hands, trying to contain her tears, when the wet swipe of a tongue made her jerk her head up in surprise. It was a dog, its warm brown eyes looking concerned … for her.

"Hello," she whispered, straightening. The dog was quite large with black around its muzzle, on its ears and over its eyes. Its ears were pointed up, alert and ready. The rest of its body was a caramel color of varying shades, except for its black back.

Reaching an unsure hand out, Eir added, "What's your name, handsome?" The dog sniffed her outstretched hand, its long, pink tongue darting out to lick her. Surprised, Eir gasped, then laughed out loud. The dog's tail began to wag then, and it bestowed another long swipe of its wet tongue onto Eir's face this time.

"Fuck, Sophie! No!"

Eir's eyes shot to the side just as the fog disappeared. A man stood there, and Eir's stomach did a little flip-flopping motion at the sight of him.

"I'm so sorry," the man said, looping what looked like a broken leash through the metal hoop on the dog's collar. "She doesn't normally just run off like that," he added, glaring down at the dog.

"She?" Eir squeaked.

The man looked at her again, and Eir's stomach flip-flopped doubly hard. His gaze was fixated on her for a moment before he shook his head as if to clear it. "Yeah. She." He looked at the dog again, whose tongue was lolling out of the side of her mouth. Eir giggled at the sight of the dog's angry owner and the seemingly unperturbed canine.

A smile broke out on the man's face at the sound of her laughter, abruptly stopping her.

"No, don't stop," he said. "You have a beautiful laugh."

Eir sighed. "I don't have anything to laugh at right now, I'm afraid," she admitted, dropping her eyes from the intensity of his hazel gaze.

"Do you mind if …"

Eir saw he was gesturing toward the seat beside her. "Please," she replied.

She watched as he made himself comfortable. He was wearing a pair of sweatpants, sneakers and a comfortable-looking jacket with a hood.

"I'm Mason," he said, "and that is Sophie," he added, gesturing at the dog, who was yet to move from Eir's feet.

"Sophie? She's beautiful. What kind of dog is she?"

Mason smiled, his eyes crinkling a little in the corners. "A German shepherd. A highly intelligent, loyal and mostly well-behaved dog. She's been with me for over nine years now." He rubbed her head affectionately.

"Mostly well-behaved?" Eir inquired.

"Mostly, but not always, because she disobeyed my order for her to stay when she came running over here to you."

"Oh!" Eir gasped. "I'm so sorry."

"It's not your fault," Mason replied. "Sophie obviously knew something was wrong, so she came over to help."

"What do you mean?" Eir replied, her voice soft, her eyes lowered.

Mason paused. "Sophie's a therapy dog. She helps me with … some ongoing issues I've been having."

"I see," she said cautiously, still staring at Sophie. The dog crept forward a little and rested her head on Eir's lap. She lifted her hand, but hesitated, turning to look at Mason for permission.

"Go ahead," he murmured, his eyes intense.

Eir rested her hand gently on top of Sophie's head, right between her ears.

"You have a beautiful smile," Mason said, jolting Eir; the smile she had been unconsciously wearing melted away. "What's your name?" he asked when she had the nerve to look up at him again.

"Eir," she practically whispered. She wasn't sure what it was about this man, but she found herself drawn to him … perhaps it was just because of his beautiful dog and his overwhelming sadness.

"It's nice to meet you, Eir," he said, offering her his hand. As she took it in her own, Mason's eyes suddenly widened, and Eir felt a familiar warmth against her palm.

She slid out of his grasp and stood up, nervously smoothing

non-existent wrinkles from her coat and pulling its collar closer around her neck. Sophie walked back two paces and sat down again, staring at her. It was uncanny how in tune the dog was with Eir's feelings, but she shouldn't have been surprised. Animals were very receptive to strong emotions and hers were all over the place—so all over the place that she had inadvertently begun taking away some of the pain Mason had been feeling, out of habit, without conscious thought.

Mason was flexing his hand into a fist over and over again. "What just happened?" he asked, staring at her in awe.

"I …" *Oh, no.* "I have to go. I'm sorry." Eir threw the words at him over her shoulder as she rushed away. She had to get out of there. Fresh tears began leaking from her eyes and she wiped them away.

"Hey! Eir! Wait, please," Mason called out after her.

She didn't know what it was about him—the tone of his voice or the compassion she could sense in him—but she stopped, her chest heaving up and down. He touched her shoulder as he reached her, and Eir found herself relaxing against his hand.

"I'm sorry if I upset you," he said apologetically. "Let me make it up to you."

"Make it up to me, how?"

His eyes left her face, suddenly shy. "How about breakfast?" he asked.

Her traitorous stomach decided to growl at that point, effectively answering for her. She wrapped her arms around her torso in a vain attempt to cover the sound, but Mason grinned.

"I'll take that as a yes, then?"

Eir's stomach fluttered for a whole different reason then. "Okay," she replied, allowing Mason to lead them out of the park towards one of the many cafes that ran along Tremont Street.

He was heading towards one of her favorites called the Thinking Cup.

"Just hold up for a minute," Mason said a few feet from the door. He'd stopped behind her, pulling a piece of material from his pocket. After getting Sophie to sit down, Mason fitted a black and red 'Service Dog' coat over her back and secured the buckles.

"All set," he said a moment later, holding Sophie's leash loosely in his hand. "Are you ready?"

Eir nodded and began towards the front door, but before she could pull it open, Mason swept in and did it for her.

"Thank you," she said in a small voice, watching Mason's lips turn up in a small, appreciative smile as she walked past him and into the cafe. They found a table near the back and looked over the menu before deciding.

"So, Eir, what'll it be?"

"I think I'll get a chocolate croissant and a hazelnut latte." Eir closed the menu and looked at Mason. "What about you?"

"Actually, that sounds pretty damn good," he said. "I'll get the same. Be back in a minute." Then to Sophie, he said, "Stay."

Eir watched him move towards the counter to order their breakfast while Sophie watched her with soulful brown eyes. Eir looked down at the dog. "What?"

Tilting her head to the side, Sophie looked at her a moment longer before settling down onto the ground at her feet.

Mason returned then, sliding into his chair and shaking his head. "She's sure taken a liking to you," he said.

"I can't imagine why," Eir replied.

"I can." Mason's words were barely audible and she chose to ignore them. "So, Eir, what do you do for work?"

"I, umm, I work at Mass Gen. I'm a nurse."

"Oh, wow. A nurse?"

She looked down at the tabletop, but not before she caught a wicked smirk tilting up his lips. She could feel a blush heating up her cheeks. It wasn't the first time she'd received this kind of reaction—men seemed to enjoy the fact that nursing was her profession. She checked over her shoulder, praying to see one of the waitresses walking over with their breakfast.

"How do you like being a nurse?"

"I love it," she replied honestly. "I love being able to help people … you could say that it's in my blood." Eir shrugged, meeting his intense gaze, seeing the admiration in his eyes. "So, what do you do?" She had to get away from talking about herself.

"I'm in security."

What follow-up questions were there for that statement? "That's nice."

He laughed. "I guess you could describe it that way." His grin was infectious, and Eir found herself returning it.

"Two hazelnut lattes and two chocolate croissants," the waitress trilled brightly as she approached the table, balancing a tray on one hand while she unloaded its contents.

"Thank you," Eir told the young girl once she was done.

"No problems. Was there anything else I can get for you?" Her Boston accent was heavy.

"We're great. Thanks," Mason answered. The girl blushed, bobbed her head and turned to walk away.

"So tell me more about the hospital and being a nurse."

Eir took a sip from her mug after blowing gently across the surface. "There's not much to tell, really."

"Well, how about you start by telling me how long you've been a nurse." Eir swallowed hard. "A long time." *A really, really long time.* She hoped he wouldn't ask for an exact number of years.

"Where did you study?"

All right, this one was easy. She'd gone back to university about five years before to keep her registration current. "Johns Hopkins."

Mason whistled. "Impressive." He picked up his croissant and brought it to his lips. Eir watched him carefully, enjoying the way his tongue ran along his bottom lip before he took his first bite—it was almost like he was savoring the flavor before he'd even had a taste.

"All right, so I know you're a nurse …" he said, placing the croissant back on his plate. Eir took the opportunity to take her first bite of the buttery pastry in front of her, suppressing a light moan as the rich flavor hit her tongue.

"Tell me about your family," he said.

Eir swallowed her bite of croissant and met his steady gaze. "I had ten sisters, but …"

Her hand curled into a fist, her fingernails digging into her palms to stop the tears from falling. She gasped when Mason placed his incredibly large, incredibly warm hand on hers.

Drawing in a shuddered breath, she looked up at him. "But many of them have died, so there are only four now—five including me."

"I'm sorry." Mason's thumb ran over the back of her knuckles, calming her down. "I can understand why you're so sad," he added.

"H-how?" she stammered.

He grimaced, pulling away before looking down at Sophie. The dog's head lifted and cocked to the side. "Sophie knew," he said. "She's very good at sensing people's emotions, but even better at sensing sadness."

He held Eir's gaze, almost willing her to accept his answer. Eir took another sip of her latte.

"What about you?" she asked to steer the conversation back on course. "Tell me about your family. Do you have any brothers or sisters?"

Mason got busy staring at the table. He cleared his throat, took a sip from his coffee and met her eyes. "I had a brother, but he passed away a little over ten years ago."

Eir reached over and touched his forearm, squeezing it gently. She could feel his pain hovering just below the surface, but she made sure she didn't take it away. One slip-up had been enough.

"I'm so sorry, Mason. Losing a sibling is hard no matter how long ago it happened."

Placing his other hand over hers, he said, "I know it's stupid—he's been dead so long—but sometimes …"

He drifted off, lost in his own memories. Eir said, "You don't have to talk about him, really. Not if you don't want to."

As she removed her hand, she noticed the time. Was it really that late? She stood up abruptly, rattling the table and unsettling Sophie. "Oh, I'm sorry. I have to go." Giving Mason an apologetic smile, she tucked her chair back under the table. "Thank you for breakfast. I'm sorry, but I have to be at work in half an hour."

"It's no problem. It was nice to meet you."

"Likewise." She bent at the knees to pat Sophie on the head. "It was nice to meet you, too."

As Eir left the cafe, she felt a sliver of weight from the emotional load she'd been carrying for a month lift from her shoulders.

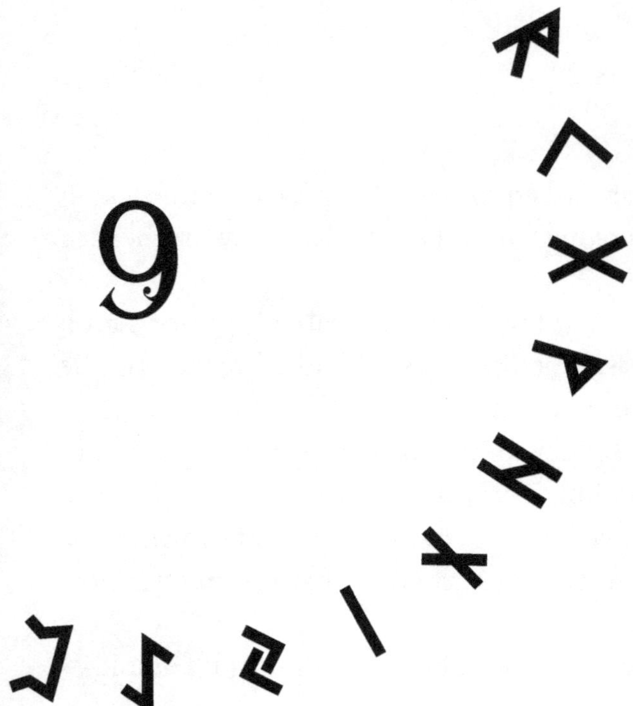

9

Taer dropped down into a defensive position, lowering herself closer to the floor. Korvain was standing about six feet away from her, his dark eyes traveling over her body, looking for an opening in her defense. Grasped lightly in his hand was a curved blade, his preferred weapon—a karambit.

She was unarmed—his ideas, not hers—and she was painfully aware of all the places he had already nicked her with the blade he was currently wielding. Blood covered nearly every inch of her bare skin, some wounds already healed and some weeping fresh crimson tears. Smatterings of red adorned the blue mats that had been set up to save cleaning up the floor of the Eye after their training.

"Take it easy on me, okay?" Taer muttered, not taking her eyes off the threat in front of her. Korvain was deathly still. Not even his massive chest moved; only his nostrils flared as he breathed in and out.

"Darrion won't be taking it easy on you, Taer, so I won't be taking it easy on you." She swallowed the lump in her throat as Korvain added, "I'm not going to try to cut you anymore, but if I do, you'll heal."

Somehow that didn't make her feel any better. Taer licked her lips. "All right, let's do this." She maintained her stance, keeping her center of gravity extremely low in hopes of countering the Mare's coming attack.

Korvain's top lip curled off his fangs in a shit-eating grin and then he was nothing but a blur of movement. He began twirling the blade around, trying to draw her eyes to the weapon and away from his body, making it harder for her to anticipate what was coming. He came at her quickly, flipping the weapon across his palm. His arms—thickly corded with muscle—flew at her body, and Taer automatically brought her elbows up, shielding her neck and torso.

As soon as she was in position, Korvain appeared to stop, then shifted his weight low to match hers and, with a feint on way to draw her defenses, secured one of her arms, and swept her feet out from beneath her, collapsing her to the floor. Taer was vulnerable now; she tried to protect herself, but he slapped her hands and elbows away, leaving her torso wide open. Within the space of a heartbeat, the tip of his blade was less than an inch away from her carotid.

Taer was breathing hard, the adrenaline dump coursing through her blood like a freight train.

"Not bad, Taer," Korvain said, dropping his arm and stepping back. "Not bad, but not good either. You need more practice." With his finger threaded through the ring of his blade's handle, he flipped the curved metal back around so she could see the light gleaming off the surface.

"I've never done that before," she spat out when she was sure her voice wouldn't tremble, angry that Korvain was being so hard on her. She stood up shakily. "You could have killed me."

Adrian had been training her, but she only realized now that perhaps he hadn't been the right person for the job. He had been too emotionally attached to her, his love for her blinding him, making him go easy on her. No, what Taer needed was someone who had no qualms about killing another living being. She needed someone who wouldn't think twice about sinking the blade of a knife into someone's heart.

She needed Korvain.

"I wasn't trying to kill you. I was trying to get a reaction out of you."

"I reacted out of instinct," Taer replied, pacing the length of the blue mats, the disapproving tone of his voice infuriating her.

"Instinct is only part of what you need when you're fighting against a bladed opponent. You need to be able to read them. You need to be able to anticipate what they're going to do."

"And how am I supposed to do that?" she spat back. "Tell me, how am I supposed to learn how to read someone and know what they're going to do before they *actually* do it?"

The muscles in Korvain's jaw jumped. "Time, Taer. It takes time."

She stopped in front of him. "It's been a month already, Korvain. How much longer is it going to take? We should have started the day after ... after ..." *Adrian died.* "We should have started as soon as I was healed."

Korvain's eyes grew darker. "You weren't ready to start training then, Taer. And from what I've seen, you aren't ready for the training you need to fight Darrion now."

Taer was seething. From between clenched teeth, she said,

"You promised me you'd help me kill Darrion."

"*Kill* Darrion, yes," he said, "Not *be killed by* Darrion. There's a big difference, Taer." He shook his head. "You're exhausted. I've been watching those circles under your eyes get bigger and darker. You're hardly sleeping, or eating for that matter. You're still grieving for your brother." Korvain sighed. "Maybe we should put all the physical training on the backburner for now."

"Wait, what?" she sputtered. "You aren't going to train me at all now?"

He rounded on her, his anger making the shadows in the room shiver. "Did I say that?" he boomed. "I said we wouldn't do the physical stuff. There's so much more you have to learn if you want to get your revenge on Darrion."

Angrily, he shoved the mats out of the way and began resetting the tables and chairs that had been stacked around the perimeter of the room while they were training. Taer watched him, her anger building from a simmer to a rolling boil.

"Are you going to just stand there and watch me?" he snapped. "Bryn needs to open up the bar in less than an hour, and I still need to bring Eir home from her shift at the hospital."

Taer glanced at the clock above the bar. It was already half past six. They'd been training for nearly eleven hours straight, and all the physical work was taking a toll on her body. She could feel that, but she wouldn't ever admit it to Korvain.

She looked at her bloody limbs. "I'll get blood on everything."

He growled, stalking around the room, positing the chairs around the tables he'd already set out.

Finally finished, he shrugged into the jacket he'd brought down with him that morning and turned to leave. Before melting into the shadows, he paused and turned to Taer.

"I know you can't see it now, but I am helping you get your

revenge, Taer." She glared at him, refusing to be cowed by the hard glint of rage still there in his eyes. "I can't stop you from looking for Darrion, but don't do anything stupid, okay. It's not just him we have to worry about. Odin is still out there, too, and you've got just as big a target painted on your back as any of the Valkyries."

Without waiting for her reply, Korvain stepped through the back door and into the closest shadow, fading away. Turning back around, she walked a few steps before she felt her knees buckle. She hit the ground, exhaustion rolling through her—a tsunami-sized wave that threatened to drag her under and never let her surface again. She was so goddamn tired, but she couldn't rest, which left her with the only other acceptable option of hunting down potential leads on Darrion's location.

After finding a spare hoodie in the staff room, she stepped out the back door and into the alleyway. The night was cold, a fine, misting rain falling, leaving small droplets glistening on every surface. Taer started walking, drawing the hood up to cover her head and face.

She didn't have any particular destination in mind, but when she dragged her attention off the slick concrete, she saw where her sleep-deprived brain and wandering feet had inadvertently taken her. She looked up at the brick facade of the War Hammer, quietly grinding her teeth together. She hadn't wanted to go back there so soon. If Aubrey had any information for her yet, he would have showed up at the club.

But now that she was there, she wondered whether Aubrey was in there right now, or was he out hunting down leads, trying to find out where Darrion was, as he'd said he would? It was too soon. Turning to leave, Taer stopped when she thought she heard Aubrey's voice drifting from further down the road.

"Couldn't stay away, could you?"

Taer turned to tell him to go to hell when a breathy female voice answered him instead.

"Not from you," she replied. Taer peered out to see Aubrey pinning a woman against a Lexus parked a little further up the street, his thigh between her legs, his hands on either side of her shoulders, gripping the top of the car. He leaned his face closer to hers, whispering something into her ear.

Aubrey looked like he'd just stepped out of the pages of *GQ*. Dressed in a charcoal gray suit and white open-necked shirt, he seemed to ooze sexuality and danger. Taer could see how well his clothes fit him, clinging to every sculpted muscle in his back and shoulders … his ass.

Taer forced her eyes off him and looked at the woman. Where Aubrey was dressed impeccably, she was dressed like she'd shopped in the kids department. In a miniskirt two sizes too small and a scrap of material masquerading as a shirt, she looked as if she was enjoying whatever Aubrey was saying to her, her nipples taut against the fabric hugging her breasts.

A strange feeling began to unfurl in Taer's belly at the sight of them and twisted sharply when Aubrey's mouth met the woman's, when his hands tightened in her hair, tilting her head back in a display of dominance and aggression.

Biting back the growl rising in her throat, Taer retreated into the safety of the shadows, hating how her heart was pounding against her ribs, how sharp and disjointed her breathing seemed to be. She didn't have time for this shit.

Too jacked up to fade, Taer walked back to the club, forcing the image of Aubrey and that … woman … far from her mind. She wouldn't allow herself to be distracted, and she certainly wouldn't dwell on the fact that Aubrey was probably already fucking the bitch in the back of that Lexus.

She had only one use for the light elf, and that was to find Darrion. Nothing more. So why did the sharp pain in her belly return at the thought of him with another woman?

10

"I don't know how you do it, but I don't want you to stop."

Galen inclined his head to Henry Craine, acknowledging the compliment that had just come from the mob boss's lips. Craine was the top of the food chain when it came to organized crime in Chicago, and if there was one thing Galen had learned about the bastard in his short term working for the current mob boss, it was not to fuck around with him.

Galen had seen almost all of them come and go; he'd worked for the biggest names to ever grace the newspaper headlines—Colosimo, Torrio and Capone, Ferriola, Carlisi and LaPietra. Rhys and Galen had seen them all rise through the ranks, had seen them dominate and had seen them fall.

"I've got another job for you." Craine slid a manila folder

across the table purposefully, his dark eyes on Galen's face. Galen reached for the thin cardboard, pulling it in front of him and studying it.

The mark was someone Galen had never heard of before. The three grainy black and white photos showed a young man with dark hair and eyes.

"His name is Anthony Allesi. He's been skimming my product and selling it on the side, lining his pockets with *my* money," Craine told him. Galen looked up at the man from under his lashes for a moment, seeing the anger darkening his already dark eyes.

"I want him dead, and I want it to send a message to anyone else in my operation who thinks running their own outfit at my expense is a good idea."

Galen smiled coolly. "It's no problem."

"You have twenty-four hours. I want him gone before he can distribute the current cut he's taken from me." Craine stood up from behind his desk, offering Galen his hand like he always did. He was firmly of the belief that it wasn't a gentlemen's agreement without sealing the deal with a strong handshake.

They shook, then Galen slipped his jacket from the back of the chair and stepped from the room, shutting the door behind him.

Craine's bodyguards were standing on both sides of the door, passively staring at nothing in particular. Galen could smell the tang of gunpowder on them; it seemed they had both gotten a little trigger happy within the last few hours.

Not a surprise.

After they handed back his machete in its holster, Galen looked down the hall. A dozen feet away, Rhys sat in one of the chairs against the wall, his expression blank. His eyes cut to Galen when he heard his footsteps.

Galen strolled from the office, the details of his target neatly tucked away in his head. Without needing to look over his shoulder, Galen knew when Rhys pulled up behind him.

"We've got twenty-four hours," he muttered, fixing the collar of his shirt and tucking it under his leather jacket.

Rhys stayed silent, but that wasn't anything new. The ride down in the elevator was quiet except for Rhys's steady breathing. They stepped out of the glass and metal building into downtown Chicago, the rush of the night-time pedestrian traffic beginning to thin out. Galen settled his attention on the skyscrapers all around him, thinking.

"I want to take care of this sooner rather than later," Galen told Rhys.

"Fine by me," Rhys replied darkly, the malevolent grin in his voice unmistakable, and they turned down an alleyway so they could fade to the address written in the dossier. On the way they passed a man who was just stepping out of the darkness. Their eyes met, and Galen thought he recognized him for a moment. Overhead, the guttural caw of a raven floated over the sound of traffic. Galen turned to watch the man walk across the street, keeping his head down.

"What is it?" Rhys asked, following his gaze.

"Nothing," he muttered. "I just thought I recognized that guy."

Rhys squinted after the man. "Let's get this hit done."

Galen shook his head, trying to shake the feeling that he'd seen the man before. "All right, let's go."

A moment later, they were standing across from a warehouse tucked away behind some other industrial buildings.

Galen pulled out his machete from the holster under his jacket while Rhys fingered the handle of his hunting knife. Bladed weapons were better than firearms—less noise, more intimate fighting, bloodier deaths. All of these things made Galen tick. It was what made him feel alive.

They both watched on for an hour or so, noting how many people walked in and out of the building, what pieces they were carrying. There were maybe a dozen people inside, Galen thought. A dozen they could most definitely handle. Galen and Rhys were stronger and faster than the humans, who really didn't stand a chance against a couple of trained killers like them.

"Ready?" he asked the other Mare.

After a curt nod from Rhys, Galen moved towards the building, staying within the shadows to hide his approach. A man stepped from the doorway, huddling up against the brickwork and shivering in his coat. Pulling a cigarette from his pocket, the man put it in his mouth and attempted to light the end. He cursed every time a strong gust of wind extinguished the flame before it could take. Eventually, he turned around and huddled near the wall—turning his back to Galen in the process—and flicked the flint with the pad of his thumb.

Galen could see the glimmer of a dancing flame; it burned bright orange for a moment before guttering out to leave the man's face in shadows once more.

Fading directly behind the human, Galen drove the tip of his machete straight into the back of his neck, angling the blade upwards into the base of his skull while covering his mouth with a hand. The human dropped to the floor soundlessly, Galen cradling his fall before pulling the knife free and running its sharp edge across the front of his throat.

When the man was quiet, and only the sound of blood escaping his body could be heard, Galen signaled for Rhys to move in. Galen stood up, picking up the body and dragging it out of sight, then followed his best friend into the harshly lit warehouse. Sure they could have faded in, but where was the fun in that?

The humans stopped what they were doing when they saw them both, some stepping back a fraction when their eyes found Rhys. The smell of fear hung heavy in the air, and Galen soaked it up. There really was nothing a Mare liked better.

Galen and Rhys were among the humans before they had time to register that they were under attack, weaving around gun muzzles pointed in their directions and ducking under sharp blades aimed for their chests. Before any blow could land, Galen would fade to a new position, confusing his opponent, opening them up for a fatal hit. He made sure his kills were extra violent—instead of going for a straight slash to the throat, he chose to cut open the humans' bellies first to let their intestines spill out onto the floor. He materialized directly in front of one human, wrenching the butterfly knife the man had been brandishing free of his hand before he could strike. With practiced movements, he slid the man's own weapon into his solar plexus before punching the handle in and up, into his heart.

When there was no other movement in the warehouse, Galen looked up to see where Rhys was. The Mare was literally dripping in warm blood, the spray from severed arteries covering his face and neck until only his stark white teeth and pale blue eyes could be seen.

Taking a look around, Galen counted fourteen humans. Their blood was pooling on the floor around their dead bodies.

"Let's go find Allesi."

Stalking through the warehouse, Galen was surprised he hadn't already seen the cocksucker. Perhaps he was the kind of man who didn't like to get his hands dirty. Yeah, that had to be it. After scouring the lower level, Galen moved towards a set of metal stairs. Music was pouring out from under the door of the room perched at the top.

Rhys followed at his back, protecting him against possible attack. There was no doubt in Galen's mind that Rhys would give up his life for him. His loyalty was embedded in his DNA.

There was a small window beside the door. Galen looked in, seeing the man from the dossier asleep in an office chair—his legs propped up on a desk covered in bricks of white powder. Galen frowned. For someone who was supposedly running a clandestine operation, it didn't seem smart to fall asleep on the job.

Bringing the tip of his machete up to the glass, Galen tapped once, twice, three times. Allesi awoke with a start. The man blinked dumbly at the bloodied weapon, a crease forming between his brows … then his eyes widened as he realized the blade was attached to a hand and that hand was attached to Galen.

Allesi began reaching under his arm, but Galen stopped him with a measured shake of his head. The man froze, thinking for a heartbeat before going for his weapon in any case. Before Allesi could point the muzzle at the window, Galen and Rhys were already inside the room, sharing the same air, breathing in his fear and his anger.

"Who the fuck—" he sputtered, stopping abruptly when Galen *tsk-tsked* him as though he were a recalcitrant child. He really was in no position to be making demands. After hauling him out of the chair, Rhys pressed the length of his bloody hunting knife along Allesi's neck.

"You've been a very naughty boy, haven't you, Allesi?" Galen taunted, looking the man square in the eye. Allesi's brown eyes widened with fear, a new wave of the acrid stench hitting Galen's nostrils. He breathed in deeply, holding it in his lungs for a moment.

"Oh, God," Allesi whispered, realization dawning. "Whatever

Craine is paying you, I'll pay you double," he said, his voice quivering.

Galen stared coldly.

"I … I can give you a cut of my profits." Allesi spoke rapidly, his voice getting higher.

"How much?" Galen inquired, meeting Rhys's eyes with a smirk. He liked this game.

"Three percent."

"I'm sure you could do better than that," Rhys murmured darkly beside his head.

Allesi's whole body shook, his bladder releasing in fear. Galen stared down at the puddle of piss collecting on the floor before looking back into Allesi's face.

"F-f-five percent," Allesi stammered.

"Ten," Galen countered, thoroughly enjoying himself.

The human's eyes darted around wildly. "Ten," he agreed, still shaking, still stinking of fear. Galen looked at Rhys and stepped back. The human's shoulders slumped, his whole body relaxing at his newfound sense of freedom. Allesi had thought his "deal" was enough to change Craine's order to kill him.

But he was wrong.

Rhys struck like lightning, driving his blade into Allesi's side.

Allesi screamed out wordlessly, dropping to the ground, clutching his side. Blood gushed from the wound, soaking the threadbare carpet beneath their feet. Galen rolled him over until he was on his back and stared down at him.

"Consider this your one and only warning from Craine." The words were slow and deliberate, meant to taunt him. Galen stood back up and brought the blade of his machete down across the man's throat. Allesi's head rolled beneath the desk, a bloody trail following its path.

Galen met Rhys's greedy yellow eyes. "Let's make sure we send the right message."

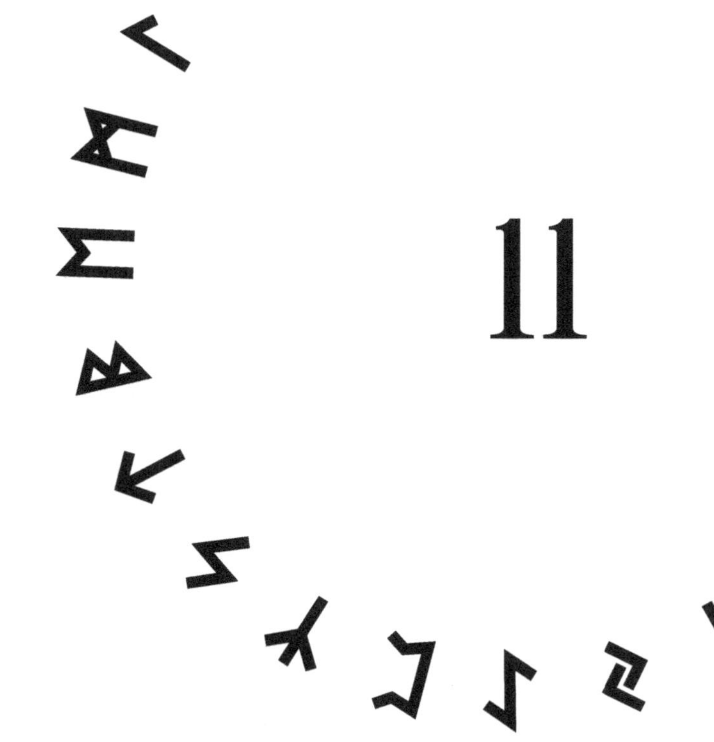

11

T aer ignored the yells from the line of humans, gods and demigods waiting to get out of the cold and into the Eye as she stepped past Mav and into the club. The Valkyrie's midnight and cornflower blue eyes remained cold and detached as they watched her. Not once had Taer seen Mav display any emotion other than cool indifference.

Mav's black sword sat starkly against the skin of her neck, naturally drawing the eye to the thick scar marring the Valkyrie's otherwise perfect skin on her throat. Taer had never been told what had happened to Mav, but as she touched her own scarred throat, she understood why Mav wouldn't want to discuss it very often.

The wall-length bar on her right was crowded with people already, Mist and another young woman, a human, serving the five-deep line of clamoring gods, demigods and humans. Taer pushed her way past them all, brushing off the casual pats to her ass as she did.

She was halfway through the crowd when she heard a crash and a loud shout. Her head spun around toward the bar, and she saw one of the young human women Bryn hired as a bartender grimace and clutch at her forearm with a white-knuckle grip.

"What the fuck happened?" Mason barked from behind Taer. He pushed forward, scattering the patrons at the bar waiting to be served. Taer followed in his wake, taking up her position beside him.

"I broke a goddamn bottle and cut myself, that's what's happened," the woman yelled, pressing the towel Mist passed to her against her forearm.

"You're out," Mist said the instant she got a good look at the wound. "But—" the woman protested.

"Elli, you're out. Go to the hospital. Get that wound treated and come back tomorrow."

Taer watched as Elli's eyes hardened, her shoulders bunching up in anger.

"Elli," Mason said. "You heard Mist. Go get that cut seen to."

Elli's brown eyes swung to Mason, holding his stare for a long moment before she ducked under the end of the bar and pushed through the "Staff Only" door.

When Taer looked back, Mist was staring at her. "You know how to pour a drink?"

Taer shrugged.

Mist sighed. "Guess that'll have to do." Throwing a shirt at Taer, she said, "Go get changed, then come and help me out. We're swamped tonight."

Taer didn't want to be there—it was too damn noisy and her nerves couldn't really take it—but before she could back out, Mason took her by the elbow and led her away.

"You need to help out. Your nerves will be fine. Just keep your head down and do as Mist tells you, okay?" His words were spoken quietly—gently—and when she looked into his hazel eyes she wondered how he'd known. Was she wearing her wariness so openly on her face?

He sighed. "It's a long story." Opening the door Elli had just disappeared through, Mason gave Taer a little shove. "Go on now. You're wasting time."

Taer wandered—slightly dazed—down the hallway and into the changing rooms. The tang of blood hit her senses first, followed by anger, then tears. She found Elli angrily stuffing her apron and a bar shirt into her locker.

"How is it?"

"Still bleeding," Elli shouted, slamming her locker door shut with a clang. Shouldering her bag, she turned and left the locker room, taking her swirling anger with her.

"What a bitch," Taer muttered under her breath as she pulled off the hoodie and T-shirt she'd been wearing and put on the one Mist had given her. After washing her face and finger-combing her dark hair and putting it in a high ponytail, Taer checked her reflection, seeing the scar at the base of her throat.

She pressed her fingertips to it, hating it was on show. Maybe she could …

Bang! Bang! Bang!

"Taer?" Mason called. "You need to get out here now!"

With a resigned sigh, Taer pushed through the door, coming face-to-face with the human. His eyes did a quick survey of her body, his gaze not lingering anywhere in particular. He gave her a reassuring nod then walked back into the belly of the Eye. She followed, seeing there were at least double the amount of people crowding at the bar now.

"Taer, get your ass back here!" Mist called.

"Get over it," she told herself sternly. "You have knife fights with the scariest male you'll ever know, so you can do this."

Letting out a sharp breath, she stepped behind the bar and looked at the closest customer. The human stared at her scar, and she barely resisted the urge to stab him in the eye with a broken bottle.

"What are you having?" she asked. She had to listen hard to hear the guy's reply as he yelled it over the music. After she'd served him two beers, he paid and she moved on to the next customer.

After about six hours of this, the crowd started to drop off and Taer felt as if she could breathe again. She slumped against the bar top, staring out at the thinning crowd. Exhaustion completely and utterly owned her body, but she figured it was better than the alternative of reliving her brother's agonizing and drawn-out death.

She spun around when someone grabbed her hand. It was Mist, shoving a fistful of money into her palm. Taer gave her a quizzical look.

"Your share of the tips from tonight. You did well, Taer." Mist turned back to wipe the bar down. By the time everyone had filed out, and the bar was clean, the lights had been turned on, chasing away the shadows.

"Tay?" Korvain asked behind her. Taer looked up to find him standing at the bottom of the stairs leading to the upper levels of the club. "What are you doing behind the bar?"

"Mist asked me to fill in when Elli cut her forearm on a glass bottle," she said, shoving the cash into the pocket of her sweats.

Korvain leaned up against the side of the doorway, his dark eyes assessing her. "How are you feeling?"

Translation: Aren't you tired?

Taer shrugged. "I'm surviving."

Korvain frowned, but said, "Come on. I want to teach you something."

"Tonight? Now?"

He arched a dark brow at her. "Weren't you the one complaining that I wasn't teaching you fast enough?"

"We're going to do weapons training right now?"

It was true that this was exactly what Taer wanted, but why the change of heart?

Korvain shook his head. "No. I'm going to start your mental training tonight." Before she could baulk at his offer, he said, "Not negotiable. Come on."

Taer looked at Mist, who only shrugged at her. She followed Korvain's broad back to the elevators up to the apartments. Taer could still feel the stifling tension between them from their earlier argument.

She cleared her throat and leaned against the side of the elevator car, facing Korvain. He looked relaxed, but looks could be deceptive.

"Is Bryn still worried about Darrion coming after the other Valkyries?" she asked to break the stiffness between them. "Is that why you're taking Eir to and from work?"

He turned to her. "It's not Bryn who's worried. It's me. I don't trust that he's just gone into hiding. He has to be planning something. He has to be coming for me, or you …" He paused. "Or the woman I love," he tacked on quietly.

Taer stared at him, dumbstruck, and Korvain averted his eyes—looking at the sealed door of the car.

"You love her?" she asked just as quietly.

Korvain's jaw flexed, and he refused to look her way. He was shutting down, unwilling to share any more with her. A little over a month ago, she would have seen his love for Bryn as a weakness and made some smart-ass comment, but since losing Adrian, her perspective had changed. Loving someone wasn't a weakness. It took strength to trust someone else with your heart, but it took more strength to know that maybe they might be taken away from you sometime soon.

"I'm happy for you, Korvain," she said without looking at him, joining him in staring at the doors as the car glided to a stop. She let him lead the way out and followed him into the apartment.

"Get showered. I need you relaxed for what we're going to do."

Taer didn't fight him on it. After training all day and then having drinks spilled on her all night, she was in desperate need of a shower. Once she'd toweled off, she tied her hair into a high bun at the top of her head and padded into the living room, where Korvain was waiting.

"Lie down on the couch," he said from the armchair across the room. Taer did as he instructed, propping her head and shoulders up with a few cushions.

"Now, close your eyes." He waited until she had before speaking again. "Over the next few nights, we'll be focusing on some other skills that will help you defend yourself against non-physical attacks by Darrion." Taer sat up and opened her mouth to argue, but Korvain simply spoke right over her. "And my decision to stop training you with weapons still stands. You're not ready for that yet."

Lying back down and closing her eyes, Taer crossed her arms over her chest. "And you think this will protect me better than being able to wield a sword or a dagger or anything else pointed, dangerous and likely to perforate?"

"Against Darrion? Yeah, I'd say so."

"So, what could possibly help me defend myself against him?"

"Dream walking."

Taer had heard only the strongest and most pure-blooded Mares had that ability. "Are you sure?" she asked, cracking one eye open to look at him.

"We won't know until we try it. Now, close your eyes and relax your mind—just let it go blank."

Taer placed her interlaced hands on her stomach, let out a breath and did as Korvain had asked. She tried to make her mind blank, but instead her thoughts went to the many ways she could torture and kill Darrion. It was just too bad that he could only die once, really. That motherfucker was going to suffer for killing Adrian.

"Tay? I said relax," Korvain said, his voice barely a whisper.

"I am relaxed," she spat back.

"No, you're not. Your knuckles are white. What are you thinking about?" Taer opened one eye and looked at her hands. Sure enough, they were both white, the bones straining against her skin. Forcing her fingers to relax, she flexed them a few times before trying again.

"Better," Korvain said. "Now, I want you to think of Eir."

"Eir?" she asked, her brows pulling into a confused frown.

"Yeah. Think about the color of her eyes and hair, think about how she smells, the color of her skin. Think about it all. Are you doing that?"

"Yes," Taer replied, thinking hard about the Valkyrie lying in a bed on the opposite side of the wall, no more than fifteen feet away from her. She imagined herself looking deeply into the goddess's royal blue and teal eyes.

"Okay, good," Korvain said, but his voice sounded distant

now. "Look around. Can you see a door somewhere?"

A door? Taer looked away from Eir's blue-ringed eyes and took in the room she found herself standing in. The walls were a brilliant, pearlescent white. Completely pure. The floor was the same. She thought it was stone she was standing on, but it was warm and seemed to absorb her weight effortlessly.

"Find the door, Taer," Korvain urged, his voice sounding fainter this time. Taer took a few steps forward, the white walls giving way to more white walls. She looked behind her on instinct, jolting back in surprise. Just to the left of where she'd been standing was an old wooden door with iron studs protruding from it.

"I see it," she replied, not sure whether Korvain could still hear her. She felt like she was completely alone in this place.

"Good. That's good. Open it."

Taer's hand stretched out to the small iron ring in the middle and twisted it. She was sure it would creak and groan, but it opened smoothly. On the other side, she couldn't see anything but blackness.

"It's dark. I can't see anything."

"That's all right. Step into the room anyway. Trust me."

Taer swallowed the lump in her throat and stepped through the door. She expected to fall straight through the darkness, but was surprised when her foot hit spongy green grass instead. Slowly, like the rising of the morning sun, light filled the space. Taer blinked, looking around. She recognized where she was after a few seconds: Boston Common.

Suddenly there was a dog bounding towards her ... no, not towards *her*—towards Eir. Taer could see her now, sitting on a park bench directly in front of her. Her head was down, her face covered, and Taer could hear the gentle sounds of her sobbing.

The dog's pink tongue whipped out of its mouth and swiped across the back of Eir's hands. Gasping, the Valkyrie sat back in surprise.

"Hello," she said, reaching out an unsteady hand. "What's your name, handsome?"

Taer watched closely as the dog licked Eir, causing the Valkyrie to laugh out loud. The dog took this as an invitation to keep going, this time landing lick after lick on her face.

"Fuck, Sophie! No!" Taer heard a voice and turned in time to see Mason come running up to the dog. Mason apologized, and when Eir laughed again, his whole expression softened. Taer had wondered before why Mason's eyes always looked so haunted, but now—while standing with Eir—he looked so at ease ... so happy.

Did they know each other?

"Taer? Come back to me now." Korvain's voice seemed to boom in her ears. She looked over her shoulder, expecting to find him standing there, but there was only the expanse of park at her back.

"I don't know how," she replied, keeping her voice low, afraid she'd be heard.

"Think about where you are right now, in this realm."

Where was she? Taer squeezed her eyes shut even tighter and thought about the apartment, about the couch she was lying on in the living room. She opened her eyes when the scent of Korvain's skin trickled into her nose.

He was looking down at her seriously. "What did you see?"

"Eir was in the park," she replied, sitting up and realizing how stiff her muscles were after the grueling workout earlier. "Was I in her dream?"

"Yeah, it sounds like you were. You did really well, Taer. It took me nearly three cracks at this stuff before I even got close to the hallway into someone's unprotected mind. It looks like you're a natural."

Taer's chest puffed out a little with the praise, but if it was that easy for her, wouldn't it be just as easy for someone else to infiltrate *her* dreams?

"Don't worry. Not all Mares can dream walk. Your private thoughts are safe if you follow the proper precautions," he said, answering her unasked question. The concern must have been written all over her face. "Try to get some sleep now. Your body needs to repair itself. We'll start practicing some shielding techniques over the next few days."

Too exhausted to argue, she got up and slid into the bedroom she shared with Eir. The Valkyrie had her back to Taer, her chest rising and falling steadily under the blanket draped over her. Getting into bed, Taer slid down into the pillows, drifting off into what would no doubt be a restless and nightmare-filled sleep …

———

Taer awoke suddenly when she sensed something wasn't quite right. The base of her neck tingled in warning. Blinking rapidly, she looked around the endless black hallway she found herself standing in. She realized she was in someone's dream … but whose?

Looking over her shoulder, she found a door. Letting out a steadying breath, Taer pushed against the pale wood, the barrier giving way easily. Remembering what Korvain had told her, she stepped through the doorway and into the inky blackness on the other side. Taer waited for the pinprick of light in front of her to grow and expand, to reveal where she was.

She was indoors. A king-sized bed upholstered in black leather with blood-red sheets took up most of the room. On either side of it sat bedside tables with black lamps and shades. The lamps were both turned off, but there were some candles in small glass jars scattered on both tables, all flickering with a warm light.

Taer let her eyes drift. The walls were painted dark gray, and almost looked black in the dim light. There was very little furniture in the room, except for a footstool sitting at the end of the giant bed. She walked over to one of the bedside tables and picked up the book lying there.

The copy of Jane Austen's *Pride and Prejudice* was well worn, the pages dog-eared, the binding frayed and warped as if it had been read a thousand times before.

"I was wondering how long it would take you," a male's voice said behind her. Taer spun around, dropping the book to the floor. It landed with a dull *thud*, matching the hard throb of her heart pounding against her rib cage. Aubrey stood on the other side of the room, a towel wrapped around his waist, his pale skin glistening with droplets of water.

He sauntered towards her, his hips swaying provocatively. "Despite my lack of attire, I must say this is rather a pleasant surprise."

Taer's eyes fell from his face to chase a rivulet of water that ran down the smooth expanse of his toned chest and stomach before enticingly disappearing into the towel. Her mouth was suddenly dry as desire coursed thick and fast through her blood. The hammering of her heart in her ears only confirmed what she already knew: she was attracted to this male. She swiped the tip of her tongue over her bottom lip, and Aubrey's normally luminescent eyes darkened a fraction when they darted down to watch.

He smiled at her lazily, the gleam of lust in his eyes unmistakable.

"Couldn't wait to see me again?" he asked in his practiced drawl, his lip still hitched up in that grin that seemed to quicken Taer's breathing. He was trying to throw her off balance, and she wouldn't let that happen.

Boldly, she let her eyes wander back down his torso. Aubrey laughed, a husky, throaty sound, causing Taer's blood pressure to spike.

"Like what you see, Little Girl?" he asked, amused.

Taer tilted her chin in defiance at his assumption, even though it was true. He had a warrior's body, although not like Korvain's. Korvain was pure muscle and size. Aubrey was much more slender, but his stomach rippled with solid muscle, and his shoulders and arms were highly defined.

"And if I did?" she shot back, enjoying the hint of surprise on his handsome face.

He grinned salaciously. "Then I'd say we'd better do something about that. I'd hate to leave you wanting."

He let the towel around his waist drop to the ground. It pooled at his bare feet and Taer's breathing hitched. His semi-erect cock was growing larger, longer and harder under her steady gaze, and the desire she felt for him multiplied a hundredfold.

Taer met his hot gaze once more, her face blank. "Was that *little* stunt supposed to impress me?" she asked.

Aubrey's smile widened, one hand coming to rest on his heart. "Oh, how you *wound* me, Little Girl," he simpered. "But no matter how cool you play this, I know you're just as attracted to me as I am to you." He approached her gracefully, his scent swirling around them, drawing her in closer. He was only a few inches away from her now, the flickering candlelight dancing over his bare skin. Taer swallowed hard, her eyes darting back to his face when he spoke again. "I knew you were there, watching me with that woman."

He reached up to touch the strands of hair that had come loose from her bun, sliding the silken lengths behind her ear. Even though he hadn't physically touched her skin, she could feel his hands as if they were touching every inch of her body … intimately.

"I said I'd find you when I had the information you needed— so why else would you seek me out, hmm?" he asked, his breath warm on her skin. "Just admit it to yourself. You. Want. Me."

A shuddered breath left her lungs, her eyes sliding shut. She wanted to surrender to him, but that wasn't why she had accepted his help. She'd accepted it because he said he could get her close to Darrion.

And just like that; Aubrey's spell was broken.

Taer woke with a gasp, suddenly, as if she'd had a bucket of ice-water thrown on her, her eyelids fluttering rapidly as she took in her surroundings. Her own bed. Her own room. Eir sleeping in the bed nearby. She had made it back, but how in hell had she ended up in Aubrey's dream in the first place?

12

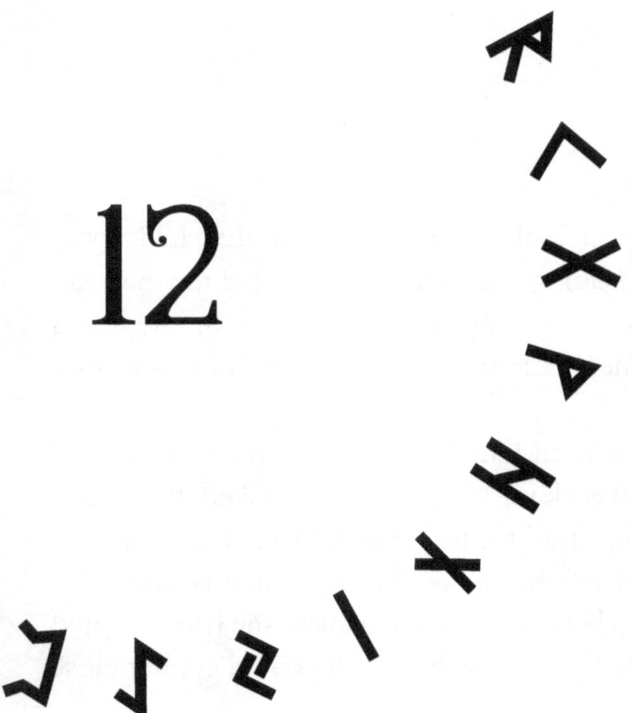

Ten years had passed since the death of Darrion's parents and little sister, Ara. Ten long years in which thoughts of avenging his family had burrowed into every single cell in his body, festering until as a young Mare he was left hell-bent on taking from Odin what Odin had taken from him.

Njord's army had grown exponentially in that time. They had followed in the wake of Odin and his Valkyries, combing through the devastation they'd left behind, seeking out the dark elves who had slipped through the cracks and survived. These Mares were the most dangerous. They had nothing left to lose and everything to gain by training to become killers.

Darrion wiped the sweat from his brow, his eyes on the blood splashed all over the rough ground. Some of it had been soaked up by the sand thrown on the hard-packed floor. Some was dull and old against the dark dirt.

And none of it was his.

Arthon—his opponent—blinked up at Darrion from the floor, his blood streaming out of the cuts to his head, lip and neck. He cradled one elbow in his hand, holding his broken arm close to his body.

That thought alone brought a sadistic smile to his lips. When Darrion fought, he fought until blood was spilled and his opponent's body was broken—and even then he didn't stop.

"I think you broke my arm," Arthon mumbled, spitting blood out as he spoke. Darrion's shoulders lifted slightly. He wasn't about to waste his fucking energy on any more movement than that.

"He could have killed you," another voice said. Darrion regarded Njord, who had appeared from one of the many tunnels leading around their guild house. The Vanir god looked like a proud father, beaming at the good deeds of his son. "But he didn't because I won't allow it."

Arthon's eyes lowered in deference. "Yes, master."

Njord frowned at him. Darrion watched Njord take in Arthon's injuries, taking stock of them, calculating where and when Darrion had struck. "Get your wounds attended to," he ordered.

Without making eye contact, Arthon struggled to his feet. One of the other Mares rushed over to help him, holding him up and leading him toward a room off the main tunnel that housed a crude medical station. As Mares, the superficial damage they suffered could be healed, but for broken bones and more serious internal injuries, it took time.

Turning, Njord asked Darrion, "How long did it take you to inflict that much damage?"

Darrion shrugged. "Forty-five seconds."

"You could have done it in thirty." Njord's retort wasn't meant to rile Darrion, but it had that effect.

"I'll do better next time," he ground out.

The god regarded him for a moment. "I have no doubt." He walked away, indicating to Darrion he wanted him to follow. "How was he until he started bleeding out?"

"He was good."

"But not as good as you."

"Nobody is as good as me," Darrion replied simply. He knew he was a natural—born to it. He understood that being a farmer, tilling the fields with his father, wouldn't have satisfied this dark desire Njord had nurtured within him.

Thinking about his father and the life he could have been living brought him up short. He hadn't thought about that before. All he'd ever considered was finding bloody revenge for his whole family's death.

"What is it?" Njord asked, taking Darrion by the arm and leading him further away from the other nearby groups of Mares still sparring.

"Why is Odin doing this? Why is he hunting my people down like dogs?"

Njord seemed to think about that for a moment. Eventually he said, "One fears what one fails to understand. Odin is no different … and dark elves are some of the only beings in all the Nine Worlds that don't bend to his will."

"But *why* would he want to control us? What use do we have? We have no powers like the gods."

The Vanir gave him a knowing smile that Darrion couldn't decipher. "You are probably unaware of this, since you came from a poor family, but with special training, a Mare can be quite dangerous. With the right information and knowledge, they can become something special …" Njord trailed off before adding, "They can become Shadow Walkers."

"Shadow Walkers?"

"Yes. Those of pure blood, and I mean *pure* blood, were able to wrap shadows around them, to conceal themselves. They could become invisible, making them the most feared creature in all of the Nine Worlds—even feared by the All-Father."

"What happened to the pure-blooded Mares?"

"There are none left now. Odin wiped them out. He has been persecuting dark elves for over one hundred years, wiping out entire generations without a thought other than to strike first and strike hard.

"So what some families started to do was capture a light elf— usually a male—and force them to bed one of their females. The light elves' paler features are dominant, so most of the offspring would have their blond hair and light eyes."

Darrion touched his pale hair absently, staring at Njord with wide blue eyes. The Vanir nodded in silent understanding.

"You inherited the paler traits, but your sister and mother had the darker features."

Darrion had often wondered why he'd looked so different from his sister and mother—and why his father looked more like a light elf. "My blood is not pure," he reflected. "I can never be a Shadow Walker."

"I don't want you to be a Shadow Walker." Njord stepped closer and grasped Darrion's shoulder lightly. "I want you to become the Master of Shadow Walkers."

Darrion's brow knitted together. "And how is that possible, when I'm not even worthy of calling myself a real Mare?"

Njord laughed and swept Darrion around by his shoulder. Darrion saw immediately what the Vanir was showing him: every single pair of eyes in the room was locked on him, fear and uncertainty simmering just below the depths.

In his ear, Njord whispered, "You don't need to be worthy. All you need is the determination to take what you want. All you need is their fear." He gestured to Darrion's fellow trainees, still staring at him. "All you need to do is control them with this fear and you will dominate them."

Darrion grinned. He liked the sound of that. "How?" he asked.

"Who is the best out of the group? Is it Arthon?"

"Yes."

"Kill him." He said the words so calmly, as if asking Darrion to fetch him a cup of water, not kill a fellow trainee.

"Now?" Darrion asked.

Njord studied his face, searching for something. "Make them fear you. Make them uncertain of their position in our army."

"*Our* army?"

"That's what we've been doing, Darrion. We've been building an army against Odin. I'm training *them* to become the most lethal killers so that *you* can get your revenge on the All-Father. But in order to have their respect and their fear, you need to do as I ask."

Could Darrion kill the other Mare? He weighed his master's words carefully as he considered his reply. He stared into the god's glowing green eyes as an idea took shape.

"I've got a better idea."

13

The heady scent of blood was floating on the air. This, accompanied by the panic and fear tainting the wind, drew Loki in. He was surrounded by warehouses, obviously in the more industrial part of town. Up ahead, shouts of surprise and pain echoed, and Loki knew without seeing it that it was going to be good.

Loki moved towards the sound, and as he got closer to the source, he could see the first of the bodies lying on the ground outside the door. Getting down onto his haunches, Loki got a better look at the corpse. The wound to the back of his neck looked as if it had been angled up, the weapon being driven into his spine to kill him instantly. There was blood everywhere, growing tacky around his body.

The light spilling out of the nearby door drew Loki's attention.

Standing up from his crouch, he entered the warehouse, hitting the wall of blood, seeing the carnage. There were more than a dozen bodies with at least a dozen different fatal wounds. Loki was impressed, and curious to know who had orchestrated such a beautiful scene.

But as he looked around a little more, he realized that he hadn't even noticed the best part. In the middle of the room, Loki found a disembodied head positioned so it was looking up. Droplets of blood decorated the ground, a small perimeter of red circling the head. Loki's eyes rose to the rafters, a gratified grin spreading across his lips. The body strung from the steel beams was still leaking, the victim's life blood dribbling and seeping all over the bare concrete floor. His belly had been cut open, the intestines spilling out and dangling, suspended in the air like a macabre chandelier of human blood and flesh.

"Let's get out of here," a voice said, and Loki recognized it immediately. Stepping behind a tall wall of wooden crates, Loki watched Galen and Rhys descend the staircase at the back of the room and wander casually through the warehouse. They were covered in blood and gore, both of them wearing satisfied grins. They faded from the scene as the wail of sirens started in the distance.

The human authorities must have been on the way. Not wanting to be seen, Loki left the warehouse and staked out a spot in the shadows to watch. Within moments, the flash of red and blue lights reflected off the windows and steel doors of the surrounding buildings.

The first car pulled up, the word "POLICE" stamped across the front door. Another three cars followed, lights blazing, and the men from the first car got out. They both unclipped the snaps across their weapon's holsters and kept their hands on the grips as they walked towards the front door of the warehouse.

Their eyes were on the first body as they passed it, but they pressed on. The man in front drew his weapon and led the way inside, his partner closely following behind him. Loki's eyes moved to the other officers, now filing in behind the first two cops. He could see the wariness in their eyes as they passed him.

Staying back and out of sight, Loki drew closer to the door, watching the humans survey the scene in front of them. One of the younger ones suddenly doubled over, the contents of his stomach spilling out onto the floor a few feet away from one of the corpses.

"Jesus fucking Christ, Moloney," someone said. "You're fouling up the crime scene. Take it outside."

The cop—Moloney—jolted upright like a puppet attached to invisible strings and turned around, wiping a shaking hand across his mouth. He didn't even see Loki standing there as he staggered outside.

"What a goddamn mess," another cop said, crouching down to inspect one of the bodies that had had its throat slashed.

"I haven't seen anything like this before," said another, bringing his hand up to cover his mouth and nose, trying to smother the smell of rust and spilled bowels.

"Who do you think is responsible for this shit?"

"There's only one man who could order a hit this violent." The man who spoke had a hard, square jaw, his mouth set into a grim line. Loki recognized this look. It was the look of a man who had seen too much.

"You've got a real hard-on for Craine, don't you, Bray?" another cop said, this one a lot rounder and softer than Bray.

Bray ignored the comment. A drop of blood fell on his shirtsleeve, and he looked up at the ceiling. Taking a step back, he uttered, "Holy mother of God."

The statement drew the attention of the other cops, their gazes also gravitating to the rafters. Two more men gagged and fell to their knees.

"Do you know of any other man who would order that?" Bray demanded, gesturing to the body hanging from the roof. "This has to be Craine's doing."

The other man's lips thinned into a hard line. "Okay, let's say for argument's sake it is, what's the motivation?"

Bray was already walking toward the stairs. "All right, so we know Craine is the biggest importer and distributor of coke in Chicago, right?"

"No, we *think* he is," the other man said. "We haven't been able to pin a goddamn thing on him. It's like he's fucking coated in Teflon—nothing sticks."

At the top of the metal staircase, Bray paused and turned around, his gun in hand. "I'd bet a year's wage there's something inside this room that will tell us everything we need to know."

He twisted the handle and stepped into the room, gun raised. Less than a minute later, he was on the small landing once more.

"Well?"

"Nothing," Bray replied bitterly, holstering his weapon and descending the stairs. His boots thumped against the metal. "Tell me the medical examiner is here already. I need to get out of here as soon as fucking possible."

14

Eir was just finishing getting dressed when there was a small knock on the door. She'd been in a daze since she'd woken up that morning. Last night, she'd dreamed of Mason again. They were still in the park, but it felt different this time, though she didn't know how to explain it. It was almost as if there were unseeing eyes watching her, which made absolutely no sense at all.

"Eir?" Korvain's dark voice came through the door. "Are you ready to go?"

With one last look at her reflection, Eir opened up the door. The Mare filled up the space between the jambs, and for a fleeting second, the fear rose up in her. She worked hard to push it back down. She could trust Korvain. He'd proven himself time and time again—it was just the old panic rising up in her. It was like trying to tell a cat not to fear a dog; it was instinct. Pure and simple.

"Morning," she said, giving him a tentative smile. "I'm ready."

Korvain led the way from the apartment and down to the lower levels of the club they now all called home.

Getting used to living with the other Valkyries had been surprisingly easy for Eir.

She hadn't realized just how much she'd missed them living alone—and now there were only five of them left, the sisterly bond she felt for her fellow Valkyries was ten times more potent.

Once they were outside the bar, Korvain waited for her to close her eyes to fade. As her body dematerialized, she felt Korvain follow her to the darkest section of the hospital parking lot.

They walked the rest of the way in silence, the sound of her shoes dainty compared to the harsh crunch of Korvain's boots over the hard concrete.

"What time do you finish?" he asked.

"It's a twelve-hour shift, so around eight tonight. I'll let you know if I'm running late."

"Okay." Korvain didn't take his eyes off the people and cars around them, always checking for potential threats. Once they got to the doors of the emergency department, he pushed her gently in the direction of the entrance. Eir walked through, the harsh sting of antiseptic hitting her nose the instant she was over the threshold.

Before she disappeared through the "Staff Only" doors, she turned and waved at Korvain.

"Wow, Eir, he's like … smoking hot," Stacy said from behind the receptionist's desk as she passed.

That brought Eir to an abrupt stop. "Excuse me?"

Stacy indicated to the main doors. "That guy!" she exclaimed. "Talk about tall, dark and dangerous."

Oh, if only she knew. Eir shrugged. "I guess."

"Is he single?" the receptionist continued.

"Ah, no. He's dating my sister."

Stacy's face fell. "Too bad." She turned away, but stopped. "Hey, did you hear about that murder in Chicago?" she asked. "It's all over the news!"

"No, I didn't."

Stacy leaned in as if she were divulging a secret. "The cops found this warehouse filled with at least a dozen bodies. Apparently it was some mob boss. It looked like it was personal, too, because there was one body that had been strung up from the rafters." She glanced conspiratorially over her shoulder. "They haven't released this information yet, but my brother was one of the first cops on the scene and *he* told *me* that the body had been decapitated. They found his head on the floor below the body, positioned so it looked like he was staring up at his own corpse."

Eir felt her stomach turn. "Why would someone do something like that?" She already had a pretty good idea of *what* could have caused that kind of damage.

Stacy shrugged unapologetically, a gleam of excitement in her eyes. "I don't know, but whoever did it, my brother said they're good. They haven't been able to find a shred of evidence at the warehouse. It's as if they don't even exist."

She had a dreamy sort of quality to her voice when she spoke, making Eir shiver. "Anyway, I'll see you later," she chirped before going back to work, answering phones and filling out paperwork.

Eir shook her head. The murders sounded like a Walker hit. Could it have been Darrion in a fit of rage? But why? From what Korvain had told her, Darrion was a methodical killer, so the rage theory didn't fit. And Chicago seemed like a strange city for him to be working in.

She went into the change room to get into her scrubs, only to be ambushed by one of the oncology nurses in the hallway.

"Eir, I'm glad I found you. I could really use your help right now."

"Of course, Mark. What can I do?"

Mark looked up and down the hallway surreptitiously, leaning in closely to speak into her ear. "I need your special hands to work their magic."

Mark—whose real name was Eolas—was a light elf who blended in well with the humans. It was only times like this that he let her see just how much he knew about her.

"Of course," she replied. Eir knew her secret was safe with Mark. She followed him to the bank of elevators, standing beside him as they waited. "Who is it?" she asked him quietly, as another nurse and two doctors joined their waiting group.

"An elderly gentleman. He's going to get his diagnosis and treatment options this morning, but he's already in a lot of pain. I'm not sure how much more he can take. I was hoping …"

"I'll do what I can," she said, squeezing his forearm gently. When her palm connected with his skin, she could instantly feel Mark's distress for his patient. "It's going to be all right."

Mark placed his hand over hers and squeezed it briefly before releasing her. The elevator arrived and they all got on. A few minutes later, Eir found herself being ushered into a private room on the fifth floor.

The man lying on the bed was incredibly still, with just his chest rising up and down shallowly with every pain-filled breath. Mark walked towards the man and touched him gently on the shoulder.

"Mr. Adamsen?" he asked gently. The man's paper-thin eyelids opened, his pale, cracked lips contorting into a grimace. The man blinked a few times, and Eir watched as his hands curled into weak fists at his sides. "I've brought someone here to help take the pain away," Mark said.

He beckoned her forward, beseeching her with his eyes to do something for the man. Eir approached the bed, breathing in the scent of sickness through her nose. She knew without putting her hands on the old man that he didn't have long left.

Mark spoke again. "Mr. Adamsen, this is Eir. She's just going to touch your chest, and you'll feel better. I promise."

The man's eyes focused on Eir for a moment before the slightest nod of his head said she could continue. Flexing her hands a few times, she lifted them up and placed them gently on top of the thin scrap of material covering Mr. Adamsen's torso. She could feel the wiry hair of his gaunt chest through the gown, could feel that his body temperature was a lot cooler than it should have been.

Eir's eyes slid shut when the rush of pain coursed through her body, making her heart pound faster. She stumbled back a little from the force of the cancer invading his frail body, but was able to keep her hands on his chest.

He had no hope.

Mark took hold of her upper arm, supporting her against the tide of pain ripping through her body. A few seconds later, Mr. Adamsen groaned in relief, his body becoming lax under Eir's healing palms. After a few more seconds, she pulled away and took a few steps away from the bed.

"Is it bad?" Mark asked, pressing her shoulders so she'd sit down on the only chair in the room. Eir brought her hand to her forehead, noticing the shake.

"It's aggressive. It's in his lymph nodes and in nearly every organ." She blinked up at the light elf. "He doesn't have long."

Mark's eyes hardened. "It's worse than we thought, then. I'm not sure his body can even handle the treatment we have planned for him."

Eir slumped forward, feeling as useless as she'd felt after taking her sister's pain from her. She had only deferred it for Kristy, and even then, it hadn't stopped Loki from killing her twin in any case.

Taking away the pain when it was this severe always took it out of her. She was used to doing small things, like regulating breathing or improving circulation. Her palms began to burn and, seeing her discomfort, Mark took one hand in between both of his and started to rub the pain away.

"Better?" he asked.

She bit her lip, hastily pulling her hand free of his grasp as the doctor walked into the room. Mark stood a little straighter, she noticed, too.

"Mark? Are you ready?" the doctor asked. Eir didn't know the man personally, so she stood back and tried to blend into the background. A few times, Mark's eyes flicked over to her, but Eir tried not to notice.

Eir stood off to one side as they explained to Mr. Adamsen what the combination of chemotherapy and radiotherapy would do to his already ravaged body. Hair loss. Anemia. Fatigue. Nausea. He'd have it all, and even then there was no guarantee that he'd beat the cancer, given his age and ailing health. The doctor was so matter-of-fact about the whole thing that she wanted to throw her hands over her ears and stop listening. He was treating Mr. Adamsen like he was already dead.

"Eir?" Mark said gently, taking one of her hands.

Her gaze landed on her hand and saw how well it fit into his. She liked him, but she wasn't interested in having a relationship with him. His face fell when she pulled away, but it only lasted for a moment.

He said, "Thanks for coming in to help. He's sleeping peacefully now."

Eir looked over his shoulder and saw Mr. Adamsen was indeed resting, his breathing even. "That's good."

"Look, Eir … I know there's a policy about this and everything, but do you think you'd like to have dinner with me sometime?" he asked, hope shining in his eyes.

She took a step away. "That's really nice of you to ask, Mark, and I'm flattered, really, but—"

Mark stopped her with the wave of his hand. "It's okay, Eir. I just thought I'd ask." He sighed. "Have a great rest of the day," he added, a little too brightly.

And with that, he turned and left the room. Giving him a few minutes' head start, Eir left the room, too, making her way down to the elevators to get back to the ER. She just needed to get lost in her work for a little while.

15

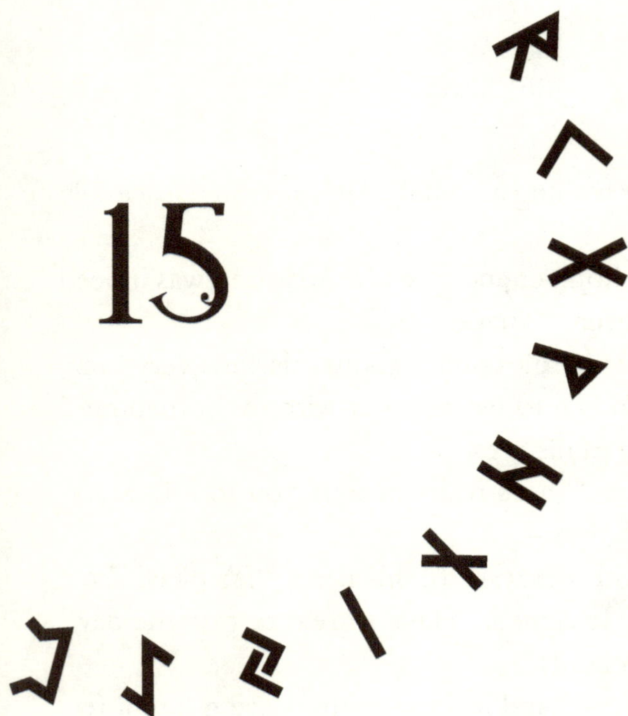

After a fitful sleep that saw most of the day disappear, Taer was on the floor in the living room, the news showing on the muted TV as she did some stretches to loosen up her muscles, tight and cramping from the previous day's training.

Bending one leg and placing her foot near her groin, Taer leaned her chest towards the ground and stretched out her arm until her hand were wrapped around her foot. She felt the pull all the way through her hamstring, but she leaned even further forward, making her muscles scream. She welcomed this ache, trying to take her mind off the accidental dream walk she'd found herself in—the events still running like a movie reel in her head.

"Like what you see, Little Girl?"

Aubrey's words echoed through her head, taunting her. All right, so maybe she was attracted to the bastard, but nothing was ever going to happen between them. All Taer needed him for was to help find Darrion. After that, he would be nothing more than a goddamn memory.

"But no matter how cool you play this, I know you're just as attracted to me as I am to you."

Taer huffed and increased the stretch, hoping the pain would take her mind off that smug bastard.

But no matter what she did, or which part of her body she pushed to the very limits, she couldn't get her mind to focus.

"I knew you were there, watching me with that woman."

She closed her eyes, letting out a slow breath. Behind her eyelids, the image of Aubrey standing with the towel pooled around his feet, his magnificent body on show, all for her, was like torture.

"Taer?" Korvain asked, touching her on the shoulder, wrenching her from her thoughts. She blinked rapidly at him standing in front of her.

"Yeah?"

"How are you feeling today?" he asked, concern in his voice.

Blowing out a frustrated breath, Taer said, "I slept like shit. How do you think I'm feeling?"

Korvain grunted. "You slept most of the day."

Releasing her stretch, Taer gave her other hamstring the same treatment. "Is that a problem?"

"Of course not," he replied, taking a seat on the couch behind her and pulling out his karambit to clean.

"Will we be doing any training tonight?" she asked.

The Mare shook his head. "Not tonight. Dream walking takes a toll on your energy levels—even more than physical training does. Tomorrow night, maybe."

"We could do some weapon training instead?"

His eyes shifted from the blade. "No, Taer. We've already discussed this," he replied darkly, "and I'm not willing to discuss it further. My decision is final."

Turning away from him, Taer swallowed down her anger and disappointment. If he wasn't willing to teach her, she would just have to find someone else to do it.

"I have to go downstairs and help Bryn open up," he said. "What are you doing tonight?"

Taer shrugged, focusing on the TV. "Not sure yet. Might just watch some TV or something. Maybe there'll be a good movie on later."

The dull rasp of a blade being put back in a holster whispered behind her. "I'll check in on you soon, Taer."

She waved him away and pretended to be transfixed on the TV instead. When the apartment door shut behind him, Taer stood up and got showered and dressed.

She had somewhere she had to be.

———

Pushing into the War Hammer, Taer was too pissed off to acknowledge the stares and marched to the same booth she'd seen Aubrey at before. The bastard was sitting there, looking relaxed, with a woman—a different woman from before—straddling him, happily rocking backwards and forwards in his lap. He glanced up at her arrival, a cocky grin spreading on his lips. Taer wanted to wipe the damn thing off with the blunt end of a bar stool.

"Caught you at a bad time?" she asked sweetly. The woman turned around with a gasp, giving Taer a dark look.

"Give us a minute, Ava," Aubrey told the woman in a steady drawl, patting her on the ass she as extricated herself from his lap. Ava left them in a hurry, Taer's eyes following her as she did. When she was out of sight, Taer turned her attention back to Aubrey, who was giving her a narcissistic smile.

Dick.

"Girlfriend?" she asked caustically, hating that anger she heard in her voice.

Why should she care who Aubrey fucked?

"Just a girl," he replied, readjusting himself openly. "To what do I owe the pleasure? Two visits in less than twelve hours." He ran a hand over his stubbled jaw. "Aren't I the lucky one?"

The reminder made Taer grind her teeth together. "That was a mistake," she replied, "and not the reason I came here."

Aubrey's pale brows rose. "A mistake? I wouldn't have called it that, but do tell me what the other reason is for you coming to see me."

"I need to know whether you've found out anything about that Mare yet."

"The guild master?" he clarified. Taer gave him a tight nod. The light elf leaned back in the booth, his fingers interlacing on top of the table. "Not yet."

Taer was seething. "Is that because you've been too busy … entertaining the opposite sex?" she asked.

A lazy smile hitched up one side of his delectable mouth. "Jealous, Little Girl?"

Taer frowned. "Of her?" she asked, angrily indicating the direction the female had disappeared in. "You've got to be fucking kidding me."

"If you're not jealous, why are you so angry right now?"

"I'm not angry, Aubrey. I'm fucking pissed off. You said you could help me find this male, but so far I've not seen you do much else other than womanize and philander. If you can't help me, just say so, and I'll go find someone else who can."

"You didn't mean a single thing you've just said," he retorted, leaning forward, ensnaring her with his searing gaze. "If any of it were true, you wouldn't still be standing here. So, tell me the real reason you came."

Taer didn't like how intuitive he was, but he was right. She hadn't come down here simply to chew him out for not finding Darrion yet. She had come here to ask another favor, but was afraid of what he would ask for in return. He hadn't asked for anything the first time around, but now she would be asking a lot more of him.

"I need another favor," she begrudgingly replied, the words like ash on her tongue.

"I'm all ears."

Cursing under her breath, Taer forced herself to look him in the eye. "I need weapons training."

Both of his brows rose this time around. "Why would a sweet young girl like you need weapons training? And why would you think *I* would know anything about weapons?"

Planting her palms on the table, Taer leaned down, making sure Aubrey could see just how serious she was. "To torture and kill the bastard that killed my brother," she replied darkly. "And you haven't lived as long as you have without knowing how to fight," she added.

The light elf's expression sobered, his gaze intensifying. "So that explains the pain in your eyes," he commented softly. There was pity in his tone, and Taer hated to hear it. Straightening, she tried to put as much distance between them as she could. His expression hadn't changed, forcing her to look away.

"Will you help me or not?" she asked, knowing there really was nowhere else for her to turn.

"Of course," he replied unhesitatingly, and her eyes darted back to his face.

"Just like that?"

He shrugged. "Just like that."

There had to be more to it than that. "What's it going to cost me?"

"Your name."

"That's all you want? I tell you my name and you help train me?" she shot back incredulously.

He smiled, but it lacked the cockiness she was used to. "Is that so hard to believe?"

She wanted to tell him yes, it was, but she wouldn't push the issue. He had agreed to train her, and it had cost her a hell of a lot less than she'd expected.

"When can we start?"

"When will you tell me your name?" he returned, one brow cocked.

Taer looked away, indecision about his motives plaguing her. She'd already come this far, though. Facing him once more, she said, "It's Taer."

"Winter Fox," he said, the true meaning of her name on his lips sending shivers down her spine. Fuck, she had to get better control over her mind and body while she was around him. Pissed off with herself for letting him affect her so much, Taer turned to leave, but paused when Aubrey spoke again, his silky voice drawing her back like it was a drug and she was the addict.

"Tell me something; do you like to read classic books?" he asked casually.

Taer's shoulders tensed. "Not really had much time to read," she replied warily.

"You should find the time. I could lend you a copy of my favorite book, if you'd like?"

"And what's that?" she asked.

His expression was mocking. "Jane Austen's *Pride and Prejudice.* You *have* heard of it, yes?"

Taer cleared her throat, refusing to acknowledge that she had. Instead, she said with a shrug, "Can't say that I have."

Aubrey stood up and moved towards her, his body lithe and graceful. "I'll bring you my copy sometime." His voice was inviting.

Reaching up, his fingers grazed Taer's cheek. The pounding of her heart intensified, and she prayed he couldn't hear it.

"Come back here before closing. We'll start training then."

———

It was close to three in the morning when Taer returned to the War Hammer. She had tried to talk herself out of going more than a dozen times, but she always came back to the fact that she needed Aubrey, even if she didn't want to admit it in so many words.

The street was quiet as she tapped on the door. She was dressed in a hoodie and sweats, the bitter wind blowing right through her. Cradling her upper body tightly, she tried to fight off the chill as she waited for the door to open. There was a shuffling of feet on the other side, then the door was pulled open by Alistyre. The dwarf gave her a reproachful look.

"What are you doing here?" he asked gruffly.

"She's here to see me, Al," Aubrey said from deeper inside. The dwarf looked over his shoulder, grunted and stepped back from the door. Taer pulled the top of her hood down and walked inside. Aubrey appeared from the back of the bar dressed in a black singlet and black track pants, his feet bare.

Against her better judgement, and in direct contradiction to her own pep talk to not become ensnared by the light elf, Taer couldn't help but peruse his body when she saw him. Forcing her eyes away, she found him watching her, amused.

"Enjoying the view?" he asked.

She shrugged easily, dismissing his question. "Where will we be training?" She looked around the empty bar, noticing the relics from their old worlds hanging from the walls for the first time. Among the dwarves' axes were elven shields and bows as well as battle horns and helmets.

"Upstairs."

His answer brought Taer's eyes back to him. "You live here?"

He shook his head. "I never said that." Before Taer could ask any more questions, he turned around and walked back the way he'd come. "Are you coming, Winter Fox?" he called, mockingly.

Cursing quietly under her breath, Taer stomped after him, finding the light elf waiting at the bottom of a set of stairs.

"After you," he said. Pushing her shoulders back and tilting her chin up, Taer marched right past him and up the stairs. She felt more than heard him follow, the heat of his body pressing up against her. At the top of the stairs she reached a door and pushed it open.

The space was huge, at least as big as the bar below. Each corner held different equipment: daggers and hand weapons, sparring mats, grappling dummies and targets. On the floor, blue mats had been spread out, covering the entire surface.

"Where would you like to start?" Aubrey asked, his voice a seductive whisper from right behind her. His hand brushed against the back of her neck. Startled, Taer spun around and reflexively swung her arm out. Aubrey caught her by the wrist before the strike could land, his fingers cinching shut.

Taer struggled to free her arm from his grasp, but Aubrey just flexed his arm, dragging her closer to his body. On instinct, Taer went still, her face mere inches from his. She was staring into his pale eyes, those infinite grey windows to his soul.

"Lesson number one: be prepared for anything." His breath was a warm breeze across her cheeks, his cinnamon scent wafting over her. "And lesson number two: strike only when you know you will inflict damage."

Releasing his fingers, Aubrey gently pushed her away and dropped his arms. "How much training have you had?"

"Not enough." Taer hoped he couldn't hear the tremble in her voice.

"It shows." Walking in a tight circle around her, he seemed to watch her and ignore her at the same time. "What do you want to know?"

"Everything."

He paused and turned to her. "That's a lot. Narrow it down for me."

Taer thought about it for a moment. "I need to know how to defend myself against a bladed weapon."

"What kind of bladed weapon?"

"Throwing knife," she replied automatically, remembering Darrion's proclivity for daggers.

"Okay. It's a start." Aubrey walked over to what looked like a metal tool chest. Pulling open the top drawer, the light elf withdrew a double-edged knife and turned to face Taer.

He weighed the weapon in his hand carefully, walking back towards her.

"A throwing knife," he said, presenting the weapon. "Deadly, if you know how to wield one successfully."

She stared at the metal weapon. It was probably no more than seven and a half inches long with a silver and black finish on the blade. The brushed steel reflected light while the black oxidized steel seemed to absorb it.

"But beatable?" she asked. She needed it to be beatable. Taer had worked with long and short swords with Adrian, but he hadn't wanted to show her any more weapons.

He shrugged, the muscles in his chest and shoulders rippling beneath his pale skin. "At a distance? No. In close quarters, perhaps."

"Show me."

Aubrey gave her an indulgent look. "I will, but I want to see how you handle one first. Have you ever thrown a blade before?" Taer shook her head. Aubrey walked over to one corner of the room and pulled out a large wooden board and an A-framed stand. Setting it at the other end of the room—at least forty feet from her—he made his way back to her, and she couldn't help but notice the way his hips swayed.

Coughing, she pinned him with a hard stare and muttered, "It's too far away for me to hit."

He only shrugged in reply and handed her the knife, handle first. The cold steel hit her palm, but it warmed to her body temperature almost immediately. "Close your eyes," he ordered. Taer blinked at him. "Close your eyes," he repeated. "I'm not going to do anything to you, Winter Fox," he added with a self-assured grin. "No matter how much I want to."

"Why?" she asked, and she realized her mistake as soon as the word had left her lips.

His grin turned lascivious. "I want you to feel the balance of this weapon," he replied, but his eyes were saying so much more.

Letting out a breath, Taer weighed her options. She had to trust him at least a little. He was training her, after all. Against her better judgement and every instinct she had, Taer closed her eyes.

Aubrey shifted closer to her, making Taer stiffen in response. She brought the blade up, tilting it in his general direction. "Relax," he whispered. "I'm not going to touch you until you ask me to, Taer."

"That'll never happen," she spat back. Aubrey chuckled and moved away.

"I want you to get a feel for this weapon. Unwrap your fingers from the hilt and let the knife find its natural balance in your hand," he ordered gently.

Taer relaxed her hand and let herself feel the metal, how the steel felt against her skin.

"Can you feel it?" he asked beside her.

"Yes."

"Good. Open your eyes. Now, the trick to throwing a blade is having a firm but not too tight grip. These blades don't have a guard, so be careful with your fingers."

"Am I holding it properly?" she asked, stretching out her hand to show him.

"Don't worry about that so much. I want to see what your instincts are when it comes to a blade. You might just be a natural."

"All right," she submitted. "We'll try this your way, I guess."

There was a low chuckle behind her. "Throw the blade."

She drew in a deep breath, concentrating on the steel in her hand. She had no idea of the correct technique, so she just brought her arm above her head and threw the blade with as much power as she had.

The ring of metal slicing through the air sounded for a moment before a loud *thunk* and an even louder clattering sound made her eyes open wide. The blade was lying on the bare floor about three feet from the wooden target. The hilt had hit the target but then bounced away. She looked at Aubrey.

"You do not have a natural ability for throwing knives."

"No shit," Taer muttered, going to collect the steel from the floor. She handed it back, being careful not to brush his hand as she did. "So, clearly I can't use a throwing blade. But that's not what I want to know." Taking a step towards him, she watched his eyes widen and nostrils flare. "I want to know how to defend myself against one. What if my opponent has one? What then?"

Aubrey's clear eyes narrowed on her face. "You know who killed your brother, don't you?"

"And I'm sure you know who killed him, too," she retorted, holding back the grief that threatened to spill out with her words. How could he not know? He wasn't a fool. She was looking for Darrion, and although she hadn't told him why, he must have put two and two together by now.

She said, "Teach me how to defend myself against someone who uses throwing knives."

Aubrey studied her for a long minute. "You've got balls, Winter Fox. I'll give you that." He walked a few paces away and then turned to face her again. "You can't defend yourself unarmed against someone with a throwing knife who attacks from a distance, especially against someone who is as … proficient with the blade as Darrion is. But if you can get close to him—inside his guard—then you can defend yourself."

Taer's eyes locked on Aubrey. "Drill me on that then. I want to attack Darrion in a way that will leave him unable to fight on his terms."

Aubrey gestured at her hoodie and sweats. "What have you got on under there?" he asked.

Taer looked down at herself. "A singlet and underwear," she replied, brazenly meeting his gaze.

Heat flared in his eyes. He reached out a hand and plucked one of the strings from her hoodie, playing with the end. "Lose the hoodie. Keep the sweats."

Taer's mouth was suddenly dry. She didn't want to expose her scar to Aubrey, but she really didn't have a choice. Sliding her arms from the sleeves, she pulled the hoodie over her head and threw it against the wall.

Aubrey's eyes were focused on her chest when she looked back at him.

"Enjoying the view?" she asked, turning his own question back on him.

His pale gray eyes met hers. "Would you hold it against me if I said I was?" he asked.

"That's so not going to happen," she muttered. "Can we get on with this?"

Aubrey's eyes drifted down, and she could see the moment when they found the scar at the base of her throat. "Who did that to you, Taer?" he asked darkly, his hands clenching tightly at his side.

Taer's hand automatically rose to her throat. "I'm not discussing that with you, Aubrey," she warned. "You said you'd train me, not interrogate me."

He stared at her again, the set of his jaw firm and unyielding. "Fine." Bending his knees, he lowered his body into a fighting stance she recognized well. "Just remember that you wanted this."

They were the last words he spoke to her as he became of blur of shadows and silver arcs, his smooth, sinuous movements silent except for the *whoosh* of steel cutting through the air. She had known he'd be proficient with a weapon, but she hadn't realized just how good he'd be. It was almost as if he were a completely different person when he had a blade in his hand.

Taer did her best to dodge each attack with a well-timed pivot, or by ducking the swipe of the blade, but she quickly became aware of how futile fighting at close quarters was. Still, Aubrey barked orders at her, correcting a stance, or trying a new position.

By the time they were done, Taer had shallow cuts on her forearms, the tops of her hands, her throat and face. The superficial damage was already beginning to heal, but the smudges of her dried blood served as a reminder of just how lethal Aubrey really was.

Taer doubled over, her breaths coming out in a harsh staccato rhythm. She could hear the pounding of blood in her veins, feel her sweat mingling with the blood that covered nearly every inch of her upper body.

"Again," Aubrey said—not even a little bit breathless.

They were continuing? Aubrey gave her a look that told her to toughen up and face him again, and she suddenly wished for one of his seductive smiles, his usual teasing tone.

"You're letting your emotions get in the way," he said matter-of-factly. "Remain detached. Remain unaffected and you can overcome any enemy."

She hauled her body upright, ignoring the sharp protest of her muscles and readying herself for the next onslaught.

With every movement, she was aware of her injuries, aware of how Aubrey was cutting her in the same place two or three times. Fresh blood tainted the air, somehow fueling her to fight harder, to move faster, but her arms and legs screamed with each contraction of her muscles.

She forced all rage, anger, grief and pride from her body, focusing everything she had on the fight, and suddenly found that she could anticipate his next move, and counter it, but she was still too slow.

They continued in this way for what felt like hours, until her entire body begged for release. Taer had just been knocked down and was picking herself up again when Aubrey abruptly stepped away. "Good," he muttered, wiping his blade with the end of his T-shirt. "Enough. We'll start again tomorrow."

Taer was disinclined to argue with him after the beating he'd just dished out. She pulled the slick fabric of her singlet away from her sweat-drenched body to wipe her forehead.

"Put this on before you get cold," Aubrey said, handing her the hoodie he'd retrieved from the floor.

"You're asking me to cover up?" she said incredulously, taking the sweater and pulling it over her head.

"I promise it'll never happen again." He paused, then added gently, "Regretting asking me to train you now?"

"Why would you ask that?"

He reached out a hand to brush against her cheek, but Taer dodged it, glaring at him.

"Because it appears as if I've hurt you."

"You haven't hurt me," she replied, turning around and walking to the door. She stopped there, not turning back around. "Because you can't hurt what's already broken."

With her words still hanging in the air, Taer went down the stairs and left the War Hammer, a new sense of accomplishment unfurling in her belly.

16

The fire in the corner of the room was the only source of light. Darrion grunted as the first slice of the sharp blade ran through his skin between his shoulderblades, the skilled hands of another god carving out the words that would forever be inlayed in his skin.

Njord was standing beside Darrion's head, naked from the waist up. In his hand, he held one of Darrion's newly forged throwing blades, pressing the tip against the inside of his own wrist.

With each stroke of the blade in Darrion's back, Njord made another stroke against his own skin. The sharp tang of blood filled the room, but Darrion didn't know whether it was his blood, or Njord's, or perhaps it was both of them blending together.

"Blood for blood, Darrion," the Vanir told him.

"It's ready," the other god said, his voice like gravel under the heel of a boot.

"Good." Njord moved from Darrion's line of sight, coming to stand over his back. "Mix my blood with the ink, Aurvandil, then rub it into his skin."

Darrion felt the ink being dribbled over his back, pooling between the muscles and sinking into his skin. Aurvandil's rough fingers began prodding and pushing it into the shallow grooves in his back. He clenched his jaw in agony as fire and ice mixed together surged through his body.

"How do you feel?" Njord asked, wrapping a swathe of cloth around his own bloodied wrist. Darrion pried open his eyes and stared at the god.

"As if on fire," he gritted out. "Is that normal?"

Njord's face was serene. "I have not done this before," he replied. "But I hope any discomfort you're feeling will subside soon."

Darrion ground his teeth against the pain. "Why am I the first?"

The god smiled fondly at him, the look paternal and loving, but he did not reply. "Come. I want to show the others what they all will want."

Darrion maneuvered himself off the table, looking back at Aurvandil who had scored his flesh, standing there with the blood and ink on his hands. Aurvandil stared back blankly until Darrion looked away. Picking up his shirt, Darrion followed Njord from the room, stepping onto a small landing that looked over the great hall where twenty Mares were waiting.

"This is what those of you who pass the Final Test will receive to show your loyalty to me and to Darrion."

Turning his back, Darrion showed the other Mares the ink on his back.

"Blood for blood," Njord boomed. "Odin has hunted you

down for as long as I have been breathing. He has killed your kind in unprovoked attacks. He has decimated villages. He has slaughtered your mothers, your fathers, your sisters and your brothers. He has murdered your wives and killed your children."

Grunts of assent and growling rage greeted the Vanir's words.

"But that's not going to happen anymore. We will hunt *them* down and slaughter *their* families."

The small group of Mares roared in agreement, fueled by the vehemence of Njord's speech.

"I have brought you all here. I have trained you so that you may fulfil your deepest desire—revenge on the Aesir, who have taken from you what you most love."

Darrion could feel their growing thirst for blood prickling against his skin. They were building themselves into a feral frenzy, and he couldn't help but be dragged along, joining them in the calls for revenge.

Njord turned back to Darrion, triumph shining in his eyes. "Let the Final Test commence."

Darrion turned back to the Mares, still crying out for blood. He called out the names of those who had been training for the ultimate battle. Each one knew there could only be one victor in this fight, and they were all more than willing to give up their lives if they should fall.

The five combatants lined up in front of Darrion, bloodlust, fear and writhing hatred of him shining in their eyes.

Darrion called for calm, addressing the five Mares awaiting their deaths. "Each of you may choose the one weapon you would like to use in this fight. There are no rules. This is a fight to the death. Each of you will demonstrate to me why you should be part of this army. Only the strong survive."

The Mares all grunted their assent, taking the opportunity to size each other up.

"Blood for blood," he said under his breath, staring down at them, then stalking away to join Njord. They stood together on a raised platform overlooking a section of the great hall barricaded off by wooden palings, benches circling the outside of the ring. Sand had been thrown on the floor to soak up the large amount of blood that would be spilled.

The five dark elves filed into the ring, each of them armed with the weapon of his choice—a sword, a war hammer, a mace, a battle ax and a scythe—and Darrion began to wonder who would be left standing at the end.

The Mares stood in a circle around the arena. Some were dressed in nothing more than a loincloth, while others wore a sort of armor over their chests. The crowds' excitement was palpable, the yells and chants making everyone crazed, making them salivate to see the first blood shed.

Njord raised his arms in front of him, calling for a silence that came in an instant. "The fight ends when only one Mare is left breathing." His voice pulsed with power. Turning to Darrion, he said, "At your master's command, you will start."

Darrion could feel every set of eyes on him. He stared at the five Mares, each of them twitching or shuffling from foot to foot … except for one. Arthon stared hard at Darrion, waiting, watching for the signal for the bloodbath to begin.

Darrion gave an almost imperceptible nod of his head. Arthon was the first to strike. Wielding his battle ax like it was an extension of his hand, he slammed the blade into the rival Mare standing directly on his right. The weapon lodged in his back, but Arthon was already there to pull it free, bringing it down once more across the back of his opponent's neck as the Mare fell to his knees. Bone and metal collided and his head went rolling across the sand. The amount of blood that poured from the wound was astounding, but Darrion watched on blankly.

He kept his eyes on Arthon, only occasionally letting his attention drift to the remaining three. The Mare with the scythe was battling the mace-wielding elf, unable to deflect the blows from the much heavier weapon. Despite his clear disadvantage, he moved the scythe with a grace and expertise Darrion had not expected.

Narrowly avoiding a mortal blow to his head, the male swung his long-handled weapon in a smooth arc, the air whistling as the blade cut through it. At first it looked as if he had missed his target … until the other Mare began to stagger around wildly, dropping his mace to the sand. Darrion wanted to slide forward, to get a better look, but he stayed where he was, watching as the injured Mare dropped to his knees.

A river of blood began to flow from his neck, streaming down his chest. Darrion's eyes cut back to Arthon to see him make his killing blow, his battle ax becoming lodged in his opponent's sternum.

Standing on the fallen Mare's foot, Arthon wrenched the weapon up through his opponent's sternum and out through his chin. The Mare's chest and neck split open, blood now flowing like a swollen river down his body and into the sand.

Covered in gore, and with his last victim toppling over behind him, Arthon turned around to face his final challenger.

One half of the small crowd was chanting Arthon's name while the other half were calling out the name Zarail. The male with the scythe—Zarail—surveyed the crowd for a second, before locking his eyes on Arthon.

Zarail was relatively unscathed other than a small slice to his upper thigh. A rivulet of blood ran down from the wound, getting matted in the hair on his legs. Arthon didn't appear as if he had just fought for his life at all; his breathing was steady, and a smirk pulled up the corner of his mouth.

He was cocky, but Darrion knew that cockiness could get you killed. As soon as you thought you were better than your opponent, you gave them permission to be just that.

The watching crowd was clamoring for more blood now. The screams were deafening. Darrion's gaze landed on Njord, who was watching him intently rather than the fighting before them. He looked back in time to see Arthon fade and then rematerialize behind the other Mare. Arthon brought his arms above his head, as if to strike his opponent in the back of the head with his ax, but Zarail was too fast. Spinning around, he brought the long handle of his scythe up horizontally above his head, blocking the attack, but sacrificing the length of his weapon. The ax's blade bit through the staff easily, leaving Zarail with a simple curved blade and a foot of wood.

Backing away, Zarail stripped the wood from the blade and readied himself for Arthon's attack. A cocky grin pulled at the corner of Arthon's mouth before he struck at Zarail with the speed of a viper. Driving him backwards with blow after blow, Arthon pressed the other Mare up against the wooden barrier, holding the razor-sharp blade of his ax at Zarail's throat.

Zarail's fingers released the curved blade in his hands, the steel falling noiselessly to the sandy floor. The crowd began to chant for Arthon to make the kill, to finish the fight and claim his title as the first of the *agarwaen*.

Arthon looked over his shoulder first to Njord then to Darrion, looking for instruction. Darrion's eyes flickered to Zarail, seeing that he had already faded from Arthon's ax blade. A split second later, the Mare spun back around, but it was already too late.

Zarail had scooped up a discarded sword and, with a beautiful arc through the air, removed Arthon's head with one stroke.

The crowd erupted, clambering over the wooden barrier and rushing into the arena to give their congratulations to the last Mare standing.

In Darrion's ear, Njord confided, "I did not see that coming."

"I did. Arthon was too sure of himself. Vanity and pride will get you killed every time."

A loaded silence filled the space, and the Vanir said, "Perhaps that will be Odin's downfall, also."

No. Odin's downfall will be at my hand, Darrion thought darkly.

The screams and yells of celebration suddenly morphed into screams of terror. Both Darrion and Njord's heads whipped around.

No. It just couldn't be.

Darrion was a child again, cowering in the hidden room, watching Odin and his Valkyries cutting down his entire family in cold blood.

It was happening again. Everything was the same as before.

The beautiful dance of the Valkyries' colored swords blurred through the air, connecting with the flesh of the Mares still too stunned to do anything but scream or stare. Darrion watched them all fall, one after another after another.

When the last of them had been struck down, Njord jumped over the barrier. He ran at Odin with rage billowing from his frail body, the fury of his power blowing back his hair and beard, sending it into a tangled mess around his head. Darrion was fixed to the spot, his legs like lead, watching the showdown between perhaps two of the most powerful gods to have ever walked the Nine Worlds.

"You've gone too far, Njord," Odin snarled, striding forward until they were standing toe to toe, two of his Valkyries flanking him protectively. "Do you think you can just build an army against me?"

"Any loyalty I felt towards you disappeared a long time ago."

Odin's eyes darkened. "You have no dominion in any of the Nine Worlds anymore, Njord. You had to rely on these filthy dark elves." The All-Father spat on the ground at the Vanir's feet, a nasty sneer pulling up his upper lip. "And I won't let you do this."

Suddenly, there was a strangled moan. Darrion's hands balled into fists when he saw hot blood pour from Njord's side, dripping down his leg and onto the sand-covered floor.

Too shocked to move, Darrion watched Odin pull the spear from Njord's body, reveling in the pain he was inflicting. Without another sound, Njord dropped to the ground.

This act ignited Darrion's rage. Watching the man he had come to think of as his second father die before his eyes—and at Odin's hand once more—broke something in him.

He thought he'd known the desire for revenge before. But now … now he knew what it really was. Darrion's eyes burned into Odin as he stared down at the fallen Vanir. The All-Father's head rose, his eyes meeting Darrion's. He cocked his head to the side slightly before turning to the Valkyrie on his right. She held a black sword lightly in her palm, her ethereal features beautiful, her eyes frigid.

Darrion knew what was to come. His fate would be that of all the other Mares lying dead in the sand. But he couldn't allow that to happen. He was supposed to rise up and overcome this. He was a master. His life would not end here, on this day.

He spun around, coming face to face with the Valkyrie with the black sword. His eyes settled on the thick scar running across the front of her throat. A warning growl bubbled up from her chest, her sword hand rising to strike. Time seemed to be reduced to nothing more than the breaths he drew into his lungs.

As the blade came toward his neck he saw the cool indifference in the Valkyrie's eyes. Whether he lived or died, it made no difference to her. His death was just another of the All-Father's wishes to be fulfilled.

The anger he had been carrying with him for years surged, and with it came clarity. He looked up to see the blade less than a quarter of an inch from his throat, and he did it—he did something he had been practicing with Njord, something that should not have been possible for another forty years.

He faded.

Leaving the guild house behind, Darrion disappeared into the darkness of the night, his fade taking him to the only other place he could think of.

He returned home.

17

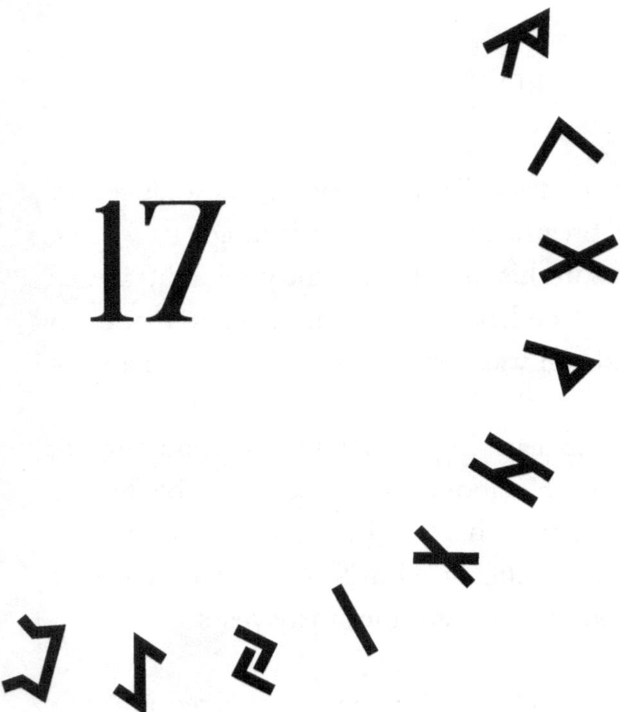

Chicago

Locating Henry Craine's offices had been surprisingly easy for Loki. Craine's face was often featured in newspapers and a magazine called *Business Review USA*. It appeared that Craine was a legitimate businessman—owner and CEO of P&C Pharmaceuticals.

Waiting until early afternoon, Loki went to the P&C Pharmaceuticals offices. Situated in downtown Chicago between a bank and a law firm, Craine's building was a monument to wealth and social stature, made entirely of thick sheets of glass and metal. Loki waited across the street, watching the reflection of the dying sun move and wink across the front face of the building.

A little before six, a Bentley pulled up to the curb. A second after that, a man dressed in a black suit left the building with two large men trailing after him. One of the large man got into the front seat while the other opened up the rear door. The man in the suit—Craine, Loki deduced, since he was the only suited man with bodyguards to have exited the building—slid inside the car, hidden from view by the dark tint on the windows. The second man stayed on the sidewalk and closed the door.

The car left, swerving into traffic aggressively. The man left behind turned and entered the building once more. Loki stared after the Bentley, fading a few blocks at a time to keep up with it. After leaving the city, they stuck to a northern route, their final destination a place called Lake Forest—a leafy suburb with perfectly manicured lawns on the banks of Lake Michigan. The town car eventually pulled into a driveway and through a gate flanked by two large pillars, surrounded by black wrought-iron fences.

The house itself was like nothing Loki had ever seen before. Made entirely out of stone, it was completely symmetrical, finished with white shutters and dormer windows. The car came to a stop at the top of the circular drive, and the large man seated in the rear got out and ran around to open up the door for his employer.

Craine climbed out, his attention on the phone in his hand, and made his way to the front door of the house. Loki stayed hidden in the shadows of an oak tree on the lawn until the car pulled away. Then, with a single thought, he faded inside, where he could hear floorboards creaking overhead.

Casually walking through the downstairs level of the house, Loki noticed the complete lack of anything personal. There were no family photos. There were no personal touches. It was entirely decorated in varying shades of beige, and he got the distinct impression that Craine hardly spent any time here.

Wandering into the kitchen, he pulled open the top drawers on the island bench, looking for a weapon he could use.

"Perfect," he said when he found exactly what he was looking for.

Pulling the meat cleaver from the drawer, he tested its edge, a smile forming when a slash of red welled easily on his thumb. Silently closing the drawer with his hip, Loki made his way to the stairs that would take him to the upper levels of the house, cleaver in hand. It was dark up there, except for a sliver of light coming from a bedroom at the end of the landing.

Whistling a little tune, Loki wandered in that direction and nudged the door open with his foot. Light spilled out of the room, creating an arc of gold on the carpet around his feet and ankles. The sound of running water came from further inside, and he could see the bathroom door firmly shut.

Flipping off the overhead light, Loki made himself comfortable on the sleek low-lying sofa in one corner of the room. The upholstery felt like silk velvet, and he knew it would hungrily drink up the blood that would soon be spilled there. After only moments of waiting, the water stopped and silence ensued until Loki saw the bathroom door handle turning.

"What the fuck?" Craine said in a surprised voice, his hand reaching out to flip the switch beside the door. He had a towel wrapped around his hips, his upper body in good shape for a man his age. Loki had time to see a handful of scars on his arms, chest and torso—bullet and knife wounds, by the look of it—before the man saw Loki reclining on the sofa. He dropped the towel and reached for the gun sitting on the bedside table to his left.

"Who the fuck are you?" Craine's voice was strong—one that commanded Loki to answer. Loki got up, ignoring his question. The muzzle of the gun followed his movements. "Stay right where you are," Craine added, his two-handed grip steady.

Loki put his hands up, still gripping the cleaver.

"Drop the weapon."

"I'm afraid that's not going to happen," he drawled back.

"Oh yeah? Well, I say it is, because I can put a bullet through your skull a hell of a lot faster than you can attack me with that cleaver."

Loki liked the sound of that challenge. "Are you sure about that?" he asked, canting his head to the side.

"You're goddamn right," the human retorted fiercely, disengaging the safety with his thumb. Loki took a step forward, but before his foot hit the floor again, the explosive crack of gunfire rang out in the room.

It was too late.

Loki was already behind Craine, one arm wrapped around his chest, the other pressing the cleaver into his carotid. "Engage the safety and drop your weapon," he said. Craine's breathing was harsh, uneven, but he did as he was told, letting the gun fall to the carpet.

"Who are you?" Craine's pulse was hammering. "Why are you doing this?"

"It's nothing personal, really," Loki told him. "You have something I want."

"What? What do you want? Is it money? Drugs? I can give you both."

"You have something much more powerful in your possession."

With one swift movement, Loki sliced the blade across the front of his throat, the sharp edge biting into the skin, muscle and sinew. The sharpness of blood saturated the air. Craine gasped, the sound bubbling and forced as he gulped for breath. Loki let Craine's body slide to the floor at his feet, the man's hard, dark eyes staring up at him, his mouth moving but not making any sound.

Loki dragged him over to the sofa and deposited him there, enjoying the way the cool fabric warmed with the color of his blood. More blood bubbled and foamed from his lips, but his eyes were wide and attached to Loki's face.

Picking up his feet, Loki arranged Craine's body in just the right way. He smiled mildly down at the man, reaching out to brush some hair from his face.

"Now, this won't hurt at all," he cooed softly, bringing the cleaver up to Craine's face once more. He let the man see the blade already stained with his blood before beginning his work.

18

Chicago

Galen's phone was buzzing silently, the vibrations traveling up and down his leg. Dipping a hand inside his pocket, he retrieved the phone and answered the call.

"Yeah?"

"We need to talk," Craine said abruptly, his voice sounding a little cooler than usual.

"I'll be there in half an hour," Galen replied, pulling the phone away from his ear to hang up.

"No!" Craine bellowed on the other end. "I need to see you now."

Galen frowned. It was unusual for Craine to make such a forceful demand. Normally, he'd work around Galen's schedule, so something big must have been going down. He hung up without confirming he'd heard the order, sliding his phone back into his pocket.

"What's up?" Rhys asked, his concentration firmly on the blade he was oiling at the dining room table.

"Craine wants to see me."

"What about?"

Galen let out an annoyed grunt. "I don't fucking know, but he sounded kind of pissy."

"Think it was about our last hit?"

He thought about that. Galen hadn't heard from Craine since leaving his office, even though he would have surely heard the news. But there had been no congratulations, no pats on the back for a job fucking well done.

Nothing.

Had Craine thought they'd gone too far? He didn't think so. The mob boss was a tough motherfucker who commanded ruthlessness from everyone lucky enough to find themselves in his employment.

His and Rhys's handiwork had made the national evening news. He'd seen the broadcast while pounding back a few beers at a local bar. Rhys had been in the bathroom getting his dick sucked.

Galen stood up from the table, raising his arms above his head and stretching out the stiffening muscles in his back. "Stay here. I'll go see what he wants."

He faded to the alleyway beside Craine's downtown offices and stepped out onto the pristine sidewalk. The sun was trying to break through the clouds, but was losing the battle, casting a strange, filtered light over the city.

Pushing into the building, Galen bypassed all the building's security guards, heading straight for Craine's goons, who were loitering near an elevator that had only one function—to take you to and from Craine's top floor offices.

"Craine wants to see me," he muttered when asked what he was doing there. "I haven't got you scheduled," Goon One replied, looking down at a small notepad in his meaty fists, his fat fingers curled around the edges of the paper.

"Are you sure it was today you were supposed to see *Mr.* Craine?" Goon Two asked.

Galen stared at the man, his eyes telling him that he was fucking tired of playing Twenty Questions.

"Give me a moment to call him," Goon One said, pulling out a two-way radio and stepping away from their group. Galen kept his eyes on Goon Two. A few moments passed before Goon One reappeared.

"He's good to go." He jabbed the elevator button with a thick finger. There was a pleasant *ding* and the doors opened soundlessly.

Galen stepped in, turned around to face the two men and flipped them off as the doors closed. "It was a real pleasure, boys."

Galen was just going to fade straight into the fucking building next time.

The elevator car didn't seem to move at all, but a few seconds later, the doors slid open on the top floor. Some more of Craine's bodyguards were standing just outside the doors, and they patted Galen down after he'd pulled his machete out from the holster attached to his back.

Another meathead opened the door, revealing Craine sitting behind his large desk, the sleeves of his white button-down shirt rolled up to his elbows, his top button undone. His dark eyes ran over Galen, who could sense there was something not quite right with his boss.

"What did you want to see me about so urgently?" he asked,

crossing his arms over his chest, feeling naked without his machete.

"Sit down," Craine ordered, indicating to a chair in front of Galen.

Galen didn't reply or comply—he just stayed where he was, staring at the Chicago mob boss. A small smile lifted the corner of Craine's lips as he leaned back in his chair, assessing Galen.

"I have another job for you."

"Okay."

"I need you to go to Boston."

A chill went down Galen's spine. Boston was home to a lot of Aesir, but also the home of Darrion—the oldest and most ruthless of guild masters. If he found out that Galen was there, he'd be paying for it in blood; no dark elf waltzed into Darrion's territory without signing their own death warrant.

Not that a human like Craine knew about the minefield surrounding guilds.

Galen let out a breath. "For any particular reason?"

"Have you heard of a club called Odin's Eye?" Craine asked, watching Galen closely.

"Yeah, I've heard of it."

"I need you to go there and just check things out for me."

"Check things out?" Galen repeated, confused. Craine was never ambiguous about what he wanted done. If he wanted someone dead, he would say so in as few words as possible. If he wanted to send a message, he would say so. This vague request was setting off alarm bells for Galen.

"Yes," Craine said.

Galen's brow furrowed. "I don't understand."

"I'm not asking you to understand," Craine spat out. "I'm asking you to follow my orders and go to Boston. Go to Odin's

Eye and find out everything you can about the place. Get them to trust you. I don't care how you do it. Twist the truth. Flat out lie. I don't give a fuck, but make sure it happens."

Galen was a hired killer, not a diplomat. "What makes you think I'm a good representative for you? Can't you send Moretti?"

Moretti was Craine's lawyer, but also his captain. He was a snake—ruthless and cold-blooded both in and out of the courtroom—but he'd been born with a silver tongue, whereas Galen had been born with a blade in his hand.

Craine's mouth flexed up in the corners. "I need your particular services for this job."

"So, you want me to kill the owner? One of the employees?" Galen asked him, fishing for more information.

"No, I think you're a little more useful than that." Craine leaned forward in his chair, resting his forearms on the blotter, pinning him with a hard and probing glare. "I know what you are, Galen."

The alarm bells were now clanging loudly. Galen jutted his chin forward slightly. "And what's that?" he asked in a deadly drawl. He had no qualms about killing the man with his bare hands if he knew too much.

"*Morier.*" The word was spoken quietly, a smug smile making itself at home on Craine's lips.

"Is that supposed to mean something to me?" Galen asked coolly.

Craine waved his hand dismissively in front of him. "I'm not going to play these games with you, Walker."

It took Galen half a second to fade from his position behind the chair and reappear behind Craine, but somehow the guy had moved with inhuman speed. He was already out of his seat, his hand wrapping around Galen's throat. Turning, Craine slammed Galen's back onto the top of the desk—the furniture creaking loudly beneath him.

Galen eyed the man above him, feeling the cold sting of metal against his temple.

"Are you going to behave?" Craine asked calmly. Galen didn't know how he'd moved so quickly, unless he was partaking of his products. That was a dumb fucking move, and he thought the mob boss would be a whole lot smarter than that.

"Well?" Craine prompted.

"Let me up," Galen spat. For a heartbeat longer, the muzzle of the gun stayed where it was, until finally Craine pulled away, placing his piece on the desk beside Galen's head and straightening his shirt.

Slowly, and with very calculated movements, Galen sat up. He stared hard into those eyes, thinking he'd seen a flicker of green in their dark depths.

Craine took his seat again, steepling his fingers under his chin and staring harmlessly at Galen. "I want you to leave in two days' time. I want you to gather as much intel as you can. Make sure you're seen. Make sure they know who you are. Am I making myself clear?"

"Crystal."

"Good." Craine stood up, holstered his piece and walked around his desk. "I'll be expecting a call from you by the end of the week with good news."

19

Mason squeezed his eyes shut for a moment, trying to collect his thoughts … and to keep his brain from fucking imploding. There was a lot noise tonight—both in his ears and inside his head. There must have been about a hundred gods and demigods down on level one of the Eye, laughing and spilling their drinks while chatting to the humans.

His eyes skimmed over the crowd again. Although he wanted to tune every damn voice out, he had to be vigilant. Korvain had given him the same spiel as before about listening out for Darrion's name in all the chatter, but so far he hadn't heard anything more interesting than how some god was going to fuck a woman against the bathroom wall.

Bryn was back at the bar, sitting at the end like she always did, watching the crowd in the mirrored-glass splashback behind the bar. Mist wasn't there, but Taer was, pulling bottles from the small under-the-counter fridges and pouring drinks.

Although she seemed a little frayed around the edges, the girl was holding her own against the demands of the crowd. Forcing his eyes away, Mason watched the trickle of people Mav was letting through. He could usually tell by looking whether they were human or not. Just to make sure, he concentrated on them, confirming his suspicions when their thoughts started broadcasting loud and fucking clear in his head.

"Hey, am I good to go on my break?" the other bouncer for level one asked.

"Yeah, take it now."

The bouncer moved towards the door leading into the staff room and offices as Mason scanned the immediate area again. A scream at the rear of the bar brought his head around. There was another shout, and a fleshy-sounding hit followed closely after it. He had been around enough testosterone-filled men to know what had just kicked off.

"Fuck!" he cursed, moving towards the fight. He should have seen it coming. Two men were throwing sloppy, drunken punches at each other, while two women were screeching at them to stop, slinging insults at each other in between breaths.

With one hand, Mason grabbed one of the men, pulling him off the other one, while still trying to keep his woman away with his free hand.

The other man, who had recovered from the last strike, was up on his feet again. He approached Mason and the man he was currently holding on to, a look of fierce determination in his eyes.

"Back the fuck up," Mason warned in a low voice. He took a moment to look around. Where the fuck was everybody else? Backup should have been streaming in by now.

The first guy wasn't listening, though. Mason had two choices: let the other guy go to grab the first one, or allow himself to get punched in the face for this asshole. The guy in his grasp was wriggling, trying to break free so that he could go for round two.

Fuck.

Mason looked up in time to see a meaty fist coming in his direction. The bastard had swung wide, catching him just above his eye. The gaudy college class ring the guy was wearing caught Mason on the eyebrow. The sharp sting told him the skin had broken. Blood was now trickling down the side of his face.

Mason recovered and stood up to see the guy coming at him again. Unable to block this second attack, Mason closed his eyes instinctively, but seconds passed, and nothing had happened. So Mason opened one lid … and then another.

A guy Mason had never laid eyes on before was standing behind the other man, a thick forearm wrapped around his throat. After a long beat, Mason snapped back into action.

"You and your buddy are out of here," he said forcefully into the human's ear, hauling him towards the door. The guy who had saved his ass followed behind him, and the two women trailed after them, still arguing over who had started what.

He handed the men off to Mav, who promptly pushed them out the door, the two squabbling women tripping out into the street after them.

Mason turned back to the guy who had helped him out, offering him his palm. "Thanks, man. I owe you."

As they shook, Mason took a peek inside his head, out of instinct, his neck tingling when he saw what the guy was.

"It's no problem. You can return the favor by getting me an audience with your boss."

Mason eyed the man. "And who the fuck are you?" Suspicion laced his voice.

The male smiled, but the action didn't reach his eyes. "Forgive my bad manners. My name's Galen and I have a business proposition."

20

Eir wiped the steam from the mirror, staring at her reflection in the slightly fogged-up glass. She was still bothered by how the doctor had treated Mr. Adamsen the previous day. She was also a little sad. Even though she didn't know the man, she had felt his pain. She knew what he was suffering, and that she could only really give him temporary relief from the pain.

Carefully, she toweled off the rest of her body, drying her hair and pulling it back into a loose chignon to keep it out of the way. Once she was dressed, she wandered into the living room, sat down and stared at the blank screen of the TV. It was too quiet, and although quiet was what she wanted, Eir realized she didn't want to be alone either.

She sighed. She hadn't really done much socializing since Kristy had died, focusing all her attention on work instead. She knew this was her way of grieving, but she had to stop it and come back to the real world.

She changed out of her pajamas and into jeans and a white blouse before walking back down to the elevator at the end of the hall. Pressing the down arrow, she waited for the car to arrive.

It hummed as it descended, the sound relaxing her, but when she stepped out and headed for the main body of the bar, the door between the bar and the hall she was standing in swung open violently, thumping against the wall.

A man she had never seen before was being forcibly led into the hallway by …

"Mason?" she whispered in disbelief.

She could have sworn her heart stopped beating for a moment. He hadn't noticed her yet and she took advantage of that by stepping against the wall, trying to make herself as small as she could.

He was dressed all in black: black pants, black button-down shirt and black boots. He had a headset attached to the inside of one ear and a microphone on the collar of his shirt. His hazel eyes were serious. He looked professional and in control—not at all like the man she'd seen in the park.

What was he doing there? Did he work at the club? Mason's head swung around suddenly. When his too-serious eyes landed on her, they widened. Bryn followed behind the two men, closing the noise of the bar out as she shut the door.

"Mason!" Bryn snarled, her tone interrupting Mason and Eir's eye lock. "Get your head back in the fucking game … and for fuck's sake call Korvain," she said, pushing the man he'd been manhandling further down the hallway and forcing him up against the wall roughly, kicking his feet to separate his legs.

Touching the tattoo on her neck, Bryn summoned her sword, and its magic hummed through Eir's body. Her own sword began to throb in response. Where Bryn's sword was golden, Eir's was violet in color. She hadn't used it in nearly a thousand years, yet when another Valkyrie's sword was drawn, she felt a desire to use hers, too.

Eir's attention went back to Mason when he touched the button on his collar and spoke to Korvain, still watching her. Eir could see the questions burning in his eyes, and she was sure he must see the same thing in hers.

Barely a minute had passed before Korvain pushed through the door. His rage roiled around him, causing the room to darken, the shadows to thicken.

"What's going on? Who the *fuck* is he?" he ordered when he saw Bryn's patting down the stranger. Goosebumps broke out on Eir's skin, and she shivered, wrapping her arms around herself.

"This is Galen. He says he wants to discuss something with me," Bryn said, staring hard at the man.

Galen cleared his throat and tried to push himself off the wall. "Yes, as I was saying before—" He grunted as Bryn slammed him back against the wall again.

Korvain clicked his teeth together noisily. "I didn't fucking ask you, did I?" He stared icily at Mason first before addressing Bryn once more. "Let's go into your office for a bit more privacy."

"Okay."

Eir watched them haul the other man into the room, slamming the door shut behind them. When Eir turned around, it was just her and Mason in the empty hallway. He walked towards her, halting a few feet away. His eyes devoured her hungrily, and Eir's skin flushed. An undeniable electricity surged between them.

"What are you doing here?" he asked.

"I live here. What are you doing here?"

He frowned. "You live here, as in you're one of Bryn's Valkyries?"

His words startled her. "What do you know of the Valkyries?"

Mason stared at her for a beat then ran his hands through his short hair in disbelief, drawing her attention to a cut above his left eye.

"You're bleeding," she uttered softly, lifting her fingers to his forehead. She began inspecting the wound, until Mason sucked in a sharp breath, the sound hissing through his teeth. "I'm sorry, but I need to see how deep it is. You may need stitches," she said. Eir began probing the wound again, determining what she needed to do.

He did need stitches, so she had two choices really: take him upstairs and patch him up, or take him into the staff changing rooms and do it there. For her own sanity, she decided to lead him into the changing room.

"Sit," she commanded, pointing to the long benches that separated the two sides of the room. While Mason settled in, Eir went to one of the lockers and pulled out the first-aid kit. Although she could have healed him, although she *wanted* to heal him with her touch, Eir chose to do it the old-fashioned way instead. The less he knew, the better.

He was straddling the bench, his hazel eyes heavy-lidded as he watched her. Eir could feel the blush traverse her neck and climb her cheeks, but she pushed the feeling of flapping butterflies in her stomach away and sat down next to him.

His large chest rose and fell as she twisted her body to face him. She took one of the sterile pads from its packaging and soaked it in saline, then pressed it to Mason's temple. His blood mixed with the saline, turning it pink, leaving faint trails down his cheek before dripping off his chin.

When the awkward angle Eir was sitting at made it too difficult for her to work properly, she stood up, straddling the bench so her and Mason's knees were touching, the first-aid kit sitting between them. She pressed a clean swab to his forehead while mopping up the excess water with another.

"Hold that there for me?" Mason's fingers grazed hers as she pulled away. Eir busied herself by searching through the kit for a small suture needle and some thread. She could feel Mason's eyes on her as she worked and the flush crept back into her cheeks again.

"This might sting a bit. Are you ready?" Her breath was embarrassingly whispery and faint.

Four neat stitches later and Eir dropped the needle and thread into her lap before finding a small sterile patch to keep the stitches clean and dry.

"I'll give you some more of these when you finish tonight," she said, concentrating on her work. "The stitches should be ready to come out in a few days."

"Will I have a scar?" he asked, his lips tilting up mischievously.

"Were you hoping for one?"

"Yeah … chicks dig scars," he added when he saw her questioning look. She laughed out loud, making the grin on Mason's face even wider, making him look younger.

"There it is," he said, his gaze hot on her face. "There's that laugh I like so much."

Eir blanched and got to her feet, dumping the used gauze and empty packaging into the trash. With her back still turned to him, she asked him the question she'd wanted to ask him for the past half an hour. "What do you know about Valkyries?"

He was silent, and when she turned around, he was looking down at the ground. "A lot more than I should," he replied, then sighed. "Look, I have to get back out there," he said, indicating the main belly of the club with his head. "Come find me after we close and I'll explain everything to you. Please?" he added when he saw her hesitate. "You need to give me more of these things anyway." Mason pointed to the gauze covering his freshly tended wound.

Eir reluctantly agreed, pushing out of the door and walking towards the elevator. She could feel his eyes on her as she walked away, but was too scared to turn around and look at him. He said he knew a lot more than he should about her world, but how could that be?

"I'll explain everything tonight, Eir. I promise," Mason called out. Eir turned to meet his gaze, feeling that same flip-flopping in her stomach as before. Thankfully the elevator arrived soon after she pressed the button. She stepped inside, staring down at the floor until the doors slid shut.

Eir let out a shaky breath and slumped against the wall of the elevator car. Waiting for three am to roll around was going to be torturous.

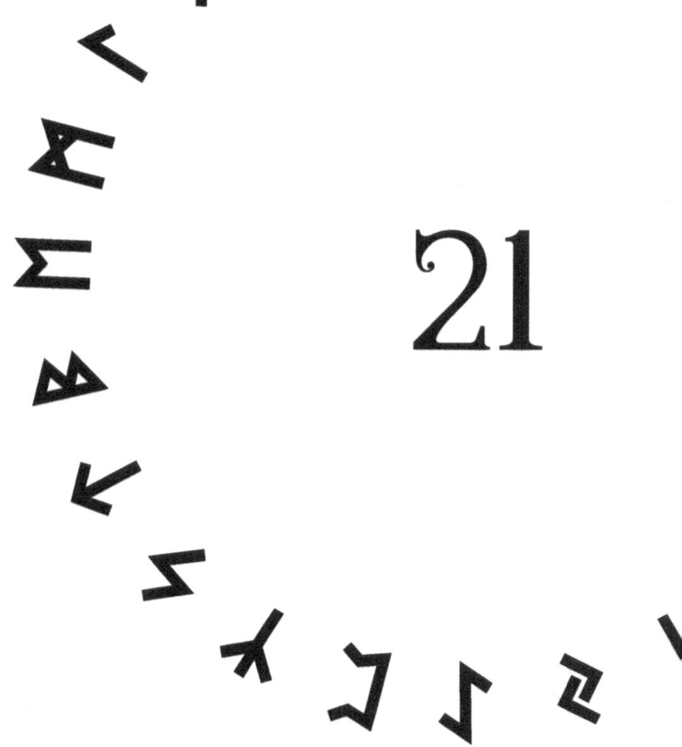

21

Mason saw Bryn emerge from the hallway that led to her office, and his shoulders immediately relaxed. He had been wound so damn tight thinking about Bryn talking to that guy, but thankfully he knew Korvain wouldn't leave her alone with the bastard.

Mason watched the goddess for a moment before he made his way over to the bar, where she was pouring herself a glass of 42 Below. He took a deep breath, steadying himself for what he was about to ask. "What did he want?"

Bryn took a sip from her drink, holding his gaze while she swallowed down the cool liquor. "He had a business proposal for me."

"Really?"

"Yeah. He was here on behalf of his boss." Bryn put her glass down with a dull *thump* after taking a long, deep drink. "Henry Craine."

Mason had heard of Craine, as had most people. He was perhaps the most ruthless mob boss since Capone had run the Chicago-based racketeering circuit in the twenties. For a few moments, he just let that information sink in. "What does he want with us?"

The Valkyrie's lip tilted up in a small smile. "He wants a stake in the business."

"Why the fuck would he think he could buy into the club? Hell, why would he want to?"

Bryn looked off into the throng of people and shrugged, taking another sip from her glass. A drop of condensation rolled down the side, slipping off the end and hitting the bar. All around them, the bar kept functioning as if nothing was wrong.

But something was very wrong.

Mason could feel it like a gentle buzzing in his ear, gradually getting louder. It was triggering his marine's instincts, setting off the alarms and telling him to keep his eyes fucking open.

"What are you going to do?"

Bryn's eyes suddenly blazed. "My business is *not* for sale. I've worked too damn hard to keep everyone I love safe to give up a stake of my home."

Mason exhaled; he was glad she wasn't even considering selling. "How did Galen take that answer?"

She sighed. "He warned that his boss would be *disinclined*—that was his choice of word—to accept a refusal." She took another sip of her drink, placing her glass down purposefully. Her eyes were still firmly planted on a spot in the distance. "There was an implied threat, and I guess I can expect another visit from him soon enough, no doubt to up the offer and sweeten the deal."

Mason dragged a hand down his face. The buzzing was growing into a persistent hum now. He didn't like the fact that Craine was sniffing around. Why the Eye, and why now? The answer hit him like a ton of bricks. Craine was balls-deep in the drug trade. What if he wanted to expand the business into Boston?

"Fuck," he muttered to himself. Bryn hardly even cast a look in his direction. Mason couldn't have Bryn exposed to that. Hell, he couldn't have Eir exposed to that.

Eir.

"Listen, Bryn, I wanted to ask you about something."

"What is it?" she asked, her gaze traveling over the crowd surrounding the bar.

He was suddenly nervous. "It's about Eir."

She looked at him, eyes hard. "What about her?"

"I, ah, want to know more about her."

Her stare said more than her words ever could. He knew she would protect all her Valkyries from danger.

"She lives here, right?" he pressed, knowing he was pushing his luck with her. After a few tense seconds, Bryn nodded. Mason licked his lips. "What else can you tell me about her?"

Bryn's mouth tightened just a little as her eyes betrayed her thoughts. Mason listened in as she tried to decide whether she should tell him any more about Eir.

"Why do you want to know about Eir?" she asked.

"She's the only one of your … sisters … I hadn't met before tonight," he replied nonchalantly. "If I'm supposed to look out for you all as Korvain's asked me to, I need all the information I can get."

It was only a half-truth he was telling her, but it sounded convincing.

"She's a nurse at Massachusetts General Hospital."

"And …" He hesitated, leaning in just a little closer, so their conversation remained between the two of them. He couldn't believe what he was about to say to her. How would she take the news that he knew all about their world? Would she shun him or welcome him into the fold? He blew out a breath. "She's one of your Valkyries."

Bryn's eyes widened for just a second before her cool expression returned. Mason leaned back against the side of the bar, his words hanging in the air between them. She couldn't deny it, and even if she tried, he'd call bullshit.

"Is that so?" Her voice was icy.

"Yes." At least she hadn't flat-out denied it.

Bryn poured herself another drink, picked up the glass and moved from behind the bar toward the door that led to her office. Mason stayed where he was until she glanced over her shoulder at him.

"Come with me."

Mason looked over at one of the other bodyguards standing by the stairs, indicating that he was stepping away for a moment. Then he followed Bryn out the side door and into her office.

Once he was settled in the chair opposite her desk, the Valkyrie began to speak.

"Who told you?" she asked, eyeing him over the rim of her drink as she took a long sip of vodka. She put her glass back down, still watching him.

"Nobody told me. I …" Mason thought carefully about what he was going to say. He'd made a blood oath to Korvain that meant he wasn't allowed to discuss Valkyries with anyone, but … he wasn't talking to *anyone*. He was talking to a Valkyrie. "There are some things you don't know about me, Bryn."

One pale brow arched. "Is that right?" she replied coldly. When he only bobbed his head in reply, Bryn's lips thinned. "Tell me exactly what it is you *think* you know."

"I know of the Valkyries and the gods. I know of Mares and

I know of Odin." Bryn shook her head in disbelief, but Mason pressed on. "I'm also aware of the Nine Worlds and the Fall."

"How?" she asked, anger burning in her voice.

At least she'd given up the pretense of ignorance. "Korvain is aware of everything I know, and how I know it," Mason replied.

"What does this have to do with Korvain?" Bryn's fists slammed against the desktop, rattling her glass. Her anger was a whole other person in the room, breathing in their conversation and spitting out a whole lot of hostility in return.

"Because Mason was the one who saved your life," a dark voice interrupted. Korvain—all seven feet of muscle-bound Mare—stood in the doorway, imploring Bryn with his eyes. "He saved your life, Bryn."

Korvain's dark eyes settled on Mason. "He can hear the thoughts of the gods," he added simply.

Bryn's chair creaked as she sat back. "Hear their thoughts?"

"Yes," Mason said with a shrug. "And I want to know more about Eir."

Bryn's eyes shifted to the glass in front of her. "Can't you just read her thoughts?" There was a derisive edge to her voice that he had never heard before.

"I don't enjoy doing that if I don't have to," he said in his defense, keeping his eyes downcast.

"But sometimes you have to?" Bryn retorted.

"His abilities have served you very well so far, Bryn." Korvain interrupted. "Think about this for a moment. This is Mason. You trust him. All he's doing is telling you something that might help to protect you better."

Her eyes rose, her voice low when she finally spoke. "But what if he tells others of us? He'll put us all in danger."

"I would never do that, Bryn."

"I have already taken care of that," Korvain said at the same time. "He has taken a blood oath. He's sworn to secrecy."

"Or what?"

Korvain gave Bryn a wicked smile. "I get to show him just how good I am at my job."

A long, heavy silence fell upon them as Bryn deliberated. "How much does he know about what happened last month?"

"Nothing."

Mason kept his eyes on the Valkyrie, hoping that his expression showed just how much he cared about her, and how worried he'd been after her abduction.

"You might as well know it all, then." Bryn blew out an irritated breath. She proceeded to tell him everything, from the death of her Valkyries to her capture, from Eir's twin sister's death to Loki's. When Mason learned of Eir's loss, he felt the pain like a sharp stab through his heart.

"And who's Darrion?" he asked, directing his question to Korvain, who was now perched on the edge of Bryn's desk, his face betraying nothing. The only reason Mason knew Korvain was pissed was that whenever Bryn had mentioned Loki or her imprisonment, the muscle in his jaw had jumped.

"My guild master. He's also the one who had charged me with killing Bryn. I still don't know where he came up with the idea, but the fact that Loki was going after the other Valkyries too makes it seem as if they were in league with each other, whether knowingly or not."

"And you have no idea where he is right now?"

"No."

The finality in Korvain's tone made it clear to Mason that this conversation was over. Hauling himself out of his chair, he stood to leave, but as soon as he reached the door, Bryn spoke.

"Thank you, Mason. I'm glad you've had my back. Loki would have eventually discovered a way to kill me if Korvain hadn't found me when he had."

Mason turned to her. "I've still got your back. And you should know I would never betray you, or the others. You mean too much to me." He hesitated, unsure how his next words would be received. "I want … I want to tell Eir about what I know."

Bryn shot Korvain a concerned look. "Why would you want Eir to know about this?"

Oh, fuck. How was he supposed to explain his way out of this one?

"Ah, when I saw her before, I kind of let the word Valkyrie slip in front of her. I was just so surprised to see her and it just kind of popped out."

"How do you even know her?" Korvain asked, his dark voice like the tip of a blade being run down Mason's spine.

"I met her in the park the other day." When Korvain glared at him, he felt compelled to add, "We had breakfast."

After a long beat, Bryn replied, "I don't see why you can't tell her. Eir can keep the secret, since it's mutually beneficial."

Mason let out the breath he'd been holding. "Thank you." As he made his way down the hallway, Mason knew Eir would have a whole load of questions for him, and he'd better be damned ready to answer them for her. He wanted to be honest with her. He wanted her to know about him—for the first time he wanted a woman to know about him and his past.

And that fucking terrified him.

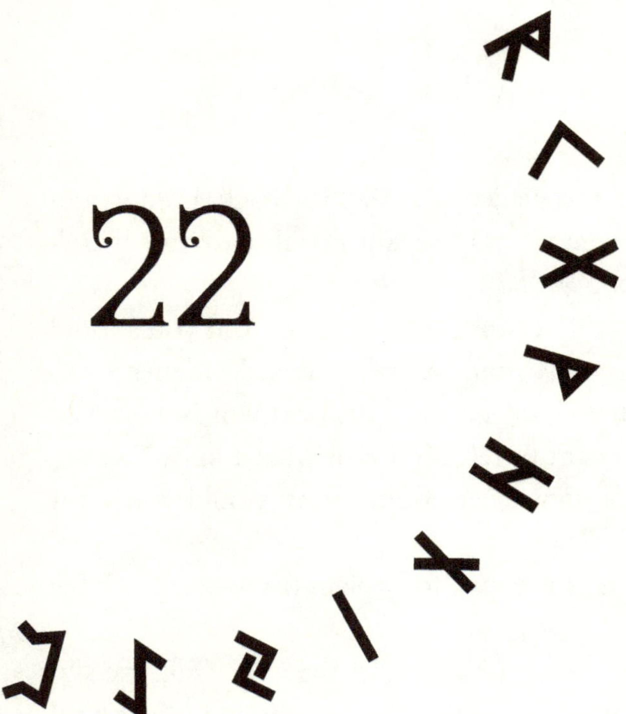

22

It was three am, and Eir was the most nervous she had ever been. Not even the excitement she had felt at meeting Odin could top the butterflies currently battering the inside of her stomach. But that was Odin. And this was Mason.

A *human*.

A man she wanted to get to know better—and that was something she had never thought would happen to her. Mason somehow knew about her, and even though she hadn't confirmed his suspicions, it didn't take away the fact that he knew *something* about the Valkyries.

Maybe he was just guessing—taking stabs in the dark. He was pretty damn close to the target for stabbing in the dark, though.

In her palm, she crushed the three gauze bandages she'd promised him, wishing she already knew what he was going to tell her. The gentle *ding* of the elevator bell brought her attention back to the present. She stared at the closed doors, willing them to open a little faster.

A few excruciating seconds later, they parted and the empty expanse of hallway opened up before her. Steadying herself with a few deep breaths, Eir forced her feet into action, her brain already running through the different scenarios. She had to admit she was surprised not to see Mason there waiting for her but also relieved at the same time. Despite being ready for him, she also felt completely unprepared.

Her sensible shoes hushed gently against the polished concrete floors, carrying her past Bryn's office, where low voices could be heard through the wooden door. Stopping at the staff room, she pushed open the door and took a peek inside.

Empty.

Mason still had to be in the main bar.

"It's closing time." Mason's disembodied voice floated through the brilliantly lit bar as Eir went through the door. On the opposite side of the room, Mason was gently ushering a young woman out into the now freezing Boston night.

The door squeaked closed behind Eir then, ruining her chances of slipping inside unnoticed. Mason whirled around, his mouth open as if he was about to say something, but he closed it when he saw it was Eir. With his lips curling up into a shy smile, she felt the flicker of heat beginning to burn in her chest.

"I thought you weren't going to show up," he said, taking a step closer. With his approach, Eir was keenly aware that she could smell the hypnotic scent of his aftershave and the fresh, clean spice of his skin. Oh, what was she doing? Her hands clenched tight around the gauze, reminding her that she had another excuse to see him.

"I had to give you these." Her voice sounded so small. Holding the bandages out, she deposited them into his open hand.

"Thanks." He shoved the gauze into his pocket, his eyes never leaving hers. "We need to talk, but I have to get home to Sophie, and I have a feeling you're going to have a lot more questions than I can answer."

What was he asking her to do?

He cleared his throat nervously. "I'm saying I want you to come back to my place so I can feed Sophie and take her out for a walk. We can chat there, and I'll be able to answer all your questions."

Eir bit her lip, her teeth digging into the sensitive flesh of her lower lip. "Please, Eir," he pleaded. "I promise to bring you back here after we're done, no matter the time."

Her head was screaming at her to reject his proposition, but her traitorous body was all for it. In the end, all she could do was nod.

"Great. Let me get some things out of my locker and we can go."

"I'll get my coat and let Bryn know where I'm going."

She soon found herself sitting in the front seat of Mason's car as he drove, her hands nervously clenched together. Bryn hadn't even blinked at her request to leave with Mason. In fact, she had smiled knowingly at Eir, telling her, 'It will be good for you.' What that meant she had no idea.

Mason drew her from her thoughts. "Are you warm enough?" he asked, adjusting the dials on the center console.

"I'm fine." She looked out the passenger window, watching the city lights flash by. It was quiet at this time of night—almost as if Boston was abandoned, and only the ghosts haunted its streets.

"I love this time of night. I love how quiet it is." Mason's voice was a gravelly drawl. Eir looked over at him, taking the opportunity to study him as he concentrated on the road. The passing street lights alternately cast his face in shadows and light.

A fine stubble was just starting to grow on his jaw, and Eir found herself wanting to reach out and run her fingers along his cheek. He turned his head slightly to look her way, and Eir averted her gaze, embarrassed.

Ten minutes later, they pulled up in front of an unassuming apartment building in downtown Boston. Maybe five or six stories high, it looked like all the other brownstones around it, but when she stepped into the lobby, Eir was surprised to see how modern the interior was.

"This is nice," she said absently, taking it all in.

He laughed gently. "Sophie and I like it just fine."

The mention of his dog brought a smile to Eir's face. She was looking forward to seeing her again.

"She likes you, too, you know," Mason told her.

Eir started. Her lips parted to ask him how he'd known what she was thinking, but she thought better of it. She was sure he would answer all her questions in due time.

They rode the elevator together in silence, Eir flushing at how close they were standing, of how his breathing had accelerated ever so slightly, just like her own.

When the doors opened, Mason allowed Eir to exit first, sweeping his arm out in front of his body. Stepping out, Eir could see that there were only two doors to choose from on this floor.

"It's this one," Mason murmured, placing a gentle hand on the small of her back, and a jolt of desire shot through her. Not for the first time, she wondered who this man was and why he made her feel the way she did when he was around. He opened the door to his apartment, and Eir stepped inside, greeted by a blast of warm air and the wet licks of an excited dog.

———————

Mason moved forward and grabbed Sophie by the collar, pulling her away from the goddess.

"Sorry. She gets really excited when I get home. She'll calm down in a minute." After getting Sophie to sit down, Mason was surprised when Eir crouched down in front of her, scratching her behind her ears and talking to her.

Mason laughed. "You definitely have a friend for life now."

Eir peeked up at him, golden highlights in her hair shining. "She really is lovely." He held her gaze a second too long, till they both felt uncomfortable, but then Sophie rolled over onto her back to get her belly scratched.

Mason was normally pretty wired after a shift at the club, and tonight was no different. He moved towards the kitchen, setting the coffee maker to start and pulling two mugs from his cupboard.

"Coffee?" he called, busying himself with getting out the cream and sugar.

"That would be great," she replied. He looked up, surprised, to find her standing on the other side of the kitchen bench. She had shucked her coat, revealing the purple sword tattooed on her neck, and her eyes were bright and curious. The doubt and unease he'd seen when he'd first asked her to come to his apartment were now gone.

"How do you take it?"

"Black."

He grunted, putting the cream and sugar away. "Me too."

The Valkyrie said nothing more while Mason waited for the coffee maker to finish. When he set the mug in front of her, Eir had perched herself on one of the stools that were stowed under the bench. He settled in against the side of the counter, staring at Eir over the lip of his mug as he took a sip.

He could tell by her face she had questions, but he didn't dip into her thoughts to confirm it. He never liked doing that in any case, but with Eir it felt like a real invasion.

The Valkyrie blew on her coffee to cool it, then took a sip. "You said we needed to talk?" she asked.

"Yeah. We need to talk. I feel I need to explain some things to you."

Eir never broke eye contact. Christ, Mason could feel the heat in those eyes, could feel the questions burning there.

"I ... umm ... I ..." Mason paused. How in the hell was he supposed to broach this subject? It had almost been easy with Bryn. With Eir, he just had no idea how to start, but he did want her to know about him.

"Look, let's just address the elephant in the room. You know I'm a Valkyrie." She waited for him to confirm her statement before continuing. "The reason I was so surprised by you knowing is that no humans know this. They don't believe anymore."

"I know a lot about your world, Eir—Odin, the Valkyries, the Aesirean gods—all of it."

"How?" she asked, her voice the barest whisper. Sophie padded over to her, sensing her distress, and placed her head in Eir's lap.

Mason looked down at the counter, the tip of his index finger running over a dried coffee ring. He'd kept his secret for nearly ten years, not telling anyone what he knew, but somehow—within the space of a month—he had not only spilled it to one of the most dangerous and feared beings in the Nine Worlds, but to his boss too, and now he wanted to tell the woman he could seriously fall in love with.

Eir reached for his hand. Her small fingers were dwarfed by

his, but the warmth he felt at her touch gave him the courage to go on.

He took a deep breath to calm his nerves, but couldn't shake the feeling that his throat was closing up, being choked by dust and debris long since settled in his memories. "Thirteen years ago, I joined the marines, and almost ten years ago I was injured while on tour in Iraq."

"Injured, how?" she asked, her tiny fingers cinching tighter around his hand. That same warmth he'd felt before in the park was back, and a moment later he could have sworn he felt more relaxed than a few seconds ago.

"My unit was in the town of An Nasiriyah. I was with three others, making our way up to the top floor of what we thought was an abandoned building. I was third in line and I think that may have saved my life."

Mason fell silent. Every time he thought about that attack, he was right back there, reliving it.

The screams of agony.

The pleas for help.

The smell of blood soaking into the dust and sand.

He was suddenly yanked back into the present when Sophie stuck her wet nose into the palm of his free hand. Pulling his other hand from Eir's grasp, Mason crouched down beside Sophie and wrapped his arms around her neck. A wet swipe of her tongue brought a measure of peace, and for a brief moment he wished he was alone.

"I'm sorry," Eir said. "This is obviously difficult for you to talk about. I'll just go."

She stood up and made her way to the door, but Mason was faster. Gently, he took her by the elbow, stopping her.

"Please, don't go." Mason's voice sounded rough even to his

ears. "I just need a few minutes."

Eir touched his hand, but instead of returning to the kitchen, she headed for his dark leather sofa. Mason followed with Sophie shadowing him. Perching on the other end of the sofa, he waited until his heart stopped pounding. When Sophie placed her head in his lap, Mason's fingers sank into the dense fur between her shoulderblades.

"There was a bomb on the rooftop. It was detonated remotely. The first two guys were killed ..." Mason closed his eyes, trying to fight off the vision of the life bleeding from his brother's eyes. "I was thrown back by the blast. I hit my head pretty hard and the same with the other guy. I was knocked out cold. It was only when I was patched up and sent home to the States that I realized something wasn't quite right."

"What do you mean?"

"I ... I could hear what people were thinking."

Eir sat back in her seat. "You can hear their thoughts?"

Mason kept his eyes fixed on his fingers in Sophie's fur. "But it's not everybody's thoughts ..." he sighed. "I didn't know what it meant at the time. It was only after a while, listening and learning, that I realized I was hearing the thoughts of the gods and goddesses of the Nine Worlds."

There. He had said it.

Now, to wait for the fallout.

Eir frowned deeply. "You can hear our thoughts?" she asked almost inaudibly.

"Yes, but it's not like I enjoy eavesdropping. It's just the side effect from the knock on my head."

"Have you ever read my thoughts?" she asked sharply.

Oh, fuck. "Like I said, I don't do it intentionally. I have to concentrate quite hard to block the voices out, and sometimes if

I don't have the energy, I just hear them."

The Valkyrie's lips pressed together. "How often do you listen in to my thoughts?"

"Never," he answered honestly. "I don't enjoy prying."

"Does Bryn know about your ability?"

"Yes. So does Korvain. In fact, I've made a blood oath with him, so that I can't discuss what I know with anyone else."

"So you've just broken your oath to tell me?"

"No. I've already spoken to both of them about telling you." He gave her a small smile that she did not return.

"Are you angry with me?" he asked after a few beats of heavy silence.

"I'm not sure," she replied. "I'm not sure how I feel about this information."

"I won't be telling anyone else about what I know. Why would I? I would have to tell them *how* I know. It's been a long time, and I've only recently told two people about it ... well, three now."

She looked up at him, her eyes searching his face. "So only Bryn, Korvain and I know about this?"

"Yes."

The goddess bit her lip, her eyes searching his face. "Why me? You didn't have to."

Mason inched a little closer to Eir. He wanted to touch her hand, her hair, her face. "Korvain found out about me when Bryn was missing last month. I didn't want to tell him, but Bryn was in trouble and I would rather die than see her hurt. I told Bryn today because I *wanted* to tell you." Reaching out, Mason took her hand in his, grateful she didn't pull away. "I want you to know about me because I think there's something here between us, Eir." She looked away, but he pressed on. "Please tell me you feel it too."

The back of her hand felt warm against his, but it wasn't that same warmth as before. He hoped he hadn't just fucked things up with her.

"I … I feel it, too, Mason," she whispered. "But nothing could ever happen between us."

"Why not?" he asked gently, stroking her silky skin with his thumb, rubbing slow, rhythmic circles over her knuckles.

"Because you're a human and I'm a goddess."

"I can't see your point," he said. "Eir, I haven't felt this spark with anyone before. Never in my life have I wanted to share things with someone like I do with you."

"I'm immortal," she muttered, looking at him. "And you're not."

"If I get to spend a sliver of your immortality with you, I'll be a happy man. Maybe we're not meant to be together forever, maybe we are, but you can't deny the electricity between us."

Eir shook her head, and Mason's heart sank into the pit of his stomach. "Why are you doing this?" she asked.

"Because I think you're worth it. You know everything about me now." *Well, almost everything,* he thought bitterly. "All I'm asking is for you to get to know me a little better. And I want to know more about you."

She seemed to withdraw into herself then. "What do you want to know?"

Mason was triumphant. She was listening to him. He had a chance here. "Every damn thing," he replied honestly.

At last, Eir seemed to relax, turning her body towards him. "You already know a lot about me. I'm a nurse, and I told you before that nursing was in my blood, but there's more to it than that. You see, I'm not like Bryn and the other Valkyries. Odin made them immortal, but I already was."

He frowned. "I'm not following."

She gazed up at him. "I'm Eir, the goddess of healing. Odin brought me into the fold for my healing abilities a thousand years ago, and instead of staying with him when Bryn left, I chose to leave too. I just couldn't see the point of serving the All-Father when the humans had forgotten about us."

"So you really are a goddess?" he asked, completely dumbstruck. "And your palms?"

The goddess looked down at her hands and shrugged. "I heal through my palms."

Mason's lip tilted up slightly. "That's the warmth I felt in the park and just now?"

"Yes. I can heal someone, or take away their pain, but I can also regulate their breathing, or help their heart to pump blood more efficiently. The only thing I can't do is cure a fatal injury or disease. That is beyond my powers."

He touched the cut above his eye. "And this?"

She sighed. "I could have healed that for you earlier, but I couldn't risk you finding out about me … but if you wanted me to, I could still heal you now?"

Mason thought about that for a minute. He'd felt just a small part of what Eir could do. He shook his head. "Nah, I'd like to keep the scar."

"Really?"

He gave her a cocky grin. "It'll remind me of you."

Suddenly bashful, the Valkyrie looked down at her hands again. "Is there anything else you'd like to know about me?"

"If you'd like to talk about it, I'd like to know about what happened to you last month."

Her whole body stiffened, and she wrapped her arms around herself, as if she were trying to hold herself together. Wrapping his arm around her slender shoulders, he pulled her warm body into the side of his, feeling her melt against him. She sobbed, her slight frame shaking, a tremor passing through her and into him. Mason willingly absorbed it, willing her to take some of his strength.

"Eir, we don't have to discuss this if you don't want to. I'm sorry I brought it up, really."

He cursed himself for upsetting her. He didn't need to know that badly, not now. If he had it his way—and he was going to make damn sure he did—he would find out soon enough. She had obviously been hurt during that time, and that thought alone had his blood boiling.

Eir's sobbing didn't let up, and her body was still shaking, but gradually she grew calmer. When he felt she could talk again, he hooked his finger under her chin and tilted her face towards his.

Her eyes were red-rimmed, her nose pink from sniffling. She tipped her head down, a curtain of her hair shielding her face from him. Damn, he had to admit that she looked pretty damn cute when she was being shy about being upset.

Pushing her hair behind her ear, he said, "Eir, please don't hide your beautiful face from me."

She bit her full bottom lip and all the blood in Mason's body traveled south. Fuck, he was a bastard for even thinking about sex while this goddess was so upset. He placed his thumb on her lip and tugged the flesh free from her teeth. He could smell fresh spearmint, feel the warmth of her each and every breath.

He leaned forward another fraction of an inch, waiting, watching to see whether she would stay or whether she would bolt. When he could see she wasn't going anywhere, he inched a little closer again.

Mason heard the hitch in her breath as he closed the minuscule gap between them, a hair's breadth away from pressing his lips against the sweetness of hers.

The sound of a phone ringing shattered the silence, shattered the promise of his lips touching hers for the first time. He cursed as she pulled away, flustered, and searched through her cardigan pocket. She glanced down at the screen for a moment, then looked up at him nervously.

"It's Korvain. He must be waiting to take me to work."

Mason looked over at the digital clock on his microwave; it was nearly five in the morning. While Eir spoke to Korvain, he listened to the velvety cadence of her voice. He let it wash over him, his eyes getting heavier and heavier.

"No, it's fine. I'm with Mason. I'm sure he can take me to the hospital."

At the sound of his name, Mason's eyes flipped open, staring at the Valkyrie, who was now looking at him questioningly. He mouthed the word "okay" to her. Her lips flexed into a shy smile.

"Ah, sure, I'll put him on. Hang on." Eir handed the phone to Mason. "He wants to speak to you for a second."

He reached for the phone, his hand steady, although his heart was jackhammering against his rib cage. "Yeah?"

"Guard her with your life," Korvain said quietly. "You hear me? If she comes to harm, you come to harm."

Mason remained mute.

"I'll take your silence as an affirmative. Take your weapon with you. If you come across anyone even thinking about trying to harm her, shoot them between the eyes." The softness of Korvain's tone was at complete odds with the ferocity of his words.

"Is that a possibility?" Mason croaked out.

"I don't think so. It's just a precaution. Put Eir back on the phone."

Mechanically, Mason handed the phone back to the goddess. She frowned slightly at the expression on his face.

After listening for a moment, she told Korvain, "I'll see you this evening when you pick me up. Okay. Thank you. Goodbye." She ended the call, and turned to Mason, clutching the phone in her lap. "I'm sorry. I shouldn't have sprung that on you. If you can't take me, I'll get myself there."

"It's no problem." Sophie lifted her head from his feet, looking at him with her big brown begging eyes. "We're not too far away from the hospital. Let me grab a jacket, and we can walk there if you're ready now. That way I can give Sophie a bit of exercise too."

23

Boston—1943

Darrion's eyes passed over the newspaper, reading and re-reading the front page article about the Allies' advances in Europe. America had been involved in the Second World War for a little over two years, and there was no real end in sight.

Not that he cared about the plight of humans.

This war of men didn't stop his line of business.

He watched as one of his concubines entered the room. Dressed in the old style, she sat at his feet, looking up at him from under her blonde lashes. Darrion only kept female Mares to satisfy his more carnal needs and the needs of his men.

Reaching out, he gently touched the cheek of the female. He thought her name was Allynna. She smiled gently at him, although there was a hint of fear in her eyes. She was right to fear him. Without warning, he grasped her chin in his hand, forcefully digging his fingers into her tender flesh.

Allynna gasped in shock, tears coming to her eyes. She whimpered when he brought his face closer to hers, putting them nose to nose, breathing in the same air. "You know what I want," he whispered harshly.

With tears silently running down her cheeks, her fingers clumsily fumbled with the buttons on his pants. He grasped a large handful of hair and held her to him as she brought him to orgasm. Satisfied for now, Darrion released her and pushed her away, staring at her swollen, gasping mouth in a detached way. Allynna scurried away from him on her hands and knees, backing up until she was pressed against the wall opposite him. Her wide, fearful eyes had yet to leave his face.

Methodically and deliberately, he redid the buttons on his pants. "Go and service any other males that require it," he commanded coldly, dismissing her.

The female did as she was bid, leaving him alone in the private wing of the house he shared with his Walkers. A former boarding school, the place he called home for now was large enough to house his Mares—nearly a dozen of them—in relative safety.

It had been a long time since they'd been attacked by zealous Aesirean gods looking to pass the time, but keeping hidden and safe was still his greatest concern. Darrion looked at the small brass clock perched on the mantle.

It was time.

Pushing himself from his chair, he made his way to the one and only entry and exit point of their guild and faded to the location of one of his Walkers' latest assignments.

Business had been good for him despite the war. Human men working for foreign governments paid big money for the assassination of major American players in the war, and Darrion's pockets had been well lined by their greed.

The target of this latest hit was a major backer in the arms manufacturing race, and Darrion didn't give a fuck as to whose side he was on. He'd sent Connak to finish the job, but although he should have been his best guy, Connak wasn't nearly as fucking good as he ought to have been. He had won his quinary test by fucking default, and his contract was finally up.

Thank fuck.

Darrion faded to the palatial house the target called home. Connak was just stepping out of the front door, wiping his hands on a rag. The Walker's preferred method of killing was with his hands. He liked to get in nice and close to his victim, to see the horror flash in their eyes, to see them silently beg for mercy and watch them feel the cold embrace of death.

Darrion stepped out from behind an automobile, asking in a bored drawl, "What did this one promise you?"

Connak's dark eyes danced with humor. "More money than I could imagine plus a free pass on the conscription."

"Humans will promise anything when their lives are threatened … but I think the same could be said for any creature of the Nine Worlds, too."

Connak's dark brows knitted together. "What do you mean?" He stowed away his rag and pulled out a thin cigarette from a gold-plated case.

Darrion began to pace around the Walker, watching him. Waiting for realization to strike. "How long have you been in my service, Connak?"

"This is my hundredth year …" He laughed. "Almost to the day."

"So it is," Darrion replied darkly. "And what will you do with your freedom, Connak … when you have it, that is."

Connak lit his cigarette with a practiced hand and shook out the match, dropping it to the ground. The end of the cigarette flared in the darkness before a billow of pungent gray smoke erupted into the air.

"I have no idea really. Maybe see what the west coast is like. Hey, I might even start my own guild."

Darrion wanted to smack the ridiculous grin off his face. Nobody completed their contract with him and walked away. After spending time training them, he wasn't about to let them go and do whatever they wanted. They belonged to him.

They would always belong to him.

Darrion casually pulled out one of his throwing knives and pretended to dig dirt out from under his fingernails. Connak watched him warily and flexed his shoulders, no doubt feeling the burn of the tattoo he had inked into his skin.

Death before dishonor.

That tattoo was also Darrion's fail-safe. No Mare under contract to him could physically harm Darrion, which meant if he were to attack them, even self-defense was out of the question.

He calmly took a step towards Connak, staring into his eyes for a drawn-out minute before viciously driving the length of his dagger into the Mare's throat. A look of shock registered on the Connak's face as Darrion withdrew the blade and plunged it in again and again and again.

When the life had left Connak's pale blue eyes, Darrion stood over his body and wiped the spatters of blood off his cheek with the back of his hand.

Korvain stood in the shadows of the large house, observing the Mare Adrian wanted to swear fealty to. The sharp tang of blood hit his nostrils as the one called Connak fell, gasping, blood foaming from his lips. Korvain could see Darrion's cold, dead eyes, watching the life drain from the Walker like it was nothing at all.

Korvain had seen his fair share of death—had even dealt out his fair share—but he had never wanted to join a guild. Once upon a time, when his kind was being hunted to the brink of extinction on the whim of a god, being a member of a guild had had its place. But now? Since the Fall?

He just couldn't see the point. He could disappear any time he liked as long as there was the whisper of a shadow he could wrap around his body. For Adrian, though, it wasn't just about protection in numbers. Rather it was about being able to protect his sister, Taer, from the predators of both their old and new worlds.

Darrion faded from the scene, leaving the body of his former Shadow Walker behind for the human police to find. Korvain returned to the small apartment he, Taer and Adrian shared.

"Where've you been?" Adrian asked, looking up from the vegetables he'd been chopping for dinner.

"I went to check out that Mare you wanted to swear to."

Adrian leaned against the counter, one eyebrow hitched. "And?"

"Have you really thought about this? I mean, *really* thought about it?"

His best friend's face darkened. "If it means I can protect Taer better, then I'll do anything it takes."

"He's a monster," Korvain muttered under his breath. "I just think there's a better way."

"There's not. He's the most feared guild master in the whole

Nine Worlds. That's why I want his protection. No one would dare take Taer if she was safe-guarded by Darrion's reputation."

Korvain cursed. "What makes you think he wouldn't take Taer and make her a concubine anyway?"

Adrian shook his head, but Korvain saw the flash of fear in his eyes. "I'll negotiate with him," Adrian said.

"You? You'll negotiate with him?" Korvain shot back in disbelief.

"I'll tell him if he touches one hair on Taer's head, I'll walk."

"What if—by some miracle—you make it through the quinary on top and you get inked? You won't be able to walk then."

Adrian looked down at the knife in his hand, his blond hair shining dully in the kitchen lights. "I don't know, but it's a risk I'll have to take."

Korvain cursed under his breath. "You haven't thought this through, Ad. We're good as we are. We've survived."

"Yeah?" Adrian asked venomously. "For how much longer? You know there are gods out there still hunting us. You're okay. You can just disappear into the shadows. Taer and I? We have to rely on our wits and fading away ... well, I'm sick of running and hiding from those bastards! I want the protection Darrion can give us."

Korvain snapped his teeth together in agitation. He had to make Adrian see that Darrion wasn't all that he seemed.

"Do you know what I saw tonight? I saw Darrion kill his best Walker because his contract was up. It was his *best* Walker and he just rammed a knife through his throat, killing him in cold blood. Tell me what kind of master that is. Tell me if that sounds like he protects what's his."

Adrian's already pale skin blanched. "Maybe there was some other reason he killed him. Maybe he'd disobeyed an order."

Korvain shook his head angrily, his hands curling into tight fists. "No. I heard their conversation. It was casual and relaxed. The fucker had no idea it was coming."

"It doesn't change anything," Adrian said. "I've already spoken to Taer. We're doing this and there's nothing you can do or say to stop me."

Korvain's black mood caused the shadows in the room to darken the walls, thickening with his growing rage. "He'll kill you, Ad. He'll kill you and he'll kill Taer and everything you fought to protect will be lost." Frustrated, Korvain left the room. If Adrian wouldn't listen to reason, there really was nothing more he could say to change his mind. He would just have to take matters into his own hands.

———————

Darrion sat in the booth of a small diner in downtown Boston, his knuckles drumming against the pale blue Formica top. He'd received a message that an untrained Mare wanted to join his guild, wanted to train as a Walker. Darrion's ranks were already full, but if the dark elf had potential, he supposed he could make an exception.

The human female working the diner by herself came over to refill his coffee cup, spilling a little over the side when she realized he was staring at her. He'd always despised humans because of Odin's fondness for them. They were nothing but bags of flesh and blood. They were weak. They were fragile. And they would all fall beneath his hand.

Just as the woman walked away, a blond male approached his table, looking nervous. "Darrion?" he asked.

Darrion looked over his shoulder, checking to see that one of his Walkers was watching the proceedings like he was supposed to. He turned his attention back to the blond male. "Sit down."

He did, and Darrion liked his ability to follow orders. The male looked uneasy, uncomfortable with the situation.

Advantage, Darrion.

He studied the Mare's features, took in his musculature, calculating whether he could be trained to become a Shadow Walker.

"Why did you seek me out?" he asked. The Mare had the height of a dark elf, but his hair and eyes were pale. If Darrion didn't know any better, he could have sworn he was a light elf, but he'd seen a flash of fang when he'd spoken, and that was an entirely dark elf trait.

"I want to join your guild."

"I already know this. What I want to know is why. Why now?"

He looked Darrion in the eye. "I need protection for me and my sister."

Sister? "I'm listening."

The male's eyes hardened, glinting dangerously. "Here's the thing: Taer is all I have left. Nobody is to touch a hair on her head." He leaned across the table slightly. "Including you."

Darrion laughed, startling him. "Who's going to stop me?"

"I will," the Mare swore. "If you say anything to her, if you look at her the wrong way, I'll just walk away. I'll tell your rivals everything I learn about you during my time training with you. Is that something you want to risk?"

Darrion leaned back into the booth, the vinyl squealing in protest with his movement. He had to give it to the bastard. He talked tough, but he wondered how he would hold up against the strenuous training. If he happened to get killed during the Final Test, his sister would be vulnerable, and Darrion could do whatever he wanted with her.

The advantages far outweighed the risks. "What's your name, Mare?"

"Adrian."

He took a sip of his coffee. "My standard contract is one hundred years."

Adrian's shoulders rolled forward with relief. "How long is training?"

"Twelve months. Maybe six if you excel. If you survive the Final Test, you will become *agarwaen*—bloodstained. The tattoo you receive when you join my guild will contain my blood. This will be our contract. Do you understand the risks? Do you know what you're asking for?"

Adrian opened his mouth to reply, but his head whirled around when someone called his name. Darrion looked up, his eyes settling on a nearly seven foot Mare with shadow-filled eyes and a snarl on his lips. His frame was stacked with muscle, his arms and legs nearly triple the size of most other Mares Darrion had seen. Darrion sensed the power within him, and that made him pay real attention.

"Korvain, I told you that you couldn't stop me doing this," Adrian said hotly.

"I know," the Mare replied, turning his dark eyes to Darrion. They stared blankly at each other for a good long while. "That's why I'm here. I'm joining the guild, too."

Darrion smirked at Adrian's outraged cry. "Why would you do that?"

"Because we stick together, my brother," Korvain replied, dragging a nearby seat close to the table and lowering himself into it. "Always."

Darrion couldn't believe his luck. Three Mares for the price of one? Hell, even if Adrian did get killed, it was worth the deal if this one, this Korvain, was part of the package.

"So what do you say?" Korvain asked.

Darrion stared back at this new male, this monstrosity of a dark elf. The power in his blood seemed to flood the air, saturating it. Darrion breathed him in, wondering how he could seal the deal.

"You ever had any training before?" he asked Korvain, leveling him with a hard stare.

The Mare's chin tilted up in defiance. "I've defended myself when I've had to."

"So you have had some training before," Darrion surmised. "Who trained you?"

Korvain's lips tightened. He wasn't going to say any more, but Darrion didn't care. He wanted this one. He could see the potential.

"My standard contract is a century."

Korvain's lip pulled up, revealing his impressive fangs, confirming Darrion's suspicions that the bastard came from nearly pure blood. "No contracts. I'll be there as long as Adrian and his sister are."

"I won't have an uncontracted Mare in my guild. You agree to my contract or no deal."

Korvain looked at Adrian. "You don't need to do this," Adrian implored. "This is my decision. It's what's best for Taer and me."

"And this is what's best for me." Turning his attention back to Darrion, Korvain leaned his huge forearms on the table, making the furniture creak beneath his weight. "Fifty."

Darrion bared his teeth. "Ninety."

Korvain's eyes narrowed dangerously and Darrion could feel the cold hatred boiling off him. "Sixty."

"Eighty and nothing less."

The Mare's hands clenched into tight fists. The leather of his jacket crackled with the flexing of his muscles. "Seventy. Final offer."

That was more than enough time for Darrion to take advantage of him. "Deal," he agreed, getting up and moving away from the table. As he passed, Korvain's fist shot out, his strong fingers wrapping around Darrion's wrist, bringing him to an abrupt stop. Darrion glared down at him.

"Taer stays under our protection," Korvain said. "You don't lay a hand on her … ever. And I do the Final Test with the current quinary."

Darrion hated being told what to do, but he wasn't stupid enough to pass up this deal. "Fine," he replied through gritted teeth. "Anything else?"

The bastard had the nerve to smile. "Yeah. To make sure you keep your hands off Taer, she, Adrian and I will live away from the guild." He arched one eyebrow in challenge, and Darrion had to bite his tongue. This sonofabitch was going to be the fucking death of him.

"I agree, but on one more condition."

"I'm listening."

"I'll be training you personally, and that's non-negotiable."

Korvain barked a throaty, mocking laugh. "You couldn't teach me anything new," he sneered.

"I bet I could," he replied coolly. Wrenching his wrist out of Korvain's grip, he stalked towards the door. "Training starts tomorrow morning," he threw over his shoulder, not waiting for the response.

He faded from the diner, completely and utterly pleased with himself. He had just secured perhaps one of the last pure-blooded Mares in the whole of the Nine Worlds—hell, maybe even the last one—and he would make the bastard pay for every single bad decision he had ever made.

24

Eir couldn't help glancing up at Mason every few seconds. She still couldn't believe how their relationship had blossomed. He knew everything about her, about her world, and she was … relieved. She didn't have to worry about trying to explain things to him.

She smiled as she looked down at Sophie. She could have sworn the dog had a huge grin on her face.

"She looks like she loves this," Eir said, breaking the silence. Mason's thoughts were obviously elsewhere. He had been distant ever since Korvain had barked something to him on the phone.

His eyes darted around them before settling on her face. The sun had just begun to rise, the first rays hitting Mason's face, highlighting the flecks of green in his eyes. "She certainly loves being taken out," he replied absently, his eyes still troubled.

"Did Korvain say something to you?" she asked when his eyes made another sweep of the immediate area.

That got his attention. "When?"

"Just before, on the phone."

There was a beat of silence. Mason pressed his lips together, his jaw tightening up too. "What can you ..." he started, looking away a moment later. "Forget it," he said dismissively.

She placed her hand on his forearm, slowing his steps. His concern for her bombarded Eir's senses. "Finish what you were going to say," she encouraged.

He met her eyes briefly then said, "What can you tell me about Darrion?"

Eir's heart stopped for a moment before resuming its usual rhythm, although it was pounding a little more quickly than normal. She honestly didn't know very much about the Mare Korvain had called master, but she feared him because Korvain feared him.

"I honestly don't know anything about him. Why do you ask?"

"No reason," he muttered in reply, still looking around, his eyes never settling on one spot for more than a few seconds.

"Is that what Korvain spoke to you about? Is that why you're being so vigilant?"

He grunted, and Eir thought it was in agreement. She smiled at his protective streak, amused by the idea that he would be able to protect her should Darrion come looking for her. She was a Valkyrie. She could summon a blade that could kill with a single stroke, yet the idea of Mason going into battle for her made those butterflies flutter in her stomach once more.

They were only a block away from the hospital now, the sun touching Eir's face, warming her skin. She sighed deeply.

"A penny for your thoughts?" Mason said.

She saw that he was staring down at her. "For the first time, I don't wish to go to work," she admitted.

"And why is that?"

She reached up and hooked a tentative hand into his elbow. "I don't want this day to end."

They arrived at the hospital entrance, where Sophie sat patiently at Mason's feet while they said their goodbyes. Boldly, he took Eir's hand in his, bringing it to his mouth and brushing his lips against her knuckles. "I don't want this day to end either."

His words were a steady rumble that sent a shiver of pleasure down her spine. Eir looked into his eyes, a blush creeping up her cheeks.

"I should get inside," she replied softly. "Will I see you later on, at the club?"

A slight smile hitched up one side of his mouth. Eir felt as if there were a million other things that needed to be said, but she found that all the air had left her lungs. Bobbing her head one final time, she turned towards the double glass doors.

"Eir?" Mason called.

She turned back.

"Thank you for being so understanding about … what I told you earlier."

She could see it pained him to say the words, but she also knew there was much more buried within him. She had felt his pain when he'd comforted her only an hour earlier.

"We all have secrets," she said. Mason's eyes shot to her face.

"That we do," he agreed. Once again he brushed her knuckles with his mouth. "I'll see you later."

Eir entered the hospital in a kind of daze. Never before had a man captivated her in this way, and she hadn't the slightest idea why.

"Damn, girl, where do you find these men?" Stacy called out as Eir approached reception. "Please tell me that kiss was more than just a friendly goodbye."

Eir couldn't ignore the flutter of excitement in her chest. She shrugged. "I'm just lucky, I guess." She moved past the reception desk and into the staff room before Stacy could launch into another one of her interrogations.

No sooner had she stepped into her scrubs and put her clothes into her locker than Mark tapped on her opened locker door. "Hey."

"Hey, Mark. How's it going?"

He looked down at his feet—a sure sign he wasn't just there for a friendly chat. "I saw you talking to a guy out the front."

"Yes?"

There was a long, drawn-out pause. Eir could practically see him trying to find the words to say to her. "Are you seeing him?" he blurted out clumsily.

Eir gazed up at him, unsurprised to see a flame of color bruising his cheeks. "I'm not sure what you mean."

The muscle in Mark's jaw bounced. "Is he your boyfriend? Are you seeing him?"

Eir couldn't tell if he was embarrassed or angry.

She laid a hand on his shoulder, clearly startling him. "Mark, he's not my boyfriend," she said. "He's just a friend who walked me to work."

The light elf looked truly relieved at the news and visibly relaxed. "Right, well, the reason I came in here was to ask you for another favor."

"Oh?"

"Yes. I want to know if you'd come and see Mr. Adamsen again. His treatment starts today, and he's nervous. I was wondering whether you could ..." He wiggled his fingers.

She smiled easily at him. "Of course I can."

Eir followed the light elf out of the staff room and to the elevators that would take them up to the oncology ward.

"So, how have you been?" Mark asked when the doors slid closed.

"I've been busy. You?"

He shrugged. "Same old, same old, I guess."

"What time do you finish?"

Mark looked down, staring at his shoes. "I finished an hour ago. I was waiting for you to come in so you could see Mr. Adamsen."

His answer shouldn't have surprised her, but it did. She really had to nip this infatuation in the bud.

"Mark, you know that—"

He waved her words away. "I know, Eir. I just wanted Mr. Adamsen to have the best around him before he went through with this treatment." He looked away. "I'm really worried about him. I don't think he'll be able to pull through this."

Eir placed her hand on his forearm, instantly feeling the fear and concern he had for his patient. This was what made him a great nurse. "I'll see what I can do for him," she said.

She knew from the last time she'd seen Mr. Adamsen that Mark was right—he probably wouldn't survive this treatment. The elevator doors slid open, and Mark placed his hand on the small of Eir's back to lead her out and towards the private room where she'd first seen Mr. Adamsen.

The frail old man lying on the bed hardly moved when she and Mark entered the room. The muted whir and subtle beep of machines filled the space.

Eir approached the bed her eyes focused on the shallow rise and fall of Mr. Adamsen's fragile chest. She looked over her shoulder at Mark, who was standing at the door to the room. He gave her a small, encouraging smile, and she turned back around.

Carefully, she drew the blanket down Mr. Adamsen's chest, exposing the thin gown all patients wore. Placing both hands on his chest, she closed her eyes and let the power that had always flowed through her veins surge into the human's cancer-riddled body. The man gasped almost inaudibly, his paper-thin eyelids fluttering, but not opening.

Eir let out a steady breath and let her power work the way it needed to. With each inhalation, she could feel the cancer in her body like it was in his, spreading through her blood, infiltrating her organs. She pressed her lips together and held on for just a little longer.

Mr. Adamsen groaned in relief, letting her know her work was done. He would sleep peacefully for a while now, but Eir would need a few hours to recover.

"Thank you," Mark whispered into her ear. She tensed at his closeness, but forced herself to relax. Casually stepping away, she turned to face him. "It was my pleasure. I'd better get to work."

She moved towards the door, letting herself out and sagging against the wall. She flexed her burning hands a few times, trying to work the tingle from her palms.

Well, one hour down. Only eleven more to go.

25

Taer felt like death. Korvain had wakened her from a brief, fitful sleep a few moments ago, but it was a mercy, really. She had been dreaming again—dreaming about blood, gasping final breaths and the undeniable stench of death. Taer would rather stay awake than suffer that dark torture.

The lack of sleep wasn't just taking a toll on her, but dragging her down into a black place where even revenge was becoming a blurry goal further and further out of her reach.

Aubrey had trained her hard into the early hours of the morning, bone-deep weariness bringing her home just before dawn. Aubrey hadn't told her whether he'd found out anything more about Darrion yet, and even though she wanted to interrogate him, she held her tongue.

Sitting up, she glanced over at the twin bed on the opposite side of the room, finding it still empty. Pushing away the sheets and dragging herself upright, Taer pulled on a pair of sweats and changed her shirt. Every muscle in her body was begging her to get some more sleep, but training was more important.

Staggering out of her room, she came face to face with a seven-foot wall of muscle and menace. Korvain regarded her, his dark eyes concerned as he studied her face. Fuck, she must have looked as bad as she felt. She looked down at her feet, hoping he would suddenly forget what he'd just seen.

But that was wishful thinking.

Korvain tilted her head up with a strong finger under her chin. "Did you get *any* sleep?"

Lie, damn it. Lie. "I got a few hours."

"You can't lie to me, Taer. I can practically smell your dishonesty."

Fuck. Taer heaved a heavy sigh. "You don't have to worry. I'm fine."

"Is it the dreams? Are they getting worse?"

Taer recoiled. How did he know? The only person who knew about them was Eir, and Taer was sure the Valkyrie could keep her mouth shut.

"They're only dreams. Just forget about them, all right?" She tried to walk away, but Korvain's vice-like grip was around her upper arm within a nanosecond.

"No, Taer, it's not all right." She stared angrily at him from under her lashes. He sighed and released his fingers. "I just want to help you, Tay, but you're making it really difficult for me."

"You want to help me?" she asked acidly. "Train me to kill Darrion and you will be helping me." This time he let her walk away from him. Entering the kitchen, she snatched a mug from the drying rack and filling it with freshly brewed coffee from the machine.

She felt the heat of Korvain's body before he spoke at her

back. "I made a promise—"

She whirled around before he could say anything further, the violent shake of her hand sloshing coffee all over the kitchen counter. "Don't say it. *Don't* say his name to me." She didn't think she could stand to hear her brother's name. The wound was still too raw, too painful to even consider speaking his name out loud.

Korvain's eyes softened as he stared down at her—almost as if he could feel her pain. Taer felt tears welling, the tears she'd never let herself shed for her brother, but she shook her head, refusing to let herself cry now. She'd made it this long. She could damn well make it a little longer.

"Tay, bottling up your feelings won't bring him back, and it certainly won't help you become a better fighter." Korvain pushed on, ignoring her protests. "You might not be ready to talk about him now, but when you are, I'll be here. Bryn will be here. Eir will be here. For you. Do you hear me?" he asked.

She wanted to slap him for being so understanding, for saying the right things to her at the right time. Logically, she knew what she was doing was counterproductive, but somehow she couldn't stop the hate burning inside of her.

"I know you don't want to talk about … him right now, but can you at least tell me about the dreams?"

Taer rubbed her temples, attempting to stave off a headache and sighed. She could give him this one concession. "Dream," she conceded. "It's just the one dream."

"Okay," he replied. "Want to tell me about it?"

Picking up her mug, Taer shuffled over to the couch and sat down, folding her legs beneath her. She couldn't believe how tired she was. Korvain didn't sit beside her. Rather he perched his muscular body on the edge of the armchair in the corner.

She could feel his steady gaze on her face as he waited patiently for her to be ready to speak.

Taer took in a deep breath and let it out, focusing her attention on her hands wrapped around the coffee mug. "I'm surrounded by blood. It's still warm. It covers my face and neck, but it's tacky like it's been there for a while." A wave of goose bumps traveled over her body at the visceral memory. She gave a small shudder.

"I can hear someone breathing ..." She frowned. "No, they're gasping, and the longer I listen, the more certain I am that I'm hearing somebody taking their last breaths. I try to move, but my limbs are heavy." Taer's throat worked over a hard lump. "I want to move, to get away, but no matter how hard I try, I just can't. I try to look around to see where the sound is coming from ... even though ... even though I know who is making those sounds."

"Adrian?" Korvain asked. Taer nodded mechanically. She was too far into her memories to care right now if he said her brother's name aloud.

"The gasping becomes a gurgle, but it starts sounding more desperate." Taer's eyes slid shut. "The sound becomes sharper and louder and there's nothing I can do to stop it. I can't even scream out to ... him. He's dying and I'm responsible."

"Tay," Korvain's dark voice cut through her. "You are not to blame. Do you hear me?"

"I hear you." And she did, but she didn't believe him.

"We're going to skip training today."

"What? No! We need to train. I *need* to train."

Korvain shook his head. "No. What you need is to sleep."

"There's no point. I can't sleep with this recurring dream."

He gently shoved her in the direction of her bedroom. "Try."

Taer was already exhausted, and she was only a few hours

into her shift down on the first level of the Eye. Solid sleep had eluded her again, but she thought she had been dreamless for at least a little while. In any case, it was enough to keep her going, to keep her functioning normally.

She looked up at the ever-growing crowd in the bar. The place was maybe two-thirds full with no sign of slowing. She kept up a steady pace serving customers, keeping in sync with Mist.

She had her head bent over a drink order when the fine hairs on the back of her neck suddenly stood on end. Scanning the crowd, she spotted the tall form of Aubrey, his height putting him head and shoulders above every other patron in the bar.

"What the fuck is he doing here?" she asked under her breath as he moved her way. And why was her heart pounding out a staccato beat in her chest at the mere sight of him?

She couldn't help but notice the appreciative looks the females in the bar—both humans and goddesses—threw in his direction, and a sharp stab of jealousy rolled through her, just as it had when she saw him pinning that other female to the side of the car with his hips.

She slid the drink she was preparing over to a human, holding her hand out to give him his change.

"Keep it," he told her with a boy-next-door wink. Taer flashed him a brief smile that didn't reach her eyes, jamming the notes into the jar beside the till before turning to serve whoever was next.

"Winter Fox," Aubrey purred, rolling his nickname for Taer around on his tongue like some illicit secret. His pale gray eyes had an almost predatory gleam. She suddenly felt out of step, like his arrival had pulled the rug out from under her feet. This building was her inner sanctum, and having him there made her uneasy.

"What are you doing here?" she asked, going on the defensive straightaway.

He cocked his head to the side like a bird, his shrewd eyes narrowing ever so slightly. His lips eventually twitched, flexing up in the corners.

"What?" she barked, irritated by the smug look on his face. "If you've just come here to stare at me, I've got better things I could be doing."

He surveyed the bar, his pale eyes taking in everything. "You know, I didn't believe you when you said I could find you here. Living among the—"

"Keep your voice down!" she hissed, cutting off his words. "This isn't the fucking War Hammer. If you need to talk, I'll take my break and we can talk out the back."

Without waiting for his reply, Taer caught Mist's attention and told her she was taking her break. Mist's eyes widened when she caught sight of the light elf standing at the bar. "Are you all right?" she asked, stepping closer to her and lowering her voice.

"I'm fine. He just wants to talk."

"How in the hell do you know him?" Mist pressed.

Taer looked over at Aubrey. He smiled innocuously at her before she turned back to the Valkyrie. "I met him a few years ago," she lied.

Mist stared at her skeptically, but said, "I'm coming to check on you in ten minutes." Her tone left no room for argument. Turning back around to face Aubrey, she waved her hand in the direction of the end of the bar.

She pushed open the "Staff Only" door, waiting for Aubrey to pass through, and noticed Mason staring at her. Mouthing the words "I'm fine" at him, she followed Aubrey into the hallway, hoping Mason didn't get suspicious and come back and check on her—or worse, send Korvain to check on her.

"Through here," she said to the light elf, leading him into the locker room. Putting her back against one of the rows of metal cabinets, she watched as Aubrey walked around the room, his eyes roving, looking at everything.

"I assume the only reason you're here is that you *finally* have information about Darrion."

"Your assumption is right." He sat down on the benches that ran down the middle of the room. "I've heard that Darrion has been seen around Boston."

Taer's heart leaped into her throat. "When?"

"As recently as two days ago."

"Do you know where he is?" She worked to keep her voice even. If he had found out where the bastard was, she was going there straight after work. "Tell me what you know."

"I have had unconfirmed reports he's been seen visiting some properties around Boston."

"His safe houses," Taer said under her breath. "Can you give me any addresses? I'd like to go and check things out," she added when he hesitated. "And don't you dare tell me to stay away."

Seconds dripped by before he slid two long fingers into his inside jacket pocket and pulled out a heavy piece of card. He stood up, and in two strides he was standing in front of her. Hesitantly, Taer reached for the card, being careful not to touch his fingers, and looked down at the embossed print. It was his name along with a phone number. Flipping the card over in her hands, she saw two addresses handwritten in the old language.

"Be careful," Aubrey murmured, his voice a lot closer than it had been before. She peered up, feeling her stomach bottom out as she stared directly into his icily pale eyes. This close she could see just how long and thick his eyelashes were. He studied her steadily, then retreated a few steps, giving Taer much needed room to breathe.

"Thanks," she said, the words barely audible over the roaring of her pulse. She didn't know whether her heart was pounding because she was one step closer to finding Darrion, or because of the light elf sharing the same air as her.

Aubrey bowed his head, one hand placed over his heart. "It was a pleasure, believe me." He looked down at his watch and frowned. "My ten minutes is up, I'm afraid," he said with a shrug. He met her eyes, a twinkle in his own. "I wouldn't want your Valkyrie to have to come in here and rescue you from me."

"Mist means well," she said absently.

Laughing, he said, "There's no doubt about that."

She frowned at him. "You're right though. You really should go now," Taer told him. "My break is over and I have to get back to work." She pushed on the door, holding it open for him.

Aubrey left the room, Taer hanging back to give him a head start. She needed the time to settle the butterflies that were going berserk in her stomach. What was it about him that made her feel this way? After a few minutes, she returned to the Eye and stepped back behind the bar. Mist raised an eyebrow at her, which she ignored. A moment later, Taer saw the crowd part for Aubrey as he made his way towards the door. Their eyes met for a moment, then his lips tilted up in a brief smile and he was gone.

26

Leaning up against the hood of his car, Mason cupped his hands over his mouth and blew, trying to warm himself up. It was damn cold outside, too cold to be standing around waiting for someone, but he couldn't help himself. He was there to see Eir, and nothing—a blizzard, a torrential downpour or a tsunami—would stop him from seeing his Valkyrie tonight.

He smiled to himself.

Although he had only known her a matter of days, he knew she was his, or at least she very soon would be. That almost-kiss they'd had was a lingering memory, always at the forefront of his mind. All he'd had to do was close that quarter of an inch between them, and he would have tasted the sweetness of her lips.

She would have tasted like honey. He just knew it. But they'd been interrupted. Mason checked the time on his phone. It was quarter past six, and just as he was slipping the device back into his jacket pocket, the glass sliding doors of the hospital opened.

He lifted his head up, seeing Eir waving at a young woman behind the reception desk as she walked out the door. When she got outside, the Valkyrie's shoulders hitched up near her ears, a shiver running down her spine. Her hands made their way into the pockets of her coat, her fur-trimmed hood like a halo around her head, making her appear even more ethereal.

Mason's phone rang, the noise cutting through the car park. Eir's gaze swung in his direction, her face lighting up. She was happy to see him, and it made him feel ten fucking feet tall. He took out his phone and pressed it to his ear as he watched her make her way over to him, a small smile in place.

"Yeah?" he said into the phone, keeping his eyes on Eir's beautiful face.

"Where the *fuck* are you?" Korvain asked. "You were due to start fifteen minutes ago."

Fuck me. "I'm here picking up Eir. I thought I'd bring her back to the club then I'd start."

"And you didn't think to tell me about this?" Korvain asked in a soft, dangerous voice. The sound of a chair being dragged across a hardwood floor cut through the line like nails down a chalkboard. "I was just about to leave to pick her up."

"Well, now you don't have to. I'm here. I'll bring her home safe and sound."

"You're goddamn right about that. Bring her home. Now."

Mason wanted to yell right back at the Mare, but Eir's warm hand on his forearm stopped him. She shook her head at him slightly, mouthing the words "Let me talk to him."

Reluctantly, he told Korvain to hang on for a second and gave the phone to Eir. Their fingers touched briefly and a surge of longing shot through his body. Fuck, he was in over his head with this woman.

He watched the way her mouth moved as she spoke to the Mare. He could hear how gentle Korvain's voice was on the other end, so gentle and so completely at odds with the menace that rippled off his body ninety-nine point nine percent of the time.

Eir's eyes remained locked on his face the entire time she spoke, smiling and agreeing with whatever the Mare was telling her.

"He wants to speak to you again," she whispered, handing over the phone. He put the device back to his ear and listened to the harsh breathing on the other end.

"Bring her home. Now." The cruel coldness of Korvain's tone rolled through Mason's body, the line dying abruptly a second later.

"What did he tell you?" she asked, gently touching his hand.

Forcing away his frown, he said, "He wants you back now, and when I get back there, he'll be tearing me a new one."

That last statement made her lips twitch. "I wouldn't worry about Korvain too much. He means well."

"I'm not too concerned about whether he means well or not. I'm more concerned about him disemboweling me … with his bare hands."

Eir placed her hand in his and pulled him off the hood of his car. "I've had a long day. Take me home?"

He huffed, but allowed her to lead him to the driver's side door. Eir opened his door for him, indicating he should get in. A secret smile curved up the corners of her mouth as she walked around to the passenger side, shoving her hands deep into her pockets. Mason started up the engine, cranking the heat to warm up the car.

"So, how was work today?" he asked, trying to distract himself from the reaming he was going to get in about fifteen minutes.

She let out a heavy sigh. "It was … intense."

"Oh?" He hated to hear her so weary. He wanted to erase every bad thing that had happened to her that day.

She sighed again, turning in her seat to look at him as he pulled out of the carpark. "There's a patient I've been working with. He's an elderly gentleman who has an advanced form of cancer. His body is riddled with it. His doctor is sure he can survive the treatment they've devised for him, but …"

He reached over and took her hand. "But?" he prompted, giving her hand a reassuring squeeze.

Her focus dropped down to his hand on hers. "But he won't survive the treatment. The cancer … it's everywhere—metastasized."

"How old is he?" Mason asked, rubbing his thumb over her knuckles. He studied her briefly before turning his eyes back to the road.

"He's lived a good life—a long life. He's in his eighties, but his family are demanding the treatment. I truly believe he would rather just pass away quickly, but there's nothing we can do. We have to obey the wishes of the family."

"I'm so sorry, Eir."

She looked up at him, unshed tears pooling in her eyes. The car in front of them slowed to a stop, giving Mason the chance to reach over and wipe the tears away.

"Please don't cry. I don't like seeing you sad."

She blinked at him, her pale lashes wet. "I don't know why this affects me so much. I've been healing people and watching people pass for as long as I can remember. There's just something about this man that makes me care that little bit more."

He picked up her hand and brought it to his mouth. His lips brushed her skin. "You care about everyone, Eir. I don't think that's such a bad thing, do you?"

She shook her head. "No. I don't think so … but enough about me. How was your day?"

Mason looked back up at the traffic. It had started moving again. "It was spent sleeping mostly. I did manage to get some cleaning done, though, and I took Sophie out for a long run before I had to get ready to head into work."

Eir laughed gently. "Look at you. I never would have pegged you for a domestic goddess." He gave her a sideways glance, thinking about how great the sound of her laughter was.

Bringing her hand to his mouth again, he said, "Well, you *are* the only goddess in this car, but you're a beautiful woman first."

The look in her eyes made his heart stutter in his chest. "You shouldn't say things like that to me," she whispered.

Really? They'd come back to that again? He thought they'd straightened all of that out before. "Why not?" he pushed, determined to get back the same Eir he'd left that morning—the Eir who had almost kissed him back in his apartment, the Eir whose cheeks flushed pink at his compliments and heated as he brushed his lips against the back of her hand.

Her chest rose and fell with a heavy sigh. "Because we're too different."

He gritted his teeth. "You can't use that as an excuse, Eir. I've already told you I don't care how different we are, and I don't see why you should either."

Her mouth popped open for a moment, but then she shut it just as fast. She looked down at her lap, but a small smile was hitching up the side of her mouth. Mason saw it and his heart soared. That smile said it all.

It said she was listening and accepting his words.

A few minutes later, he pulled his car up behind the club,

parking next to Bryn's BMW SUV.

Opening up Eir's door, Mason lead her to the back door of the club, punching the code into the keypad and opening things up.

"I was wondering when you'd get here." Korvain's throaty growl broke the spell Mason was under while with Eir. Looking up, he came nose to chest with the Mare. Tilting his head back, he met Korvain's arctic stare and felt a shiver of fear starting at the base of his skull and running down the length of his spine.

"Korvain," Eir said soothingly, breaking the tension. "Mason just picked me up from work. The traffic was bad."

The Mare's dark eyes drifted down to Eir's face, softening perceptibly. Mason could physically feel the shift in the air as the Mare became a different person around Eir. Korvain was looking her over, no doubt checking for any visible signs of damage.

"I'm going to go upstairs and get changed," Eir said. She turned back to Mason. "Thanks for picking me up tonight."

Mason was holding out hope she would press a kiss to his cheek, but she simply touched his forearm briefly and made her way towards the elevator at the end of the hallway. When he looked back, Korvain's eyes were burning.

"Pull that stunt again and I will kill you," Korvain said menacingly. Mason knew the bastard wasn't lying. In fact, he was pretty sure he would take great pleasure in gutting him.

"I won't, but I have to know why it's such a big deal."

Korvain ran a hand through his hair, his fingers flexed into claws. "I've heard that Darrion has been seen around town. He's already killed one of his own Walkers, although why he did, I have no idea."

"Fuck." The word left his lips harshly. "I'll keep my ears open for any more talk."

"Good. You've got work to do out there, and I've had to cover your ass."

That was as much conversation as Korvain was going to have, so Mason went into the locker room to change his shirt and put his headgear into place. A few minutes later, he was ready for a night of drunken humans and loud music.

Pulling open the door between the club and the offices, Mason stepped into the Eye. The floor was probably half full; the crowd was quiet compared to what he was normally greeted with. Behind the bar, Mist and Elli served drinks. Elli's forearm was still bandaged up, but she looked mobile enough.

Mason walked towards the bottom of the stairs. One of his men who usually worked in the nightclub on level two was in his spot.

"I'll take it from here," Mason told the man.

"Sure." The man disappeared up the stairs. Mason took up his position, his eyes moving across the room. Everything seemed to be running smoothly, until his eyes came to a stop on someone he had no desire to ever see again.

27

Galen stepped past the Valkyrie standing guard at the door. Her calculating eyes had studied him for a lot longer than any other human or god who had come through before him. That fact alone made him uneasy.

As she held him up, he got a good look at the tattoo on her neck. Against all logic, the blade actually reflected the image of his face back at him, and his fingers twitched to reach out and touch it. The goddess grunted and dropped her hand from his chest. He waited just a second longer before stepping into the dimly lit club.

He hadn't taken more than two steps when another hand landed where the Valkyrie's had just been. The hand belonged to Bryn's human.

"What the fuck are you doing here?" the guy asked.

"That's none of your business," Galen shot back, enjoying the way the human's eyes flared. Reaching up, he removed the man's hand from his chest and went to walk past him.

"You're not welcome here." The words were thrown at his back, stopping him. Galen turned around and faced the human once more. He lifted his lips in a smile, revealing his fangs, hoping to intimidate the fuck out of the guy.

But the human stayed strong. In fact, he didn't look at all fazed by the display.

"I'm not going to waste my time speaking to you," Galen said slowly. "Where's Bryn?"

"You *are* going to waste your time with me. She wasn't interested in your last offer, and she sure as hell isn't interested in your current one. In fact, I don't think she'll be interested in any offer you come up with, ever. The Eye is *not* for sale."

Leaning in closer to the human's face, Galen muttered his next words carefully. "I'd like to hear that from her lips."

"Do we have a problem here?" Galen broke his gaze, turning around to look at Bryn, who had come up behind them.

He smiled, making sure to look nice and friendly. Yep, that was him, Galen—totally non-threatening.

"Good evening, Bryn. I'm here—"

"I know why you're here," she said abruptly, hitching one hand on her hip. "I'm not interested."

"You don't even know what I'm offering you."

Her mouth flexed up in the corners, but the smile was cold and didn't reach her eyes. "Let me make myself clear to you here, Galen. I'm not interested in selling a share of my business—large or small—and there is no price your employer could put on it that will change my mind. Am I making myself clear?"

He returned her smile. "Perfectly. But I'm not here for that."

There was a subtle change in her expression, causing him to press on. "I understand why you don't want to sell to Craine. You don't know anything about him, yet he wants to buy a portion of your home."

"You got that goddamn right," Mason snarled at his back.

"Mason," Bryn warned. Her eyes didn't leave Galen's face. "Come back to my office. I don't want to discuss this out here."

"Bryn, please," the human pleaded. What a fucking pussy.

"Come," she said, turning around and making her way through the small crowd already in the bar. Galen followed the Valkyrie, but could feel the human following him, watching him, like he had a target on his back.

Bryn reached the door leading to the hall and waited, ushering Galen through, but she stopped Mason, waving him away.

"Bryn." His voice was strained.

"Mason," Bryn said, "I'm fine." She placed a hand on his forearm. Quietly, she added, "Just call Korvain down here. Will you do that for me?"

Reluctantly, Mason retreated from the hall, but not before he shot a dangerous look in Galen's direction. Galen gave the man a smile that said *fuck you* as a parting gift.

Out in the hall, Bryn opened up her office and waved him in. Galen looked around, walking over to the large reproduction copy of William. T. Maud's *The Ride of the Valkyries.*

Bryn stalked past him, dropping into the leather chair behind her desk. He could feel her eyes on his back, but she kept quiet. He turned around, jerking his head in the direction of the painting.

"One of your finer depictions," he said.

Bryn's eyes didn't shift from his face. "Have a seat, Galen."

He did, lowering himself into the chair opposite her. "I spoke to my boss—"

The Valkyrie put her hand up, stopping him. "I didn't bring you back here to discuss whatever new deal your boss sent you back here for."

He arched a brow. "So … why *did* you invite me back here?"

She ignored his question, just staring blankly at his face. They sat there for what seemed like hours before Korvain burst through the door, his muscular chest rising and falling rapidly with his harsh breath.

"What the fuck is he doing here again?" Korvain asked.

"I was waiting for you," Bryn said.

Well, that can't be good, Galen thought.

Korvain wandered casually around the office, the menace swirling in his eyes, which were watching Galen like a hunter watching his prey.

"What are you doing back here?" he asked, his voice low—perhaps a little too low.

"As I was telling Bryn before, I've spoken to my boss—"

"And *I* told *you* that I don't give a fuck about what your boss has to offer."

Galen sank back into the chair. He had to try another tack. Craine had told him to get close to them by any means possible. The first lie hadn't worked. Looking abased, Galen met Bryn's penetrating gaze.

"He's fired me," he said. "I fucked up and he told me not to come back to Chicago unless I wanted to be a head shorter."

"Bullshit." Korvain pressed his palms onto the desk and leaned down—getting into Galen's personal space. Galen looked into those fathomless, dangerous eyes and swallowed hard. After meeting Korvain the first time, he had done his research. He'd gone down to a bar called the War Hammer and learned all about him, in fact.

He was somewhat of a legend.

He was the only Mare ever to have negotiated his contract with

Darrion, the only Mare to be feared more than his guild master. He was rumored to be the last pure-blooded Mare in all the Nine Worlds, and that was why Darrion had wanted him. Galen just couldn't figure out *how* the bastard had gotten him to sign the contract in his blood.

"Look, I don't know any other way to tell you this. Craine was pissed that Bryn rejected the offer. I told him she wouldn't accept any offer to buy a part of this property." Galen sighed and ran a hand through his hair. "He told me not to come back if I can't close a simple deal. He'll kill me—and my brother—if I do." The lies flowed so smoothly from his lips that he hardly had to think about it anymore.

Bryn's eyes narrowed, and as he watched, Galen could have sworn that the room darkened. Every single hair on his body seemed to stand on end, and his eyes darted to Korvain.

"I suggest you leave before I remove you myself … piece by piece," Korvain said. The lights flickered, sending the room into darkness for a split second. Galen stood up and moved towards the door.

He knew when he was beaten … unless …

Turning back around, Galen tried one last thing. "If you send me back there, you're signing my death warrant."

Korvain smiled, flashing his long fangs. "Happily."

Galen licked his lips nervously. "My boss, Craine, I think he's been manipulated by someone. He's been acting really strangely lately."

Bryn and Korvain shared a look. "Why would this be our problem?" Bryn asked, mistrust threaded through her voice.

Galen shrugged, his mind working hard. "I work for him, but I'd rather not be working for him if someone else has got control of the strings now."

Korvain took a step towards him, his thick arms coming to rest across his chest. "You're a hired killer. Why would you care where the orders come from?"

Galen shook his head. "It's different. He's acting like a guild master—trying to order me to do things. I began working for the humans because I didn't want to feel as if I had no other choice, and with Craine it was always as if he presented me with a job and I could choose whether to do it or not."

"And now?" Bryn asked.

"Now I feel as if I'll be a member of the formerly-breathing-team if I return to Chicago with nothing. He'll kill me. I'm sure of it."

Korvain asked, "What do you want us to do about it? You're a goddamn Mare. Kill the bastard first."

Galen looked Bryn square in the eyes as he muttered his next words. "Give me a job here."

28

The house Darrion had chosen had been random. It could have been any house on the block in downtown Boston, but he had just walked up to this one and decided. Fading inside, he'd found a family just sitting down to eat dinner together.

One big happy family, as it were.

Seeing them sitting together—a father, a mother, an older son and a younger daughter—Darrion had to block out memories of his own family, of them sitting down together to break bread and talk about the happenings of the day. His hatred had taken over then. He hadn't thought about his family in more than a thousand years, yet the scene he had invaded was suddenly bringing all those memories back …

And he hated them.

He hated what they represented.

He hated that he would never have that again.

Ignoring their demands that he tell them who he was, he pulled a blade out and threw it into the face of the mother, seconds before fading behind the father and slitting his throat with another. The children screamed, their high-pitched cries reminding him of a screaming horse being cut down. He felt no pity. To him, they were two loud, annoying things that needed to be silenced.

He turned towards the girl first. The sound of metal slicing the air silenced her, her small body slumping down in the chair, his blade buried to the hilt in her throat. The boy stopped screaming at that point, staring blankly at the red stain spreading across the tablecloth under his sister's limp form.

He turned towards Darrion, his blue eyes blinking slowly. Darrion was sure there was more screaming to come, but the boy simply stared at him. Blood gurgled and foamed from his sister's lips, creating an eerie soundtrack. With a sneer, Darrion pulled one more blade free and flicked his wrist towards the kid's chest.

The boy winced when the knife sank home, dropping his eyes to look down at the handle. Darrion watched— fascinated—as the color drained from his cheeks and a trickle of blood dribbled from his mouth.

His upper body drooped a second later, the hilt propping him up on the edge of the table. When his body grew still, Darrion pressed his index finger against the boy's shoulder, pushing him back into his chair. Gripping the handle of the knife, he dragged it from the flesh of the boy as a trickle of blood escaped the large wound—the gash a grotesque grimace in his chest.

Some of his blood had dribbled down the handle of his knife, pooling on the table. Darrion ran his finger through the congealing pool on the dark wood table, soaking through the pristine white tablecloth. Moving to the boy's sister, he slid his weapon from her throat, too, wiping the blade clean on her shirt.

At last, he came to the mother. The look of terror frozen on her still face brought a smile to Darrion's lips. He pulled the final blade free and re-holstered it along with the others.

Darrion wandered around the lower levels of the house, inspecting every room. It would be perfect for what he required. He had needed to find a new place to stay, needed to be close to his guild. He'd been keeping his eyes on all his Walkers, tracking them but staying hidden. He knew where every single one of them was, with the exception of Nieven.

His longest serving Mare was off the grid, and had been for a little less than a week. To Darrion that could only mean one thing.

He was dead.

Darrion made one round of the house, eventually circling back to the dining room, taking in his handiwork. It was almost … poetic. The tables had turned. He was the one wielding the weapons while the defenseless family fell beneath his hand.

Satisfied the house was completely empty after a sweep of the upstairs bedrooms, Darrion went back down to the living room and dropped onto the sofa.

The night before, he had gotten into Taer's dreams just like he had been doing for the past month—ever since he realized Korvain had taken his prize from him and saved her life. Darrion was sure he was driving her insane. Every night, she had to relive her brother's death as if she had been conscious for the whole thing.

Her fear—her pure, unadulterated, raw fear—seemed to permeate the dream completely, saturating his skin, sinking into his pores and filling his nostrils. He fed off it, letting it nourish him.

It had been so easy too. Her mind was unguarded, simple to manipulate. All it took was a single thought and he was in there, taking her greatest fear and greatest regret—killing her brother—and using it, pushing against the door of her mind.

Smug, he remembered just how easily she had yielded to him. It had taken Darrion a long time to perfect the art of Dream Walking. Njord had told him he wasn't a natural, but with effort, dedication and practice, he would be as good—if not better than—any other Mare.

Tonight, Darrion would invade her subconscious again. He'd been taking it easy on her. He'd been letting her 'drive' for the most part, letting her own horrific memories run unrestrained, but tonight he was going to ramp things up a little.

Stretching himself out on the sofa, Darrion closed his eyes and thought about the young female. Her hair was thick—a glossy, black lacquer pouring over her shoulders and back. Her pale green eyes held an intelligence unexpected in a female, with a quiet spark in them. He had to admit that when Adrian had first told him of her desire to go through the training and become a blooded Walker, he'd been shocked—a feeling he hadn't experienced in a long time.

Curious as to how Taer would go, Darrion had allowed the training to commence, but made Adrian solely responsible for her instruction. From what he had seen, she was shaping up into a fine Walker, but there was no way she could pass the Final Test, not when the others in her quinary were all male and physically much more able.

And now here she was. Her brother dead; her whole world shattered; and Darrion would destroy her mind along with it. He knew she must be intent on revenge, and with nothing left to lose, Taer was a dangerous enemy.

Oh, yes, he knew she would be coming for him now. Korvain might have been Adrian's best friend, but he would give Taer the honor of killing his murderer … that is, if they could catch him.

But he never stayed in one place for longer than necessary. He knew there were a lot of people searching for him.

With his whole body relaxed, Darrion was able to find the door to Taer's mind. He looked it over, knowing every inch of it.

It was as black and as smooth and lustrous as her hair. There were new cracks in the wood, and he wondered whether his repeated invasions had been responsible for putting them there, and if her fragile mind was starting to fracture.

He hoped she was cracking. Her brother had had a weak mind too. He was easily manipulated and controlled—a near-perfect soldier.

Reaching out his hand, Darrion pushed against the ebony wood, feeling it ease open from the gentlest pressure. The space inside was black, a dream yet to form. With a satisfied smirk, Darrion conjured up his own memories of killing Adrian and made the scene materialize once more.

Without even needing to glance over his shoulder, Darrion already knew Taer was there. Stepping from the inky shadows of her own subconscious, her eyes would be running over the scene in front of her. He turned, enjoying the way her eyes widened and tears trembled on her lashes. Until now, her dreams had been from her own perspective—she had witnessed the scene through her own eyes, seeing it from down on the floor, where she had fallen—but tonight was going to be different.

29

Exhausted didn't even begin to describe how Taer was feeling. The same nightmare that had been plaguing her for over a month now was back. Only … it was worse. It was different.

And she *felt* different in it.

This time around she wasn't underneath Adrian, inhaling the scent of his blood and feeling his dead weight on her chest. She was standing apart, looking down upon the scene in a disembodied sort of way. Looking at Adrian's body from this angle made her aware of just how much damage Darrion had inflicted.

She moaned pitifully. Her brother's head was barely connected to his body, his throat a bloody, gory mess. Taer swallowed the burning at the back of her throat, unsure whether it was bile bubbling up from her stomach, or the tears she was still refusing to shed for her brother.

The hairs on the back of her neck suddenly stood on end, fear making her scalp prickle. Fighting her instincts to run, Taer took in a deep breath and let it out.

"You did this." The words were a graveled purr, the speaker somewhere behind her. She spun around, squinting at the edges of darkness skirting around her fuzzy subconscious.

"Who's there?" Her fear was receding, making way for the rage bubbling and boiling up within her. "I asked who was there!"

She knew she was alone in this room, yet she sensed a presence. A shiver ran down her spine as something touched her ear.

"Your worst nightmare," the voice said again.

"Darrion," she spat out venomously, goosebumps traveling over her bare arms.

"Yes," he whispered.

She had to remind herself that Darrion was not physically in her dream. Curling her hands into fists, she said, "You killed my brother." She wanted to rip out his black heart and burn it.

He paused for a moment, and when he spoke again, she could hear smugness in the motherfucker's voice. "Yes."

The weight of his admission left her bereft all over again, her rage draining away as she was overwhelmed by grief. "Why?" Her voice was so small and shaky that she wondered whether he had even heard her at all.

"Because I could."

The dismissive way he said it relit the spark of her anger. A growl built in her chest. "I'm going to put you in the ground, you bastard."

It was a promise.

It was a goddamn oath.

Darrion's amused laughter had her squeezing her eyes shut.

"Get in line," he whispered into her ear, his warm breath cascading over her neck. She was completely and utterly repulsed, but worse than that?

She was petrified of him.

And of what he could do to her if she was to fail.

———————

Taer had woken from that nightmare exactly five hours ago. It was just barely dawn, but she could hear Korvain moving around in the apartment. Sliding from her bed, she carefully closed the bedroom door behind her so Eir could keep sleeping undisturbed.

When she padded out into the kitchen, she found Korvain starting up the coffee machine. He looked up with a smile, which turned into a frown.

"You had another dream, didn't you?" he asked, keeping his harsh voice low so he didn't wake up the rest of the apartment.

Bristling, Taer replied, "It's fine. I can handle it."

Taking her chin between his thumb and forefinger, Korvain gently tilted her head until her pale eyes met his. His fingers tightened when she refused to meet his intense stare.

"It's not fine, Tay. I could—" Korvain clamped his jaw shut abruptly, releasing his hold on her and stepping away. His hardening eyes gave away his clear frustration.

He knew something. He fucking *knew* something. "What were you going to say?" Taer's voice was hard, icy.

"Nothing," he said quietly. Picking up a mug from beside the sink, he filled it with coffee. He was effectively dismissing her, but she wasn't going to allow that to happen. The dream was getting worse, and the only thing that would make her feel marginally better about them was to see Darrion bleeding out on the floor in front of her.

And in order for that to happen, she needed more training.

"Will we be doing any training today?" She tried to make her question sound offhand. She didn't want him to see just how desperately she needed this.

He scowled at her over the rim of his mug. "Not today," he replied, grudgingly adding, "Tomorrow, maybe."

Taer spun around. "Fine." She threw the word over her shoulder, slipping back inside her bedroom. She got dressed in a pair of gray sweatpants and a fitted black tank before pulling her hair into a high ponytail at the top of her head.

Looking over at Eir to ensure she was still sleeping, Taer opened one of the drawers in her bedside table and pulled out the card Aubrey had given her the other night. She grabbed her phone and typed out a text, then sat back and waited for the light elf's reply.

He responded almost immediately with an address, and it wasn't the address of the War Hammer.

Taer bit her bottom lip, staring at the screen. "Fuck it," she said to herself.

Taer waited until she could hear the shower running in Bryn's bathroom before she left the apartment. Once outside, she closed her eyes and faded to the address Aubrey had sent her.

She couldn't see the house from where she was standing. An imposing red-brick wall loomed in front of her, covered with creeping ivy. A black wooden gate was set into the brick, a silver box with a speaker and one button beside it. Looking up and down the quiet street, Taer reached out and pressed the button, which lit up with her touch.

"Winter Fox." Aubrey's voice came from the metal box, a mellifluous drawl. "Come in," he added, a small *snick* indicating that the gate had just been unlocked. Taer let out a breath and pushed against the gate, her eyes rising up to take in the front of the imposing house.

Taer's gaze was drawn to Aubrey waiting at the front door, no more than a dozen feet away. "I'm surprised," he said, assessing her suggestively. Dressed in a pair of dark gray jeans and a loose-fitting white shirt, he looked every inch as delectable as Taer had tried to convince herself he wasn't.

"You shouldn't be," she snapped back. "I need training. You're providing me with that."

One pale brow arched as he stepped away from the door. "We'd better get started then."

Taer stalked into the house, finding herself standing in a grand entrance way, with a large stairway leading up to the second floor directly in front of her.

"You live here?" she asked, surreptitiously inspecting the antique furniture and rich fabrics in the rooms to her left and right.

"I do," he replied close to her ear, his hot breath tickling her neck. Taer stepped forward, away from his warmth, and turned to face him.

"It's nice—a bit pretentious, but nice," she added when she saw the satisfied grin on his face. Aubrey laughed.

"Come," he said without looking back as he opened a door beneath the stairs and disappeared. A yellow glow emanated a second later, beckoning Taer to follow. She stepped forward, finding a set of stairs leading down to what she assumed was a basement. Descending the stairs, she could smell the richness of leather and the scent of cleaning products. When she reached the final landing, Taer looked around the room, taking in the sparring mats and the weapons hanging from the walls.

"Why are we here, Aubrey?" she asked, wary. She'd expected him to tell her to come to the War Hammer, as they'd trained there before.

With an aloof smile, he started to unbutton his shirt. Taer watched—unwillingly riveted—as he shrugged the shirt off his shoulders. She had to force herself to look away from his bare chest. She wasn't there to be seduced.

"Don't like what you see, Winter Fox?" he asked.

"I swear if you unbutton your jeans, I am out of here, Aubrey," she warned.

"You've seen a lot more of me than this," he reminded her. "A simple bare chest shouldn't cause you to blush this much."

"I'm not blushing," she shot back, turning her angry eyes on him. "I asked you to train me today. That's all. I didn't ask you to try to seduce me, and I certainly didn't ask you to undress in front of me."

Aubrey chuckled. "Relax, Winter Fox." Picking up a tank top slung over a weapons rack, Aubrey pulled it over his head, covering his partial nakedness. "I was just getting changed." His clear eyes studied her. "You're wound up too tight, do you know that? And do you know the best way to release that tension?"

Taer shot him a lethal look. He stepped in close to her, uncomfortably close. Taer held her ground, but his advance forced her to crane her head back.

Her green eyes were stuck on his gray, her mouth suddenly dry. One half of her wanted to get the hell away from him, but another part wanted to stay just where she was, just with less clothing on.

When all she could see was him, and all she could smell was his scent, he leaned down so they were eye to eye.

"Fucking," he whispered seductively. His warm breath caressed her skin as he spoke, her nostrils filling with the sweet scent of cinnamon.

She let out a breath, making sure her next words were filled with a snide confidence she didn't feel. "With you? No thanks."

His smile faltered. "Liar."

"I'm a liar? All right. I'll make you a deal, Aubrey. The day I voluntarily touch you—when we're not training together—is the day I'll let you fuck me."

He stuck out his hand. "Deal," he said with a cocksure grin.

Taer eyed his extended hand with contempt. "Nice try, light elf," she muttered, walking away to study the weapons on the wall. Her eyes took them all in, but she drawn to one in particular—a katana in a black scabbard with a pale green handle.

She reached out a hand to touch it, then stopped and looked over her shoulder to Aubrey for permission. She realized he'd been watching her the entire time. He gave her a small nod and Taer turned back around. She picked up the sword with both hands—one on the peg and the other on the scabbard.

Very slowly, she withdrew the weapon from its cover, revealing the smooth, dangerous blade. It was the single most beautiful thing she had ever seen in her life. All through the steel, embedded veins of pale green twisted and writhed—looking almost molten. She felt a pull towards it, as if it was in her blood to wield this sword.

"The ancient samurai warriors of Japan used these blades in open combat," Aubrey said beside her, his voice silken, and almost … reverent. "But it wasn't the Japanese who invented this blade. It was one of the gods. Some say it was Odin himself who showed them how to construct them. Others say it was Tyr, working with the Japanese god of war, Hachiman. Nobody really knows for sure, though."

Taer touched the steel, and it seemed to warm under her fingertips. In that instant she knew everything there was to know about the weapon. She knew just where and how to grip it.

Holding that blade made her feel like she was home.

Finally.

"You feel it, don't you?" he asked. He didn't need to explain what he meant.

"Yes."

The light elf shook his head. "I've heard of dark elves finding their affinity, but I've never witnessed it before."

Her affinity. Is that what it was? Taer's eyes returned to the katana resting in her hands. For Korvain, it was the karambit, and for Darrion it was the throwing knife. And for Adrian ...

A great sadness swept over her. She knew her brother had never found his affinity. He had never had this feeling of absolute ... *knowing*. It was almost as if part of her soul that had been unknowingly lost had come back to her.

"Are you ready to train?" he asked her. She looked to her right, seeing him staring at her intently.

"What weapon will we be using today?"

Without uttering a word, Aubrey picked up the other katana that had been hanging beside her green one and unsheathed it. His blade was just as beautiful as Taer's, but where hers was green, his was exquisite silver. He held it confidently in front of him, indicating that Taer should do the same.

Taer brought the sword upright, one elbow raised to the side to be in line with chest, her right hand close to the guard and her left hand snug behind it. She lowered her center of gravity by bending her knees and kept her fingers loose on the sword, instinctively knowing that this was how it was done, turning the blade out away from her skin.

She watched Aubrey about six feet away from her, adopting a similar stance, but she could see his flaws: his grip was too tight, the blade slightly turned in towards his body.

"Ready?" he asked, his expression serious. "Remember to leave all emotions at the door. I'm just a target for you. You're just a target for me," he reminded her.

She let out a breath.

Taer was ready for him, but she wasn't ready for the speed at which he struck. Within seconds she found herself flat on her back and staring up at the light elf. She should have known he wasn't going to go easy on her.

Ignoring his proffered hand, Taer got back onto her feet, making sure to keep her eyes on Aubrey the entire time. He had retreated to the other side of the room, ready for round two.

Getting back into position, Taer prepared for his next attack. She listened to her body, but mostly she listened to the blade, which had become an extension of her hand.

She was soon in a steady pattern of striking, parrying and blocking, and as the minutes dribbled into hours, her mind and body felt more in tune with her katana. Aubrey had succeeded in nicking her skin a few times, but each time they reset their stances, she could see that he had more cuts than she did.

Simulating a slash across Aubrey's belly, she blocked his counter, whirling around behind him and making a final slash down the length of his back. "Dead," she said. Dropping her stance, Taer stepped away, relaxing her body.

"Good, Winter Fox. We're done for the day," he told her, his shoulders rising and falling with his heavy breath. Nearly every uncovered inch of his skin was obscured by dark red blood. Some of the deeper wounds were still bleeding a little, but they would heal within the next couple of hours.

He looked tired, yet proud at the same time. "Well, remind me never to get into a katana fight with you," he said, his words gruff. Walking over to a trunk in the corner of the room, he pulled out a roll of paper towel, two small towels, and a small bottle of liquid.

Crouching on the mats, he motioned for her to do the same. "We have to clean the blades properly before we finish up."

Taer squatted opposite him, watching him first wipe away the blood with the paper towels before using a clean towel to apply oil to the steel. Ensuring all the excess oil had been removed, Aubrey slid the blade back into the scabbard carefully.

Taer copied each of his methodical steps, feeling a great sense of peace as she worked. When the blade was clean and sheathed once more, she stood up to hang it back on the wall.

"What are you doing?" Aubrey asked softly from behind her. Startled, Taer gave him a questioning look.

"Putting the sword back," she replied.

"That sword doesn't belong to me anymore," he said. "It's yours now, Winter Fox."

"I can't," she blurted out, going to place the katana back where it belonged.

"Don't insult me, Taer."

She hesitated, not knowing what to say.

"You know, *thank you* is the customary response to someone who has just given you a gift," he prompted.

"Thank you," she replied automatically, frowning. They stared at each other for a long moment. Then, feeling as if she'd overstayed her welcome, she muttered, "I should go. Thanks for today."

"Let me walk you out."

Taer trailed after him up the stairs and through the entrance way, where he paused. Night had already fallen. She studied him from under her dark lashes, her heart pounding out an erratic rhythm.

Curiosity made her want to stay, but she'd promised herself that

Aubrey was off-limits. Her decision made, she tilted her chin up and strode towards the door.

"Good night," she said.

Aubrey reached out, wrapping his warm fingers around her wrist. He pulled the katana from her grip, lowering it steadily to the ground. With a gentle tug, he spun her back around, throwing her off balance. Thrusting her hand out in front of her, she collided with his chest. She was six foot tall, but with him pushing nearly seven, she had to tilt her head back to look at him—exposing her throat to him.

When he did nothing more than stare down at her with half-lidded eyes, she tried to step from his grasp, but his fingers encircled both her wrists and held her against him effortlessly.

Taer's pulse galloped, causing Aubrey's top lip curled into a lascivious smile as if he knew exactly what effect he was having on her.

"I quite like having you in my home, Winter Fox," he drawled, his eyes on her mouth.

Oh, fuck. Licking her lips, she tried to break free once more, but it was like trying to break through warded steel; there was no way she was getting away unless he allowed it.

"What do you want?" Taer's voice was defiant, if also a little curious, too.

He stared at her mouth. "A taste," he replied simply, "Just a taste." Leaning in, he brushed his lips against hers. She tried to push away then, but he simply pulled her back into the hard line of his body, forcing his mouth to hers once more.

His erection pressed against her stomach, and she remembered seeing him naked in her dream, remembered her visceral reaction. She'd told him he was small, but there'd been nothing small about him. He was beautiful and she would have given anything to see his naked body again.

The moan that left Taer's throat unbidden as Aubrey's tongue brushed against her lips was met with one of his own. He let go of her wrists, his hands skimming down her body to her hips.

A wildfire of desire, of want and need, burned her blood, setting her whole world alight. She wanted more, she *needed* more of him, and every reason she'd thought up to avoid him suddenly didn't seem to matter anymore. Taer drew her arms around his neck, tilting her head toward him. His tongue swept in, teasing her, caressing her and driving her insane with every touch.

She held on tight to his arms as his mouth and his body claimed her completely. He tasted just as he smelled, but with his drying blood a coppery aftertaste, she found she wanted more …

So much more …

She was so engrossed in the feel of his hard body against hers that for a moment she forgot to breath. His breathing was rapid and ragged too. The kiss had been electric—but her promise to him rang through her head with deafening clarity. Taer realized what she had been doing. With anger filling her veins, she brought her hand up and slapped Aubrey across the cheek. The sharp crack reverberated through the room.

"That wasn't voluntary," she barked, marching through the doorway. Abandoning her katana, Taer faded directly back to the club with the smell, taste and feel of Aubrey still lingering on her fingers and in her mouth and nose.

30

A light tapping on Taer's bedroom door made her stir from a restless sleep. She was still enduring the same nightmare, but adding to her misery was the kiss she'd shared with Aubrey, his scent and taste still torturing her.

"Come in," she answered in a low voice, so she didn't wake up Eir.

Korvain stepped through the door, his broad shoulders blocking the light coming from the hallway. "Good. You're awake."

Taer tried on a smile. "You know me—I'm an early riser."

Bull-fucking-shit was what his expression told her. He knew she'd not really slept at all. He didn't need to ask—he could see it in the dark circles under her eyes and the fear in her gaze.

Taer slid from the bed and started scooping her dirty clothes up from the floor. "If you're about to give me a lecture, you can keep your mouth fucking shut," she hissed, her eyes darting to the side when she heard Eir shift in her sleep.

"You don't need me to tell you what you already know," he replied, just as harshly. "Get dressed and come into the living room when you're done. I have to show you something."

She'd planned to visit one of Darrion's safe houses today, but before she could protest, Korvain was already out the door, shutting it carefully behind him. With a heavy sigh, she stripped off the shorts and tank she had slept in and pulled on a fresh pair of sweats and a tee from her drawer.

Five minutes later, a cup of coffee in hand, Taer dropped into the seat beside Korvain. His eyes were glued to the TV screen across the other side of the living room, watching a news story about an entire family that had been slaughtered in Boston last night; they were the second in a week. A woman wearing a heavy winter coat was standing out on the street, a row of cars parked behind her and the blue and red flashing lights of police cars and other emergency vehicles decorating an otherwise normal-looking street.

"Police still have no leads in these disturbing murders, which took place somewhere between nine and ten pm yesterday evening, on a quiet street in an affluent part of Boston. No details have been released, other than that there are striking similarities between this seemingly unprovoked attack on a young family and the one that occurred not more than two days ago.

"Police are urging people to keep their doors and windows locked and to remain vigilant. This is Brenda Lee, WCVB News."

"So," Taer said. "What kind of training are we doing?"

"I'm going to teach you how to shield your mind today," he said, taking her coffee away from her. He hauled himself up from the couch, deposited her cup on a small table and sat down on the floor opposite her, his back against the armchair.

"Asshole," she muttered, knowing full well he would hear it.

He looked smug, but before she could ask what was so damn

funny, a pressure began to build in her head. It grew and grew until she felt as if her skull was going to shatter into a million pieces. Clutching at the sides of her head, she tried to breathe through the pain. Still, a scream clawed its way from her throat. Her vision grew dark and her world tilted like it was spinning wrong on its axis. She was about to pass out, and she was terrified.

Then, just as quickly as it had started, it was over. The pain was gone. She blinked rapidly a few times, and Korvain came into focus once more. Panting, Taer demanded, "What just happened?"

"I was pressing against your mind," he said. "It's a hard thing to do while you're still conscious, and it's a skill that didn't come naturally to me. I had to work at it—and what I did just then? That was nothing. I was only using the slightest pressure. If you'd been asleep, I would have slipped inside so easily."

"Where was the warning, asshole?" She felt violated. "You could have at least told me you were going to do that."

"Darrion would never tell you he was going to do it, so why should I?" He sat up and leaned closer. "And believe me when I say that you would *not* want to have Darrion inside your head."

Taer's anger surged. "How in the hell am I supposed to defend myself against that?"

"That's what I'm going to teach you," he said, leaning back against the armchair once more. "Shielding your mind is a twenty-four-seven kind of thing, Tay. It takes more concentration and strength than any physical fight ... and it is your *only* defense against a mental attack."

Grudgingly, she said, "So teach me, O wise one."

His lip quirked up a little. "I will. But I need your full and undivided attention."

"Don't you always get that from me?"

His expression sobered. "I mean it, Tay. I need you to invest in this stuff. It's important."

Taer sank back into the cushions, digesting his words. Her suspicion that he knew more than he was letting on was only getting stronger. "Korvain," she said, "you know something about my dreams, don't you? What is it? Why are you keeping things from me?"

He leveled her with a cold stare. "You're not ready yet, but everything we've been doing is to get you ready." Hoisting himself off the ground, he lowered himself into the seat beside her. "And you need to be ready. Can you just trust me a little longer? I'll tell you when the time is right."

After a moment or two she nodded, agreeing to his request. No matter what, Korvain had her back like he'd had … Adrian's. She trusted him implicitly. "So, are you going to teach me something, or what?" she asked.

Korvain reached out and squeezed her hand before standing up again. "Sure."

Five hours later, Taer felt as if she had grasped what shielding her mind was and how to do it. The idea behind it was actually quite simple. Korvain said that by holding an image steady in her mind, she could block almost any kind of breach, but she needed a lot more practice before she would be able to do it successfully.

Korvain's image was an endless ocean at night. Taer chose an icy tundra, lonely and desolate. It was how she felt deep down inside. She didn't think the ice around her heart and in her soul would ever melt.

And honestly, she hoped it never did.

She had lost too much already.

Korvain still sat across from her, his intense black eyes boring into hers as he tried once again to breach her mental shield. His attacks had been relentless and she'd had little success in keeping him out. Fresh sweat beaded on her brow, trickling down her temples and dripping onto her bare arms.

This assault continued for three-quarters of an hour before Eir came in, distracting Korvain, and his concentration dropped.

He turned to the Valkyrie. "Where are you going?" he asked.

Eir stopped in her tracks.

"I'm … umm, I'm going on a date."

Taer watched the muscle in Korvain's jaw tick angrily. "Who with?"

Even though Eir was a Valkyrie and could no doubt cause some serious damage to Korvain with her sword, she seemed cowed by the Mare.

Taer couldn't really blame her.

Korvain was as intimidating as fuck.

"With Mason," Eir answered cautiously. "We're going out to lunch together."

Taer could see how much that news upset Korvain. "Mason?" he asked sharply. "Mason asked you out?"

"Yes," Eir said meekly.

A snarl vibrated through the room and she took a step backwards. "I want him to bring you back straight after you eat," Korvain told her.

Taer was surprised. When had he become the protective father? But Eir agreed wordlessly and rushed from the apartment, closing the door behind her.

Korvain prowled over to the kitchen bench, snatching up his phone, and violently began punching the buttons. He paced until someone picked up at the other end.

"I thought I told you to stay away from her," he said coldly.

Those ten little words said so much more. Korvain was

worried—Taer could see that, and if there was one thing she'd learned about him, it was the more calmly he spoke, the angrier he was.

Korvain was silent for a moment, listening, then said curtly, "Failure is not an option, Mason."

His unspoken threat hung dangerously in the air for a moment before he hung up the phone.

"Are we done for the day?" Taer asked carefully. He spun around to face her, his face still clouded with rage.

"No," he told her, cold anger burning in his words. "I want you to try and breach my shields."

"We already know I can't."

"Yet," he corrected. "All it takes is practice, Taer. I need you to start that practice now."

Wiping the sweat from her brow, Taer twisted around until she was comfortable and then tried to do as Korvain had asked. For the rest of the afternoon, Taer worked hard. She tried everything, from trying to mentally kick the shield to concentrating on it, pushing her will onto it.

By the time Korvain had to go to work, she'd had enough of looking at that damn endless ocean at midnight. She'd had enough of him telling her she had to try harder. And she'd had enough of failure.

"How in the hell am I supposed to breach someone's shield, Korvain? You keep telling me it's important. Fine. I get that, but what you haven't told me is *how* to do it. If Darrion is an expert in this, then what hope do I have going up against him if I don't even know how to do it?"

The Mare stayed silent, staring hard at her, and Taer gave up. He was only giving her the information she needed in trickles, when she wanted the whole damn bucket poured over her. "Do you know what?" she said impatiently. "Just forget it." Bringing the hem of her shirt up, she wiped the sweat from her face. "I'm done. I can't do it anymore."

She stood up before Korvain could start chewing her out and headed down the hallway to the bathroom, locking herself in. She started up the shower and stripped off her sweat-soaked clothes. Stepping under the spray, she let the hot water carry away the stickiness and frustrations of the day's exertions.

She couldn't see how her knowledge of breaking shields could be of any use. If she couldn't get past the vast black oceans of Korvain's mind, how was she supposed to break through Darrion's—the Mare who had taught Korvain almost everything he knew?

Shutting off the water, Taer stepped from the stall and wrapped herself in a towel. Her mind was running at a mile a minute, trying to work it all out. Perhaps there was only one person who could possibly give her the answers she was seeking ... the one person she really, *really* didn't want to see again so soon.

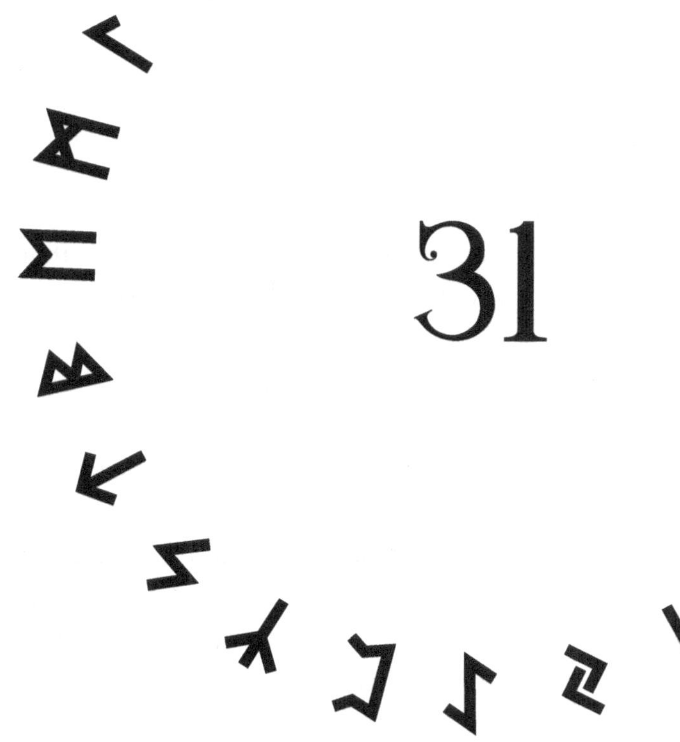

31

Eir was sitting at the bar in the Eye, watching Mist restocking the shelves, waiting nervously for Mason to come and pick her up for their lunch date. She could feel her cheeks heat at the thought. Never in a million years would she have thought she would be dating a human, but she was, and she found herself strangely exhilarated by it.

Of course, she was aware that what they would share would be just a blip in her long life, but Mason made her feel things no other man had. She had never been one to seek out male company. She had honestly never had much interest in it … until Mason, that was.

"Where are you off to?" Mist asked her, glancing up from her inventory list. With a pen balanced between her index finger and thumb, she smiled at Eir. Mist's sleek bob looked like silk under the downlights, the short length revealing the blue blade tattooed on the delicate skin of her neck.

Eir blushed again. "I have a date."

Mist's smile widened. "A date? With anyone I know?"

"Umm, Mason," Eir replied, looking down at the bar top. She waited to see what Mist would say. Dating humans wasn't unheard of for gods and goddesses, but for the Valkyries it was a foreign concept.

One of Mist's brows arched. "Really?" she asked.

Eir flushed in response.

Mist looked puzzled. "I didn't realize you two were …"

Embarrassed, Eir shrugged. "It was a surprise to me, too," she admitted. Looking up to gauge Mist's reaction, she asked, "What do you think about that?"

The other Valkyrie put her pen down and leaned a hip against the bar. "Honestly?" Eir nodded. "I think our world has changed. And if you like the guy, then I think you should go for it. I mean, look at Bryn and Korvain. She's a Valkyrie and he's a Mare. They really shouldn't even like each other, but they do. So, I think if you like Mason and he makes you happy, you should definitely pursue this." She sighed. "A lot of people search for a long time to find a person they like enough to spend extended periods of time with."

Looking down at her hands laced together on top of the bar, Eir said, "I like him. He seems like a decent man."

"He is." Reaching out, Mist rested her hand on top of Eir's. "You deserve to be happy. You've had a pretty tough time this last month, and if Mason is the man to do that, well, I'm all for it."

The door to the hallway swung open then. Eir turned her head in the direction of the doorway, her breath catching in her throat. Mason stood there with a lazy smile on his perfect lips. Dressed in a pair of dark jeans and white button-down shirt, he looked

… delectable.

"Hungry?" he asked with his cocky grin still in place.

"Famished," she replied without thinking. Mist laughed, causing Eir to blush furiously.

Mason chuckled. "I'd better get you to lunch then."

Sliding from the bar stool, Eir said goodbye to Mist.

"You look lovely," Mason murmured as she walked towards him. Looking down at her midnight blue wrap dress and ballet flats, Eir blushed again, then self-consciously met his warm hazel eyes.

"Thank you." Her reply was quiet and unsure. She had never been good at accepting compliments.

Mason put a warm hand at the small of her back, leading her through the rear door of the club and towards his car, parked beside Bryn's BMW. After opening the car door and waiting until she had slid inside, he came around the other side and climbed into the driver's seat.

Eir clasped her hands together in her lap, nervous. "Which restaurant are we going to?"

Mason started the car and reversed from the spot before he answered her. "There's a new sushi place that's opened up in Chestnut Hill." His easy expression suddenly melted away. "You do like Japanese food, don't you?" he asked, looking concerned. "If you don't, we can go somewhere else. Or we could—"

Reaching over, Eir placed her hand on his forearm. "Mason, sushi is fine … I've actually never tried it before."

He blew out a relieved breath and the smile that split his face in two warmed the cold hollow in Eir's chest. "You'll love this place then."

They drove the Boston city streets in companionable silence until Mason pulled into a parking space on the street. "The restaurant is another block away, but I doubt I could get a parking spot any closer. I could drop you off at the front if you'd rather not walk, though," he said, that look of worry washing over his features again, and Eir realized he was nervous.

Well, at least she wasn't the only one.

"Mason, it's fine. We can walk there."

Taking his hand in hers, she tried to draw some of his anxiety away.

He grunted, looking down at their intertwined fingers. "You're doing that warm palm thing, aren't you?"

"Yes, I'm doing that warm palm thing. Is it helping?"

Placing his hand over hers, he said, "Yeah. I don't know why I'm so nervous about this." She noticed a flush creeping up his neck before he added, "Maybe it's just because it's you."

The restaurant was modern, but still warm and inviting, and Eir noticed many couples having romantic lunches together, their hands touching, their eyes full of heated lust. The tables were set low to the ground, and the diners sat on mats on the floor.

The hostess greeted them with a friendly smile, then led them all the way across the room, stopping at an opaque screen. She slid open the door, revealing a room completely different from the rest of the restaurant. Instead of the muted palette of creams and peaches, the walls were painted a deep shade of red.

"Your server will be along to get your drink orders shortly," the hostess said, stepping aside. Mason nudged Eir inside gently, stepping in close behind her. The heat of his body against her back was heavenly, and her eyes shuddered closed for just a minute.

Mason led her to a seat on the right, taking her hand while she lowered herself down onto the cushion. After she was comfortable, Mason walked around the low table and took his place opposite her. The low light exaggerated the planes of his face, his hazel eyes black in the dimness.

The door slid open then and a young man stepped into the room. "Good afternoon," he said in a smooth and cultured voice. "What can I get you both to drink?"

Mason said, "I'll take an Asahi and ..." he looked expectantly at Eir.

"The same."

"Excellent," the server replied. "I'll give you a few more moments to look over the menu."

The gentle thud of the sliding door indicated his departure. Eir dropped her eyes to the menu sitting on the table in front of her. Everything looked so foreign to her. She looked up nervously at Mason.

"You'd better order for me."

"No problem. Is there anything you don't like?"

"No, I'm pretty adventurous."

The server returned with two bottles of beer with white labels and placed them on the table, along with two, chilled tall glasses.

"Are you ready to order?"

"Yes," Mason said, and rattled off a string of Japanese-sounding words which Eir could only assume were dishes on the menu. The server dutifully wrote them down, then excused himself from the room.

"What did you order?" she asked curiously, watching Mason fill her glass with beer.

"A bit of everything. If you don't like anything, I'll eat it."

Reaching out, Eir took the glass in her hand and took a sip. She didn't normally drink beer, finding the Americans' version of the drink too strange for her taste, but she found she liked this one.

Placing her glass back down, she leaned her elbows on the table.

"Tell me something I don't know about you, Mason."

He gave her a lazy grin. "There's not much to tell, really."

"Well, where did you grow up?"

"California, but my parents moved my brother and I to the east coast when I was ten and he was eight."

"What did your parents do?"

"My mother was a secretary and my dad did a million different jobs. He was in construction for a while, worked at a bar, mechanic, dock worker …" He shrugged. "All sorts."

"And you joined the marines?"

His shoulders stiffened. "When I was eighteen, I joined. There was nothing else I wanted to do. Ever since I was a kid, I was always playing soldiers and pretending I was going into battle." He swallowed a mouthful of beer.

Eir smiled. "And your brother? What did he do before …?"

"Hunter—that was his name—was always following in my shadow when we were growing up. He looked up to me, and I think that's why he also joined up when he turned eighteen. I'd already been in for two years, so I could keep an eye on him just like I did when we were growing up."

"I wish I could have met him." Reaching over, she placed her hand on his arm, but before she could take away his pain, he pulled his arm free, pretending to reach for his glass once more.

Eir clasped her hands together in her lap. She didn't want Mason to be upset. She didn't like to see that sadness in his eyes, to feel it pulse through his veins.

"I'm sorry. I just … I just …" He looked up, his eyes filled with sorrow. "Talking about Hunter still hurts."

Her heart bled for him. What she wouldn't have done to take away his pain.

She was still trying to find the right words to comfort him when a series of servers suddenly whisked into the room, covering the table with plate after plate.

As the servers left, Eir stared wide-eyed at all the food.

"Try this one first," Mason said.

"What is it?"

"Gyoza—deep-fried dumpling. Try it."

Picking up her chopsticks, she held them like he was and picked up the small parcel of food. Bringing it to her mouth, she bit into the little half-moon-shaped pastry. The crunchy outer casing gave way to a deliciously soft filling of meat and vegetables. She couldn't contain the moan erupting from her lips as she chewed and swallowed. Mason watched her, captivated, as she ate.

When she had taken her last bite, she wiped her mouth. "Aren't you going to have some?"

The heat in his eyes was unmistakable, causing that familiar flush to take over her body once more.

"Mason—" she began, flustered.

He grinned at her, reaching over to the gyoza plate with his chopsticks and picking up one. He popped it in his mouth and chewed, his eyes never leaving hers.

The rest of their lunch went in much the same way. He would suggest something, she would try it and find that she liked it—except for something called *tsubugai kimuchi*, which Mason told her, after she'd eaten it, was sea snail with a spicy Korean sauce.

Four bottles of beer and two very full stomachs later, Mason paid the bill and led her from the restaurant by the hand. Once outside, the spell of their hour and a half together was broken. This was the real world.

He pulled her into him, his hands finding her waist as if they were always meant to be there. "I had a really good time," he said, his eyes dropping down to her mouth. Eir chewed her bottom lip nervously.

"Me too."

Tucking a stray tendril of hair behind her ear, he added, "We should do it again."

"We should. Look, Mason, I'm—"

Her phone rang in her bag, interrupting her. Mason released her so she could pull it from her bag. With her eyes on him, she answered the call.

"Yes?"

"Eir? It's Mark. I didn't know who else to call." He sounded harried and stressed.

"Mark, just calm down."

At the sound of Mark's name, Mason's eyes narrowed, his nostrils flaring. She touched his cheek gently and turned around.

"What's the matter?"

"It's Mr. Adamsen. He's … he's not doing so well. Please, Eir, I need you to see him."

"Mark, surely there's someone else there, something the doctors can do."

"*Please.*"

She couldn't say no to someone in need. "I'm leaving now. I'll be there in a half an hour."

"Hurry."

The line went dead and she turned back around. The look on Mason's face made her stomach drop to her feet.

"Who was that?" he asked.

"Mark. Another nurse I work with sometimes. He's having a small crisis with one of his patients and needs my help."

"And this Mark guy …?" Mason pressed. Stepping closer, he cupped one hand possessively behind her neck, his thumb tracking over her pulse on the side of her throat.

"Is just a friend," she said with a smile. "You're cute when you're jealous," she added.

"I'm not jealous," he replied.

Eir leaned in and pressed her lips to his stubble-covered cheek. "Can you take me to the hospital?"

———

Eir couldn't stop her fingers drumming silently on the top of her thigh. The traffic was unbearably slow, and Mason got caught at every red light.

"Are you all right?" he asked, pulling to yet another stop.

"I'm fine … it's just …"

"What is it?" he asked, taking one hand off the wheel and resting it on her knee. She looked back out the window.

"I'm worried about Mark."

In the reflection, she saw one of his brows shoot up. "What did he say to you exactly?"

"It wasn't what he said—it was more his tone. He sounded so … desperate."

"I'm sure whatever it is, you'll be able to help."

When they pulled into the staff car park at Mass Gen, Eir looked up at the building, a feeling of trepidation weighing heavily on her.

"Maybe I should come in with you," Mason muttered.

"No, it's fine. I mean, what could possibly happen to me here? I'm perfectly safe."

"Still … how long do you think you'll be?"

"I'm not sure. An hour? Maybe two?"

Checking his watch, he said, "It's three o'clock now. How about I come back in an hour, and if you're going to be any longer, you can give me a call before then to let me know?"

She popped open the door. "That sounds good." Collecting her bag, she got out.

The passenger window wound down after Eir slammed the door, and Mason called out, "Everything will be okay, Eir. I know it."

She turned to wave goodbye before heading towards the entrance, anxiety gnawing at her gut.

Not two steps into reception, she found Mark there waiting. He took Eir's elbow firmly and steered her toward the elevators. He jabbed at the elevator button, his grip dimpling her skin.

She pulled out of his bruising hold. "Mark, tell me what's wrong."

His eyes darted to hers, but he didn't answer her until they were safely inside the elevator. She noticed then that his skin was a little paler than normal. She placed a hand on his forearm, letting herself feel what he was feeling.

Anxiety.

Fear.

Sorrow.

And all so potent. Pulling free from his grip, she stepped away from him.

"Mark, tell me what's happened."

He looked pained as he spoke. "It's Mr. Adamsen. He's … dying."

This news didn't surprise her.

"He was due to start his treatment on Monday."

"All right, but I'm not sure why I'm needed. You know there's nothing I can do. If it's fatal, it's fatal."

The elevator doors opened and Mark hustled her down the hallway towards oncology. When she stepped into the room, it was filled with people she had never seen before.

An older woman sat in a chair beside the bed, clutching Mr. Adamsen's hand. Another younger woman stood behind her, her hands resting on the older woman's shoulders.

A younger-looking version of Mr. Adamsen stepped forward and Eir surmised he was his son. "Who are you?" he asked, spitting the question at her, a look of hatred in his eyes.

"Mr. Adamsen, my name's Eir. I'm one of the nurses here at Mass Gen. Mark has asked me to come in and see your father."

Mr. Adamsen's eyes cut dangerously to Mark. "How is she going to help? Is she going to somehow make that … that damn *cancer* strangling his body disappear?"

"Mr. Adamsen, please," Eir started. "I've been consulted about your father's treatment before, so Mark asked me to come down."

"Can you cure his cancer?" he asked venomously. Eir tried not to take his words to heart. He was angry and frustrated and he was lashing out at anyone unfortunate enough to be in his path.

"No, sir, but—"

"Then there's no reason for you to be here." He stalked away, running his hands through his hair.

"Brian, please calm down. Think of your heart," the younger of the two women said, her pained expression telling Eir she had to be his wife. Mr. Adamsen's son looked up at the woman and touched her cheek gently.

"I'm sorry, Melody. I just …" His eyes darted to his father on the bed, and he ran his hand through his hair again. "I feel so damn helpless."

"I know you do, my love. But we have to let the doctors do what they do best and heal him." Melody's voice was steady and calm, and seemed to be having the desired effect on Brian's nerves.

"Can you take his father's pain away?" Mark asked into Eir's ear. She shivered at his close proximity, and for the first time his attention made her truly uncomfortable. She focused on Brian, silently asking for permission to approach his father. After a long, hard glare, he nodded slightly before lowering himself down into the only other free chair in the room.

Eir approached the bed cautiously, her eyes taking in the almost imperceptible rise and fall of the old man's fragile chest. It had barely been a day and a half since she'd last seen Mr. Adamsen, but he had deteriorated to a point where she wasn't sure what she could do for him anymore.

Flexing her hands into fists a few times, she reached out and pulled the sheet down a little and placed her hands on his chest. The immediate rush of pain pushed all the air from her lungs. She gasped, sucking in large gulps of air and trying to force her healing energy into him …

But it didn't work.

It seemed to be bouncing right back at her. His body was rejecting it. She tried again, even though she knew it wouldn't work. She couldn't force anyone to heal if their body wasn't willing to accept it.

Pulling back, she repositioned the sheet with shaking hands and stepped back from the bed.

"He's too far gone," she said softly. "I'm so sorry."

The shrill bark of alarms suddenly filled the room. Mark rushed towards the bed, checking the monitors and looking at Eir frantically. Another nurse bustled into the small room, shouldering past her. Moving to the wall to stay out of the way, she watched as two doctors and another nurse ran into the room.

Brian jumped up from his chair and marched towards to Eir. "What did you do to him?" he demanded, taking her forcefully by the arm.

"Brian, what are you doing?" Melody cried, her attention torn between her husband's actions and those of the doctors.

A heartbeat later, Brian released his fingers reluctantly, his eyes burning into Eir. Eir stepped away from him, rubbing at the red marks on her arm and trying to get her breathing back under control.

"Eir, can you please take his family out?" Mark asked from near the monitors, obviously unaware of the altercation that had just taken place.

Brian's face reddened. "I'm not going anywhere!" he yelled, rounding on Mark and moving to stand by his father's bed. Eir's eyes darted to Mark, looking for guidance.

"It's fine," Mark said. "Just take Melody and Mrs. Adamsen out to the waiting room. I'll bring them news as soon as I can."

She beckoned to the women to follow her. Walking numbly down the hallway, she showed them into the waiting room and asked if there was anything else they needed. When they were settled, she headed back to Mr. Adamsen's room.

The alarms had stopped ringing; all she could hear now was Brian yelling ferociously at the doctor. "Do something! Why are you all just standing around?"

"Mr. Adamsen, you have to understand," the doctor began, his tone pleading. "Your father has a DNR in place. We have strict instructions not to resuscitate him if his heart stops beating. This was your father's wish."

"He would never sign anything like that!" Brian roared, pacing the room like a caged lion.

"Mr. Adamsen, there really isn't anything we can do. It's a binding contract that we must honor."

Brian glowered at Mark, then at the doctor. His nostrils flared angrily, his mouth set into a thin, hard line. He looked ready to kill someone.

"Brian–" Eir began, drawing those blue eyes—those cold, angry blue eyes—to her face.

She shuddered and took a step away.

"I'm sorry," she said before leaving the room. Walking as fast as she could without actually running, she made it to the elevator and pushed the button. She felt as if she had just witnessed something private and meant only for the eyes of Mr. Adamsen's family.

At last the elevator arrived with a muted chime, and she was relieved to see it was empty. Stepping inside, she pressed the button on the panel. She could still hear Brian Adamsen's shouts from down the hall.

Looking down at her feet, Eir prayed the doors would shut immediately. She didn't know how much more she could take. Her wish was finally granted, the doors closing gradually—inch by excruciating inch—until they suddenly sprang open once more. Startled, she looked up to see a hand forcing the doors apart.

Brian Adamsen stormed into the elevator, the doors sliding shut without any hesitation this time. His eyes were wild with grief.

"Mr. Adamsen, I'm so sorry for your loss."

"I don't want your pity," he said, his fist coming out to punch at the emergency stop button. The car lurched to a stop, throwing her against the wall.

"This was your fault."

"Mr. Adamsen—" The words died on her tongue as his hands wrapped tight around her throat. She clawed desperately at her neck, trying to pry his fingers away, gulping for air as her vision went fuzzy around the edges.

She could feel his hot breath on her cheek as the world turned black, his closeness ensuring she could hear every single word. "You did this. Whatever you did to him caused his heart to stop."

Eir sucked in a shallow breath. "No … it was the cancer …" she gulped, her lungs beginning to burn. It was hopeless. He was too strong. She couldn't fade with the adrenaline pumping through her bloodstream, and not being able to reach her sword meant there was nothing more she could do … except …

Swinging her arm out wildly, she depressed nearly every button on the side panel, hoping to hit the emergency button again. The elevator started with a shudder and then came to a stop again almost immediately, the door opening within seconds onto the lower floor. Adamsen released her and she collapsed. Air rushed into her lungs, filling them almost painfully. She drew in gasp after gasp as a huge wave of relief washed over her.

Crumpled on the floor of the elevator, Eir hardly noticed her attacker leaving. The last thing she remembered was drifting off into unconsciousness, and she welcomed it.

32

With his leg bouncing up and down furiously, Mason's eyes were fixed on the door on the opposite side of the room, and had been fixed on that same damn door for the past hour.

Why hadn't they come out yet?

He looked up at the ceiling, as if all the answers would be revealed there. Fuck, he wished they would be. He had no idea what was happening, and it was driving him insane.

After dropping Eir off at the hospital, Mason had returned to his apartment to find Sophie collapsed on the living room floor, completely still and with foam caked around her mouth. He'd thought she was dead, but after feeling that she was still warm, he knew there was a chance that she could make it.

He'd scooped her up into his arms and carried her out to the car, sliding her onto the back seat and throwing a blanket over her barely moving form. Seeing her so helpless and not knowing what to do had been frightening.

Now he was the one feeling helpless. He'd arrived at the vet, they'd taken her into the back and he hadn't heard a peep since. He refused to let his mind wander to the worst-case scenario. Sophie would pull through this. She had to. He simply didn't know what he would do if she were to …

He couldn't even think the word.

Standing up, Mason began to pace around the vet's waiting room. His hands clenched into fists as he thought about just barreling into the surgery to find out what was happening. He would have to get past the nurse at reception first, of course. She looked over her half-moon glasses at him, as if she had heard his thoughts. He gave her a flat look and collapsed back into his chair.

Hours passed, or it could have been minutes. His grief was messing around with his head. It was the sound of his name that brought him around.

"Mr. White?"

He stood up instantly, approaching the vet, a middle-aged woman in a white coat.

"What's happening? How's Sophie?"

"Mr. White, we still don't know what's wrong. We've run a number of tests, but they have all come back inconclusive."

"So you don't know what's wrong with her at all?" he demanded.

"Not yet we don't. We still have a number of tests we can run, but I'd like to keep her overnight and hooked up to an IV to keep her hydrated."

Mason stared, almost zombie-like, at the doctor. "Do whatever tests you have to do. It doesn't matter how much it'll cost. She's worth every damn penny."

"Of course. We'll do everything we can for her." Her hand

came up to rest on Mason's shoulder briefly—awkwardly.

"Can I see her before I go?"

"Sure. If you'd like to follow me," she said, leading Mason through one of the doors behind the reception desk. They walked down a short hall before the vet stopped at another door and opened it. Mason followed, stepping into a room with cinderblock walls and a linoleum floor. Around the perimeter were metal cages, around half of them containing dogs in various stages of recovery. Despite the number of animals, it was oddly quiet.

Sophie was lying on her side in a cage. Her front left paw had been shaved to clear the way for an IV inserted into her vein. She didn't even lift her head up when he walked into the room.

Getting down onto his haunches, Mason crouched in front of her cage, wanting so badly to soothe her the way she had soothed him so many times in the last nine years. Somehow she had always known how to make him feel better, even if it was by just being there.

"If you like, you can open the door."

Mason looked up at the vet before doing exactly that. Sophie's eyes opened at the soft squeak of the metal hinge, but closed again quickly. Scooting a little closer, Mason reached in and stroked her back.

She whimpered at the touch, making Mason's heart clench tight in his chest. "Do you have any idea what's wrong with her?" he asked, his throat rasping out the words.

"Not yet. It could be a virus, or she could have eaten something she shouldn't have, or she could have been bitten by a spider or a snake. There're a number of things, and we just have to narrow it down, but that's going to take time."

He was so damn helpless.

"Is there anything you can do for her now, though?"

The vet stuck both hands into the pockets of her white coat. "She's comfortable for now. The IV is keeping her hydrated, and I've put some antibiotics through just as a precaution. But …"

"But?"

"There's nothing more we can do right now. I've sent her bloods off to the lab, but until they come back, I won't know how to treat her, other than to do what I'm already doing."

Mason looked back at Sophie, the labored rise and fall of her chest the only movement. He didn't want to leave her while she was suffering.

"Do you mind if I sit with her for a little while?"

The vet gave him a sympathetic look and retreated back through the door. Alone in the quiet room, with nothing but the occasional small whimper from one of the other dogs, Mason's thoughts caught up with him.

What would he do if Sophie died?

He knew it sounded stupid. She was just a dog. But she had been the one constant in his life for nearly nine years. She was his rock and the one thing that could calm him down when he was having a flashback. She could read him like no one in his life ever could.

So what would he do without her there when he woke up in the middle of the night, drenched in sweat and reliving the trauma?

What would he do when the feelings of guilt and hopelessness overwhelmed him?

Leaning back against the cage, Mason kept one hand on Sophie while his eyes slid shut. Damn, he was so tired. If he could just get a bit of sleep …

"Mr. White?" Mason woke with start when a light hand landed on his shoulder. Looking around in confusion, he blinked at the bright lights of the vet surgery. The vet was crouched beside him, her face a few inches away from Mason's.

He scrubbed the heel of his palm over his face. "What time is it?"

"Just after half past six. The surgery's closed and I'm afraid I'm going to have to ask you to leave." She looked at Sophie. "Don't worry about Sophie. We'll take good care of her."

"Will you be keeping an eye on her? Overnight, I mean?"

The vet pursed her lips. "We don't normally do that, but since she's really on the borderline, I'll be back in in a few hours to check on her."

Mason got to his feet; his legs tingling from being in the same position for so long. "Thank you. I'll come by first thing in the morning to see how she's going."

"No problem, Mr. White. I'll see you then."

Mason walked out into the cold night. His whole body felt numb. He had just reached his car when he felt a strong pull between his shoulderblades. His blood burned and hummed and then his body shook as he was thrown violently against the side of his car.

"Where were you?" Korvain asked in an icy drawl, his face so close they were sharing air, but Mason was too numb to be frightened. He felt as if he were floating, watching the scene from a distance, not really there.

He stared at Korvain, waiting. The air seemed to thicken as the Mare drew the shadows in around them. His eyes grew darker and darker, until Mason was left staring into bottomless, cold orbs of blackness.

"Where is she?" Korvain's voice was hostile and rolling with menace. "Where. Is. Eir?" he demanded, every single word enunciated carefully.

Eir.

That one word brought Mason out of his haze.

Eir.

"She said you were going to bring her home today after lunch."

Eir.

Lunch.

Dropped her at the hospital.

Promised to be back there within an hour.

"Fuck," he said. He had to get to the hospital. Eir was waiting for him. Mason pulled at the handle of the door, wondering why the door wouldn't budge. Looking up, he saw that Korvain had his meaty fist planted against the top of the door.

"Where is she?"

"I had to drop her off at the hospital a couple of hours ago. She got a frantic phone call from one of her colleagues, asking her to come to the hospital, asking her to help him with something."

His lips twisted into a snarl. "Two hours ago?"

Mason looked away, suddenly ashamed. It was actually closer to four hours. "I was supposed to pick her up after an hour unless I heard differently from her."

"And you didn't, I take it?"

Mason dipped his fingers into the front pocket of his jeans and retrieved his phone. A blank screen greeted him. "My phone's dead."

Korvain cursed and, reaching past Mason, opened the car door. He shoved Mason inside, then materialized next to him in the passenger seat.

"Drive."

———

By the time they reached the hospital, Mason was in a cold sweat. He couldn't afford to lose Eir as well as Sophie in the same day. Korvain had kept grumbling under his breath about what would happen to him if Darrion had got his hands on her. Mason prayed to a God he didn't believe in that she would still be there when they arrived.

As soon as he had parked the car, he was out of it and running towards the hospital doors, Korvain following silently behind him. Mason made a beeline for reception, slamming his palms down on the desk when he got there. The young woman looked up, startled. Her eyes soon found Korvain, though, and instead of paling with fear like any normal person would, she actually blushed.

"I'm looking for Eir," Mason said. The girl looked back at him reluctantly. "Ah, give me a moment to see whether she's come back from her CT."

CT? What the fuck had happened to her?

Biting his tongue, he waited for her to explain. Korvain wasn't so patient.

"What room is she in?"

The young girl's eyes widened at the ferocity in his voice.

"Second floor. Room twenty thirty-eight."

Korvain walked off to the elevators, leaving Mason to follow like a fucking puppy. Inside the elevator, the lights dimmed as Korvain's anger grew, the air thickening to a point where Mason began struggling to breathe.

The doors sprung open and Korvain stalked out into the busy corridor. Every single set of eyes turned to him as he passed. Mason followed behind him again, looking at the room numbers as he went by them.

Twenty twenty-six.

Twenty twenty-eight.

Twenty thirty.

Up ahead, Korvain disappeared into a room.

As Mason caught up and stepped through the doorway, he had no idea what to expect. Would Eir be all right? What had happened to her in the time that he'd left her at the hospital?

Korvain was bent over the bed in the center of the room. His shoulders were so wide that Mason could only see Eir's blanket-covered legs sticking out the end.

"Are you all right? What happened to you?" Korvain was asking gently.

"What are you doing here?" Eir asked him in a scratchy voice. "How did you know this was where I was?"

Korvain stared menacingly over his shoulder at Mason. When he turned back to Eir, he said, "Mason told me he dropped you off here."

"Is he here?" she asked, her voice spiking with what sounded like excitement.

Korvain growled but stood to one side as Mason answered. "I'm here."

She was pale—her normally golden skin looking lackluster under the harsh clinical light. She was dressed in a hospital gown and looked incredibly uncomfortable in it, tugging at the white cotton sheet to cover her chest, but her delicate neck was exposed—and all around it there were long, dark, finger-sized bruises.

Pushing his anger deep down within him, Mason mentally counted to ten and breathed out.

"What happened to you?" Walking to the side of the bed, he took one of her hands. She was warm and he felt calmer for touching her.

"It was nothing."

"Those bruises around your neck don't look like nothing," Korvain said darkly.

Eir's eyes flickered to him before gravitating back to Mason. "It was a dying patient's son. He was upset that there was nothing we could do to help his father when his heart gave out. Mr. Adamsen had a DNR in place, and we have to respect those wishes. His son didn't take that so well, I guess." Eir's eyes dropped to the hand Mason was gently cradling and her fingers curled around his.

"I left the room to give the family some time to grieve." She looked at Mason once more. "I was in the elevator. He slipped in at the last minute and pushed the emergency stop button. I tried to give him my condolences, but he said that it was my fault."

"How could that have been?" Mason asked, gently running his thumb across her knuckles.

"I had tried to take away his father's pain, but his body was rejecting it. There was nothing more I could have done for him."

"So the bastard blamed you for trying to help his father?" Korvain asked, his jaw bulging.

"Yes. I tried to reach my sword, but his hands were wrapped entirely around my throat. I think I managed to hit the emergency button again, because the doors sprang open and he walked away. That's the last thing I remember. When I woke up, I was in this bed … I don't even know how long I've been here."

"Not more than a couple of hours," someone said from the doorway. Mason looked up to see a man in a white coat enter the room. Embroidered above his chest pocket was the name *Samuel Bridges, MD* in black thread.

The doctor approached the bed warily, guardedly studying Korvain. The Mare stepped away and the doctor stared down at Eir. "How are you feeling?"

"Fine, other than a sore throat."

"The sore throat shouldn't last more than a few days. I have the results of your CT. Everything is fine—no concussion from that bump on the head you took." His eyes went first to Mason, then to Korvain. "So if these two men are here to escort you home, I'll get your discharge papers in order."

"Thank you, Doctor Bridges."

The doctor bobbed his head, giving Mason a smile then Korvain a nervous look before leaving the room.

"Mason, can you pass me my clothes, please?" Eir asked, pointing to the chair behind him. As Mason handed her the dark blue dress and matching lace bra their eyes locked, their fingers touching.

Korvain cleared his throat noisily, breaking their moment. Mason glanced at the Mare briefly before turning back to Eir.

"We'll let you have some privacy."

Korvain pushed off the wall as Mason walked around the bed.

"Mason?" Eir asked softly.

"Yeah?"

"Would you stay, please? I'm … too afraid to be on my own just yet." Korvain huffed impatiently. "I'll be waiting outside," he announced, pulling open the door and stepping out into the hallway.

Mason watched him go and was still facing the door when he said, "Okay, but I'll keep my back turned."

Fuck, was that his voice? He had some serious gravel going on.

The hospital bed creaked as she slid off the mattress, the whisper of clothes on skin following soon after.

"All right, you can turn around now," she said.

Mason spun around—quite possibly a little too eagerly—and swallowed. She looked every inch the goddess that she was. Then he saw those bruises again and the anger threatened to take over.

He closed his eyes and counted to ten once more. It was at a time like this that Sophie was needed.

Closing the distance between them, Mason gently slid his fingers over each and every purple mark.

"I'm fine," she told him, touching his hand.

She was far from fine, but Mason dropped his hand, pressed a kiss to her forehead and pulled away.

"We should go. You must be tired after your ordeal."

She bowed her head. "You're right. Take me home?"

Tugging at her hand, he led her from the room, meeting Korvain out in the hall.

"Are you ready?" Korvain asked, placing a hand on the small of Eir's back and leading her back towards the elevators.

"I have to sign the discharge papers," she said.

"It's already taken care of. I just want to get you home," Korvain told her, almost curling his body around hers as they walked. This rubbed Mason up the wrong way, but he realized Korvain was definitely the right person to be looking out for her. Obviously he couldn't be trusted to do the job himself. He'd had no idea she was in trouble. He'd been so absorbed by Sophie that nothing else had mattered.

Mason trailed them out the front door and started to head for his car, but Korvain stopped him.

"I'm going to fade back with her so you can't fuck it up again. Get straight to work when you get to the club. I'll take care of Eir."

The words stung, but Mason nodded and unlocked his car. As he watched them fade from sight, he sighed. What the fuck was he doing getting further involved in their world?

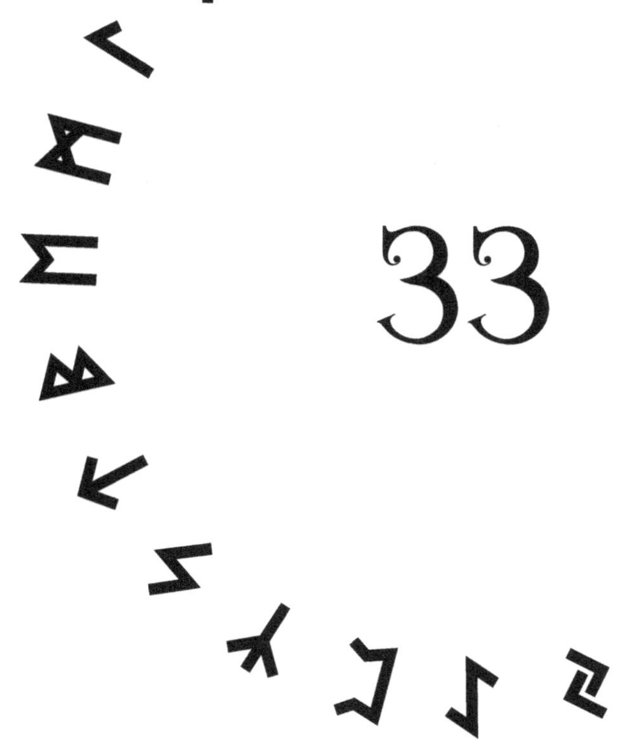

33

Taer shrugged into the holster that would house her Beretta, feeling the loss of the katana she'd had in her possession only briefly. And thinking about the steel made her remember—with startling, erotic clarity—what had happened between her and Aubrey. It turned out that her promise to herself meant pretty much nothing, because as soon as his lips had touched hers, she had wanted him.

Still wanted him.

"Get your head in the fucking game," she told herself, sliding her weapon into the holster under her arm. Picking up her jacket from the bed, Taer stormed out of the apartment and rode the elevator down, her teeth grinding the entire time.

Once she was outside in the alleyway, Taer pulled out the card Aubrey had given her with the two addresses scrawled on the back. Neither of them were that far from where she, Korvain and Adrian had lived before.

Closing her eyes, she felt the pull of her fade. The air shivered and the next moment she was standing opposite the ruin of her former house. It had been a month since she had been there, but it felt like yesterday.

The battered chain-link fence running along one side of the driveway was slightly charred from the ferocity of the fire, but the neighboring house had escaped the flames. It looked as if someone had bought the cursed land and was building again because earthmovers were in place—monstrous, empty and silent in the darkness.

Sighing, Taer turned her back on what had been her home and started in the direction of the first address, only four blocks away. Looking up at the building, Taer searched for any indication that it had been warded. Darrion's paranoia wouldn't have allowed him to stay anywhere unprotected, so there had to be something.

The house itself looked just like all the others in the street. Two storys high, with tired yellow paint flaking off the siding, the front porch railings leaning precariously off the edge. The whole structure looked about ready to fall. Some of the windows had been broken, the contents of the house probably already stolen and sold for drug money.

She inspected the doorframe closely, only noticing the protective rune carved into the wood once she had rubbed some of the dirt away. It was a crude spell, but it meant Taer couldn't fade in.

Checking over her shoulder to make sure there was nobody else around, she grasped the handle and forced the door open. A bell chimed inside, but other than that, there was no sound. Once inside, she pushed the door until it was just closed, but not on the catch. Her eyes swiveled around, taking in the ruined furniture and the rubbish all over the floor. It looked as if squatters had already moved in.

Gripping her Beretta, she flipped off the safety and moved through the lower level before taking the stairs up to the second floor. In each of the rooms, there was more evidence of humans squatting there—including a lot of drug paraphernalia.

She was in the final bedroom at the end of the hall when her pocket began to vibrate. It was a text message from Aubrey. *War Hammer* was all it said. Taer deleted the message and shoved her phone away.

Taer made her way down the stairs. She was whisper-quiet on the treads, keeping her ears pricked and her eyes moving. Darrion hadn't used this place in a long time it seemed. Pulling open the door carefully, she slipped outside onto the front porch and looked around the street.

Nothing was moving.

Taer holstered her Beretta and faded to the War Hammer, looking up at the building with trepidation when she got there. She pushed against the door and into the bar. As soon as Taer stepped into the dim space, all eyes were on her, just like her last visit—but this time none of them had a predatory gleam. She grinned inwardly, striding past the gods and goddesses, elves and dwarves, all sitting around and drinking.

Her eyes snagged on the same Mare who had confronted her before. The asshole. His gaze dropped as soon as their eyes met. It was another set of eyes that caught and held her attention.

Gray ice.

Haunting.

Taer lifted her face towards Aubrey, who was sitting at his booth in the back. The low lights did nothing to hide his other-worldly beauty, nor could they hide the danger and sexual electricity that oozed from his body. Longing shot through her unbidden as she gazed at him.

Aubrey's upper lip twitched in amusement, his fingers casually drumming on the tabletop. Taer felt as if she was rooted to the spot, her body warring with her head. She should have just ignored his demand that she come and see him. She was about to flip him off and stomp out of there until she saw what was resting on top of the table.

Pushing her shoulders back, she walked toward him, stopping a dozen feet away. "What do you want?" she asked, her eyes on the katana laid across the table as his long fingers caressed the scabbard.

"What a dangerous question," he drawled. Her eyes shot back to his, finding amusement dancing in those gray-ice depths. "To give you back what's rightfully yours," he eventually added, his voice a silken caress.

"I don't want it," she lied, her eyes dropping down to the steel and lingering there. When she looked up, Aubrey's expression had darkened, his eyes the color of lead. He stood up abruptly, scooping up the katana as he did, and advanced on her. Every inch of his body told of his lethality, and yet Taer held her ground.

"I made a mistake yesterday," he said with a sigh. "I had no right to kiss you like that. It won't happen again until you ask me to." He moved even closer to her, whispering, "And I won't fuck you until you beg me to, so think of this as an apology. Please."

Taer looked down at the blade. She could feel the call of the steel. She didn't want to be indebted to him in any way, but the sword was a part of her now—not something she desired but something she needed. She wrapped her hands around the peg and the scabbard, accepting both the gift and his apology. Aubrey's mouth lifted into a satisfied smirk before he turned away and sat back down again.

"This doesn't change anything between us, you know, Aubrey,"

Taer said, taking a few steps forward to set the katana down on the table. "You're training me. That's all."

He shrugged lazily. "If you say so," he replied. "But since you're here, I've also got something else for you."

"Unless you can tell me where Darrion is, I don't need anything else from you."

"It's something of mine I've seen you admire." From under the table, he pulled out a book and laid it on the table. Taer leaned forward to read the title.

Pride and fucking *Prejudice.*

"Is this some kind of joke?" Aubrey looked affronted, and she would have taken him seriously if it weren't for that slight curl to his top lip.

"A joke?" he asked.

She reached for the book, but Aubrey was faster, slipping the hardback away from her. She huffed under her breath, looking around to see who else was watching their little exchange.

"No, this isn't a joke, Winter Fox." His voice was quiet, but the amusement was still there, in his eyes, in his voice. "Everyone should read the classics."

"Look, I didn't come down here for this shit, Aubrey. You wanted to apologize? You did it." Picking up the katana, Taer turned to leave.

"There's something else you need from me, though, isn't there?"

She turned back to him. "Fuck you."

He laughed at her outraged expression and she turned to stalk away. "Ask me what you need to know, Taer," Aubrey called out after her.

"What would it cost me this time?" she replied hotly, despising the way she'd been forced to turn to him once more. But what choice did she have? Korvain wouldn't tell her what she needed to know, and there was nobody else who could possibly know what she was going through.

He leaned forward, his elbows resting on the table. "Sit down, Winter Fox." His tone was more serious now.

Sliding into the booth, Taer kept her eyes trained on Aubrey. She stayed like that for a few minutes, silent, waiting for the simmering of her rage to die down.

"Are you going to ask me the question you have poised on that distracting tongue of yours?"

The mention of her tongue made Taer's mind flash back to that kiss, the way that his tongue had moved, the way his body had felt against hers. She exhaled deeply, angry with herself for allowing him to kiss her in the first place. "What do you know about breaking through mental shields?"

His lip quirked up slightly. "Now, why would I know about anything like that?"

Her hands curled around the katana beneath the table. "Just a hunch," she replied, matching his nonchalant tone.

He laughed, throwing his head back. "I like you, Winter Fox," he said when his laughter died down. "I like you a lot. Do you want to know why?"

She shook her head.

"I like you because even though you pretend to hate me, deep down you can't stay away from me. So you make up little stories and lies so you can come and see me once more."

"You were the one to ask me down here," she bristled.

"True," he conceded, "but you didn't have to come." He leaned back again, stretching out his legs, brushing past Taer's thighs. She slid her body away, frowning.

"I think you find my ego irresistible," he said.

Taer snorted and looked away, her eyes landing on the cover of his book. "So, what's the book about?"

"A strong-minded young woman bullied by society into finding a wealthy husband."

Really? "I wouldn't have pegged you for a chick-lit lover."

Aubrey touched the cover fondly. "Ms Austen is quite the storyteller."

"How does it end?"

Aubrey slid the book over to her. "Read it and find out."

Taer let her fingers glide over the worn fabric cover. There was no noise, except for the quiet murmurs of other patrons. "Are you going to answer my question?" she asked reluctantly.

Aubrey sighed. "To break someone's mental shield, especially a trained Mare's shield, is perhaps the most difficult thing there is to do."

"But it is possible."

Stiffly, he said, "Of course."

Taer licked her lips, feeling the flicker of hope sparking. "How?" she asked.

His gaze bored into hers. "Everyone fears something, Winter Fox. Even a Walker." He sighed. "Come back to me tomorrow night. I have someone I want you to meet."

34

Mason's hands tightened on the wheel as he made the short drive back to the club from the hospital. Even though it was barely a six-mile trip, it was more than enough time for Mason to play and replay Korvain's words in his head.

I'm going to fade back with her so you can't fuck it up again.

Again.

Goddamn him, but Korvain was right.

I'll take care of Eir.

He pulled down the side alley to park behind the club, bringing his car to a stop beside Bryn's SUV. Putting it into park, he popped open his door, letting the cool, crisp air swirl inside. He breathed it in, letting it blow away some of his anger and frustration.

He had no right to be pissed at Korvain. The Mare was just trying to protect the Valkyries, but Mason felt like *he* should have been the one to look out for Eir. He had never felt this strongly about a woman, never felt an intimacy so intense. He felt as if he could finally be whole with Eir in his life—but already he had let her down, seen her hurt. He wasn't strong enough to protect her.

With a sigh, he hauled himself out of his car, his eyes downcast … which was why he didn't see Korvain coming. One minute, Mason was upright and breathing, and the next he was kissing the asphalt, struggling to suck in enough oxygen and nursing a pain in his stomach from a punch he thought had bruised his internal organs.

Hot breath steamed onto his face, and Mason opened his eyes, finding himself nose to nose with Korvain. Korvain bared his fangs before speaking in a low, controlled voice. "You are not to see Eir anymore."

The shadows around them darkened perceptibly with Korvain's building rage. And with that, any reply Mason could have given died on his tongue. Even though it would kill him, Mason knew Korvain was right. He would only hurt Eir more if he stayed in her life, and he couldn't stomach the idea of her coming to any more harm.

"Am I making myself clear?" Korvain asked. His voice was calm, but the shadows around them grew darker.

Mason agreed stiffly. The Mare stepped back, staring down at him, his arms held close to his sides, his hands curled into tight fists.

"You're not going to fight me on this?" he asked incredulously.

Carefully, Mason sat up, propping himself up against the car. Peering up at the Mare, Mason replied, "Do you expect me to?" He sighed. "Look, I get it, all right? I've fucked up my one and only chance with her, and I knew I only had one shot. So you're right. I'm going to stay away from her."

Korvain stared at him, his eyes boring into Mason's skull.

"You're serious?" he asked.

Mason didn't break his gaze. Korvain's shoulders relaxed and he held out a hand to haul Mason to his feet.

"I respect you, Mason," Korvain said, leaning in close, "but if you'd told me to fuck off just now, I was going to put a bullet in your brain, and I really didn't want to do that."

Mason stopped breathing for a few seconds and only drew breath when his lungs began to burn. Korvain stepped away. "I expect you on the floor in five minutes."

Four and a half minutes later, Mason was standing in front of the stairway to the upper levels of the club. His face was blank, his hands crossed in front of his body, but he kept his eyes moving, scanning the crowd, as he listened to the thoughts of the gods and goddesses drinking at the club that night.

Over five hours had passed and Darrion hadn't been mentioned once by anyone. Mason was starting to think the bastard was a ghost, and Korvain was just chasing his tail trying to find him.

"Everything all right, Boss?"

Mason turned towards the voice. Sam, one of the younger bouncers at the club, was staring at him curiously. He couldn't have been older than twenty-three at the most, but Mason knew for a fact he was a good guy. Hell, he had hand-selected him. He had seen something in him that reminded him of his brother.

"Yeah. I'm good." Mason paused, wanting to take the focus off himself. He didn't want to talk about personal shit at work. "I had something on I couldn't miss." *Fuck, I said too much.* "Don't you have somewhere to be?" he asked impatiently, his eyes making their way back to the crowd. That was when he noticed Bryn walking towards her office. Turning back to Sam, he said, "Actually, stay here. I need to speak to Bryn for a moment."

Mason strode off before the younger man could answer,

catching up to Bryn in the hallway. The Valkyrie stopped when she heard the door close behind her, looking back.

"Mason?" she asked. "What's the matter?"

"I need to speak to you." The words were barely audible over the pounding of blood in his ears.

"About what? I'm kind of busy."

"I just wanted to say I'm sorry … about Eir. I shouldn't have let it happen. It's my fault."

Bryn's expression softened. "It's fine, Mason. She's all right now, maybe just a little shaken up, but she'll recover. Believe me, she's been through worse."

Mason wanted to say more, but now wasn't the time. Bryn saw him hesitate.

"Was there something else you needed?" she asked.

Shaking his head, Mason said, "No." He retreated back into the club, knowing that he needed to drown himself in running the club's security just so he could stop thinking about Eir and Sophie and everything else that was fucked up in his life.

35

An Nasiriyah, Iraq—2003

The sound of the blast was still ringing in Mason's ears. The high-pitched buzzing was intermittently drowned out by shouting, but Mason couldn't focus on what the words were. His face was covered in dust. He could feel the grittiness of it even under his eyelids, in his mouth, under his tongue.

Something hot was running down the back of his neck into his shirt, and down the side of his face, and his first thought was that it was his blood. There was no other explanation. Lifting his hand up to feel the wound felt like a near impossible feat, but somehow he did it.

He sucked in sharply, the stab of pain confirming what he already knew—he had taken a blow to the back of the head, and as his fingers probed the gash for shrapnel, he let his eyes survey the damage around him.

Jagged slabs of collapsed brick wall and rubble were everywhere. Red dust covered what remained of the partly caved in walls and roof. He'd been with three other marines, but he couldn't get a visual on them through the suffocating dust. As his hearing gradually came back, Mason could hear the sharp *crack*, *crack*, *crack* of automatic gunfire coming from the street, could hear the yells in the distance.

Blinking, still dumbstruck by what had happened, he forced his brain to snap into action. He had been trained for situations like this. He knew what to do. Mason bent his legs, inspecting them to see whether there was any other serious damage that would prevent him getting back on his feet and getting to fucking work.

When he couldn't feel any pain, he got up on shaky legs, holding himself up against what was left of the wall he'd been thrown back against. Looking down, he saw the blood on his hands and on the floor.

Fuck.

With his hearing finally cleared, Mason was able to home in on where a cry for help was coming from. A few yards away, he could see a pair of boots sticking out from underneath some debris. Staggering over to them, he hauled the steel bar and crude bricks off, tossing them aside and getting his first good look at the marine on the ground.

It was Shane, the guy who had been standing behind him. Mason felt the adrenaline hit his bloodstream as all his training fully kicked in. He did a quick inventory of Shane's injuries, noting the blood trickling from a cut above his eye and the strange angle of his arm.

"I'm going to get you out, Shane," Mason told him. He just had no fucking idea how that was going to happen. From the noise outside, it sounded as if their whole platoon had been ambushed and was now under attack. They needed an evac. Mason grunted as he lifted a tangled mess of metal and bricks off Shane's legs. Shane looked up at him, dust covering his skin, blood still streaming down one side of his face.

"How are the others?" Shane asked, spitting out blood after he spoke. The red stain immediately soaked into the sand and dirt.

"I don't know. I've only just come to myself."

"Mase, you need to check on them. I'll be fine."

Mason wiped away some of the blood and sweat from his face with his arm, desperately looking around them. He had no fucking idea where to look. All he could see was dust, broken chunks of red brick and twisted reinforced steel.

Turning back to Shane, Mason asked, "Is your radio still working?"

Using his undamaged arm, Shane checked over his equipment. "I think so."

"Call in an evac."

Over the crackle of static and Shane's low voice, a muffled moan came from the far end of the ruined room. Mason took a few steps toward the sound, coming upon a bloody arm. As he got closer he saw that the arm belonged to Derek, but he clearly hadn't been the one moaning. Derek's sightless eyes stared up at him, a large hole in his chest exposing his rib cage and shredded internal organs.

"Mason? Who is it? Are they okay?" Shane asked from across the room.

"Derek didn't make it," he rasped back after a moment. "He's gone."

"Fuck."

Mason forced his eyes away, concentrating on what was really important. There was still one more person in that room with them.

He looked around, attempting to filter out the external noise, and strained his ears to pick up the slightest sound. He was rewarded half a minute later when those stifled moans he had mistaken for Derek came again. Listening hard, he followed the sound to a place where one solid section of wall had fallen, crushing his brother's body.

Mason dropped to his knees beside his brother's head—the only part of his body still exposed.

"Hunter," Mason said, his heart in his throat. Hunter's eyes were shut, but at the sound of Mason's voice, they fluttered open.

"Mase?" he asked, his voice thready. Mason looked down the length of brick wall hopelessly, unable to see how Hunter was going to survive.

"You're bleeding," Hunter said, jerking Mason's gaze back to his brother's face. The edge of the wall was just below his collarbones, but he didn't even seem to notice.

Mason touched the side of his face. "Just a scratch."

"How are the others? Did they make it?"

Mason looked over his shoulder, first at Shane and then at Derek. "Yeah, they both made it," he lied. "And you're going to make it too."

Hunter began to cough, great racking hacks that seemed to shake his entire body. Blood bubbled up from his throat, spilling out of the corner of his mouth. Scarlet fingers ran down his cheek, dribbling onto the floor beneath his head.

Mason knew his brother was drowning in his own blood, his lungs filling up with each shallow breath he sucked in. Mason rested a hand on his shoulder, praying he wasn't hurting him in any way.

"The evac will be here soon, Hunter. Just hang on, all right?"

His brother grimaced, blood staining his teeth. "We both know that's not going to happen, Mason."

Mason's throat began to burn and his eyes stung. Roughly, he wiped the first tears away with the back of his hand. "Don't give up on me, Hunter. You're going to make it through this. Five more minutes, max, and we'll have you on your way to the hospital … Hell, maybe they'll even send you home, you lucky prick."

Mason forced a smile onto his lips even though his heart was breaking. He was supposed to be looking out for his baby brother, not preparing him to die. If only he'd taken his position in the line, then it would have been Mason under the slab of bricks and twisted steel with Hunter comforting him with hollow words and empty promises.

A nearby explosion rocked the building, sending small plumes of dust into the air once more. They were vulnerable just sitting there holding their dicks and waiting for an evac. Mason stood up and looked around for a weapon, finding his M4 buried under the rubble beside the pool of his blood. Slinging the rifle over his shoulder and positioning it between his shoulderblades, he turned to his brother. "I need to make sure our location is still secure, okay? Just hang in there."

There was a large hole in the wall, and standing to one side of it, Mason searched the short stretch of dirt road between them and the building beside them, trying to get some idea of what was happening. The sound of gunfire being hurled back and forth was irregularly broken up by eardrum-shattering IED explosions. Mason crept forward a little more, trying to get eyes on anyone from his platoon, but he couldn't see the main road. If they were trapped inside the town, their only hope was getting lifted out of there.

"Where's that goddamn helicopter?" Mason said under his breath, raising his eyes up to the sky. The cloud of smoke and dust had dissipated, leaving them wide open to further attack. Peeling away from the wall, Mason walked back over to his brother. As he approached, Hunter began coughing, worse than before. Blood foamed from his mouth, creeping down his chin in a fresh wash of red. Mason crouched down, gripping his brother's shoulder. Hunter's face was ashen, his skin clammy.

He wasn't going to make it. Even if the medics got there in time, there was no way they could lift the weight of the wall and expect him to survive. In some sick way, that hunk of clay, sand and mortar was keeping him alive.

"Mason?" Hunter said, his voice low and weak. "It's all right, you know."

Mason frowned. "What is?"

"I'm going to die. I know it. You know it. The medics will know it as soon as they get a look at me … And that's okay."

Fresh tears stung Mason's eyes. "Don't talk like that, Hunter."

His brother laughed, which only made him cough even harder. Mason laid his hand on Hunter's forehead in an effort to soothe him.

There was a sudden noise, and Mason's heart kicked up a notch as he spun around, aiming his M4 at whoever was about to come through what was left of the doorway.

Tense seconds passed, his skin twitching. He stayed there for what felt like a lifetime, weapon aimed, heart beating erratically, before he realized he was hearing things.

Nobody was coming.

He turned back to Hunter, expecting him to make a joke about his big brother being too fucking jumpy for a marine. Instead, Hunter's unseeing eyes stared up at the busted-open ceiling above him. He had died, and Mason hadn't even seen him take his last breath.

———————

Mason had laid awake all night thinking about everything that had happened to him in his life … starting with his brother's death. He had carried the guilt of not taking better care of him on his shoulders for ten years, and the wound still felt just as raw as ever.

And then there was Sophie. Not having her there, being without the familiar weight and heat of her body against him while he slept, felt truly alien to him.

He checked the clock, seeing there were still another four hours before he could go and see how his girl was doing. Four fucking hours to sit and stew over all the mistakes he'd made in his life.

And now he could add leaving Eir alone to that ever growing list. She'd been hurt and he'd inadvertently been the one to let it happen. When his brother had died he'd felt helpless, and he'd hated it. He had never wanted to feel that sense of hopelessness ever again. But yesterday, he had. And now there was no coming back.

Knowing that he wouldn't be getting any rest, Mason rolled off the bed and pulled on his sweats. If he couldn't sleep, he'd run his body into oblivion.

Out in the cold early morning, the crisp air cleared away some of the cobwebs, but the niggling fear that Sophie wouldn't pull through this okay was still there.

After running for three hours, Mason returned to his apartment with sweat soaking his clothing and running from his face. He showered and dressed in record time, snatching up his keys and jogging downstairs to his car. The vet's office would be opening in half an hour and he wanted to be there first thing.

Mason had been pacing the parking lot for a quarter of an hour and was waiting at the door when the vet's assistant flipped the 'closed' sign around to 'open'. He reached for the handle as he heard the final *snick* of the lock and walked straight in.

"How is she?" he blurted out. Thankfully, it was the same woman who had been working the day before and she recognized Mason. He didn't know what he might have done if she'd played twenty questions with him.

"Mr. White," she said gently. "Doctor Greyson has only just arrived. She was here for most of the night, but had to return home to get some sleep."

Mason bobbed his head to show he was listening.

"If you'd like to take a seat, though, Doctor Greyson will come out and collect you in a few moments."

Mason wanted to demand he see Sophie right away, but the stern look on her face made him stop. Instead, he collapsed into one of the waiting room chairs, his foot tapping impatiently on the floor.

A few minutes later, Doctor Greyson appeared from the back rooms and Mason stood to greet her. From the look on her face, Mason knew he wouldn't like what she was going to say.

His mouth went dry. "How is she?" he croaked.

The vet looked grave. "I'm sorry to have to tell you this, Mr. White, but Sophie passed away in the early hours of this morning."

After staggering back a few steps, Mason dropped back into his chair. Sophie was dead? *His* Sophie? No, this couldn't possibly be happening. Mason was vaguely aware that Doctor Greyson had lowered herself into the chair beside him.

"I'm so sorry for your loss."

Mason stared at her numbly. This was his fault. He should have been more vigilant about what Sophie was eating. He should have noticed something was wrong before she'd even gotten sick.

"Can I go and see her?"

The doctor shared a look with the nurse, who had heard the entire sad conversation. "Sure you can."

Doctor Greyson led him through into the back rooms. Everything looked the same as it had the previous night, but everything was so very different.

Mason looked down at the cage Sophie had been in, expecting to see her still lying there, but it was empty.

"I've moved her into another room."

Mason followed the vet into yet another room, this one tiled floor to ceiling in stark white. Metal trolleys with surgical tools were arranged around the perimeter of the room, and a large surgical light was positioned over a stainless steel table in the center. A sheet had been draped over a body on the slab and Mason knew it was Sophie without having to ask.

He approached the operating table reluctantly, hardly breathing. Reaching out his hand, he pulled the white sheet down, revealing Sophie's head and shoulders. Her eyes were shut and she looked as if she was just sleeping peacefully.

Running the back of his fingers along her muzzle, he so badly wanted her to be warm, wanted her to sit up and lick his fingers like she always did.

But she was cold.

A drop of moisture fell onto the back of his hand, and he scrubbed away the other tears pooling in his eyes. He didn't know what he would do now. Whenever his anxiety hit, Sophie had always been there to help him calm down again.

And now she was gone.

He was alone with his memories, with his dreams, with his fears.

"Was she in any pain?" he asked almost inaudibly.

Doctor Greyson shifted behind him. "She had been in some pain earlier in the evening, and I'd given her something to make her more comfortable, so no, I don't believe she was in any pain when she passed."

Mason was thankful for that. "Good. That's good ..." He paused. "What's going to happen to her body?"

"That was something I wanted to discuss with you. You have two choices, really. You can have her cremated and have her ashes returned to you, or, if you'd prefer, I can call in a service that we use to dispose of the body in a respectful way."

For Mason there was only one acceptable option. "I'd like to have her ashes."

"Okay. I'll have the nurse organize that service for you."

Mason reached out and unhooked the chain collar around Sophie's neck and let the links fall into his jacket pocket with a gentle *chink*.

"Is there anything else I need to do here?" he asked. "Anything I have to sign?"

"The nurse will help you with all of that. Would you like a few more moments with Sophie?"

Mason shook his head. "No. I think I'm done here. I have to get to work, anyway." He turned around and stretched out his hand toward Doctor Greyson. "Thanks for everything you've done for Sophie. I really appreciate it."

The vet shook Mason's hand. "I truly am sorry, Mr. White. I can see she was a much loved part of your family."

Mason left the vet surgery in a kind of daze. Signing all that paperwork had made everything seem so final, so permanent. In the space of twenty-four hours, his whole life had changed. He had somehow won and lost Eir, he had lost his best friend, and now he was going to quit the job that had once saved his life.

What did he have to live for?

Nothing.

At.

All.

———

Half an hour later, Mason pulled his car into the rear car park, taking his usual spot beside Bryn's SUV, and let himself in through the back door. The place was quiet, as he'd expected, except for the rapid tapping of fingers on a keyboard coming from Bryn's office.

He knocked gently, waiting until Bryn gave the okay to enter. She was sitting behind her desk, focused on one of the computer screens in front of her. Mason cleared his throat, and the Valkyrie's eyes lifted to his face.

"Mase? What's up?" she asked before her gaze settled back on the screen. Mason let out a breath and sank into the chair opposite her desk.

"I needed to talk to you about something, Bryn."

"All right," she replied, distracted.

"And it's kind of important."

It was either his tone or the words, but Bryn stopped typing and sat further back into her seat. Her attention was on him now, and even though that was what he had wanted, he squirmed under her scrutiny.

"What's so important, Mason?"

He met her intense gaze. "I'm sorry to do this to you, Bryn. Believe me when I say that I don't want to say what I'm about to say to you."

"Mason, you're scaring me," Bryn said. "Tell me what's going on. Please."

"I'm sorry, but I'm going to have to hand in my notice … effective immediately."

Bryn frowned. "Why are you doing this, Mason? What's happened? Does this have something to do with what happened to Eir?"

Mason dropped his eyes to the desk. "Not entirely."

"Are you not happy here?"

His eyes darted back to Bryn. "Of course I'm happy here. Bryn, you and the club are my life."

"So, why are you leaving us, leaving me?"

Christ. "I'm not," he replied. "I wouldn't."

Bryn stared at him for a long minute before asking, "Mason, do you remember the day we met?" He nodded. "You were this close," she showed him her thumb and index finger, less than a quarter of an inch from each other, "to ending your own life."

Fuck, how had she known that?

"And don't even try to deny it. Mav told me all about what she felt off you that day. What I want to know is *why*. What's happened? Because I'm not letting you just walk out of here without giving me a good reason. I simply won't let you drop off the face of the planet and out of my life."

She got up and walked around to sit on the desk in front of him. "Mason, you mean too much to me." Her words were soft, and for the first time, Mason truly saw and felt the depth of her love for him. "So, tell me what's really happening with you."

"I've just got a lot on at the moment, and my work is going to suffer. I won't allow that to happen. You and this club are too important to me."

"I can respect that, Mase, I really can. But you don't have to quit on me. How about you take a bit of time off to get your head back on straight? Come back in a couple of weeks when you feel like you're ready to."

That wasn't what Mason wanted. He needed a clean break.

"I'm really sorry, Bryn, but I have to quit. I'm … I'm relocating to Florida," he lied.

"Florida? Why?"

He shrugged. "I need a change."

Bryn exhaled slowly. "Okay, if that's what you want to do." She stood up and Mason did the same. Wrapping her arms around his neck, she pulled him into a warm embrace. Against his neck, she said, "I'll miss you Mason."

"I'll miss you too, Bryn."

She pulled away, staring at him, trying to figure him out. "If you don't find what you're looking for in Florida, come back here to me, will you?"

"I wouldn't want to be anywhere else, Bryn, but this is something I have to do."

Mason left Bryn's office with his decision to leave weighing heavily on him. He hadn't felt this bad since that day over ten years ago when he was getting ready to end it all. He was right back to where he had started.

And he needed to get away from it all.

He didn't drive off straightaway; he just sat in his car in the parking lot outside the club contemplating his options. He had two really, although one of them wasn't that great. He could eat a bullet, as he'd intended to, or he could do what he'd told Bryn he'd do and move. Where? Fucked if he knew. Florida? Chicago? Cali? He supposed it didn't really matter. He would be miserable because he wouldn't be in Boston.

After three-quarters of an hour of contemplation, he turned

the key and fired up the engine, making his final drive home from the club.

36

Darrion's eyes twitched open, surveying the loft apartment he had taken this time around. There had only been one human living there along with three cats. He had killed the woman, but allowed the cats to live.

He liked how arrogant they were.

The apartment itself still smelled of the woman, her stench in every fiber, every fabric, on every surface. Darrion clenched his teeth against the odor so close to his face, his head resting on the woman's pillow.

He closed his eyes once more and let his mind drift to thoughts of Taer. She had to be close to cracking. He had been tormenting her relentlessly, and nobody could withstand that much without fissures forming in their sanity.

Normally, he could blow right past Taer's non-existent mental shields, breezing right into her weak mind. But it was different tonight. She actually put up a fight. When he first thought of her, he found the endless expanse of an icy landscape, bare of any trees or shrubs, and felt a frigid wind against his face. Looking to the left and right, he could see there was nothing else in sight.

He laughed at her attempt at keeping him out and then blew past the shield of her mind with one thought. The whole scene seemed to shatter, as if a stone had been thrown at a piece of glass. Giant cracks formed, spidering out from the center, and it crumbled around him in sharp shards that glanced off his body.

Behind the shield, the long hallway of Taer's mind was revealed. Darrion began walking down the hall, his footsteps echoing around him as he approached the glossy, black door that would give him entry. Anticipation was making his heart pound with excitement. Tonight was the night he would break her.

He could feel it.

Reaching out, his fingers wrapped around the cold metal knob. The door opened about an inch before suddenly shutting in his face with a sharp *bang*.

What the fuck?

Darrion tried again, but this time the door didn't move at all. With gritted teeth, he tried one last time before shoving his shoulder into the wood. A harsh curse escaped his throat as he was thrown back again. Staggering to his feet, he scowled at the lacquered wood until the sound of a dark voice gave him pause.

"Leave."

Darrion frowned, taking a step closer to the door. Was that …

"Korvain?" he asked.

"Leave, Darrion. I won't tell you again."

Is he telling me what to do? Darrion threw his head back and laughed. The sound boomed loudly around the dark hallway, ricocheting off the walls like gunfire. In a few steps, he was back in front of the door, his mouth less than an inch from the wood.

"This little bitch's mind belongs to me," he said in a controlled voice. "You can't protect her twenty-four hours a day, Korvain."

In an equally restrained voice, Korvain said, "If I didn't want to give Taer the pleasure of killing you herself, I would let you in here right now and finish you myself. But your death will be at her hands and nobody else's."

"Do you really think she would be able to take me on?" Darrion laughed again. What could one female do against him? He had centuries of training, centuries of experience and centuries of pain to fuel his ever present rage. Lowering his voice, he added dangerously, "I'll finish the job I started when I killed her brother. I'll finish it with her. You can tell her that, too."

"I wouldn't be too hasty to judge what Taer is capable of now, Darrion."

Darrion gave a primitive snarl. He was so close to breaking Taer, and he wouldn't sit back and let Korvain fuck it all up again. He had interfered in his plans once before, and Darrion wouldn't let it happen again.

Stepping back from the door, still glaring at it, Darrion pulled out of Taer's head. Blinking up at the ceiling of the apartment, Darrion sat up, with Korvain's final words still taunting him.

"Motherfucker."

37

The ocean was absolutely infinite, the surface of the water as smooth as glass. An icy wind blew across the surface, carrying with it the tang of salt. Taer shivered, fear skittering down her spine. She wrapped her arms around herself in an effort to stave off the cold.

She had wanted to do this.

She had wanted to get inside his head, but …

It was almost as if Korvain's shield was as aggressive as the man.

Gritting her teeth, she forced Adrian's death on Korvain's mind, making him relive it in every terrifying detail as she'd had to for the past month in her dreams. She made him experience it all—the scent of blood, the gasping of Adrian's final breaths, her feelings of desperate despondency.

She didn't know what she'd expected to happen, but she'd at least expected *something*. There was no response, nothing changed—she'd had no effect at all. If anything, the wind that had been blowing only got stronger, sending Taer's loose hair billowing behind her.

She tried again, upping the intensity of her attack, summoning all of her anger and grief. She concentrated on her pain, feeling the first tears of frustration fall down her cheeks. The wind was blowing even harder now, and Taer had to widen her stance to stay upright. If it were to get any stronger, she would lose her footing completely.

After a third try, Taer decided to give up on that particular line of attack. Reliving her brother's death wasn't working. She had to think about what would really upset Korvain. What did he love? Well, Bryn obviously, but Taer had already tried that angle without success. She had to think about what was really going to hurt him. Failing Adrian was something she knew had wounded him deeply, but he felt no fear in facing the memory. So what did he fear? Discouraged and frustrated with herself, Taer went through all her possible options again.

There was only one more thing she could try. Taer focused on her own near death, but instead of seeing herself recovering from her injuries, she forced the idea of her dying from them on him instead.

Soon she noticed the whipping wind was starting to die down. She watched on as the still black water began to ripple. Taer concentrated on the thought of her own death, waiting to see what would happen next.

The water grew choppier and choppier. Soon it was as if a tempest was raging around her, yet she was untouched. She squinted at the ocean in front of her as a visible channel formed in the water, growing deeper until she could see the sandy bottom right in front of her feet, as though a pathway had opened up for her. A high wall of water stretched up on both sides of the chasm, defying logic and gravity.

Taer stepped from the stone she had been standing on down onto the sand, the black walls of water looming above her. As she took another step, she waited to see if the walls would stay up, wondering if she was about to be drowned.

When it was clear that nothing was going to happen, she turned around again and started walking forward. After more than an hour she came to a blood-red door at the end. Reaching out a hand, she twisted the doorknob and pushed into the room.

It was completely dark—not even a pinprick of light was able to get inside—but Taer tamped down her fear and stepped forward. All she could hear was the sound of her breathing—and how it changed when she was suddenly thrust up against a wall with something sharp pressed into her throat.

Warm breath feathered across her cheek. She swallowed, feeling her throat work past the sharpness of the knife.

There was a growl, then she heard Korvain curse.

Taer gasped and her eyes flew open as he shoved her forcefully from his mind. She sat up, hearing the sound of angry footsteps coming down the hallway. A second later, Korvain was there in the doorway, staring menacingly down at her. He gripped her by the upper arm, yanking her out of bed, out of the bedroom, and dragging her into the living room, where he pushed her roughly onto the couch.

Korvain's shadow tracked across the carpet as he stalked in front of her. She watched him cautiously, seeing how tightly wound he was.

Eventually he stopped, spinning around to face her.

"How did you do it?" he roared. From the corner of her eye, Taer could see the shadows from around the room gravitating toward him.

"How!"

Taer jumped, peering behind him to see if they'd woken Eir or Bryn. "I'm sorry," she said. "I didn't think it would really work."

"You got past my shields. How did you do it?"

Taer blurted out the answer without thinking. "I projected what I thought was your greatest fear onto you." The words tumbled from her mouth almost too quickly for her to understand.

Korvain cursed. "Why?" he demanded, spittle flying from his lips. "How did you know how to do that?"

Taer shrugged. "I was just trying some different things out to see what would get past your shields."

He rounded on her again. "Why didn't you warn me you were going to do that?"

She shrugged again.

"Fuck!" Korvain dropped on to the couch beside her, his head in his hands. After a few minutes, he lifted his head, his dark gaze meeting her green eyes. "I need to tell you something."

Taer blinked at him. At least he sounded more reasonable now. She stared at his face, noting the dark circles under his eyes. "Okay." She sank back into the cushions, drawing her knees up and wrapping her arms around them.

His chest rose and fell with a deep breath, and the gravity of what he was about to say settled between them with an almost physical weight. "I've been watching your dreams."

She frowned. "Watching them? What does that mean?"

"I've been inside your head while you've been sleeping."

"But how? Since our shielding lesson, I thought I'd been protecting my mind."

"You have been, but your mental shields are still weak. For someone like me or Darrion—"

"Darrion?" she interrupted. "What does that bastard have to do with anything?"

"Your nightmares? Darrion's behind them."

What. The. Fuck?

But then she thought about it. Darrion was part of her dream. She'd assumed she had just imagined him, conjured him up … but this made more sense.

Darrion was tormenting her.

"Last night we had a confrontation."

"Why wasn't I aware of this?" she snapped, standing up and starting to pace, needing to physically burn off her agitation and to give herself some time to come to grips with what she was being told. "Why couldn't I feel you inside my head? Why couldn't I feel Darrion in there?"

"We can both shield ourselves to avoid detection."

Taer shot him a glare, but kept moving. "You need to explain this to me, Korvain. I need to understand what's going on."

The Mare sighed. "Darrion has been causing your nightmares. He told me he's been trying to break you."

"Why?"

He shrugged. "He's a sadistic bastard. He was probably doing it because he could … or he might be punishing me through you for taking you away before he could finish the job."

Hearing that made her hate him just that little bit more. She hadn't even known she was capable of that much hate. But with Darrion, her loathing seemed to know no bounds.

"All right, so he's fucking with me. How can I stop him?"

He leveled her with a dark stare. "You kill him."

"But how? We have no idea where he is."

"We don't know where he is *physically*, but we don't need to know that. You got past my shields, and they're on par with Darrion's.

So all you need to do is break Darrion's shields like you did mine and kill him within the dream."

38

Galen stared down at the phone in his hand. It had been ringing every five minutes, and would continue to ring every five minutes until he picked it up.

His last meeting with Bryn hadn't gone as he'd planned. He had thought he'd be able to at least get a job at the club for his efforts. Instead, he was told in no uncertain terms that if he set foot there one more time, it would be his last day on Earth.

The phone was finally silent in his palm, the screen showing he had ninety-seven missed calls from Craine and ninety-seven voice messages Galen had no desire to listen to.

Four minutes and fifty-five seconds later, the screen lit up once more. With a sigh, Galen bit the bullet and pressed the accept button, putting the call onto speaker so he could have the ass-chewing in stereo.

"Galen." Craine barked his name, making Galen grind his teeth. Craine had turned into a goddamn guild master with his demands, and there was a reason Galen hadn't wanted to belong to one in the first place.

"Craine—"

"I want you back here."

Galen sank further back into the pillows propped up on the headboard. That was the last thing he'd expected to hear. "When?"

"Now." Craine hung up, and the screen went dark. He wondered why Craine wanted him back so soon, and the lie he told Bryn suddenly felt as if it might be true. What if he'd had enough of Galen's fuck-ups? What if it had been a test and he'd failed miserably?

He stood up from the bed, pocketing his phone and snatching up the handles of his small duffel bag. Closing his eyes, he faded back to Craine's office in Chicago. He stepped through the lobby doors and came face to face with Craine's two henchmen.

"Gentlemen," he drawled.

"Come with us," Goon Two said, his tone business-like, his face completely blank.

Galen's eyes darted to the face of the other guy. His expression was just as serious.

Fuck.

Instead of replying, Galen waited for them to turn around and lead the way over to the bank of elevators. Goon One's chubby finger jabbed at the button impatiently. Craine must have been riding their asses while he'd been gone.

The doors opened, revealing the elevator's mirrored walls and white marble floor, and all three of them stepped inside. While he waited for the doors to close, Galen made a decision that would no doubt raise a lot of questions.

He turned around to face the goons and waved at them before

fading from sight. Rematerializing straight into Craine's office, Galen found the man leaning back in his chair, his fingers steepled under his chin, his expression almost expectant.

Craine pressed a button on a small metal box set on his desk, and there was a crackle of static before he said, "Send Rhys in."

Galen studied Craine as they waited for his best friend. The sleeves of his crisp, white shirt were rolled up to his elbows, the top two buttons undone. Galen had never seen the mob boss without a tie before, and it looked … strange.

"What took you so long?" Craine asked in an icy tone.

Galen dropped his duffel at his feet. "I stopped to chat to your henchmen. They're assholes, you know that?"

Craine remained stoic, his dark eyes reproachful. The door opened at Galen's back then, drawing Craine's gaze. Without turning around, Galen knew Rhys had just joined them.

"Sit. Both of you." Galen didn't like his tone but bit his tongue and sat down, staring at the guy. He didn't quite know what was different about him. He seemed a whole lot more irate than usual. Rhys took the seat beside Galen, his attention on Craine also.

"Tell me about what happened to you in Boston," Craine said.

Galen recounted the whole story, from his first meeting with Bryn to the final one, making sure to give him every single detail. Craine was nothing if not meticulous when it came to the details of his business. When Galen was done, Craine sat forward in his chair.

"Is that everything?"

Galen said, "More or less."

"Tell me about the layout of the club."

"From what I can tell, the club is spread over three levels. I only ever saw the lowest level—the Eye—and that's where the office is."

"What's Bryn like?" Craine asked and Galen found the question odd.

"She's stunningly beautiful, but as tough as nails. She's independent, but she surrounds herself with … people who have her back, no matter what. She's almost untouchable."

Craine's lip quirked. "So, how were you able to … touch her?"

"I have my ways of getting past hired muscle," he replied, watching Craine's dark eyes. He sighed. "I guess it doesn't matter how I did it, just that I did." He spread his hands out in front of him. "I got an audience with her. I made up a story about you wanting to buy into her club. She rejected it. I tried again. I lied to get her to give me another chance, but she rejected that too. In the end, I had no other choice but to give up."

"Why?" Craine asked, steepling his fingers again. His gaze settled on Galen's face, his stare burrowing in under his skin.

"I like my head just fine where it is," Galen answered with a shrug. "And I doubt she was bluffing. The guy she keeps around is a Mare, and from what I found out, he's the last pure-blooded Mare."

"Will he bleed if you cut him?" Craine asked quietly.

"Of course."

"He can be killed, then," stated Craine simply.

"Of course he can, but I'm no match for him. I doubt there would be any fucker out there who could take him on and survive."

Galen watched the mob boss's eyes flash green. He squeezed his own eyes shut and took a deep breath. He needed some more fucking sleep.

"There are some out there who would gladly take on the Mare," Craine said.

"Maybe, but Boston is off-limits for you now."

As soon as the last word was out of Galen's mouth, Craine was out of his chair, his chest rising and falling as his nostrils flared. With his hands planted on the desk in front of him, he said, "Don't you dare tell me where I can and cannot conduct my business."

Galen kept his expression vacant, but on the inside a shiver of fear sliced through his body. He could see Rhys tense from the corner of his eye, every muscle in his body ready to fire into action should the threat become something more.

After a long moment, Craine sat back down again. "I want you and Rhys to go back there. I need this Mare removed from the equation."

"You want us to kill him?" Galen asked, incredulous. Craine was asking the impossible.

"You said yourself that he bleeds. He can be killed. But if you don't think you're good enough to do the job, I could find someone else."

Craine's meaning was loud and clear: what good were they to him if they couldn't follow orders?

Galen glanced at Rhys, his friend giving him a tight nod. They would get this done.

He looked back to Craine. "We'll leave tonight then."

Both Mares stood up, Galen picking up his duffel and leading the way from the room.

"Galen," Craine called out as he reached the door. "I need to speak to you alone for a moment."

Rhys snarled quietly under his breath, giving his friend a look that said not to do it, but Galen only shrugged. "I'll see you at home," he told Rhys, squeezing his shoulder.

Galen turned back around, dropping the bag and facing Craine.

Rhys closed the door behind them, sealing them in the room together.

"Our business relationship is finished, Galen," Craine said. "After this job, we're done. Do you hear me?"

Galen wasn't particularly surprised, nor was he particularly upset about it. Without saying a word, he scooped up his bag and turned his back on the mob boss.

It wasn't the end of the world. Galen knew there were plenty of people around who liked the idea of having a hit man on call. Hell, maybe he'd even go and work for Craine's competitor just to piss the bastard off.

Galen froze, his hand already on the door handle, when the sound of metal on metal echoed around the room. Without turning, he tried to fade from the room, but the distinctive *thwack* of silenced gunfire pushed all the air from his lungs.

A burning tore through Galen's back, his legs falling out from beneath his body. He dropped to the floor, boneless, weightless, and the side of his face pressed into the tightly-looped pile of the carpet. The dull thud of footsteps filled Galen's ears and he swiveled his eyes upward.

Craine stood over him, a gun in his hand. Galen tried to fade, but his body—which had felt so weightless before—now felt like lead. He couldn't move his legs and he knew the brand-new bullet in his spine was responsible for it. The injury wasn't life-threatening. Galen could heal the wound, but somehow he didn't think that was going to happen this time around.

The warm muzzle of the silencer was suddenly pressed to Galen's skull. His heart rate sped up and his mouth went dry. Craine leaned down, his warm breath feathering over Galen's cheek. A smirk pulled up the corner of his mouth ... and then there was only darkness and the sound of a bullet firing from a chamber ringing around the room.

39

Eir hit the end call button on her phone for what felt like the hundredth time and lay back on her bed. Every time she'd called Mason that morning, it had rung out, and the knot in her stomach tightened.

Korvain's dismissal of Mason the night before was still weighing heavily on her mind. She had tried to talk to Mason once they'd returned to the club, but Korvain had told her he had to start his shift right away.

She'd wanted to go downstairs and speak to him herself, without worrying about having Korvain looking over her shoulder, but had decided against it. She didn't really want to disturb him while he was working.

But it was mid-afternoon, and Mason should have been awake by now … so why was he screening her calls? Discouraged, she decided to do something drastic. Stripping out of her sweats, she got dressed and left the apartment, planning to sneak out the back door of the building.

She was pushing against the metal bar across the door that would take her into the alleyway when she heard his voice.

"Where are you going?" he asked, his voice a dark drawl. Eir spun around, her heart trying to claw its way out of her throat. She was suddenly mute, her mouth dry.

"Where are you going?" he asked again, pushing himself off the wall he'd been leaning against. The shadows that had been wrapped around his body drifted away, melting off and melding with the others.

"Just out," she stammered, dropping her eyes to the floor. "For a walk."

"I can't let you do that, Eir. You know why."

She kept her eyes firmly on the ground.

"Where were you really going?" Korvain asked, his voice lower than before.

Taking a risk, she answered, "To see Mason. He's not answering my calls, but I guess I can see him tonight at the club." Korvain's expression changed from anger to … pity. "What's wrong?" she asked, the knot in her stomach intensifying to the point of pain.

"Mason won't be coming in to work tonight."

"Why not?" she asked, afraid of the answer he was about to give.

"He quit this morning. Said he was moving to Florida or something."

"Florida?" she squeaked. Why would he move to Florida? Maybe he had family there she didn't know about. Maybe he just wanted to be as far away from Boston as he could without leaving the east coast. Maybe he just needed some warmer weather? She had no idea, and all the other reasons her brain was throwing up were unbearable.

"I have to go and see him." The words popped out of her mouth before she knew it, causing his hard eyes to hold her in place.

"I've already told you I can't let you do that."

"Then come with me," she blurted out desperately. She knew he wouldn't go for that idea, and after their little showdown the previous night, there was no way Mason would be happy to see Korvain either.

He looked incredibly uncomfortable for a split second before his mask of indifference was back in place. "I doubt that's a good idea."

Eir looked around the hallway, not knowing what to say, what to do. "What about Taer? She could come with me." Korvain seemed to think about it, but she could tell he was going to say no. She pressed on anyway. "She'd be able to protect me if something were to happen."

The Mare's lips thinned into a hard line. After uncountable seconds of silence, he agreed, telling Eir to go up to the apartment to get Taer. She rode the elevator up to the top floor and stepped back into the apartment.

"Hey," Taer said when she saw her. She turned off the TV and twisted her body to face Eir standing beside the kitchen bench. "What's happening?"

With her heart pounding in her ear, Eir said, "I need a favor."

"What do you need?"

Eir didn't know how to say what she wanted to. "A bodyguard."

"A what?"

"A bodyguard," Eir repeated. "I need to go and see Mason."

"And you want me to be that bodyguard? What does Korvain have to say about it?"

"It was his suggestion. So, can you spare an hour so I can go and see him?"

"Are you ready to go now?" Taer asked. Eir was surprised; she'd thought Taer would be reluctant to do anything so trivial.

"Really?" Eir said.

Taer stood up and walked towards the front door, slipping her arms into a jacket that had been hanging from the back of a stool. "Sure. Why not?"

"I just … I would have thought babysitting me would have been the last thing you wanted to do today."

Taer kept her pale eyes on Eir's face. "You saved my life, Eir. I owe you."

She gave the young Mare a tentative smile. "Thank you."

A few minutes later, they were standing in the alleyway behind the club. Together they faded to Mason's apartment only to find he wasn't there.

"Can we try one more place?" Eir asked, already walking in the direction of the only other spot she could think of that he would go. The two of them remained silent on the walk to Boston Common.

And that was where she found him, sitting alone some distance away on a park bench.

Turning to Taer, Eir said, "He's here."

Taer looked over Eir's shoulder before her pale green eyes returned to her face. "Will you be all right?"

"Yes, thank you."

Taer's eyes flickered to Mason once more. "All right."

Eir watched Taer walk out of the park, until she was out of sight, then turned around to face Mason, heaving a sigh as she did. She had no idea what she was going to say to him. A thousand and one thoughts had run through her mind about what she *could* say to him, but now she was faced with him, the words escaped her.

Approaching the park bench cautiously, she was stunned by how sad he looked. What could have happened, that he would choose to quit his job and leave the state to move to Florida?

It wasn't until she was standing right beside him that he looked up. His eyes were puffy and red like he'd been crying. Eir lowered herself into the seat beside him, her hands interlaced in her lap. She gazed at him, wishing she could do something for him, to help fix whatever was wrong.

He turned his head away, looking out at nothing in particular. Eir reached out her hand and rested it on Mason's. She gasped at the strength and volume of his grief, but his thoughts were so muddled she couldn't make out what was wrong.

She squeezed his hand and turned to look out at the park. It was a sunny afternoon, and young mothers with their children were taking advantage of the unseasonably warm weather, playing with a ball on the grass or feeding the ducks.

Mason's misery—and it really was misery—bombarded her, but she kept her hand wrapped tightly around his large hand, trying to bring him some comfort. She sat there, waiting for him to be ready to talk, until the sun began to set and the chill of the early winter night seeped into their bones.

He still hadn't moved.

When darkness fell completely, and Eir could see each breath she took on the air, she finally spoke.

"We should get you home."

If he had heard her, he showed no sign of it. But his shoulders rose and fell, his chest expanding and contracting with a deep breath.

"She's gone," he said softly, and Eir had to lean in to hear the words clearly.

"Who's gone?" she asked.

He turned to her, fresh tears streaming down his face. His expression was pained, his lips twisting into a grimace. "Sophie."

Eir put the words together in her head. *Gone. Sophie. Sophie was gone.*

"What do you mean, gone? Did she run away?"

Mason shook his head. The movement seemed to pain him as much as the words he'd just spoken. "She's dead."

Dead? "What? How?"

"I came home yesterday afternoon after dropping you off at the hospital and she was lying on the floor of my apartment, hardly moving and foaming at the mouth."

Eir's hand went to her mouth in shock. "I'm so sorry, Mason."

He shrugged slightly and stood up, still not letting go of her hand. He led her out of the park and toward his apartment. The silence enveloping them was only punctuated by the steady sound of their feet on the slick pavement.

Traffic streamed by them: people returning home from work, or from picking up a few things for dinner that night. It all seemed so normal, but for Mason and Eir, it was anything but normal. Even though she had only known the man for a week or so, she knew the depth of love he'd had for Sophie.

His heart must have been aching with her loss, and she wished she could have done more for him. When they reached Mason's apartment, he opened the front door and stood back, letting Eir walk in first. She instantly felt Sophie's absence.

In the near darkness, she walked over to the island bench separating the kitchen and the living space and turned around, putting her back to the kitchen and facing Mason.

Without looking at her, he walked over to the couch and began toeing off his boots, kicking them aside haphazardly.

She followed him, padding to the couch and sinking into the

cushions beside him. Pushing off her flats, she curled her legs beneath her body, and just … waited.

"Would you like to talk about it?" she asked five minutes later, her voice too loud in the silence.

"About what? She's dead, and I couldn't protect her, even though she protected me for nearly ten years."

"This isn't your fault, Mason. You do know that, right?"

"I couldn't save her," he muttered, letting his head fall back against the couch. "Just like I couldn't save him."

"Who, Mason?" Eir asked gently, letting her head rest on his shoulder as she took his free hand. Pain and anger filled her, but this wasn't as fresh, nor was it as potent as before, and she realized that this was an older wound—something he had been carrying around with him for a long time.

"My brother, Hunter."

"The one who passed away?" she asked.

"I told you he died just over ten years ago, but I didn't tell you how."

"And you don't need to, Mason. You don't have to talk about him if you don't want to—especially now that …"

"Sophie's dead?" He laughed derisively. "Believe me; talking about Hunter will be a nice distraction."

"Mason, please—"

"You deserve to hear this, Eir. I should have told you before, and after everything that's happened, it will make more sense to you now."

She sat up and leaned back against the arm of the couch, facing him. "All right. If you're ready to talk about him, I'm ready to listen."

She was willing to wait as long as it took. His head was still tipped back, his Adam's apple working over an invisible lump.

Five minutes passed … then ten … then fifteen. Eir was ready to get up and offer him a drink when he said the words that had been weighing him down for just over a decade.

"I killed my brother."

40

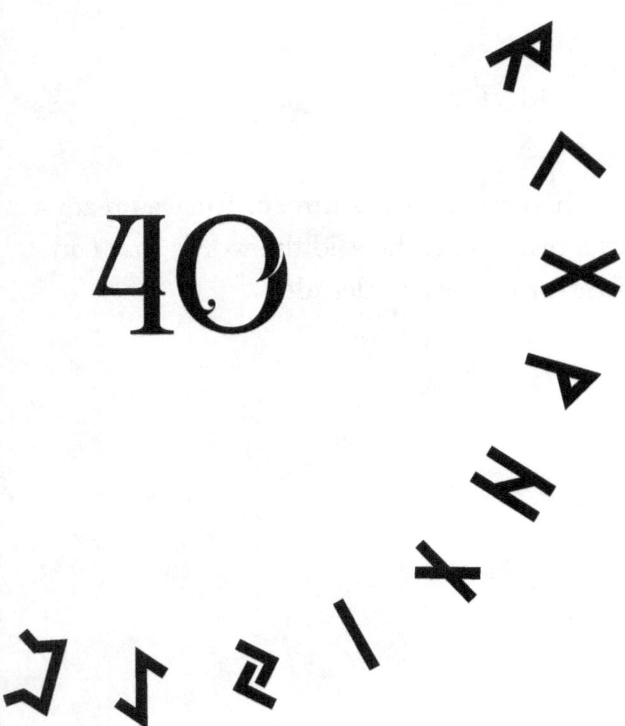

I killed my brother.

Mason let the words settle between them, giving Eir the opportunity to run if she wanted to. He cast a sideways glance in her direction. She was still there, and showing no signs of wanting to bolt. He willed the words he had buried so deeply to come up, to finally be heard.

"You already know this part, but I need to tell you again so I don't miss anything out." Mason inhaled deeply, letting the breath out. "My unit was sweeping a building in An Nasiriyah. I was in a squad with three others, and we were making our way up to the top floor of a small apartment building. I was third in line and I think that may have saved my life. There was a bomb on the roof, and it was detonated. The first two guys were killed …

"I was thrown back by the blast. I hit my head pretty hard, and the same with one of the other guys." He was simply regurgitating the words, unable to deviate from the version of the story he had played and replayed in his head countless times. "I was knocked out cold, and the other guy—Shane North—had a broken arm, a bad cut above his eye, a concussion and a sprained ankle. I managed to get to my feet and went to check on the others. Some moaning led me to Derek, but I'd been mistaken. He was already dead—a hole the size of a watermelon in the center of his chest.

"That was when I realized the sound was coming from the fourth marine in our squad—" He swallowed thickly. "From my brother, Hunter."

Eir gasped quietly at that admission, but he pressed on—unwilling to dwell on it any longer than he had a million times before.

"When the bomb had gone off, it had partially caved in the roof. There were smaller pieces of reinforced steel and bricks from the blast everywhere, but there were a few larger chunks that had fallen too." Mason looked at her, reaffirming what he already knew—that telling her was the right decision, no matter how painful it was.

"I found Hunter buried beneath one of the walls. It had been knocked down in a complete slab and crushed him. All I could see of him was his head and shoulders. He was still lucid, coherent even. He told me that it wasn't my fault he was dying, but I just couldn't believe him."

"Why not?" she asked gently.

He swallowed again. "Because I had let him go up the front. If it had been any other time, I would have pushed Hunter behind me, to protect him like a big brother should, but I'd let him take the lead."

"Oh, Mason, you couldn't have known," Eir whispered.

His chest expanded and contracted with a deep lungful of air. Then another. And another. But no matter how many deep breaths he took, he still couldn't fight the tears that were building. He swiped at his eyes with the back of his hand, looking away, not wanting Eir to see them.

"It doesn't change anything. I let him take the lead. I let him die. If I'd been up front like I should have been, Hunter would still be here."

Eir wrapped her warm palm around his wrist. "But *you* wouldn't be here," she pleaded. "Mason, look at me …"

He lifted his gaze to hers.

Her fingertips grazed his cheek. "If you'd died, I wouldn't have met you, and I just know my life would have been empty without you in it."

He gave a harsh laugh. Even though her words warmed him, he still couldn't see past his mistake of letting his brother get killed. "You're a goddess, Eir. And I'm just a human. You would have been just fine." His words were more severe than he'd intended them to be, and he stood up, his back to her, trying to break the spell he always seemed to be under when she was near him.

He felt the heat of her body before the words were spoken. "I may be a goddess, but I'm still a woman, Mason. And for the first time in thousands of years, I suddenly feel like I'm living … and it's thanks to you."

Her hand rested on his shoulder. When he turned to face her again, he saw compassion in her eyes, and sadness, but also something else—something he had wanted to spark within her. Lust.

"I lost my sister," she whispered. "I thought I'd never recover from the loss, but you've helped me do that."

He felt as if his blood was on fire. Her hand moved from his shoulder up his neck, her touch awakening his body. Her pink tongue darted out of her mouth, swiping along her bottom lip.

Eir's breath was steady, but he could see how her pulse pounded against her skin. She raked her fingers through his hair, her nails scraping against his scalp. Mason's eyes fluttered shut, his breath uneven.

He felt her mouth move against his, her lips warm and supple. Mason let out a groan, his hands finding their way to her slender waist.

Her body melted into his, molding into him like they had been made for each other. He pulled her in tighter, relishing the feeling of her close to him … finally.

He broke away from the ecstasy that was Eir's mouth, and she arched her head back as he made a trail down her throat, sucking, licking and kissing his way to the dip between her collarbones.

"Mason," she panted, her fingers running through his hair, her nails scraping the back of his neck. "Make love to me." Her pleading words were the sweetest song to his ears. "Let me heal you."

Bending his knees, he scooped her up and into his arms, a small, greedy growl escaping his throat. Her slight weight felt amazing cradled against his chest. That was where she belonged, where she would always belong.

Moving swiftly, he carried her toward his bedroom, nudging the door closed behind them.

Gently placing her down on the bed, he just took a moment to look at her—at the angel sprawled out on his mattress.

Eir propped herself up on her elbows. "What's wrong, Mason?" she asked, worry creeping into her voice.

He tried to reassure her with a gentle smile. "Nothing's wrong. I was just looking at you … you're too beautiful to be real." His voice was rough, but he meant every damn word.

Her cheeks flushed at his compliment, her eyes dropping for

a moment before they flashed to his face. "You are too," she whispered sweetly. Biting her lip, she looked away, but this time only for a moment. "Make love to me?" she asked again.

Mason dropped to his knees at the edge of the mattress, his hands wrapping around her thighs, dragging her body back down and to the edge—closer to him. Her breath hitched in her throat as she looked down the length of her body at him.

He grinned wickedly, trailing his fingers down over her knees and across her slender calves until they reached her delicate ankles. Mason gently massaged the arches of her feet, placing kisses along her instep.

"You are so beautiful," he said again, unable to stop the feelings from pouring out of his mouth.

She smiled shyly in response, but her eyes told him all he needed to know. Reaching over, he opened the bottom button of her blouse. He watched her face for any signs that she didn't want this, but he saw no hesitation. All he saw was … heat. Mason's fingers stretched out for the next button along and opened it.

She shivered when the pads of his fingers grazed the sensitive skin around her flat belly. Once he'd undone all her buttons, her blouse fell open, revealing the perfection of her skin.

Her chest rose and fell quickly as his eyes ran over her body, his brain taking in every detail. She ran her tongue over her bottom lip, moistening it, and Mason nearly lost his mind with need. Lowering his head, he placed a kiss above her navel, his tongue darting out to taste her skin. He groaned low in his throat at the flavor of her. Her fragrance was a heady mix of vanilla and roses, the scent going straight to Mason's head.

Eir buried her fingers in his hair, urging him on. His lips moved higher and he kissed her stomach, the muscles in her torso contracting as his mouth moved over her warm flesh.

He kissed a path up between her breasts, tilting his head to the left and right to kiss the soft mounds, then on to her neck. Mason's tongue darted out to run along the length of the violet sword tattooed there, hesitating when the warm, supple skin he was expecting was in fact hard and cold.

"Please don't stop," Eir begged.

"I wasn't going to," he replied, kissing the tattoo once more before moving further up her throat. When he reached her earlobe, he playfully bit the flesh, and Eir moaned. Christ, he was so fucking hard already, but that little sound had somehow made him harder—pushing him to the edge of his already frayed self-control.

Struggling to control himself, he slowed it right down, placing a small kiss on the corner of her mouth, on each eyelid and on the tip of her nose before pulling back slightly.

Her eyes fluttered open, her pale lashes framing those gorgeous dual-ringed irises that all of the Valkyries had. He crushed his mouth against hers again, and her gentle moan allowed his tongue entry. He explored the inside of her mouth, possessing her with his lips while his fingers caressed her face, committing every curve and plane to memory.

Eir's hands slid from Mason's head, traveling down his shoulders, along his back and slipping into the waistband of his jeans. Her fingernails dug into the meat of his ass, and he groaned in response. He kept right on kissing her, but when her hands traveled from the back of his jeans to his front, her fingers toying with the button of his pants, he pulled back, panting.

"Stand up," Eir said, her voice silky and her eyes dark with lust. Mason moved without thinking, crawling backwards off the bed and finding his feet. Eir scooted to the edge, placing her feet on the carpet. She stood up and moved towards him, her eyes dropping from his face down along his body.

Mason's cock twitched in response to her heated look, and her eyes shot back to his face. She looked surprised for a moment before a sexy, knowing grin spread across her lips. Her fingers trailed the outline of his straining erection through his jeans.

"You're killing me here," he said gruffly, licking his lips. Eir peeked up at him from under her lashes, her lips quirking up slyly.

"I wouldn't want that, Mason," she replied, her fingers moving to the button of his jeans. He held his breath, but released it when her hands kept moving north, to the bottom of his shirt. She tugged up the fabric, exposing his stomach and chest. "Raise your arms," she said. Mason did as he was told and felt the cool air hit his skin as she pulled his shirt all the way up.

She dropped the shirt on the floor at his bare feet and stood back and stared at him. Her warm palms touched his skin, roving all over his body, giving him goosebumps. His heart pounded furiously against his ribs and the fine hairs on his body stood on end.

His eyes fell to her long neck, her slender shoulders. She was standing before him in only a bra and her jeans, and he knew he needed to see more of her. He ran his fingertips lightly down her shoulders and her arms, then cinched his hands around her waist, running his thumbs in lazy circles along her hipbones, wanting desperately to be touching even more of her.

As if reading his mind, Eir dropped her hands to the fastening of her jeans, slipping the button free and sliding the zipper down. Hooking her thumbs into the waistband, she shimmied out of them, leaving her in her underwear.

Eir kicked off her jeans, dropping her gaze to the floor. If she was embarrassed about her body, he wouldn't let her be. He curved his index finger and brought it under her chin, tilting her head up. She raised her eyes to his face.

"We're uneven," he told her, gesturing down to his jeans. Mason freed the button on his pants and slid the zipper down carefully. He looked up to find Eir watching him hungrily, her teeth biting down on her bottom lip.

Mason dropped his pants, his boxer briefs making the journey too. Eir's eyes widened as she saw how aroused he was, and she ran her tongue along her lip.

Mason reached out to cup her chin and leaned in, kissing her gently on the mouth.

Standing beside the bed, Eir could feel Mason's erection pressing against her stomach as he kissed her, her whole body coming alive with his touch. She had dreamed about doing this with Mason a hundred times, but now it was really happening.

She had never had the same hang-ups as Bryn did about losing her virginity. Odin couldn't threaten to take her immortality away from her like he did with Bryn and the other Valkyries. All Eir really wanted was to find a man she could love, and who would love her, and she thought she had found that with Mason. He was so broken, but then again, so was she. They had both lost a sibling, and they both thought it was their fault. Eir could see that Mason wasn't to blame for his brother's death—of course he wasn't—whereas she *knew* it was her that fault Kristy had been killed. Still, the fact that he felt responsible meant that he understood what she felt, what she was going through.

"Hey, where were you just then?" Mason asked, peppering her face with half-a-dozen tiny kisses. Eir hadn't even realized she had gone still in his arms. Forcing a smile, she shook her head. "Nothing's wrong. I was just thinking about how much I've wanted this."

He gave her a crooked smile. "I've wanted this too," he said, and kissed her again, deeper this time. Eir gave in to him, letting herself fall completely into his body and his touch. He moaned into her mouth, pressing his hips more tightly against hers.

She loved the feel of him against her. She loved that she was responsible for making him feel that way, for making his body respond to hers. The knowledge made her feel strangely powerful. Emboldened by that power, she reached down between them, wrapping her fingers around Mason's length and applying the slightest pressure.

When he moaned—as if he was in pain—Eir paused a moment, worried, and pulled her hand away.

"Please don't stop," he panted against her neck. "That felt so good."

She reached down once more. This time when Mason groaned, a thrill went through her.

His hands moved down her body, skimming over her torso. "I don't want there to be any barriers between us," he said before unclasping her bra. He broke off their burning kiss and tugged at the lacy fabric to pull it free.

His hazel eyes darkened as he looked at her, but the flecks of gold and green in them seemed to glow—as if fueled by his lust. He brought his hands up, cupping her now bare breasts in gentle reverence, weighing them in his large, warm palms. She groaned when his thumbs caressed her nipples, her hand gripping him tighter, making his eyes roll back in his head.

He bent at the waist, lowering his head to one of her breasts, forcing Eir to release him. She ran both of her hands through his hair, holding his head to her as he expertly tortured her with his tongue, teeth and lips, tugging at her peaked nipple.

"You taste so good," he said, his voice vibrating through her. She shivered, goosebumps breaking out on her skin. Eir could feel her knees giving way, but Mason scooped her up and moved towards his bed.

He laid her down gently on her back and lay on his side facing her. He cupped her breast again, his thumb and forefinger plucking at her hardened nipple. Eir let out a shuddering breath, focusing on how he made her feel.

She pressed her legs together to quell the intensifying pulse building there. Mason gave her breast one last caress before his fingers began inching further down her body. He stopped and met her eyes when his hand reached the edge of her underwear.

She could see he was asking permission, and she gave it with the slight bob of her head. His fingertips skimmed over the lace, reaching between her legs. Eir gasped as a surge of electricity rushed through her body.

His smirk told her that he knew what he was doing to her. He pulled his hand away for a moment, then swept it down again, between her thighs. The more times he did that, the hotter and more wound up she became.

It got to a point where she was begging Mason just to touch her, without her underwear in the way. She watched as his fingers slid under the pale blue lace. Eir hadn't thought the sensations could have been any more intense, but she'd been wrong. Skin-to-skin contact was so much better.

"Christ, Eir, I want to taste you."

"Taste?" she asked.

He flexed his fingers against her clit, making her arch her back. "Taste," he repeated on a growl.

"Oh," she breathed, lifting up her hips as he tenderly removed the scrap of lace from her body. He took his time, sliding her underwear down her long legs leisurely, deliberately. His eyes never left hers and that complete focus from him made more moisture pool between her thighs.

He flicked the lace over his shoulder before lowering his face to the juncture between her thighs. The first dip of his tongue set every one of her nerve endings on fire. She moaned, spurring him on.

He alternated between long, languid strokes and sharp flicks of his tongue. The pressure kept on building, building, until it reached a crescendo that Eir had no way of escaping.

She felt the ecstasy sweep over her body, starting in her center and working its way through her body like quicksilver. Her spine arched off the bed, but Mason stayed with her, his fingers wrapping around her hips, bringing her back down onto the mattress. With one final stroke of his expert tongue, she gave in—screaming and gasping—to her pleasure.

When her head cleared, and her eyes fluttered open, she found him staring down at her, a satisfied expression on his face.

"That was …" she began, but couldn't find the words to finish her thoughts. She was too strung out, a slave to Mason and what he could do to her body.

He licked his lips seductively, and she felt the muscles in her lower belly tighten. She didn't think she could be ready for another orgasm like that, but when Mason looked at her in that way, she felt as if anything was possible.

The mattress shifted as he crawled up to lie beside her. She let her gaze travel up the length of his muscular body until she reached his face. She reached down and wrapped her fingers around his erection, reveling in how it twitched against her palm.

She slid her hand down further to the base, then back up

again—always watching his face. His eyes were closed; his mouth was slack. Eir continued, tightening her grasp a little, enjoying his sharp little intakes of breath. She was on her third pass when Mason's hand landed on hers, stopping her.

"If you keep going, I'm not going to be able to last." His voice was rough. He slid her fingers free, bringing her hand up to his mouth and placing a gentle kiss along each of her knuckles. Moving down, he brushed his lips against the delicate skin of her inner wrist, then made his way down to the crook of her elbow and on to her shoulder, her neck and then her mouth.

"I need you," he commanded possessively, nipping at her collarbone.

"Yes," she breathed. "Yes."

Grazing his teeth along her skin one final time, he leaned over and pulled something out of the top drawer of his bedside table. Mason moved off her, tearing the foil packet and rolling the condom over his length. Eir watched on—fascinated—before he pinned her lower body to the bed, his erection lying thick, hot and heavy between them.

Now she was nervous. There had been other men before who had touched her, who had brought her to orgasm, but never as intimately as Mason had in the last hour.

Propping himself up on his elbows, Mason looked down at her, his hips cradled in the dip of hers, the tip of his erection now pressing against her.

"Are you ready for this?" he asked. "We can stop."

"Mason, no. I don't want to stop. Just … take it slow, okay?"

"I wouldn't have it any other way," he replied, gently easing into her. Eir gasped, and he stopped, breathing hard. A frown formed between his eyes. "Eir? Are you a virgin?" he asked, uncertainty tainting his words.

She looked away but nodded. Mason tilted her face back to his.

"Don't hide from me." He smiled gently. "You should have told me."

She could feel the tears beginning to form. "I didn't want to seem inexperienced."

Leaning down, Mason kissed away the first tear that slid down the side of her face. "Don't worry about that," he whispered.

Eir stared up at him, unable to believe that Mason could have been any more perfect.

"Do you want to keep going, or would you like me to stop?" he asked, his eyes serious. She knew if she'd told him to stop that he would have.

Just like that.

"Don't stop," she breathed, leaning up and claiming his mouth with her own. Sliding her tongue past his lips, she felt him groan against her, his hips starting to move once more. Eir tried to breathe through the pain, telling herself that it was necessary and that it would be over soon.

Mason found his rhythm, but still went slowly, like he had promised. She could tell he was struggling with the pace, but he didn't speed up and he wasn't too rough with her. He simply made love to her, just as she'd asked him to.

"Oh, Christ, Eir." His words were muffled against her neck. "I'm not going to last."

"That's okay," she said. "You've given me a mind-blowing orgasm. Now it's my turn to give you one."

She tilted her hips up, giving him a different angle, a deeper angle. The sharp pain brought fresh tears to her eyes, but she forced them away. She didn't want Mason to know he was hurting her.

She urged him on by meeting him thrust for thrust until his

whole body began to shake.

"I'm so close."

"I know," she said. "Let go."

Mason's eyes squeezed shut for a moment, his body shuddering above her. He gave a loud groan and was finally silent, the only noise his labored breathing mingling with her own.

After a few long seconds, he propped himself up on his elbows and gazed down at her. "That was amazing," he said, running his thumb along her bottom lip. "How was it for you?"

"Perfect."

"I didn't hurt you?"

She shook her head. "I knew it was going to hurt, but you made it bearable. You made me want to do it again."

His mouth turned up in the corners. "You do?"

"Only with you. I only want you, Mason. Always."

"Yeah?" he asked, still smiling.

"Yeah. I knew you were special when we met. Now, I know why. You're caring and loyal, sweet and considerate. You're everything I want in a man."

Mason leaned down and kissed her deeply and passionately. "I really care about you, Eir. I know I shouldn't say it so soon, but it's true, and I don't expect you to say the same back to me—"

She stopped him talking with a kiss. "I know." She wasn't sure she was ready to bare her soul to him yet, but she knew her feelings for him were like nothing she had ever felt before.

Very carefully, he slid free of her body and propped himself up beside her, cradling her close to his chest. She could feel her eyes getting heavy, but she wouldn't let sleep dissuade her from asking what she really wanted to know. Clearing her throat gently, she asked, "Mason, why were you really running?"

He grunted, as if he'd been almost asleep. "What?" he asked, his voice rough.

"Why were you really running?"

His breath was warm against her neck. "Because if I couldn't look after Sophie, how was I supposed to look after you? I'd already let you down once by not being there for you. What if next time I'm too late?" He drew her close against him. "I couldn't live with myself if you were seriously injured and it was my fault. When … when Hunter died, I was very close to ending it all then, too."

"What stopped you?"

He chuckled. "It was Bryn, actually. She saved me by giving me a job, by giving me a purpose in life."

"Bryn is pretty amazing that way."

"And she also brought me to you. And for that I will be eternally grateful."

They were quiet for a moment. "Please don't leave me," Eir whispered. "Not when I've just found you."

Mason's arms tightened around her body. "I'm not going anywhere."

41

aer paused briefly before walking into the War Hammer. Alistyre gave her a leery stare as she passed the bar on her way to Aubrey's booth, hidden out of sight at the back. He was supposed to be introducing her to someone today, but he wouldn't tell her who it was, and the uncertainty was setting her nerves on edge and tying her stomach in knots.

She reached the final barrier between her and Aubrey, the half wall sheltering the elf from view of the general public. Taer let out a breath, shaking out her arms and loosening the tightness in her neck.

Rounding the corner, Taer let her gaze first settle on Aubrey. Her body heated in its usual way as his eyes perused her leisurely. He gave her a grin loaded with sexual tension. For the sake of her sanity, she forced her focus somewhere else, concentrating on the unfamiliar male sitting beside the light elf.

She knew he was a Mare with just a look, but she couldn't have been sure he wasn't a Walker. His dark brown hair was brushing the tops of his shoulders, his ice-blue eyes wary as he watched her. His skin was pale, and his mouth was a little too full for a male.

"Sit down, Winter Fox," Aubrey murmured, amusement in his voice. Taer shot him a nasty look before pulling out a chair from a nearby table and sitting down.

"Who's he?" she asked tersely.

"Winter Fox, this is my associate, Zarail."

Zarail nodded stiffly, his tight expression unchanging. Taer kept her face blank as she stared at him. She didn't know him. She didn't know what to think of him, and until she did, she would treat him as if he was her enemy.

"Why is he here?"

"Zarail has some information about Darrion that you might find … enlightening," Aubrey said seriously.

"What does he know?" Taer directed her question at Aubrey.

"I know a lot," Zarail replied, his voice much gentler than she had expected it to be, drawing Taer's eyes in his direction. "Darrion and I were trained together by Njord."

"Who?"

"Njord was the god who recruited us after our families were killed by Odin and his Valkyries."

Taer heard the undercurrent of rage in his words. "So this god—Njord—trained you?"

"Yes, he did."

"Why would he do that?"

"He was building an army against Odin, using our rage and thirst for revenge to his advantage." Zarail's gaze hardened. Odin had hunted their kind since time began—Taer knew that. What she hadn't known was that someone had tried to form an army against the All-Father.

"Darrion was part of this army?" she asked.

The Mare shook his head. Taer was confused. "But you said—"

"He wasn't part of the army. He was the *leader* of it. Njord made Darrion the master of us, and it was a job Darrion took very seriously."

Taer sank further back into her chair, her mind churning. "What's your beef with him?" she asked. She saw Aubrey's pale brows shoot up. "Why now?" she clarified.

"I'm sorry?"

"Why am I only hearing about you now? What's the catch?"

Zarail and Aubrey shared a look.

"Winter Fox, you have to understand something about Darrion," Aubrey said.

Taer seethed, her mood going from pissed off to downright irate. "Oh yeah? What else is there to understand about him? I've seen firsthand how sadistic he can be." Pulling down the neck of her shirt and hoodie, she revealed the thick, ugly scar across the base of her throat. "I've *felt* it. So don't fucking try to lecture me about the intricacies of Darrion's cruelty."

Her words came out as a savage snarl, but it looked as if neither of them had heard a word she'd said. Their eyes were on her neck. She adjusted the collar of her hoodie to cover it up and they looked away.

"Darrion did that?" Aubrey asked fiercely. He looked ready to kill Darrion with his bare hands, and the thought ... warmed Taer.

Taer sat forward in her seat, elbows on the table. She needed answers, and she needed them yesterday. "You said you know Darrion? Then tell me this—what's his weakness? How can I get to him?"

Zarail looked at Aubrey uncertainly. "You can help each other here," Aubrey told him, his voice still stained with anger.

When Zarail hesitated, Taer turned to Aubrey. "What's this all about? And who the hell is he?" She glared in Zarail's direction. "I want to know what's going on here!" When neither of them answered her, she stood up abruptly, her chair rocking precariously, nearly toppling over.

"Winter Fox—" Aubrey began.

"Fuck you," she snapped.

"*Taer*, wait."

She stopped.

Against her better judgement, she turned back around.

Aubrey sighed. "Sit back down and I'll tell you everything."

Crossing her arms over her chest, she stayed where she was, waiting for him to give her something, but it was Zarail—not Aubrey—who spoke.

"Over a thousand years ago, we tried to take Darrion down."

"Who's *we*?" she asked, being careful to keep her anger in check.

"Me, along with another trainee called Arthon. We had a plan to destroy both Darrion and Njord on the day of the first ever Final Test."

"How?"

"We contacted Odin. We told him how to find the hall where Njord trained us."

"In exchange for what?" Taer's voice betrayed her impatience.

"In exchange for a guarantee that Darrion would die. The plan was for the All-Father and his Valkyries to raid the hall and kill everyone except for Arthon and me, but—" He hesitated. "We were both involved in the Final Test, and we knew that one— maybe both of us—could die."

The Mare sighed in relief, as if saying the words had lifted their weight. "We were the final two in the arena. I was forced to kill Arthon just before Odin arrived. I was able to fade out of there, so I had no idea whether or not Darrion had been killed. It wasn't until late in the eleventh century that I realized he'd survived the raid and he was … thriving.

"For centuries, I've watched Darrion amass power and Walkers. He rules with an iron fist, giving his Mares no choice but to give their lives to him. I've watched him kill his longest-serving Walkers when their century-long contracts were finished. I've watched him threaten the lives of his Walkers' families in order to keep them in line."

There had to be more to it than just that, Taer thought. What did Zarail have to gain from Darrion being taken out of the picture completely? She didn't know Zarail, but she could see he wasn't some goddamn good Samaritan.

She let her silence do the talking, and when Zarail stared back blankly at her, she turned to Aubrey. "Can I speak to you privately, please?" she asked, her jaw tight. When his top lip curled up in a sly grin, she resisted the urge to slap it off his face. Getting to her feet, she stalked further into the back of the bar, feeling Aubrey following behind her.

"What is it, Winter Fox?" he asked.

"I'm not buying it, Aubrey. What's the fucking catch? Why are you introducing me to this guy now? Why not the first time I asked you about Darrion?"

Aubrey sighed, and she noticed just how weary he looked. "Zarail is a business associate of mine." Taer rolled her eyes at his words, but he pressed on. "I'm looking to expand our business and Zarail is going to head it up."

"I still don't know how I come into your grand plans here."

Aubrey's eyes darkened. "Aside from being thoroughly

enjoyable company, you're also the key to removing Darrion from the equation. You want him dead, and so does Zarail, although I believe you'll be more successful in your attempts."

Taer snorted. "I don't see how. Zarail has over a thousand years of fighting experience on me."

Aubrey shook his head. "That's where you're wrong. Yes, he trained to become a Walker, but once he faded from that arena, he swore he'd never do it again. He swore he'd never kill someone because he'd been ordered to.

"Plus, you and Darrion have a stronger connection than Zarail and Darrion do. He's not even sure that Darrion remembers him, really."

"How am I supposed to help? What do you want me to do?" she said, exasperated.

"All you have to do is kill him—remove Darrion completely. You'll have your revenge and the way will be paved for us to expand our business ventures."

"And how in hell am I supposed to do that? I have no idea how to hurt Darrion. As far as I know, he was born to some goddamn heartless monster and he has ice running through his veins."

She saw a spark of something in Aubrey's expression—guilt, almost—and was instantly wary. She spun around to walk off, but his strong fingers wrapped around her wrist. She pulled free immediately.

"Winter Fox," he pleaded, "just hear us out."

She bared her teeth at him. "Or what, huh? You're not going to help me by telling me what I need to know?"

When Aubrey only blinked back at her, she knew the answer. "You've got to be fucking with me, Aubrey."

"Taer?" Aubrey whispered, his hand coming up to caress her cheek. It was her name on his lips that stopped her from pushing him away. Her eyes fluttered shut, her heart so desperately wanting him to say it again. "Please. We both benefit here," he said. "We all want Darrion dead. You have the skills; we have the information you need to make it happen. Don't let your pride get in the way of that."

Taer's rage was still simmering below the surface when she returned home to the club more than an hour later. She'd returned to the table, sat down and listened to everything Zarail had to say. She'd learned what she'd set out to learn—now all she had to do was get into Darrion's head and destroy the bastard.

Korvain and Bryn were sitting quietly on the couch together when she arrived back at the apartment. With Bryn's head resting on Korvain's chest, their legs were twined together as they watched the early-morning news bulletin. There was another story about a Boston woman who had been killed. The police still had no idea who was committing the crimes, but they were warning citizens to be aware.

She slipped away into her bedroom unnoticed, shutting the door firmly behind her. Peering over to Eir's side of the bedroom, Taer was relieved to see the Valkyrie wasn't there.

Things with Mason must have gone well. Taer found herself smiling at the situation. She'd hoped Eir would find some happiness again after Kristy's death, and if that was with Mason, then she was truly happy for her.

Placing her katana beside her, Taer stretched out on her bed, her hands behind her head. She was still mulling over the information Zarail had given her, trying to figure out how she was going to go about attacking Darrion's shields. She rested one hand on the handle of her sword and closed her eyes.

She allowed herself to remember the Darrion she had known, conjuring up the terrifying images of her brother's former master. She forced herself to remember the last time she'd seen him—the time when he had killed Adrian and left her to die, surrounded by his blood.

She could feel the sharp bite of his blade at her throat; she could smell the metallic tang of the blood. As the memories bombarded her, her breathing grew quicker and harder until she was panting, her stomach in tight knots and sweat pouring down her back. It was only when she moaned, when the sound seemed to echo as if she was standing in some vast space rather than her bedroom, that she realized she had infiltrated Darrion's dark and diseased mind.

Opening her eyes, Taer cautiously looked around her. She was standing in a room, the roughly hewn wooden floorboards creaking under her weight. The room was filled with a warm light, although she couldn't see where the source was coming from. With her hand tightening on her blade, she looked over her shoulder.

She saw a stone fireplace, the cold ashes from the last fire still lying in the hearth. Something caught her eye there in the ashes—something small. Crouching down, she rested her sword across her lap and fingered what appeared to be a bronze brooch. She scratched at its surface, revealing what looked to be Odin's valknut—three interlocking triangles.

It seemed to have been thrown into the fire and forgotten about, but it was well known that dishonoring Odin in such a way was to bring wrath down on whoever had committed such a crime. Taer threw the bronze back into the ashes and looked around the area surrounding the fireplace. To the right, there was a small hatch in the wall, the door opened just a slice. Without bothering to look inside, she stood up and turned around, her sword hanging down at her side.

On the wall to her left, she saw a door—the wood held together with large iron rivets. On the wall to her right, she saw a mirror image of the first door, and in front of her was a third door, but this last one looked as if it had been sealed up tight.

She stepped towards the first door, the one on her left, her fingers reaching out to touch its iron handle. Turning the ring, she pushed the door open slightly, waiting to see if someone or something would come to investigate.

When nothing happened, she gently toed the door open further, holding her sword before her as the light from the joining room spilled out onto her feet. Looking through, Taer surveyed a room identical to the one she was standing in.

It was empty, except for a fireplace, a sealed-up door on the adjacent wall and another door directly opposite her at the other end of the room. Taer walked quietly through the room, keeping her senses alert. She glanced at the small hatch and the fireplace as she passed, noticing the same dead ashes in the hearth as before, but also noticing the charred piece of jewelry she had thrown back in.

Taking a closer look, she could see the imprint of her thumb from where she'd wiped it clean.

"Impossible," she breathed, looking back toward the door she'd come through. She stood up and strode back to the doorway, looking inside. The room she was staring at was identical to the one she was standing in.

What. A. Mindfuck.

Marching over to the sealed door, she pressed her nails into the edges, trying to find a way to open it. But no matter what she tried, no matter what she did, the door simply wouldn't open. Then she went back and tried the sealed door in the first room. It was the same there—the door was fastened shut. Approaching the door she hadn't opened on the other side of the room, Taer twisted the handle and pushed the door open. It mirrored the other two rooms, right down to the smudge of her fingerprint on the valknut in the ashes.

Taer realized then that this was Darrion's mental shield, and she needed to break through it, just like she had broken through Korvain's. She thought back to her conversation with Zarail, trying to remember everything he'd told her.

"Darrion liked to think he was better than all of us, but he went through the same shit we had all been through. His family had been slaughtered by Odin and his Valkyries, just the same as ours had. But for some reason, his rage was a lot more potent than ours.

"I never found out exactly what had happened to them, but it had to be more than just simple slaughter. Anyway, he ruled us with Njord by his side. He was ruthless in everything. He was the best fighter there was. He didn't seem to fear death and that gave him an edge over everyone else."

"Was there anything you saw that could be used to exploit him?" Taer had asked.

Zarail seemed to think about her question for a minute before saying, "There was one thing that happened that seemed to ruffle his feathers."

"And what was that?" she'd asked, practically smelling the blood in the water.

"There was one Mare who walked away once he'd seen what Njord wanted us to do. You see, Njord wasn't just training us to just go after Odin. He wanted us to go after all the Aesir—male, female, old or young—it didn't matter to him. Njord wanted them all dead.

"This Mare and Darrion had been close. I'd heard they'd come from the same village before Odin had swept through it like a plague. One day, this

guy decided he couldn't kill anyone anymore, not without a reason. Darrion tried to reason with him while we were all eating together one evening. The guy wouldn't listen and left the table, telling Darrion he was mad if he thought fighting the Aesir was going to bring his family back.

"Just before he made it to the door, Darrion was up from his seat, stalking towards him. I watched him pull a blade from the holster on his thigh and wrap one arm around the guy's chest from behind. He spun them both around to face the room. Darrion's eyes were wild. He bared his fangs and stabbed the blade into the other guy's throat repeatedly while eyeballing every single one of us.

"He was sending a message, and we got the damn thing loud and fucking clear. Once the guy was on the ground, Darrion snarled three words which have stayed with me since then."

"What were they?" Taer had asked, her mouth dry and the blood pounding furiously in her ears.

"Nobody leaves me."

Taer focused on producing a fantasy meant to break Darrion's mind. He wasn't afraid of losing his guild. He was afraid of losing his Mares' loyalty. She conjured up an image of Korvain walking away from him, then another of Adrian not dying, but instead standing up to Darrion's threats and cruelty.

She made him believe that Adrian had beaten him and walked away with her, safe, vowing to never serve him again. Taer watched as the door in front of her began to shudder and shake—not noticeably at first, but soon the vibrations became more violent. It shook so much that cracks began to form in the wood surrounding it, the timber splintering into jagged shards.

The sound was deafening, but Taer stood strong, her blade ready. She waited until the door slid open slightly, and with the handle of her sword gripped tightly in her palm, she walked towards it, wondering what she'd find on the other side.

With her sword raised, she reached out and pushed the door open the rest of the way. Stepping over the threshold, she found herself in darkness. She blinked when a flicker of light ignited in front of her, revealing another aged door directly ahead. It was identical to the door she had just come through, and she hoped once she stepped through it, she would be in Darrion's mind—in his dreams.

Loosening her grip on her sword, Taer pressed her free hand against the wood, feeling its coarse grain beneath her fingertips. The door opened silently, and Taer took a moment to collect her thoughts before stepping through it.

She walked through a shroud of darkness, the blackness seeming to thin out the further she walked into the recesses of Darrion's mind. The gentle lilt of the old language suddenly filled her ears, and the silhouettes of two small figures crouched down close to the floor appeared gradually through the haze.

Breaking free of the last of the black fog, Taer found herself in a familiar room with a fireplace and three doors. In front of her were a little boy and an even younger looking girl. Their backs were to her, their focus on something on the ground in front of them.

Taer approached them cautiously, gazing over the boy's shoulder. They were playing with a set of carved wooden animals and dolls, giving voices to the figurines and laughing at what they were saying to each other.

"Darrion? Get you and your sister washed up for dinner," a woman said behind Taer. Spinning around, she saw a woman with raven-dark hair dipping a wooden spoon into a cauldron hanging over the fire burning in the hearth.

"Five minutes more, Mamma," the little girl pleaded, looking up from the game.

"Now, Ara. Father will be back in from the fields any moment and he'll be hungry. Now, go with Darrion and clean your hands," their mother replied, not even looking away from her task.

The girl looked at her brother. "Dar, can we still play later?"

Darrion gave his sister a lopsided smile. "Sure, Ara, let's just do as Mother wants now and we can play after dinner."

Taer backed up a step as the two rose to their feet. She got her first look at a young Darrion and the sister who never had the opportunity to grow up. His blond hair was very pale, and his eyes incredibly blue. If she didn't know any better, she would have had him pegged as a light elf for sure. His sister, on the other hand, had the typical coloration of a dark elf—dark hair, dark eyes—just like their mother.

They walked straight past her and through the door to Taer's right. A few moments passed before they reappeared again, the front of their tunics wet from where they'd wiped their hands dry.

As they walked past her, Taer stuck her hand out to touch Ara's hair, her fingers drifting straight through the little girl. From the corner of her eye, Taer noticed the wall shimmer a little; Darrion's dream shivered at her interference.

Taer didn't know what that could possibly mean, but before she had time to think about it any further, the large front door opened and a tall, strong man stepped inside. Taer could see the family resemblance.

"Pappa!" Ara squealed, throwing herself at her father's legs and holding on tight. Darrion followed his sister, wrapping his arms around his father's waist while their mother came over to her husband to plant a chaste kiss on his cheek. The husband smiled lovingly at his wife and scooped Ara up into his huge arms. He wiped his sweaty forehead on her, the little girl squealing and trying to wriggle free of his grip. The male laughed, the sound booming around the small room. The love he had for his family was almost blinding.

Taer's eye caught that same shimmer as before, except this time it seemed to be a little stronger, blurring the scene in front of her. As she watched, young Darrion and his family faded in front of her eyes.

"How did you get in here?" The dark, dangerous voice filled her ears, fear skittering down her spine, chilling her skin and turning the blood in her veins to ice. Her fingers squeezed the grip on her sword as she turned around to face her brother's killer.

42

Darrion stood barefoot in the middle of the room. The cramped, wooden house had given way to a vast, wall-less black space. His pale blue eyes narrowed as he took in the katana clutched tightly in her hand.

"I asked you a question. How did you get in here?"

Taer couldn't tell if he was afraid or just pissed off that she'd been able to get past his defenses, but in the end, it didn't really matter. She had made it. She had gotten past his mental shields and made it inside his twisted mind to finally confront him …

And that thought gave her strength.

She had done it. All the training Korvain had given her, all the times he had told her that she wasn't ready to face Darrion, and she had still done it. She smiled to herself, refusing to answer Darrion's question.

The Mare returned her smile, baring his fangs at her. "I see Korvain has taught you well, if you've been able to get past my defenses, but did he teach you how to survive once you were through, I wonder?" he asked, his hand dipping into his pocket casually.

Taer's whole body tensed and her fingers cinched tighter around the handle of her sword, but then she relaxed her grip. She held all the power in this little exchange. *She* had invaded *his* dream. Darrion liked to think he was holding the gun, and she let him think that, but it was her finger on the trigger.

Darrion leered at her and began jiggling the contents of his pocket around. A muffled clicking sound filled the empty space, seeming to echo around Taer. Her eyes darted down as he pulled out the contents of his pocket to show her.

"Your brother's teeth," he said, watching carefully for her reaction. Taer didn't give him the satisfaction even though inside her anger was clawing and scrambling to get out. "I would have liked to remove them while he was still able to feel pain, but," Darrion shrugged indifferently, "you can't have everything, can you?"

Taer couldn't stop the growl vibrating from her throat. "Killing you is going to give me so much pleasure," she retorted, her voice morphing savagely, as the green veins forged into the katana flared brightly for a moment.

"Promises, promises," he replied brashly, dropping Adrian's teeth back into his pocket. "I'm the only one here who'll enjoy that particular pleasure. Let's just hope you last a lot longer than your brother did."

Taer shrugged. "I think you're forgetting who's in control here, Darrion."

"Is that so?" His benign smile unnerved her more than she wanted it to. His cockiness had to be a bluff—a cover. She was the one who was in control. She could kill him, right here, right now.

Her grip tightened on her katana. "The only one who's dying is you, Darrion."

His expression cooled. "Do you think you can kill me just because you've found your affinity?" he goaded, trying to throw her off her game. "You know your brother never found his, but I wasn't surprised by that. He was never a born Walker. I only took him on because Korvain would have walked away if I hadn't, and I couldn't have had someone else controlling the last pure-blooded Mare in all the Nine Worlds."

Taer made sure she stayed emotionally detached even though what Darrion was saying made her want to kill him a thousand times over.

He laughed. "I see Korvain's coolness has rubbed off on you," he said, his hands already on two throwing blades. With the smallest movement of his wrists, he flung them both at her.

The sharp bite of blood hit the air, a small crimson spray decorating both of her cheeks. Taer's eyes widened when she realized what had just happened. Darrion shouldn't have been able to harm her. She had infiltrated *his* dream, not the other way around. Suddenly, Korvain's warnings held much more weight. Darrion was obviously more powerful than she had ever thought.

It didn't matter. She would kill him, and the victory would be even sweeter knowing she was the underdog. Taer wiped the blood away from her face. "You missed," she said with a bold smile.

"I never miss," he replied smugly, launching another knife at her. She tried to dodge it, but Darrion's reflexes and strength were too great. The blade lodged in her shoulder, blood oozing from the wound a few seconds later. Wincing, Taer pulled it free and dropped it to the ground.

"You'll run out of knives soon," she taunted, bringing her

katana up in front of her, her two-handed grip showing her white knuckles.

Darrion smirked. "I'm just toying with you, Taer."

She bared her teeth at him. "You've had plenty of opportunities to kill me in my dreams. Why haven't you done it yet if you've got such a hard-on to finish what you started?"

Her question only broadened his smile. "Oh, Taer, if you don't know how I like to prolong suffering, you truly don't know anything, do you? I would have played with your brother a lot longer if he hadn't made me angry. I'll admit that I lost my control back then, but I'll more than make up for it by torturing you."

She ground her teeth together, not wanting the words to have such on effect on her … but they reminded her too much of how she had gotten Adrian killed. But before she buckled under weight of her guilt, she remembered Aubrey's words.

Remain unaffected and you can overcome any enemy.

Determined, she told herself she was better than this. She wouldn't let her emotions get in the way.

Detached.

That was the way she had to be.

Darrion was just another target she had to hit.

Taer moved in, confidently handling her sword, letting her affinity for the steel take over. She swung at him, aiming for the top of his collarbone, but Darrion faded just out of her reach as the *swoop* of metal through air sounded, the tip of her blade only inches away from drawing blood. Taer spun around, her eyes flashing with anger.

She saw him launch another blade her way, but she deflected the attack with her sword, the clang of steel on steel ringing through the non-existent room.

"Too afraid to face me like a man?" she spat, stalking towards him.

"Me? Afraid of a little girl?" he retorted. "I don't think so." He grabbed another blade, but held onto it this time. Darrion surged towards her, thrusting the weapon with exquisite skill. Taer knew the length of her blade gave her an advantage, but she was slower, and Darrion was going to exploit that weakness.

Getting inside her guard, he dragged a deep swipe across her ribs with the tip of his dagger, her close-fitting shirt splitting apart in a rush of blood. Pushing the pain away, Taer brought her blade down over her head. Darrion danced away just in time, but he wasn't fast enough to miss the sweep of her leg.

He went down hard, his eyes flaring with a potent mixture of anger and surprise. Taer sent him scurrying backwards on his hands and feet as he dodged a flurry of swings from her katana.

In the next breath, Darrion had sprung to his feet and maneuvered his body around, circling behind her. Taer followed his every move, careful to make sure she didn't stumble and fall like he had.

"You're getting sloppy," Taer shot at him, her fangs bared.

His gaze dropped down to her side. "I'm not the one leaking all over the place."

Keeping her eyes trained on his body, she said, "Don't speak too soon."

Shifting her feet, she closed the space between them, her katana ready to draw blood. She brought the weapon up across her body.

Darrion kicked his leg out while her sword was raised, his foot landing directly against her sternum. She jerked backwards with a curse, dropping the steel as she fell. Her fingers grasped desperately for the handle again, finding it. But before she could bring the sword up off the ground, Darrion slammed his foot down on her lower arm, pinning her there and sending pain shooting through her body.

Taer's chest heaved up and down, her options running through her head. From the corner of her eye, she could see one of Darrion's knives lying on the ground, her blood still wet on the blade. If she could just reach it ...

Taer bit back a scream when Darrion began to grind his heel into her flesh. She tried to twist away, but Darrion put more pressure on the joint between her wrist and hand, taking pleasure in the way her bones ground together. She let go of the katana.

"I'm going to enjoy watching you suffer, Taer. I'm going to make you regret ever coming to me like this. And if you think death is going to give you any peace, know that you're wrong. I will make sure you survive this, and I will torture you in your dreams until you break."

"You're a sadistic sonofabitch," she spat back. "But at least I know you'll only be breathing for a few more minutes."

He glowered at her, and using his total focus on her face, Taer reached out until her fingers curled around the hilt of the dagger still lying on the ground. Before he could react, she drove the biting edge into the bone of his bare ankle. The howl that erupted from Darrion's mouth was primal, setting all the fine hairs on Taer's arms on end. He leaped off her, staggering back one step and then another.

Adrenaline surged through Taer's bloodstream and she jumped to her feet. Darrion's attention was on the dagger buried in his foot, the bloody tip protruding out the other side. He wrapped his hand around the hilt, dragging it clear of the bone it was embedded in. Before he could straighten, Taer snatched a handful of his hair and smashed his head against her raised knee.

She took great satisfaction in hearing the unmistakeable crunch as bone met bone.

Blood erupted violently from his nose. Taer closed her eyes and mouth against the spray, her face now covered in both her blood and his.

Darrion lurched backwards before landing heavily on his back, the air wheezing from his lungs. Blood poured from his broken nose, rushing down his chin and cheeks, splattering the floor around his head.

He was blinking as if he couldn't quite understand what was happening to him. Swaying on her feet, Taer walked over to her katana. She tried to pick it up with her damaged hand, a small cry escaping her lips as she realized her wrist was too badly broken. Using her left hand instead, she grasped the handle and brought the sword up in front of her body.

Darrion was still down, still gasping for oxygen. His blue eyes were fixated on her face as she loomed above him, and he reached up with one hand as if he could touch her, as if he could stop her. His mouth opened and closed sloppily. Was he trying to mock her … or beseech her?

Without saying a word, Taer drove the length of her katana through his solar plexus, pinning him to the ground. As she stood above him, her hand still on the handle, her breathing ragged, Taer found she was unable to enjoy the way Darrion's eyes widened in surprise and pain. She had thought she would get some sort of satisfaction from gaining the upper hand over her brother's killer, but somehow she just felt hollow inside.

Blood foamed from the corners of his mouth, joining the fresh rivers flowing from both nostrils. The smallest sound of protest broke past his throat, but that was all she heard. Darrion was unable to hurt her any more than he already had.

Using the last of her energy, and with one swift movement, Taer withdrew the sword from his body and drove the tip straight through his eye. Darrion's whole body went rigid for a moment, his neurons still firing until the very end, before slumping against the floor completely. The last breath he would ever breathe hissed from his broken body, signaling the end.

She pitched to one side when a sudden, intense pressure began building in her skull. It was as if her whole body was coming apart at the seams, like her bones were suddenly molten and ready to burst from beneath her muscle and skin. The intense pain tore a scream from her throat just as her eyelids were forced opened in the conscious world.

With her chest heaving up and down and sweat breaking out over her entire body, she barely registered the hands squeezing her shoulders or the dark eyes peering into her face.

All she could feel was a creeping … emptiness inside her. Darrion was dead, but somehow it didn't feel real. She could feel the fresh blood on her face, could smell the tang of it, but even those tangible signs weren't enough for her.

Someone shook her shoulders and she blinked slowly.

"—Taer!"

Her world was tilting on its axis, and she felt precariously close to the edge. Taer fought against the feeling, focusing on what she now recognized as Korvain's voice. This was familiar. This she knew.

"Korvain," she croaked, still fighting the rolls of nausea.

His gaze dropped to her body, to the blood that was caked all over her skin. "What the fuck happened to you?" he demanded. "You're covered in blood."

"Darrion," she said, her dry throat stopping her from saying any more.

"Darrion did this to you?" he snarled. "I'm going to end that motherfucker myself."

Taer shook her head, the slight movement hurting her whole body. "Darrion's … dead," she whispered, right before a waterfall of blissful, pain-free darkness crashed over her.

Taer blinked against the weak lamplight beside her bed, her right hand coming up to shield her eyes.

"Try to lie still for a little longer," Eir said from across the room.

Taer dropped her hand and turned her head slightly to the left. The Valkyrie was sitting on her bed with her back pressed against the wall, her legs brought up to her chest. The large circles under her eyes said it all. She had been doing some serious healing, and if Taer had to guess, she'd been the one on the receiving end.

"Your wrist isn't completely healed yet, but I took away most of the pain," the goddess said. "As for your other injuries, they're healed, too, although the internal injuries will still cause you a little pain and I'm afraid I can't do much about the scarring."

"How—" Taer rasped. She coughed, winced, and tried again. "How long have I been sleeping?"

Eir looked at the clock beside her bed. "Six hours maybe—not too long."

Taer let the reality of what she'd done sink in. Darrion was dead. She had avenged her brother, and released every single Mare still bound to him through the blood contract.

"Is she awake?" Korvain asked quietly from the doorway.

"Yes. Come in," Eir said, sliding off the bed and excusing herself from the room. Taer watched Korvain take up Eir's former position on the opposite side of the room, his expression serious.

"Tell me everything."

Taer did exactly that, recalling every detail of their fight. By the time she was finished, the serious expression on his face had been replaced by a look of pride.

"There's just one thing I don't understand," she said. "He was able to hurt me even though I was the one who had infiltrated his dream. How was that possible?"

Korvain shook his head. "Darrion had many secrets, Taer. I don't think anybody truly knew the extent of his abilities or skills."

Taer reflected on his words for a moment. "Why did I feel like my body was being torn in different directions when he died?"

"I suspect it's because you were in his dream, and once he was killed, you were violently withdrawn from his head." Korvain shrugged his broad shoulders. "I've never killed someone in their dreams before. I wasn't sure it was even possible, in fact."

She frowned. "Wait. You wanted me to kill Darrion in his dreams even though you weren't sure it could be done?" Korvain nodded. "That's fucked up," she added bitterly.

The bastard had the nerve to smile at her. "I've never seen someone with such an instant talent for dream walking, Taer. Even though it killed me to do it, even though it went against every instinct I had to protect you, I could see no other way. You needed to be the one to kill him. It was risky, but I had to plant the idea in your head to see whether you would try." His smile grew until she could see the tips of his fangs. "And it was worth the gamble, wouldn't you say?"

"You're an asshole," she mumbled, still unable to believe he would do that. Looking down, she could see the dried blood still coating her body. "I need to take a shower."

Korvain got up from the bed. He helped her to stand and led her into the bathroom down the hall, which took a lot longer than normal since her whole body ached. When the door was firmly shut behind her, Taer stripped out of her bloody and torn clothes, dropping them to the tiled floor. Shuffling to the vanity, she stared at her reflection in the mirror above it.

The blood on her face had been cleaned off, but there were still smears here and there. Her eyes drifted down to the mottled skin surrounding the larger, deeper wound on her shoulder. Darrion had inflicted two wounds on her now—two wounds too deep and too savage to heal properly. She would carry them for the rest of her life, and she swore then and there that she would wear them with pride.

Because she had defeated the one who had taken so much pleasure in her pain.

She had taken his pleasure and made it her own.

Darrion was dead.

And Adrian had been avenged.

EPILOGUE

Henry Craine brushed some lint from the lapel of his white shirt and placed his gun on the desk blotter. The sharpness of gunpowder was still an acrid sting in his nostrils, but as he looked down on the body of his former employee, he felt …

Nothing.

Galen had been a pawn.

He had been a sacrificial lamb, and his work had great value to Craine. Glancing at the gold face of his watch, Craine picked up his suit jacket and shrugged into the expensive black fabric. The garment fit him like a glove, and he took delight in knowing it had been paid for with blood money.

Stepping over the corpse on his office floor, Craine opened the door and stepped into the large foyer. One of his bodyguards was standing beside the elevators, and when he turned his head he found another staring impassively in front of him.

"Leaving for the evening, Boss?" the first guard asked, his hands still clasped together in front of him.

"Yes," Craine replied.

The man turned and jabbed at the button beside him, the elevator doors opening swiftly with a small chime. The bland music piped into the car leaked out into the foyer as Craine stepped inside the car. He kept his eyes on the bodyguard stationed across from the elevators, keeping his expression tight and in control. Once the door had closed, though, Craine turned to look at one of the mirrored walls.

Slowly, the image in the reflection started to melt away. The black eyes gave way to pale green, the dark hair to blond. With one final shudder, Loki threw off the last of his disguise and gave himself a Cheshire-cat grin.

Everything was coming together as he'd wanted it to. Galen had played his part, and now Loki would take over. He had wanted a way into Bryn's inner sanctum, and from what Galen had told him, that was exactly what he had. They would recognize Galen at the club now, which meant that Loki could simply assume his identity and walk right in there.

He was the ultimate Trojan Horse.

But he knew Bryn's Mare had to be removed from the scene if he was to succeed. So his plan now was to go to Boston to do exactly that. He would have his revenge on the All-Father by snatching away his precious first Valkyrie.

Loki hit the emergency stop button on the elevator, bringing the car to a smooth stop after a slight shudder. Looking back at his reflection in the wall mirror, Loki started to change his appearance once more. Within seconds, Galen was staring back at him. Loki's mouth flexed, trying out his new fangs and his new body. It was a lot stronger than the human's had been, and he could feel the energy flowing through the muscles and bones.

Punching the button to get the elevator going again, Loki rode it all the way down to the bottom, stepping out into the lobby. With a new sense of purpose, he strode from the building, fading directly to Boston and setting his plan for revenge into motion.

ACKNOWLEDGMENTS

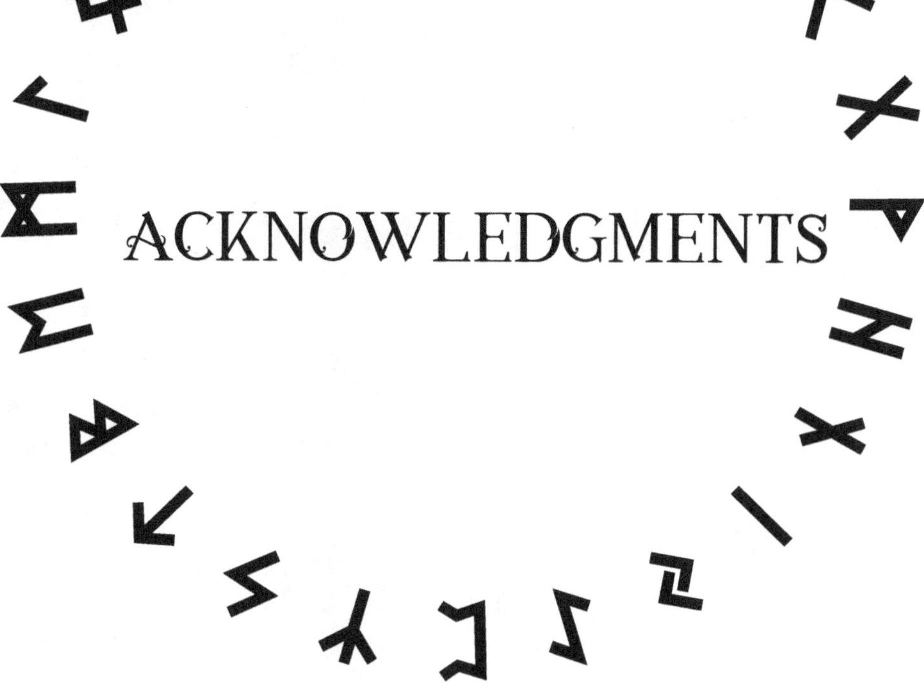

I wrote this book while I was pregnant with my first child. I also went through the whole editing and re-editing process between nappy changes and midnight feeds. I sacrificed spending time with my baby girl to have *Revenge* ready to go out into the world, but that wouldn't have been possible without some pretty remarkable people. I couldn't have done it without the help of my truly amazing husband, my friend Katie or my in-laws and my mother, who all traveled great distances to help out when they could.

A special thank you to my husband; his wealth of military knowledge and personal experiences has helped shaped Mason into a 'real' marine. There aren't too many men out there who wouldn't bat an eyelid answering questions about guns and war zones.

I also need to say thank you to my brother. As with the first book, he kept me on track and focused on the end result.

REVENGE

2

GODS & MONSTERS

www.ingramcontent.com/pod-product-compliance
Lightning Source LLC
Chambersburg PA
CBHW060734190726
48285CB00001B/197